ALSO BY MICHAEL BYERS

Long for This World

The Coast of Good Intentions

PERCIVAL'S PLANET

PERCIVAL'S

PLANET

a novel

MICHAEL BYERS

HENRY HOLT AND COMPANY

NEW YORK

Henry Holt and Company, LLC
Publishers since 1866
175 Fifth Avenue
New York, New York 10010
www.henryholt.com

Henry Holt ® and 🛡® are registered trademarks of
Henry Holt and Company, LLC.

Library of Congress Cataloging-in-Publication Data
Byers, Michael.
    Percival's planet : a novel / Michael Byers. — 1st ed.
        p.   cm.
    ISBN: 978-0-8050-9218-9
    1. Tombaugh, Clyde William, 1906–1997—Fiction.   2. Pluto (Dwarf planet)—Fiction.
    3. Discoveries in science—Fiction.   4. Astronomers—United States—Fiction.   5. Farmers—
Kansas—Fiction.   I. Title.
PS3552.Y42P47 2010
813'.54—dc22   2009040107

Henry Holt books are available for special promotions and premiums.
For details contact: Director, Special Markets.

First Edition 2010

Designed by Kelly S. Too

Printed in the United States of America
10   9   8   7   6   5   4   3   2   1

This is a work of fiction. All of the characters, organizations, and events portrayed in this novel are either products of the author's imagination or are used fictitiously.

For Paul and Margaret, and all their children

The Vision of Timarchus, as told by Plutarch

As soon as he entered the cave, a thick darkness surrounded him; then, after he had prayed, he lay a long while upon the ground, but was not certain whether awake or in a dream, only he imagined that a smart stroke fell upon his head, and that through the parted sutures of his skull his soul fled out; which being now loose, and mixed with a purer and more lightsome air, was very jocund and well pleased; it seemed to begin to breathe, as if till then it had been almost choked, and grew bigger than before, like a sail swollen by the wind; then he heard a small noise whirling round his head, very sweet and ravishing, and looking up he saw no earth, but certain islands shining with a gentle fire, which interchanged colors according to the different variation of the light, innumerable and very large, unequal, but all round . . .

This sight pleased him very much; but when he looked downward, there appeared a vast chasm, round, as if he had looked into a divided sphere, very deep and frightful, full of thick darkness, which was every now and then troubled and disturbed. Thence a thousand howlings and bellowings of beasts, cries of children, groans of men and women, and all sorts of terrible noises reached his ears; but faintly, as being far off and rising through a vast hollow; and this terrified him exceedingly.

A little while after, an invisible thing spoke thus to him: Timarchus, what dost thou desire to understand?

And he replied, Every thing; for what is there that is not wonderful and surprising?

CONTENTS

I

STELLAFANE
1990

The astronomer's wife is on her knees in the garden, facing away from him, stabbing at the soil with a silver trowel, her head covered with a big straw gardener's hat that is in fact a thrift-store sombrero whose dangly felt pompoms she long ago snipped off. During the winter when the garden is mostly dormant the mutilated sombrero lives on a hook in the laundry room, and it is one of the trusty signs of spring that Patsy has taken it down and pulled its little beaded cinch snug around her jaw and bulled her way out into the yard in just a track suit, despite Clyde's mild suggestions that it might be too early. Clyde is a sort of worrier, it must be said, but not so much that he is moved to go outside to help her. Besides, he gets cold easily now (he is eighty-four) and the cartilage in his knees is mostly gone, so that from time to time through the usual ache will come a spike of pain, always accompanied by the same musical, ivory *klok* of bone meeting bone. Instead he watches her from the kitchen table, where he is sitting with a glass of water and a small, colorful arrangement of pebbly pills, as bright as aquarium gravel, and with the afternoon's mail stacked in front of him. Their kitchen is dark, paneled in fake pine, and the appliances are the avocado green that was once stylish but which is now a source of cringing embarrassment to their daughter, Jean, who cannot help herself from picking at the Formica countertops when she comes to visit. "It's so *dingy*," she tells them, but Clyde can't see it. Well: doesn't care. He finds his kitchen fine as it is. From his seat he can see the garden and the neighbor's high paling fence threaded with the mean whips of bougainvillea and the giant primary-blue sky of March in New Mexico. And he can keep an eye on Patsy, in case she needs him.

He makes his way through the mail, pressing out the creases in the bills and paying them, one at a time, from the checkbook, keeping the balance in the register as he goes and setting the used envelopes aside to serve, later, once they have been scissored into squares, as scratch paper for telephone messages. (This also drives Jean around the bend, her father's habitual and unnecessary and, it seems, aggressive frugality. In private Clyde admits to himself that he takes some goading pleasure in what it produces in Jean, her dependable fury, her outraged sadness at her fading parents—well, it is what they have between them, it is better than nothing.)

The mail is bills and advertisements and nothing unusual; and then, like the prize in a box of Cracker Jack, at the bottom of the stack of mail he finds an invitation to speak at Stellafane, a society of amateur telescope makers, who convene an annual meeting in Vermont. He is still occasionally invited to things like this, but since most people suppose he is dead it does not happen as often as it used to. The invitation is for July.

He goes out into the garden, holding the letter, bright in the sun.

"Well," Patsy tells him, "that's very nice."

"I think I'm going to go."

"All right." She settles back on her haunches. "You ought to find somebody to travel with."

"You could come."

"Pfah. Not on your life. *That* crew." She means the enthusiasts and hobbyists who have made such a pet of her husband over the years. It is not jealousy but its opposite, the conviction they do not appreciate him sufficiently. Clyde likes this position, secretly shares it, and makes a feeble show of pretending otherwise. "What about Sarah?" she suggests.

"Well—if she'd want to."

"She might." She drives her trowel into the crunching soil. "Help me up," she says, and extends an arm. "We'll go call her."

Sarah is their granddaughter, their only grandchild. In 1990 she is twenty-two, having graduated the previous spring from Indiana University in

Bloomington. She is still living in Bloomington, working in the IU botany lab studying grains and grasses. As it turns out she is pleased to travel with her grandfather, of whom she is simply and excellently fond. Besides seeming to like him for himself, she is of the opinion that having Clyde Tombaugh as her grandfather is a cool and incidentally useful thing. When she is out to impress a boy or make herself feel better about something, she has him to resort to, the story of Planet X. Clyde enjoys holding this position in Sarah's life, which feels like something resembling his due. His granddaughter doesn't know the whole story, of course, which is just as well. For certain reasons of his own, he has never told her the whole story.

For that matter he has never told Patsy the whole story either. Or anyone.

Sarah arrives in Albuquerque in the middle of July. She resembles Clyde, in parts: she has his narrow shoulders, his blunt squarish head smoothly indented in places like a salt lick, his very white skin cool to the touch. All her own is the knowing stance, the tilt of the head down and to the side, and with this a habit of observing you through her hair with an air of tolerant skepticism. What in her mother is harried and punishing is in Sarah set back and noncommittal. But when she smoothes her hair from her forehead and puts it behind her sizable ears, you can be sure she is about to tell you something you don't necessarily want to hear. You can't fool Sarah.

On the flight to Boston, Clyde has the window seat and Sarah sits beside him. She has a new boyfriend, she informs him: Dave, a graduate student in the Indiana music conservatory. "Guess what instrument."

"Piano," Clyde says.

"No."

"I wanted to learn the piano once," he tells her.

"Guess again."

"Flute."

"No."

"Triangle," Clyde says.

"*No.*" She bats him. "He's not *gay.*"

"Well, *I* don't know. Guitar."

"Tuba!" She leans away from him, grimacing, horrified. "Can you believe that? What's *wrong* with him?"

"Somebody has to play it."

"Not necessarily. I went to a recital and he played a piece called something like Dance for Three Tubas. He couldn't find two other people in the world who played tuba, I guess, so he played the other two parts himself and taped them and then played the last part live on stage! By himself!"

"There must be other tuba players in the music school."

She hefts herself upright. "I don't know. He has to lug the thing around with him everywhere, in that giant case. It's like having the most enormous dog."

He is not very good at this, but sensing that Patsy would want to know he asks, "So, do you like him?"

"Oh, I *love* him." She grins. "He's *ridiculous*. He has a little tiny Honda Civic that he rides around in with his great big tuba. And," she finishes, "he's from *Canada*."

The talk he will give at Stellafane is the same one, really, that he has always given, amended marginally to account for differing audiences. The version he has written out for this trip is for the telescope makers, the tinkerers. They cannot really imagine what it was like to grind a nine-inch mirror themselves, in the middle of Kansas, in 1928, with the materials he had at hand. But he wants to give them a little bit of an idea. "Read my talk," he says to Sarah. He tugs the pages from his satchel and hands them across to her. It is handwritten in his tidy blue script, a few pages. She turns them over silently.

When she finishes she says, "I always forget how young you were."

"Twenty-two," he says. Then, realizing it: "As old as you are, in fact."

She hands him the papers. "I guess that makes *me* a dud."

"Well, that's—" He shakes his head. It is too wrong for words. "No."

"No, I'm sort of, you know—joking. *Sort* of! Maybe. I don't know. I'm just—" She reaches into her own satchel and tugs out a Walkman. She unwinds the cord from the earphones, inserts the jack into the tape player, and places the earphones over his ears. She presses PLAY.

He hears tuba music, oomphing and bumbling, elephants in tutus. Her face is alive with embarrassed delight.

"Isn't that *ridiculous*," she says.

———

By the time they land in Boston his knees are so sore he asks Sarah to fetch a wheelchair. It is only slightly humiliating to be wheeled by his granddaughter through the terminal. *This nice girl is mine*, he wants to crow. He satisfies himself with the envying glances of other fogies in their chairs, pushed by indifferent airport workers in untucked blue shirts, name tags flapping. No one will spill *him* onto the concourse linoleum like a sack of potatoes.

They rent a car and head north, away from the rosy brick-and-glass towers of Boston, north through Massachusetts and into New Hampshire. Sarah drives while Clyde watches the countryside. He has never been to New Hampshire, and he is pleased to see that it looks more or less as he has imagined it. It is late afternoon, warm, verging on evening, and the orange summer light leans over fieldstone barns and farmhouses until these give way in turn to long stretches of silent dark forest. The road is narrow, the painted lines nearly worn away. A first star comes out: Deneb, bright point of the summer triangle. The sky is purple above the trees.

Stellafane is just over the Vermont border, a little encampment in the woods. A sign at the gate reads PLEASE ONLY PARKING LIGHTS AFTER DARK. They creep up the dirt road, under the pine trees, then emerge onto an open hillside under the stars. Dozens, hundreds of people, it would seem: red-capped flashlights are bobbing everywhere. At the top of the hill stands a timbered house, pink in the glow of their parking lights. "That's where we're supposed to check in," he says.

"You *sit*," Sarah insists, and hops out and prances around the front fender and disappears inside. There is a flash of light, a glimpse of a desk, a bulletin board pinned with papers. A minute later she emerges with a bearded, wild-haired man, exactly the sort Patsy dislikes, in a dark T-shirt and pale shorts and tennis shoes and a beer gut. This man puts his hands on his thighs for support and peers into the car. "Mr. Tombaugh?" He extends a hand. "Mike Cornish."

"Yes. Hello."

"It's an honor, sir, to finally meet you."

They shake hands. He does like hearing this. "Thank you for the invitation."

"Well, it's about time we had you here, isn't it?"

Clyde answers, "I should say so."

Mike Cornish grins through his beard, showing a giant's gappy choppers. "You're in the founder's cabin. We'll bring you some breakfast tomorrow morning around ten o'clock. If there's anything you need, I'll be here for a little while and then I'll be over on the hill. But there'll be somebody at the desk all night."

"When do I speak?"

"After breakfast. Around eleven, all right?"

The cabin turns out to be a cedar A-frame, down another dirt road and under the pine trees again. Sarah hefts their bags from the car, arranges everything inside. There is one bedroom downstairs, another in a loft up a spiral staircase. "I'll arm-wrestle you for it," she tells him.

"No thank you." He sinks into the armchair. So much travel has unsettled his bones; he still feels the plane swaying beneath him, the thrumming of the tarry seams in the old highway. He is not surprised to note a hippyish air to the cabin: knotty pine walls and Navaho rugs—imitations, he sees at a glance. The fluorescent light from the entryway lays a cool green light over everything. He misses home, where he would now be napping in the corduroy armchair in front of the television. But he will not complain. He is a guest. He is being paid. It is work.

"I hope this is all right," he calls up to Sarah.

She pops her head over the railing. "It's *so* cool. I'm going to change and go out and look around. I saw people with their telescopes out. You want to come?"

"I'm going to rest," he says.

"But you're their *hero*," she smiles. A minute later she comes bumping down the stairs in a puffy blue parka and gray fingerless gloves. She has washed her face, and there is something clarified, uncomplicated, in her examination of him. She gestures: "So—I'll just be out there somewhere if you need me."

"Watch out for oddballs."

"Takes one to know one," she answers.

When she is gone he goes to the phone. He is surprised to find a dial tone. He calls Patsy. "You're alive," she remarks. "Are you bothering Sarah?"

"Not much, I guess," he says. "She told me about this new boyfriend."

"Dave? Dave's not new. Dave's been in the picture for—oh, at least a year, it must be."

"Well, I've never heard of him."

"You must have. He's the musician."

"The tuba player?"

"Well, that's him. I don't know, Clyde. You've heard of him before." There is something unmoored in her voice. Clyde misses her, worries over her. It is hard to be apart. "Is it cold there?" she asks.

"It's all right," he answers.

"It's nice here, but I didn't go out at all. I just lay around like I was no good. I just hate it when you go away." She sighs. "You know, I get all weedy."

When Sarah comes in a few hours later Clyde is in bed, not quite asleep. But for her sake he lies still while she washes and climbs the creaking spiral stairs to the loft. It rains that night, and a piney campground smell leaks around the aluminum window frame above Clyde's big iron bed. He wakes to the old sound of rain on the roof. He listens for a while, just enjoying the sound. A farmer's son, he never loses interest in such things. And it rains so rarely in Albuquerque. He buries himself deep beneath the knotted quilt with a sigh of sudden happiness. He misses Patsy, but it pleases him to have a bed of his own, a little camp bed under a slanted ceiling and the crinkling sound of the baseboard radiators expanding and contracting. It reminds him—oh, faintly—of his boyhood home. That vanished white room at the end of the hall—

About ten years ago Patsy got sick and went to the hospital and he was alone in their bed for weeks, which was entirely different. Silent, terrible nights, when they thought they were going to lose her.

He turns from this, listening to the rain again.

He sleeps long and late, and the next morning he eats the delivered breakfast: eggs, toast, coffee in a carafe, sausages, bacon, all things he really shouldn't be eating but which he does, greedily. Coffee is especially forbidden. As Sarah thumps down the stairs he stops himself like a dog caught with a roast. But she flumps herself into a chair, not noticing, not knowing what the rules are. "I had a dream I was watching this parade," she tells him. "And there was this sort of tow truck, and it was pulling this big, uh, sort of a house, and the idea was you were supposed to see how people lived in the house, it was the parade of How to Live."

He will have just a *little* more coffee.

"I have the most obvious dreams," she says. "Like I'm in third grade. Oh, man, by the way, you should *see* some of these telescopes they have. Until it got cloudy it was amazing. I saw Saturn, I saw Jupiter and all the little moons. And also, by the way, everybody can't wait to hear you."

"Too bad for them."

"You are totally a myth and a legend to them and you know it. Seriously, it was like being a princess in disguise."

"The Princess of Pluto."

She grins, points a strip of bacon at him. She is too pleased, she can hardly bear it; she flushes into her plate.

As for Clyde, he urinates six times in half an hour, and then his face goes a little numb and his hands start shaking, so much that he draws blood shaving under his big flat chin. When they go out a little while later to walk up the road to the main camp there is still a scraped irritation. And his knees are pretty bad this morning, after all that sitting yesterday, so it is a slow trip, a quarter mile; but he wants to walk it. It is more dignified. When they reach the top of the hill, they observe that the timbered main house is in fact pink, as it had appeared last night. And beyond it he sees now what was hidden in darkness: a long green slope hemmed at the bottom and at either side with great trees; and on the hillside an array of tents, and at the very bottom of the hill a small wooden stage and a lectern. And hundreds of people, stirring around their tents.

"Your people," Sarah whispers.

He has to pee again in the pink house, the offices of Stellafane; he shakes a few shy hands on his way in and out, and then he spends twenty minutes or so making his way down the hillside through the mob of campers. He shakes more hands. He signs things: old photographs of himself that he exclaims at; what appear to be photocopied announcements of the discovery of Planet X from the Harvard College Observatory; photographs of Lowell Observatory—and also maps of Vermont, and dollar bills, and chewing gum wrappers, he goes from one to the next, his signature always perfectly legible because it is never otherwise. Sarah walks with him, taking his elbow over the humpiest parts of the grass, hovering nearby when he is thronged. He is cold, he notices absently, but he is too busy to really pay attention; he has his windbreaker on, and his khaki pants, and his comfortable brown shoes, and people are making a fuss over him. Well, he likes it.

At the bottom of the hill Mike Cornish greets him. "You sit here," he orders, and Clyde sinks into a folding chair on the grass beside the little stage. He plunges his hands into the linty pockets of his windbreaker and shivers once. His granddaughter is sitting on the grass a ways up the hill; she sends him a sporty little wave. The four legs of Clyde's folding chair do not all meet the grass at once, so he finds himself rocking slowly from one triplet of legs to another as Mike Cornish begins the introduction, the story as it is known, in outline: the years in Kansas as a boy, making his own telescopes. The surprise summons to Lowell Observatory, as a young man with only a high school degree. There, the endless starfields to be compared. And at last the discovery.

Clyde listens with pleasure; but something odd is beginning to happen to him, possibly having to do with the coffee. There is a feeling of peculiar displacement, of being relocated somehow—that he is being gently separated from his own body. Possibly he is having a heart attack. He finds, in the afterglow of all the attention, and after that excellent, illegal breakfast, that he doesn't really mind. It is as good a place to die as any. Patsy will make it all right without him. He has left the checkbook balanced, anyway. Then Cornish finishes, and Clyde is still alive, but still in his strangeness, and he hoists himself out of the chair and climbs to the stage, which has a nice smell of new plywood and gives a little under his small weight. He has the indistinct sense of people shifting on the hillside, and then he gathers everyone is rising to their feet to applaud him. It takes eight steps to arrive at the lectern, when he turns and faces the crowd. He has been applauded before. He is used to it. No, he is not dying. Not yet.

So what is it, now, that is producing this rich sensation in his throat, not of sentiment but of something entirely else? He draws his speech from the inner pocket of his windbreaker and, unfolding the pages, presses out the crease against the edge of the lectern. The Vermont sky is gray. The air is weirdly clammy. The trees hang motionless. People are sitting down again. He looks up at them. He adjusts the microphone.

Then he sees. It is the tents. That's what it is. The tents on the hillside, all massed together like that. Suddenly the ache in his knees is gone. Those tents on the desert, in Flagstaff—and then he sees it all again. In an instant, he sees everyone. Alan Barber and his beautiful girl charging desperately up the hill around the fossil pits, around the white tents standing on the hillside. And all that blood. And the rich man, and the fighter, and the painter, and the dinosaurs, and the mad Empress Constance, and the planet that wasn't there—

It is so much. The huge, secret story that no one knows. In all its many parts, too much to tell.

His granddaughter watching.

He opens his mouth to speak, and the story comes back.

II

CERTAIN ISLANDS SHINING

1928

1

Beginnings.

In the pearly light of that lavender half hour before dawn, in the green yard of a rented farmhouse seven miles from the town of Burdett in western Kansas, Clyde Tombaugh is bent over, working, wearing a rubber-coated canvas apron that covers him from collar to shoes and two gauntlet gloves splashed dark red with iron sesquioxide, so despite his tortoiseshell eyeglasses there is an air of the butcher about him, of the slaughterhouse. His hair is slicked back, but from time to time as he works leaning over at the grinding post a chestnut lock slides forward into his eyes and he shakes it back with a toss of his head.

He is gripping a dowel with two hands. To this dowel he has screwed an oak disk about the size of a lunch plate, and to the underside of this piece of oak he has glued a fat glass disk, and using the dowel as a handle he is gently grinding this glass disk against the top of an old blue oil drum to which he has glued a second glass disk. This grinding action, glass-on-glass, sends up a faint liquid abrasive noise, the sound of two palms brushed together. It is a quiet place, all right; you can hear every grain of this and the breathing of the horses in the barn and, from inside the house, the creaking of his mother's footsteps as she comes downstairs to the kitchen. Clyde goes on grinding, three circular swiping strokes performed with two hands on the dowel, a motion like stirring a cauldron, and then a single forward-and-back pistoning stroke, after which he takes one step to the left around the oil drum; then he executes three more circular stirring strokes and another forward-and-back before taking another step leftward, and this pattern continues unvaryingly and without rest except when his hair falls into his eyes. Around the perimeter of the drum he has worn the grass away in a circle.

Around him as he goes on doing this the summer morning lightens and the birds begin to lift from their sleeping places in the brush and climb into the air after the morning insects. Maggie stirs in her stall, and the farmyard begins to smell of the water in the ditches. The oats stir in the first breeze beyond the wire fence, and the stars fade, and at last when the sun is almost up Clyde stops and straightens and walks away from the grinding post, still in his apron and gloves.

You can only do so much, is the problem, and this is about the most he can do.

In the middle of the lawn he works off one gauntlet, then the other, dropping each in turn. He reaches behind his back and unties his apron strings and lets the apron fall. He kicks off his galoshes and his boots and then goes ahead and strips down naked in the brightening morning. You don't want to get anything on your mirror once it's this far along, is the idea, something that falls out of your clothes or even the snap of a button against the glass is enough to ruin everything.

Naked, barefoot, he pads across the grass to the pump. He has a farmer's tan and is very lean through the ribs, and his legs are shanky and pale. Under the pump he douses his feet and calves and hands and arms, cold as hell, the water smelling of the distant prairie bedrock, and finally he folds his glasses and ducks his head under, scrubbing at his hair. Then he wicks his hair back and sets his glasses on again and inserts his feet into the galoshes, and wearing only these he pads across to the grinding post and grabs the dowel and turns it up.

The nine-inch circle of glass cemented to the oak plate is very smooth and ever so gently curved. A faint gray paste clouds its surface. He takes it over to the pump and douses it clean. When the gray paste is gone from the disk it appears brilliantly smooth, delicately concave, flashing blue-gray in the early light.

Well, it is a beautiful thing, and he is about half done, but this is as far as he can go without a very cool, very still room to run the Foucault knife-edge test in order to see the hundreds of microscopic flaws that remain. In practical terms the best place to run the test would be a gigantic root cellar. But they are tenant farmers and their farmhouse has only a coolhouse and no cellar at all; nor do any of the surrounding farms have a cellar of adequate size. In the past he has tried to make do with what is available, he has tried to run this test in the barn, and in the parlor, and in the upstairs hall; but with the air currents and temperature variations it is hopeless. It is the usual halfway point at which he has always been stuck before, good enough for a kid he supposes but if anything has come to him recently it is the fact that he is no longer a kid. So he takes the glass to the barn and wraps it in a chamois and sets it on the shelf with his many supplies, his Archangel commercial-grade pitch and Snow's grafting wax and boxes of Carborundum and Wellsworth emery in increasing grades of fineness. He has finished three telescopes to date, each slightly better than the last but none of them actually any good at all, none of them able to resolve anything clearly, though his Uncle Richard in Illinois has yet to complain, sending the money for them dutifully. It is a sort of charity but Clyde sure as hell works for it. The money from Uncle Richard trickles into his college fund, and together with this year's big profit on the fifteen acres of oats—they are a little late to harvest because it has been dry but it is a good sturdy crop—his father has agreed Clyde will take his savings and go up to Lawrence for college to study astronomy or probably engineering or both. With the rent due on the farmhouse and the acreage they cannot afford to send him otherwise; and even handing over the oats has required some straitening around the house, which no one has complained about, but which Clyde feels keenly, so that for once he does not protest his mother's various economies. He eats everything that is put before him, no matter what it is, and so does everyone else.

Well, he is standing naked in the barn, Maggie looks at him funny from over the top of her stall. "Don't worry, baby," he tells her, tucking the mirror onto the shelf, "I don't like you in that way."

Later he is dressed and chopping weeds in the tomato garden when he hears the steam tractor roaring down the farm road. It is his father coming back from the Steffens', towing the thresher. Clyde leans the hoe on the fence rail and followed by Kelly the dog he takes himself up onto the back porch, where there is a galvanized washtub and the friendly wringer with its two fat lips, and up in a corner there is also a wren's nest, no one having quite the heart to knock it down after little Charlie saw the birds building it there. Through the door is the kitchen, of which Clyde takes very little notice except to pour himself a cup of coffee and mention "pop's coming" to his mother's broad back.

"*Oh*," she curses. Then, shouting to the ceiling: "Roy!"

Clyde goes slurping at his coffee through the kitchen door to the dining room, also more or less out of his usual purview, although if pressed he will notice that a sort of corner or edge of the room has been given over to Mrs. Tombaugh's ideas of the domestic, where a nouveau lamp in verdigris with a maroon beaded shade stands on a walnut table and a tawny velvet sofa sits under the windows. A spinet piano is here, too, well polished but not much used except when Mrs. Tombaugh is feeling somber and full of some old childhood gold. All these items have traveled from Illinois with the Tombaughs and have since acquired a weary look, defeated by the need to reconcile themselves to the move, six years ago, to being forevermore in Kansas and therefore out of the main line of things.

Roy comes ducking down the stairs wet-haired and wearing a look of good-humored toleration. He is sixteen and boxy around the shoulders and his hands are as hard and thick as a man's. "Why, it's honored brother," Roy remarks. "Aren't you looking rested. A quiet life has such clarifying effects on the complexion."

"When'd you get in?"

"I have no idea what you're referring to, honored brother. I was here all night." Roy pulls out a chair and sits. "And I trust you to maintain as much in front of the local authorities."

"Who was it?"

But Roy only grins and looks up with satirical admiration at his mother as she brings him his breakfast. "Mama!" he croons.

"You're a bad boy," she tells him.

"Oh mama, I'm only making friends."

"See to it you don't make anything else."

"A hot rejoinder from an unexpected quarter!" Roy cries. Then he falls to his biscuits and eggs and sucks noisily at his coffee, and Clyde, not wanting to give Roy any further satisfaction, puts down his cup and goes out to await their father in a responsible fashion. Behind him he hears his mother shooing Kelly out the back door, the screen door slamming.

———

The steam tractor with its giant black iron wheels comes roaring into the yard, towing the thresher, a murderous many-jointed machine a story tall and outfitted with dozens of killing blades. His father drives the whole stupendous rig with a deadpan nonchalance that will just drive you around the bend. His father's knowing distaste for his life, his sardonic acceptance of the whole raw deal, you just want to shake him. If you think you're so damned great and above it all then why don't you get us the hell out of here, is the idea.

His father parks the steam tractor and kills the engine and the whole world goes quiet again. The big machines are owned in common by a dozen farmers up and down Route 11 but it falls to the Tombaughs to perform the maintenance on the thresher, or really it falls to Clyde because he knows what he's doing and he's got a knack for the polishing and the sharpening, also he's got the equipment. He charges everyone ten dollars for the whole job, which takes about a week, money that with the income from the oats will also find its way into his college fund. His father swings down from the big open seat and wiping his hands on a rag comes across the grass.

"It's in the usual sorry state," his father says. "Those Steffens get lazier every year, I think."

"Yes sir."

"Didn't even offer any breakfast."

Clyde takes this as an invitation, so he says: "I had mine."

"All right." His father knows all about Clyde's frustration at being trapped here for six years. What Clyde has trouble figuring is whether his father envies him for his impending escape, or considers his small ambition foolish, or feels some combination of the two. Or whether something else entirely is at work. "You finally give up on that mirror," his father asks, glancing behind him into the farmyard.

"I got it as far as I could," he says. "I can't get any further."

"Story of the world, son."

"Yes sir."

His father hands him the rag with a wry grin. "I guess Richard'll pay for it anyhow, won't he."

"Yes sir. I wouldn't, if I was him."

"No accounting for Richard," his father admits. "But you take what you can get and don't worry about it too much."

"It's just junk, that's all," Clyde shrugs.

His father sighs. His trapped and frustrated son. "Well what else do you expect it to be, Clyde. Look what you've got to work with around here, for chrissake. What the hell do you expect."

"Yes sir," he says. "I know it, believe me."

"Well then," his father says, heading past him to the house, "if you know it, maybe just don't look so damned sorry for yourself all the time."

"I am not sorry for myself," Clyde answers, once his father is gone.

Down at the thresher Clyde unslings his tools on the grass. The thresher smells of hay and oil. He bangs the hollow flanks of the machine with a soft fist and figuring he is part owner too he hoists himself into the leather captain's chair and enjoys the view for a minute. You can see to the Steffens' farm and the fields swaying in the summer breeze. The thresher has its own engine and is steered by a wheel and the throttle is on the wheel, a grade-choke. Squeezing it now produces a little squeak and somewhere a valve flaps open and fuel seeps upward. He lets it go and climbs down again and begins the work of a week. He fetches a stool from the barn and uncinches the first belt from its driver and heaves it forward onto his lap, a hard rubberized canvas tongue. With wirecutters he snips away the worn steel cable that knits the ends of the belt together. Then he sews, with a needle the size of a penknife, a new cable back in. The used cable he rolls into hard spools. He does this for eight belts. Then he begins sharpening the first of dozens of disk blades. He stands in his shirtsleeves beside the gigantic machine with his file and his slurry of Carborundum with the iron guards up and the long jointed cutting arms revealed, an enormous metal crab all unhinged in mechanical sleep. The tending of giant dumb things, the farmer's lot. Tending the giant dumb earth itself. He swings the disks free of their housings and wearing canvas gloves he hones them to a fatal sharpness while the fields ripen. From the edge of the yard he can see straight down the road to Burdett. There are girls he sees in town, around the Bijou or coming down the library steps, who wear Cuban heels and flowered dresses, and at the drugstore counter they sit up on their stools and cross their legs to show a soft hairless portion of calf. If it was a perfect world all day they would coast up in their roadsters and he would invite them to sit on the grass beside him. They would cross their ankles and admire his superior technique with the file:

Say Clyde?

Say Sadie.

How come you work so darn hard, anyhow?

(Swab, swab.) Man's got to work, I guess.

Don't you want to talk to me?

Ain't this talking?

Don't you think I'm pretty?

Oh, I guess the clocks keep running when you go by.

Do you like my legs?

Sure.

Do you like my hair?

It's all right.

What about these? Do you like these?

At college he can not only pledge but he can go out for the track team and save up a little money and get himself a car.

He leans over from the stool and pulls a stalk of grass and taps it gently against the blade. The top of the stalk falls away.

You end up deciding things sometimes, or things just seem to end up decided for you. All that week he watches Roy dog it in the kitchen garden and the barn and watches his father plod out to tend the failing fences as his mother sets her pies on the windowsill. She is pregnant again, all right. Another mouth to feed. And little Charlie comes spinning out into the yard running after Kelly, and Kelly barks like crazy, twisting and snapping at the air in her animal happiness. You watch your little brother to make sure he doesn't cut his head off against the disk blades. The oats grow up healthy past the fence. And before you leave for Lawrence you think maybe it'd be nice to have a telescope that would really work, or it'd be nice to do something all the way through for once, in a way that satisfies. Charlie would like it. It would give Roy something to think about. And his father, sure, that defeated son of a bitch. Make defeat what you expect and it's all you'll ever get.

So one afternoon he ends up standing out in the side yard. The root cellar will have to be big as hell, because of the focal length, it will have to be nearly thirty feet long is his first figure. But when it's done he can really finish the mirror, finish it so it can actually resolve a planet. When his father comes in from the fields that afternoon he finds Clyde putting out stakes in the grass. He passes by the first time without comment. But then he makes an excuse to be out in the yard so he can mention, "It ain't even our house."

But you just let this go, because you're just about gone from here, you can do whatever the hell you want, can't you. Because you're on your way to a place where things go the way you plan them.

2

It is around this time, although still a few months before he will meet Clyde, that Alan Barber is booting his way up the steep dark hill to Lowell Observatory with Dick Morrow beside him, and they are singing all the dirty parts of "Let's Do It" they can remember, all the way down to the goldfish in the bowls. The road is rough-cut into the side of the mountain and full of switchbacks and Alan can feel the stones pressing through the soles of his Masterpiece All-Leather boots. He is heavy with dinner and he loves this clear high-desert dark, five thousand stars swimming above him, and sure he can carry a tune, can't he? He is a right fine Irish tenor as far as that goes and he doesn't mind belting it out into the trees. If you happen to be standing at the Observatory gate you can hear them coming up the road long before you see them; somewhere down there in the nighttime there's a pair of voices rising out of the forest. And when they finish Dick calls out in his Brahmin tootle, "All right, Barbie, give it over," and Alan pulls from his trouser pocket the flask and without a word removes the cork and hands it across.

Dick drinks, hands the flask back, with that easy uncaring he was born to, and that Alan can't help admire. Alan's managed the clothes all right, and something of the style, and by manners and with a glance at how they each present themselves you'd think they were two old boys with nothing to distinguish one from the other, Harvard all the way. But

Alan suspects he is too much of a striver to ever quite fit in with the very toppers. Who can blame them really. You never quite trust someone who wants what you have so badly, you never know what they might be willing to do to get it.

Below them is the town of Flagstaff, a spangle of small light: the brick downtown, the sandstone courthouse, the two sprawling sawmills, the brick train depot with its lamps along the trackside in expectation of the night's travelers. It is a little Arizona village at the edge of Indian country sending up a nighttime whiff of woodsmoke. Alan reels a little as he is still not used to being up in the mountains; it still surprises him, in a fashion, how all this stuff can be piled up in one place, sort of how it keeps from falling over. He says, "You'll show her a good time, that's all." Florence Chambers, Dick's girl, is coming to visit from Cambridge. "Take her to see the Grand Canyon."

"Sure," says Dick, "if she hasn't run off with someone already. Run off with Shapley, for all I know."

"You think Shapley'd even know he was getting the rush."

"Someone else. Some damn cousin of hers."

"You're a damn cousin, Dickie," Alan says.

"So," Dick growls, "you don't want to be the one to pave the way. Proven fact you want to be the one who comes after. People get worn out chopping down the virgin brush."

"Can it, would you? She'll come."

"Sure," Dick answers peaceably, "I know what you've got for her."

Alan has learned that when you are attacked you must go on the offensive, so he says, "If I ever did make a pass at Florrie we'd be up in Michigan about now setting out the lines together."

Dick snorts. "Cooking on a skillet around the campfire. Imagine Florrie."

Alan unpockets the flask again and takes his own last after-dinner measure then hands it across. "Everything would be very fine. Very fine. And the life would be good. And the viewing would be very fine."

"Just see Florrie around a campfire." Dick is enjoying this now. "Ruining her shoes."

"Take her out in the Stutz."

"Well, the Stutz," Dick admits. "Actually that's an idea."

They round the last switchback and Dick swigs the flask empty and pockets it himself. Together they have agreed it is Alan's job to keep Dick on pace for a pint a day and that is the end of the day's pint. Usually it lasts longer than this but maybe the man really is worried about Florence coming. As far as Alan knows, Dick has no cause to worry, but he doesn't know everything. He and Dick have been acquainted for four years at Harvard, where they are studying under Harlow Shapley, and they will both be going back to Cambridge for a final term beginning in September. And then they will be returning in January to begin the photographic hunt for Planet X, which is scheduled to resume in the winter after a suspension of twelve years since Percival Lowell's death left his observatory in limbo. Now with the matter of Lowell's will finally settled, there is enough money to train a new pair of technicians to search for Planet X again. So Alan and Dick are spending these months together, learning the ropes of the place, practicing deep-field exposures, learning how to run the horrible Bosch comparator, getting an idea of what it might be like to be an employed astronomer on the hunt for a missing planet. Lowell Observatory is a second-rate place, it is generally agreed, staffed by old men and with a notorious history of crackpottery. But it's at least something, and Alan for his part is willing to entertain the idea that Percival Lowell, for all his confirmed nuttiness—his assertion that the canals on Mars were built by a race of benevolent superbeings, for example—might have been right about a few things, and that there might just possibly be a ninth planet out there, another gentle gas giant waiting to be picked out of the stars. The orbits of the outer planets are perturbed by *something* unseen; that much is known definitely. And the lovely, musical laws of orbital resonance, which describe the complex, predictable patterns drawn by gravity in a field of orbiting dust of a certain size, do suggest there should be at least one more large planet sailing out at the edge of the solar system.

Add to this the fact that he is sort of in love with Lowell Observatory anyway, a poor boy from Ohio one generation out of the stony fields of County Athlone and no mistake he can feel sort of baronial here walking the creaking corridors, it is Harvard on a private budget, it is the sahib's big house above the Martian hills. Who wouldn't want to stay? As for Dick he thinks the idea of Planet X is a crock and just wants the hell out of

Massachusetts and Flagstaff is as good a place to go as any, Dick would take a posting to Maselpoort or even Calcutta if it meant steady access to hooch. And while Lowell Observatory is not officially a part of Harvard it is everything but, it's a natural place for a certain sort of Harvard man to go—the sort who's a little out of the usual run of things.

So they are friends, possibly rivals, in equal measure. They are a funny pair. They sing together, they drive the telescopes, they slog themselves through the nasty work of picking over plate exposures with the comparator, and they don't buck too much out of respect for local feeling. Dick Morrow is an awkward-looking animal, very tall, ears standing out from his head and showing a fine network of capillaries, a large, lobed skull made of several internested spheres like a grasshopper's head. Meanwhile Alan is a foot shorter, and dark-eyed, and wears his hair like Valentino, and believes he gives a better first impression. But Dick is rich as hell, and Alan isn't, and this more than evens the score.

And in fact Alan does have a thing for Florrie. But it's a hopeless thing, and what can you do, Dick and Florrie are cousins, old Boston people who go back forever. Alan's love for Florence has to it a delicious hopelessness, the sort of thing you might sing about even, and that you almost feel does you credit. Sure, you don't stand a chance, but ain't life beautiful, ain't you a beautiful chump in your sweet longing? It's so rich you can use it as fuel. As fire. And sure, maybe you give Dick the flask a little more often than you should, to give him a little push toward whatever edge might be handy. You're still his pal, all right, and you consider yourself a pretty decent type, but that doesn't mean you need to save him if he's not looking to get saved.

The steep road levels out and passes beneath the iron entry gate that reads LOWELL OBSERVATORY, and beyond this is the dusty lot where the astronomers park their cars. At this dark hour it is empty except for Vesto Slipher's beat-up Model T and Carl Lampland's slick new Buick. In daylight you can see two of Lowell's four telescopes from here, including the big Clark observatory, which is not a dome-top but instead a funny clapboard structure shaped like an upside-down paper cup. It is set out on the hilltop in a clearing in the pines, and inside hangs the silver Clark telescope, forty feet long, riveted together in sections like a submarine. The observatory smells of Vesto Slipher's blended perique and machine oil and, faintly, of the doggish, vegetal pile of Navaho blankets heaped against the wall. During the lean years while Constance Lowell battled her husband's will things deteriorated somewhat, the pie-pan now used as a lens cap, for example; but here is Vesto Slipher, the famous director, contributor to Hubble's great theory of the expanding universe, respectable as hell in his gray three-piece suits and a short-cropped head of gray hair and the pale somehow scholastic look of the dressed-up farmer. "Boys," he greets them, in the red-lit darkness of the observatory's interior. "You took an ax to the distillery, it smells like."

"Mr. Barber made me do it, sir," Dick says.

"Shame on you, Mr. Barber," Slipher says mildly, as with a practiced speed the director heaves himself up a stepladder and grasps a rope and tugs. The upper roof panel bangs open to admit the cool night air and a narrow strip of stars is suddenly visible. Then Slipher pulls on the roof itself, which begins its massive jolting and turning, the whole upside-down cup of the observatory roof rolling on its Model-T tires and making the sound a barn would make if it found itself rolling along a highway. When the narrow roof slot is aimed where he wants it Slipher leaps lightly down and comes forward rubbing his hands.

"Barber, it's you first tonight."

"Yes, sir," he says, "I was afraid of that."

There is an art to moving the Clark and after three weeks he has yet to really master it. You are not supposed to sweat this sort of thing but what else is he going to do, with these two estimable gentlemen watching him? He grabs the twin handles on the base of the Clark and leans forward. There is as always a moment of leaden resistance before the telescope's inertia is overcome. Then it moves gracefully on its iron pivot, the great length of it alive in its oiled momentum, and smoothly Alan guides it up the sky and then it is going faster than he wants it, suddenly, and he leans hard on the barrel and brakes the motion and he is lifted up on his toes a little. When it stops he presses his eye to the finder and immediately blows a fat raspberry at himself. He has missed Tau Cygnus, their guide star for tonight, by three degrees at least.

"Some dance, Barbie," Dick says.

It is not the worst thing in the world as he is a mathematician really and astronomy is a sort of outgrowth of his attraction to the field of orbital mechanics. So he can tell himself he is not really supposed to be any good at the equipment. But it is embarrassing to be so clumsy. He gives the Clark another ungentle shove. Finally the old girl settles on its target, then he spins the brass wheels until he has the bright speck centered. "All right," he calls at last, and locks it in.

"That's the spirit, Barbie," Dick calls from the shadows.

"Nuts to you," Alan says.

Slipher says, "You're not *too* fast, anyway."

Dick cries, "Oh, you have no idea, sir. You should see him get the speed up at parties."

"Mr. Barber goes to *parties*. That's hard to believe."

"Well, of course we never invite him, sir, but he just comes along. Somehow he always finds out, and once he's there you can't really turn him away."

"You can just be more *forceful*," Slipher says. "He'll get the picture eventually." The director is kneeling in the darkness; now he opens his leather satchel and removes a heavy square object about the size of a magazine. This is the photographic plate. With two hands he slides the plate into the camera like a man setting a tray into a beehive.

"You know we can do that, sir," Alan protests. "We did it all the time at Oak Ridge."

"You think you can," Slipher answers, "but this is a very sensitive machine."

Dick collapses into the pile of blankets and sighs heavily. "You know something I always wondered, sir, Mr. Director, sir, is what the hell kind of name is Vesto Slipher, anyway?"

"What kind of name do you think it is, Mr. Morrow?"

"Martian, sir," Dick tootles, "no doubt high-class Barsoomian, sir."

This earns him a little snuffle of laughter from Slipher as he is buckling the camera together. "All right," the man says, straightening in the red light, "you're all set. See you in two hours. Don't let her slip."

"No, sir," Alan says.

"Don't drink too much," Slipher warns.

"No, sir."

"I know *you* won't," Slipher answers. Then he is gone across the lot to the 42-inch reflector, and they are left alone with each other in the dark as the wind comes up and shivers the rafters of the big observatory. Dick has settled into the pile of blankets and calls up drowsily, after a while, "What *I* remember is you making a pass for her."

You don't move your eye from the objective in case the guide motors slip, which they will do with fair regularity on the Clark.

"That's what she says, anyway."

"Dry up, would you?"

"My own girl," Dick says, wonderingly.

The hours to kill at a telescope—you just can't get around them. What he would do for a radio up here. And if the station were on all night. "Florrie's a nice girl," Alan finally admits. You can't go on the offensive all the time; it's just too tiring. "We all know it."

"A nice girl," Dick repeats.

"Aw, Dick, leave it alone."

There is a noise of offended incredulity and the sound of Dick rising to his feet. You never know when Dick is fooling with you, exactly, and Alan fears for a minute he's going to come over and horse around with the telescope, but Dick is still too sober for that. Instead he just sighs and shrugs off the thumping Navaho blankets and heads for the door.

"You have a good night with yourself," Dick says, and then he is gone.

It is the first time this has happened, and you can probably put it down to Florence's arrival. Alan can almost sympathize. And he can run the plate himself, come to that. Every twenty minutes Alan closes the shutter and gets up on the ladder and moves the roof, then gets down and aims the telescope again and opens the shutter again to resume the exposure. And two hours later when the first plate is completed and Mars has risen above the treetops he takes a few minutes to gawk at it, though it's not on the program for tonight. There it is, big as anything, a red ball of stone with its own atmosphere and more to the point its own careening momentum around the sun and its own strange moons, a system of tidal frictions and planar geometry standing there against the black of space, pure pretty mathematics in action; you can stare at it all night and watch the moons move a little and more or less hear the machinery humming. It is what he's here for, isn't it. To find the ninth planet, whatever it looks like, wherever it is. And sometimes he takes a little reminding.

He is still staring at it when Slipher comes back to switch plates for the new exposure. "Nice of you to take the overnight shift, Mr. Barber," Slipher offers.

"Yes, sir," he says.

Slipher slips the old plate into his leather satchel; this is a delicate business of lowering the heavy thing into its slot and you can't help hold your breath as it happens. "Where does he get it, Mr. Barber, have we found this out?"

He watches the plate slide home safe. "Mexicantown, as far as I know."

"Oh, that's a shame. I'd think he'd have a nose for the decent source, at least." Slipher's voice is avuncular in the darkness. "The good stuff doesn't make you such a mean son of a bitch, either. Just sort of smooths you right out."

"I don't think he minds much where he gets it."

"As long as it takes him where he's going," says Slipher. "Well, there's something to that."

"I try to keep him on course."

"That's decent of you. You want to get that new plate in."

"Me, sir?"

"If you don't mind," Slipher says, heading for the door. "Unless you've been drinking too."

"No, sir," he answers. It is the first sign of favoritism from Slipher and Alan is interested to note how little it bothers him as he lifts the heavy new plate from its sleeve and fastens it into the camera.

When he goes to fetch Dick to the comparator the next morning he is not in the library reading the paper and he is not asleep in bed or stirring up coffee on the stove. Alan tracks him down finally out at the barn scratching the cow Venus's head with a stick, his hat pitched back and his foot up on the fence rail.

"Lampland wants us on the Bosch."

Dick grimaces. "The only place in the world that spends its money on a *comparator*." He gives the cow another round of attention behind the ears until Venus is blinking with contentment.

"Well," Alan says, "I'm going."

"Sure, all right, never mind. Lead on." Dick tucks the stick into a crook of the fence for later and loops up his suspenders and together they go off to the Main Building.

It is dreadful work, the blinking. You have two exposures of the same area of sky—long exposures a week apart or so; then the two exposed plates, ten inches square, are placed side by side in the big new Bosch, all brass fittings and an urgent smell of electricity and heated glass. Looking through an eyepiece you can see a very small portion of one of these plates—an area roughly the size of a nickel, showing about two hundred stars. Then you hit a switch and the comparator will show you the identical area of the *other* plate. And if you have managed against all odds to expose your two plates identically—if you've got the differential right, and the timing, and moreover if the weather hasn't been hazy one night and clear the next, and if the telescope hasn't slipped or jarred or just been slightly misaimed for some reason, and then if you've managed in the basement darkroom to *develop* both plates the same way—well, then you will see the same two hundred stars, looking the same way, appear again in the eyepiece as the blinker shows you the second plate.

And if one of these stars vanishes or brightens or dims from one plate to the other, you can assume it is a Cepheid variable, and then you lift your grease pencil quaveringly into the field of view and mark the spot with a very small *V,* and you note it in the Variable Atlas notebook, and you make Slipher happy, and Shapley too, back in Cambridge. If there is an asteroid it will be a streak, visible on one plate and not the other. You mark this with an *A*. It takes Alan about ten minutes to convince himself he's found everything there is to find in a nickel-sized portion of a plate pair; Dick is a little faster. This is how the Planet X search will be conducted, hour after hour of hunting down a retrograding object, and the prospect is daunting at best.

You set the machine to automatic so it switches views for you, about twice a second. The clacking fills the little room, the sound of an idiot's metronome.

And Dick is awfully good at this; worryingly so, in fact. He tucks his tie between his shirt buttons and settles forward, all ease and naturalness, one eye placed easily against the objective and his off eye open. He is a damned plausible astronomer there. The good suit and the lanky beany frame. The hair razor-cut at the ears and the suntan and the long nimble fingers. Alan would hire him, anyway.

"You can hand it over," Alan says after a while.

"No." Dick sighs. "I guess I stuck you with the Clark last night."

It takes a good ten hours, at least, to finish a plate pair. And you can really only manage to stand at the blinker for twenty or so minutes at a time before you go blind, which is why you want a partner. And the Planet X search will involve at least two hundred plate pairs, and they will have many more stars on them, down to a magnitude of 14 or so, objects far fainter than anything any instrument at Lowell is currently capable of seeing.

When Dick finally gives over he rubs his eyes and scrubs his hands through his hair. "She's not that nice a girl," he offers, by way of apology. Then he claps him on the shoulder and steps aside.

They work until they can't see any more and finally Alan heads up for a nap before the night's observation. Your schedule is always peculiar but most days you manage two shifts of sleep, the first from around five to ten in the morning, another sort of late in the afternoon, if you need it.

Alan wakes from strange dreams and smells the stink of the rubber blackout shades and the empty afternoon mountaintop heat.

Stanley Sykes is up on the hill, hammering away at the new observatory where the Planet X telescope will go with its 13-inch triplet mirror.

Pow pow pow.

Pow.

Alan hoists himself out of bed and looks in across the hall. Dick is gone, his bedclothes in a tangle.

No doubt down in town, getting more liquor and a meal.

Alan scrambles an egg in the little kitchen and eats it on toast and makes himself a pot of afternoon coffee on the stove. Then he goes out through the screened porch and down the rickety wooden stairs onto the dusty parking lot. He lights a cigarette and strolls with it across the dirt to the clambering Baronial Mansion—Lowell's wry name for his mountaintop house, later shortened to just "the B.M." In fact it is a charming rustic twelve-room hunting lodge where the astronomer himself pitched up in his day and where his widow, Constance Lowell, still sleeps during her annual visits. Under the shady porch overhang Alan peers through the wavy glass of the front door. He can see a huge fireplace, a sofa shrouded in a dustcloth.

He peeks over his shoulder, then tries the door. It is locked, as always.

He lowers himself to one of the rusty chairs kept on the porch and pulls the scabbed ashtray to him and looks out at the mountain across the valley. It is a gentle green peak. When they arrived in June there had been snow on it, but now the snow is gone.

A bee thrums, bounces against the screen, retreats seriously into the trees.

The local Arizona and Western train whistles.

Florrie, he thinks. Florrie with the bright green eyes.

He finishes his cigarette.

Well, but he has a thought, suddenly.

He gets up and crosses the parking lot again and passes through the big doors of the reading room into the library. He mounts the spiral staircase to the balcony, the wooden treads crying underfoot. He hunts for a minute then finds *Memoir on a Trans-Neptunian Planet*. He brings it down to one of the tables, the ticking of the sidereal clock making the only noise.

Because the thing is, you can find a missing planet two ways.

First, you can catch it with the comparator. Stand there for weeks on end—no, months—peering into the Tolles eyepiece. The drudge's way, the brute's way.

The second, the far lovelier way, is to do what Lowell tried to do. You gather up centuries of observations of all the outermost planets, Jupiter and Saturn and Uranus and Neptune. You calculate the perturbations they ought to exert on one another, and you determine whether the planets themselves are where they ought to be, given what you know. And if the planets aren't where they're supposed to be—and as far as everyone knows, they *aren't*—if their positions indicate some residual influence, exerted by some mysterious, unseen body, then you calculate where this residual influence is coming from.

And then you just point your telescope there, and you find Planet X.

It is exactly how Urbain Le Verrier pointed Johann Galle to Neptune. And it is what Lowell spent his last years trying to do. What he did, in fact. The last page of *Memoir*, with a valedictory formality, holds what Lowell had determined were Planet X's two most likely sets of orbital elements.

$$\varepsilon' = 22°.1 \qquad\qquad \varepsilon' = 205°.0$$
$$a' = 43.0 \qquad\qquad a' = 44.7$$
$$m' = 1.00 \qquad\qquad m' = 1.14$$
$$e' = .202 \qquad\qquad e' = .195$$
$$\omega' = 203°.8 \qquad\qquad \omega' = 19°.6$$
$$l^h = 84 \ (7.1914) \qquad\qquad l^h = 262°.8 \ (7.1914)$$

According to Lowell, the planet would have an albedo of about the 12th magnitude, a disk of at least one arc second, and would be inclined to the plane of the ecliptic around 10°. But every search in these two locations, one in Gemini and one in Draco, has come up empty. And no one's looked since 1916. No other crackpot has taken up the banner unless you count William Henry Pickering, who is even now calculating his own residuals off in his private observatory in Jamaica, proposing one wild theory after another—that latest being the proposed Planet O, eleven times the size of Jupiter, seven trillion miles from the sun, amounting to nearly a second star at the edge of the solar system. Pickering is considered even more of a loony than Lowell, and that is saying something.

And it is just a flicker of an idea. But sometimes you get a notion and it rings sort of true. Lowell was adept, but he had some awfully strange ideas, didn't he? The Martians, most notably; but he was also notorious for his erratic nature, for sending his staff astronomers hurtling this way and that after his own latest theories, with Planet X's location changing month by month. You pursue a life's work with such fervor—well, it opens you to some faulty reasoning, Alan suspects.

He will simply recalculate Lowell's residuals. It will be a hell of a lot of work; but if he can catch Lowell in an error—correct his solution—

At any rate Alan knows it is territory where Dick Morrow cannot follow, Dick being not much of a mathematician, nothing like Alan. Whereas Florence, on the other hand, is. And this is another reason Alan is so taken with her, because she is that good, and with only half his training. It is just the sort of thing she would do, in fact, if she had a mind to.

And if he were to find a ninth planet—well, say, brother, what would she think of him then?

He pulls a pencil from his inner pocket.

Birds do it, he hums. Bees do it.

Even something-something in the breeze do it.

3

Percival Lowell was not the only wild-eyed schemer that Arizona ever attracted; indeed now in the summer of 1928 it can seem as though something in the desert air is drawing them by the carload. Tubercular patients in their last visionary days, half-mad desert seekers, white-gowned proponents of psychical truth, sunstruck mummy hunters prospecting in the Grand Canyon, dog-nipped Navaho dreamers, earnest ethnographers with their wax-cylinder recorders strapped to their horses hunting down the Hopi to quiz them on their otherworldly verb structure; you hardly have to walk a mile to encounter someone from another world who has decided the Colorado Plateau is the New Atlantis. Put these oddballs alongside the genuine cowboys and second-generation frontier sheriffs and you have a funny mix, all right. The observatory people ride the line between these worlds, being equally attached to the verifiable scientific world and to a basically fantastical enterprise. Also walking that line is a man named Felix DuPrie, who is also a part of the story that no one knows, and whose swinging orbit will, like that of Alan and Dick, also bring him to Arizona in the summer of 1928, but who, when the summer opens, finds himself very unfortunately shipwrecked with his mother on his way to the Panama Canal.

On the morning of this unlikely disaster Felix DuPrie is thirty-two, unmarried, and childless; he is furthermore the owner of twenty-six factories of various sizes, about half of which are somehow involved in the manufacture of the machinery supplied to chemical processing plants. The business of raw chemical production is such a monumental bore to Felix that he has never quite exactly determined what his company does in any detail; very generally he understands that the many sorts of DuPrie operations (the ovens, the boilers, the centrifuges) variously assist in the separation of one chemical substance from another, and recently he has overheard conversations involving the supply of phenol and formaldehyde, terms he jotted on a card thinking he might find out what they were; also wood flour, asbestos, slate dust, and calcium carbonate, which is evidently the white chalky stuff in his talcum powder dispenser. Throw it all together and you've got DuPrie and Son, annual net income of over a million dollars produced by a vast six-state operation overseen by a retinue of managers and engineers and dealers, nearly all of them still unknown to him. And despite his knowing nearly nothing useful about his own holdings, the money has continued to pile up, day after day. He has come by his disinterest honestly, he supposes; he has inherited these factories, of course, and all their attendant business, from his father, whose unpleasant red knobby nose—like Pierpont Morgan's—and clotted, spluttering way of speaking, and hopeless deadly *unimaginativeness,* all combined to drive Felix decidedly away as a young man, to the point that he found it hard to think of his father without a powerful dose of shame and loathing, which for a while he masked with a serene assumed indifference. If his father owned factories, Felix would have nothing to do with the world of matter. It was transparent, but like anyone else young Felix was blind to certain central facts about himself. So: for years after leaving Dartmouth Felix made efforts to project the matter of his soul into the Fourth Dimension. You sit and concentrate on a candle and wait for the falsities of distance and time to drop away à la Edward Carpenter. Well, supposedly. It was sort of a joke, maybe, though he made the effort in good faith. Also a sort of joke, for twelve dollars he sent away through the mail for a certificate attesting to his standing as a Minister of Light in the Living Church of Mind, which allowed him to marry people legally in all forty-eight states and included a nice stiff black-on-white placard that read CLERGY to put in his windshield to get decent parking at funerals. He even got a collar to go with it, and this proved good for a laugh sometimes; there were a few wild photographs of him marrying girls to horses, and he had a creeping suspicion that in fact Juanita Prescott was legally wed to a trotter named Homeonthehill. The marriage laws all said *parties*, and while you couldn't marry whites to Negroes the law was not specific otherwise.

Anyway he was no clergyman. This was for the best; he was too drawn to the darker arts. For a while it seemed actually possible a person could build up his telepathic abilities with a deck of symbol-cards while posting himself conspicuously in the Staunton, his long fingers spread on his temples while his pals sailed laughing past the open door of the dining room. They called him Dupe of Dope and the Earl of Elsewhere, but possibly it was not *all* bunk because once in a while as he sat in contemplation he did seem to sense some rude power nudging him from the Other Side, a blind fumbling pressure as though through a heavy curtain. In pursuit of this he took up a correspondence course designed to enhance his Personal Magnetism and followed the required diet, forgoing

> bacon
> baked beans
> beans, dried
> cabbage that is old and fibrous
> cakes
> candies not homemade
> clams

and on through the alphabet to *viscera*, "the worst of enemies as it contains the dead within the dead." The course, if followed exactly, was supposed to make him mystically powerful among other things and not incidentally *a vehicle of success in society*. What did he want to do? He had all the money in the world, so it was a real question. *If you will sit down and think for a while you will be surprised to know how much of your life has been mere drift.* This rang sort of worryingly true.

By the time Felix DuPrie was thirty his friends from the Hundred Club had all gone off to Mexico to build dams or to the white-shoe firms on Wall Street to make a million, and Felix was feeling more and more foolish about himself. He had taken his joking too far, taken it seriously, in fact, when everyone else understood all along what the aim of life was, to get even richer than one already was. So with the idea that he might become an inventor like his father, he paid for the erection of a lightning rod in the back meadow. But the books he ordered were full of equations, and as it turned out when you arranged thirty lead-acid car batteries at the base of a lightning rod you could start a pretty good fire. Still, sensing that he was on some kind of right track (it was a faint sense, something *productive* in all that blue flame), he sent away for *World Birds and Their Migratory Patterns, with Illustrated Maps,* which folded out to cover a tabletop; the magisterial four volumes of *Butterflies of the Western Hemisphere,* a Summa Lepidoptera with actual specimens that arrived in flat glass trays, five hundred examples affixed to their pins and making their infinitesimal pivots and bows when the cases were nudged into better light, "intended for museums and university departments"; and the titanic *Fishes,* seventeen thousand pages in twelve volumes whose bright flashing plates demonstrated all manner of underwater cunning.

But these were not right. They were too accessible. They had nothing of the mystery he sought. And anyhow they were too finished and serious. His years throwing himself around with mystical airs had taken their toll. He was no longer, if indeed he ever had been, a very careful or persistent thinker. He no longer, if indeed he ever did, possessed the patience for the self-flagellating misery of scholarly application. Yet he needed something he could present to his father without shame, some suggestion of a future course.

But it was not to be. His father had an attack and a month later died in bed, red-faced and speechless, as though caught in some terrible, final humiliation. Watching his father's coffin descend into the earth, Felix felt a dark flush of unexpected sadness. He had the sense to recognize that it was sadness for himself. He had never amounted to anything in his father's eyes, and now he never would. It was a sunny hilltop day in April. The breeze off the Potomac fluttered his coattails. He gripped his mother's arm as he stepped forward to toss in his handful of earth. His father, dead, in a box, in a hole. He cringed at the thought of those years of poking around in the dark. The loose talk of other worlds seemed to him callow and indecent—an obscene prodding of the mute, defenseless world of the dead. Well, here was the real thing all right, Felix old boy. Here in his hand, this moist clay. Its clinging mess, its flat stink. He dropped his handful in and recoiled at the tiny, unforgettable sound, the clattering of a few acorns across a roof. There was the permanent earth, stacked in its banded layers.

As he turned away he thought, *Dinosaurs.*

———

Dinosaurs. There are no encyclopedic libraries to order, no vast store-houses of knowledge to crush the spirit. One can travel to places like Montana, where Indians are still living in the wild, and walk where the dinosaurs walked, and literally find the bones *lying on the dirt.*

A month earlier he would have boarded a train immediately. But with his father's death a new seriousness has overtaken him. This has to do with his mother, who will now spend an hour putting herself into an elaborate black mourning dress, ornamented with a necklace of ancient Roman silver—eight rough beads strung together—only to lose heart at the threshold of the porch. Faced with the brightness of the day, she turns back, pulls off her black hat, and, sighing, faintly puts it aside. Felix's mother attends to her misery privately, in the same way she attends to the more manageable of her everyday messes. When Felix tries to cheer her up—showing her his butterflies, unfolding his enormous maps—she adopts the patient fondness she has always used with him. But she will not be budged. No matter what he does, her grief is visibly undiminished. She will do the work of mourning herself.

This has the effect of cementing him to her side. A stark, pared-down domesticity grows up between them. They appear at opposite ends of the parlor at about the same time, Felix with a deck of playing cards or a magazine that he has chosen for her in town. He brings her *Saturday Evening Post* or, because he knows she likes it for the fashions, *Harper's Bazaar.* Bent together over the cribbage board they can spend an hour almost without speaking, though each of them will point out combinations the other has failed to count. They both play to win, and in her tiny spiral notebook his mother keeps a tally of their matches. She, being the more naturally circumspect, wins more often. But his taste for the extreme and unlikely produces an occasional killer hand, which causes her to exhale and lean back in her chair and eye him, not altogether kindly, while he zips his peg up the board.

And all the while he feels, in an abstract sense, that he is still on the hunt for something. But what?

At the same time his new enthusiasm is ripening. *Dinosaurs.* Through the parlor windows he can see the green tops of two thousand trees and the shining metal spike of the lightning rod where it is slowly being entwined with ivy. In the pages of *National Geographic* he examines, with his new-found gravity, photographs of the hillside where Andrew Carnegie found his Tyrannosaurus. The names of the epochs install themselves effortlessly in the chambers of his brain: the Proterozoic, the Paleozoic, the Mesozoic, the Cenozoic, the Psychozoic. He reads the *Encyclopedia Britannica* with patient intent, making notes at the end of one of his old Dartmouth copy-books. In February 1928 he turns thirty-two, but still he waits, while inside the big old stone house with its slate roof Felix feels he is incubating a tender new form, a little plump shape, ridged and curled like a langous-tine. His new self. Then, at last, one wet morning in April, he drives him-self to the Indian Head library and stalks through the wax-smelling stacks until he comes to a single slim brown book: *Expeditions in the Bad Lands, or, My Discovery of the Dinosaur Diplodocus*, by Francis S. Langley. It is a rainy, cold day, dark and quiet. Outside, he puts himself back in the car, removes his hat and gloves and sets them carefully aside, and then, in the cold Amplex—the rain making *pock-pock-pock* sounds against the fabric roof, and the glass windshield fogging with the woolly heat of his breath—he falls finally in love. The book shows signs of impassioned juve-nile handling. Pages are missing and stained, and in particular the photo-graph of Langley posed against the eroding bank with a massive femur blunting out behind him seems to have suffered the traffic of a million boys' inspections. In his rich man's car Felix DuPrie presses out the wrin-kled page and lingers there himself. He is caught by the dark shape that seems to push from the mountainside, dumbly asking to be discovered. Something hideous about it, really. An echo of that old indecent probing, as though the brutal hidden powers of the dead earth are at last answering.

Langley was a fop and a glorifier, but in his little book Felix finds a blue-print. He will need a paleontologist. An advance man. A crew, a dozen or so. In contrast to the factories, where hundreds of men are employed in their mysterious business, this seems like a manageable number.

He is sitting in his car. The trees buffet in the rainy wind.

He can see himself like this.

Three weeks later, on another rainy day in May, he drives up to the Smith-sonian to see the famous Dr. Isenbright. The office is like a museum case, skulls and vast brown tusks mounted on the walls, books in tidy leather rows behind paneled glass. "A DuPrie," Isenbright remarks. "I knew your father."

"That's right. That's why I'm here, sir."

Gustav Isenbright is no more than fifty, a trim, compact, bald man, with a fringe of red hair hanging long over his collar. He subsides into his leather desk chair with relish. "So you've got a proposition, I hear."

"Something like that."

"There's nothing I like more," grins Isenbright, "than a good proposition." But before any business is to be conducted Isenbright serves coffee and begins to talk. Felix recognizes it as a feeling-out. Isenbright reels off his résumé: five years at Bone Cabin Quarry peeling away at the Morrison Formation from the Upper Jurassic, six thousand feet above sea level. Ten years at Como Bluff overseeing the unearthing of the Brontosaurus and the Stegosaurus. "Four hundred eighty-three parts of animals. One hundred thousand pounds of rock. Forty-four big amphibious animals, three armored, four unarmored bipedals, six big carnivores, and in *addition*"—he pauses, licks his wet, red lips—"four crocodiles and five turtles, none of which had ever been previously identified. You're familiar with Othniel Marsh?"

"Yes."

"Ran Leidy right out of business. Won't mean much to you, I suspect. But Dick Lull and I worked with O. C. Marsh for six years before all that happened."

"I read about that."

"Did you?" Behind Isenbright the rain pools at the bottom of the pane, spills over, pools again.

"I've been studying a little," he admits.

"Well, *that's* interesting. A DuPrie studying paleontology. Frankly I wouldn't have thought it." Isenbright smiles, setting his coffee aside. His eyebrows are winged feathery things, great red caterpillars. "All right. Answer me one question, Mr. DuPrie: why?"

"Why what?"

"Why this?" Isenbright gestures. "You have more money than you could possibly need. Why do you want to do this sort of work? It's dreadfully boring most of the time. And it's *very* hard."

For a terrifying instant his mind is a blank. He cannot explain it in rational terms, perhaps. Those bands of dirt, that sense of a graspable world. He begins in the only place he can: he simply reels out everything he knows. He is animated, possibly, by the sense he has of being on the track of something. He is pleased, astonished, to find his learning returns so easily to him in that solemn, rain-struck room. Fifteen minutes later Isenbright is sitting back, his hands behind his head. His expression has changed from skepticism to amused surprise, then—oh, glorious to see!—he begins to nod in acknowledgment and even to offer news Felix has not yet heard: that they may have found an Elaphrosaurus skull; that Coelurus and Ornitholestes appear to have herded and even lain eggs together, a new hypothesis based on evidence discovered just a month ago.

"I hadn't heard that."

"No. I suppose you wouldn't have." Isenbright lifts a sheaf of paper from his desk. "I haven't published it yet."

Felix takes this in. "At Bone Cabin."

"That's right. But Bone Cabin's a different place now than it used to be. Everything's underground now. No more scooping it up off the topsoil. More's the pity. Gets expensive. Twice as many heads in camp, half the time half the people aren't working. Not a place I'd recommend to an amateur. Even"—he nods ingratiatingly—"an enthusiastic one. If I were you, Mr. DuPrie, I'd follow my nose to Arizona. There are some interesting reports coming back from there about the Morrison Formation. You know what that is?"

"Jurassic sedimentary rock," he answers. "That's what Bone Cabin was as well."

"That's right." Isenbright hesitates. "You want a specific location, I imagine."

"Yes. And I'll need help gathering a crew."

"A specific location *and* a crew." Isenbright inflates his cheeks, laughs a little. "You know that sort of thing will cost you, Mr. DuPrie."

"All right."

Isenbright considers, refilling his coffee. "Shall we say, for the son of an old friend, ten thousand dollars?"

"Ten thousand dollars!" He feels the blood rising to his face. "Frankly, sir, to hell with you. I walk in here, and you see a payday."

"It's only about a year's expenses for a small operation. Think of it as a middleman's fee. You can *sell* what you find, you know. You can even sell it to *me*, if you like."

Felix huffs. "I didn't ask for anything but advice. I can find my own way if I have to."

"The hell you can. Anyway I've already given you a thousand dollars of advice getting you into Arizona. Only about six people in the world think the Morrison Formation goes that far south. But it does. And if you get yourself in there and *prove* it, you'll make a name, all right. Make it seven thousand."

"Five," Felix offers. "But I'll need good men."

Isenbright smiles. "Five thousand dollars cash." He reaches across to shake hands. "That's a good fair price, in fact. I hope you don't mind my saying your father would be proud."

Felix stands. He is by no means immune to such a statement, but he knows enough not to show it. "It had better be worth it," he says.

"Oh, I wouldn't give you a bum steer, Mr. DuPrie," Isenbright answers, returning placidly to his papers. "Remember, those aren't your bones you're digging up; they're everybody's."

"I understand that."

"Good. And I'm not shy. If I hear you're lousing it up, I'll call my men home at once." Isenbright lifts a warning finger. "So no mistakes."

Outside the rain has softened, falling on the loblolly pines that surround the Smithsonian. As he passes beneath their dark wings Felix smells a good Mainey something, arboreal and sheltering. He pulls his coat tighter about him. He feels scalded and elated in equal measure. Business done. Possibly this is what he has been avoiding all along, this unpleasantly complicated sensation of having got what he wants but making no friends while he is at it.

Happily he has friends to spare. He calls Brother 44 at the Hundred Club, and within a week everyone has heard the story. The telephone rings with inquiries. The old Dupe is really up to something now! It warms his heart to know he is still remembered by his old chums, and in the flush of this pleasure, while he is puzzling over train schedules and the tricky problem of how to get all the supplies together and sent out to Arizona, he is struck by a thought: he will not simply drive or take the train; no, instead he will buy a boat—a boat!

A *boat*, and fill it with all the necessary gear and sail it through the Panama Canal and up the Gulf of California to the bottom of Arizona. He traces the route on a map with his finger. And from there he will send the gear on overland by train car.

"By *boat*, Felix," his mother says.

"By boat, mama."

It is foolish but grand, and perhaps this is what he has been mistaking all along. Perhaps he has been foolish on too small, too personal a scale. This is what a DuPrie does; he makes these giant gestures.

"Silly boy," she says, happily.

When he looks up from the map he feels a tremor in his gut. Another whispered notice from the invisible world. Looking out over the ivy-covered fields, he finds the lightning rod shining, as though it is at last drawing a charge of power from the selfish heavens.

He buys an old reconditioned codder and rechristens it *Tarsal*. Wristbone. It has a dinghy, which he names *Metatarsal*. In June 1928 he steers down the Potomac with the storeroom full of food and five thousand dollars of brand-new equipment. His mother, her hair wrapped in a bandanna, sits beside him in the wheelhouse.

"Well, Felix," she says, "I hope we can have some fun now. This has been just a *terrible* year." She reaches into his shirt pocket and extracts a Camel from his pack and lights it. It is the first cigarette she has allowed him to catch her at. "Let's not do that again, all right?"

"Aye aye," he grins.

It is an easy trip, he has spent his share of time at the wheel, and any monkey can navigate with the U. S. Navy service 7 1/2-inch liquid compass standing up in its binnacle like a great flat skull. He keeps them close to shore, where the current is almost idle. Anchored at night he sees the motionless lights of North Carolina, the shadow of the treeline against the stars.

During the days his mother takes her Charlie Chan novels to the bow, where an awning provides shade. They anchor at sunset and at night in the sitting room they revive their cribbage games; and after an hour of this Felix retires to his own berth and tips down whatever volume he has assigned himself. *Problems in Alluvian Geology, Anatomical Distortion in the Ancient Fossil,* each of Plainfield's four articles on extinction and evolution. When his mother goes to bed she calls, "Night," in a voice of a girl, happy and unobliged to the world—it is the voice his father might have heard.

When Felix wants to ride in the dinghy, as he does sometimes, his mother takes her own turn at the wheel. He did this a few times with his Dartmouth chums up and down the Paskamansett River, as a sort of thriller, the object being to see whether you could piss standing up without falling in the drink. Here he remains safely seated as they motor along, the black stack churning out its roiling exhaust. The *Metatarsal* is a small rowboat with a white-painted bottom and sturdy oak sides, two flat benches across its width and a tidy cupboard at the blunt stern. Even when the *Tarsal* is under way it is an easy thing to launch. With a single heaving twist he can lift it from its clasps and drop it smacking into the water. Attached by its tow line the *Metatarsal* wanders for a moment until the rope goes taut. Then it snaps around and follows. To climb into the dinghy he reels it in, looping the towrope around his elbow, then makes his way down the ladder bolted to the *Tarsal*'s stern. He is conscious, as he climbs down, of the white churning, the bumping of the dinghy, the gray breadth of the ocean. When he is seated he releases the rope and waves at his mother; then she goes off to the wheel. On their way outbound from Key West he spends many pleasant hours in the dinghy, thudding along and finding, just below the surface of the ocean, an endless supply of sea life. Innocent translucent air sacs spin in momentary vortices. Waving fronds wisp into view. Now and then a clutch of tiny, milky eggs comes to light. In the hand they are rubbery and tight-skinned and smell with perfect cleanliness of the sea. Held to the sky, each one visibly contains a tiny black form. He has no idea whose eggs they are, but he eats them occasionally. They burst between his teeth and release a slippery saline fluid, tasting faintly of caviar.

They reach Cuba and put in at Havana, where they refuel and restock. Then they are off in the morning light, to the west. By evening they arrive at Guadina Bay, where they anchor in a tropical sunset. After dinner, playing cards in a pacific state, Felix finds himself asking his mother something he has not thought to ask until it is coming out of his mouth: whether his father would approve of what they were doing.

"Donovan? Well, of course he'd have a fit," she answers, "although in fact I wonder." She takes her time, contributing her two cards to the crib, turning up the six of diamonds from Felix's cut. "Once," she offers, "when he was a very young man, Don told *his* father that he was going to the Philippines to look for diamonds, which was something people did then. And his father just beat him, Felix, he absolutely *beat* him. Don's father was really just a brute, but it *was* a foolish idea. Although on the other hand all sorts of people were doing that sort of thing. Just haring off after whatever struck them. Still, your father toed the line. We all did. Or most of us. Nearly all of us. But it wasn't as though he never had the urge. Or me. I had my urges too, I suppose."

"What did he think of me?"

"Oh," she flutters, "well, Felix, you were a silly boy for a while."

The *Tarsal* creaks companionably around them.

"He put himself into his work after that. He couldn't open a diamond mine, so he built himself some factories. He expended his wild energies *there*. Other men spent theirs in the war. Your father wanted to go, but they wanted him home, you must know. Fifteen six, and a *pair*. I could have used that six *last* hand." She pegs her cards. "Two of the factories were made over into munitions production, possibly you remember."

There are depths to his ignorance he will never plumb. "No."

"It is bad, bad, bad to think about. The *number* of shells they made every day. We had just a tiny portion of them. But just the *number* of them was hard to fathom. Thousands every day." She holds her hands a foot apart. "Bullets, really, enormous exploding bullets. There were bigger ones, but we didn't make those." She watches him turn over the crib, then takes the last cards from him and begins to shuffle. "No, he got what he wanted, for the most part. So did I. As for you, I imagine he would be happy to see you had finally found something to do."

"I have, mama."

"I know." She deals, her mouth held tight against the pressure of tears. "But oh, I hated him so much sometimes," she whispers, "the things he said about you, my only child, made me want to rip out his tongue. My

mother instinct. Sometimes I wanted to run away with you to the mountains."

"What did he say?"

"That you were a Balton. That you and I were both Baltons and that we
weren't DuPries at all. As if being a DuPrie is such great shakes." She
sniffs heartily and wipes the back of her hand across her eyes. In a moment
she recovers and fans out her cards. "And now here we are, two Baltons on
the high seas. So to hell with him, anyway."

Is he upset by this? Is there some flaw in his concentration brought on by
this? It does not seem so at the time, but later he will wonder.

The next afternoon, once they are well out into the Yucatan Channel,
nearly to the other side, his mother helps him down again into the dinghy.
He performs the creeping emplacement of himself inside of it, and he pays
out the line as always. He picks up his binoculars and picks out a dark
storm, far to the north, in the Gulf of Mexico, about to vanish over the
curve of the earth. As he watches this he senses the dinghy begin to shift
a few degrees to the starboard, and he knows something is wrong. He puts
down the binoculars. He turns. The towline has come undone from the
clasp at the bow of the dinghy and is just now, even as he turns to see it
happen, slithering out around the final cleat and into the water.

The dinghy is loose.

It is at this moment—it all happens so slowly—that he notes that his
mother is still standing at the aft rail in her pants and blouse and bandanna, watching him watch the storm. She too sees the line slide from the
cleat. She sees him there, alone in the dinghy.

In a single unconsidered gesture she lifts herself over the rail and into
the ocean. She makes a small splash, then her head appears again in the
waves. Somehow this does not seem immediately dire. There is still a feeling
of things happening at half speed. He sees the rope sliding away through
the water.

His mother is bobbing.

The *Tarsal* is motoring away.

"The line!" he shouts, pointing.

She looks at him now aghast as she recognizes what she has done and
beats the water, groping for the rope. It is too far to reach. He flings himself

into the water. His shoes drag him down. The *Tarsal* is diminishing, the stovepipe belching its black smoke. He thrashes after the rope while the *Tarsal* continues its heedless progress away. The sea is slippery, and his shoes drag, and he reaches his mother where she is crying in the waves, her gray hair smacked to her skull. "There are oars in the dinghy," he tells her.

"I'm sorry!" she gulps. "I don't know what I was thinking!"

He takes her elbow, frail as a chicken bone, and they swim to the swaying dinghy. He pulls down the gunwale and levers his mother aboard from below, his eyes closed for fear of seeing something he does not wish to see. Then he cautiously pulls himself over the side while she grapples at him.

"We'll go after it," she tells him, when he is sitting upright.

"We'd never catch her." He unfastens the oars from their straps and places them in the oarlocks He takes up the oars, pulls, and turns them west.

"What are you doing?"

"Rowing us ashore. We're only about ten miles out here."

"Oh dear." Dripping, clasping her hands at her throat, she turns and looks at the *Tarsal* again. "How long before it runs out of gasoline?"

"I don't know. Days." Already it is bearing east, drifting with the current. After a few strokes he puts the oars up, unbuttons his wet jacket, hands it to his shivering mother.

She says, "When we get there we'll report it to the Navy and they'll go after it. We'll tell them who we are and they'll send a ship out to intercept it."

Even he knows this is foolish. "Take off your sweater," he says. "It's wet, and it's making you cold."

"I'm all right."

"Take it off."

Her fingers clutch protectively around her top button. "You leave me alone, now, Felix."

"You'll get cold, and you won't be able to row."

She stares him down fiercely. "I'll let you know if I'm getting cold or not, Felix. I'll warm up enough when I have a turn at that."

"Let me see your hands."

"My hands are just like your hands. I gave you your hands." She holds them out. "There they are."

They are pale things, indeed very like his own. For reasons unknown to him this sparks his sudden fury, and a thousand retorts come to him, all of them unsayable. Instead he pulls at the oars. All his work, his careful accumulation of supplies, all his planning dashed. As though she could not stand to see him succeed at last. He rows. After a while a heat begins between his shoulders. The *Tarsal* dwindles to the south and east, the black band of smoke foreshortened to appear like a hard black clot against the sky.

"I didn't want to *leave* you there," says his mother.

"Please."

"I didn't. I just didn't think."

"Please," he growls, "*don't talk.*"

She measures him from beneath her eyebrows. He looks away.

The oars are long blond paddles, varnished and veined. He watches the seawater drip from the ends of them, watches the swirling vortices bubble and vanish. He closes his eyes for a time and rows blind. When he opens them his mother is clutching her elbows, watching him still. Behind her and everywhere the ocean is peaceful. The horizon to the east is a gray line. The sun is overhead. He grows hot and thirsty. He does not stop to examine his hands, but he can feel blisters forming, liquid and slippery.

Still the *Tarsal* does not disappear. Every few minutes he catches the distant rumble of its faithful engines, dumbly motoring on.

There are no other vessels in sight.

He rows and rows.

What the boys at the Hundred Club will make of him now. The Dupe, all right. The Dead Dupe.

"It was a mistake," she says, after half an hour. "I'm very sorry."

"But Jesus Christ, woman," he blurts, "what a mistake!"

He rows.

He rows. The sun moves down the sky. He can feel its progress down his back; the light becomes richer with the afternoon. Then the sun meets the horizon behind him, and he is still rowing. All afternoon he has rowed steadily. His socks are now dry and wrapped tight around his hands, and his mother has twice spelled him, making slow, competent strokes for fifteen minutes while he lay as flat as he could on the bench, resting. As night falls he is afraid, until the stars come out, bright and many-colored, and after a few minutes of study he sees how it is possible to navigate by them. There is the North Star, which everyone knows, and by imagining longitudinal lines on the dome of the sky he can orient himself west, then adjust a few degrees to the south to ensure that they do not miss the Yucatan.

That he is capable of this does not seem strange to him, but it seems to put him into a novel position in relation to his mother, a superior one. This, added to the thing she has done, and combined with the really unbearable pain behind his shoulders, and the thickness of his thirsty tongue, sustains the dark pulse of anger in him, and to it is added something new, an urge to do violence. His mother with the onset of night has folded herself into the bottom of the boat to sleep. It would now be only a small matter to stand, step forward, and heave her into the sea.

He feels the impulse alive in him. It occupies his arms. She would make hardly a splash. A faint uncomprehending cry, then nothing. Alone on the water.

He keeps rowing. The urge diminishes. The night, vast and cool on the open sea, goes on. The stars blaze overhead. A green meteor trail goes scalding down the sky, leaving a swirling trace. He is so tired his body seems to be stuffed with cotton; his mouth is parched and tastes of rot. At some point during the night he begins to feel a sort of tugging beneath him, faint at first but gradually strengthening, as he enters the province of some current, which seems to carry him generally south and west, in the direction he wants to go, and he lifts the oars and stares at the stars on the far horizon to judge his progress.

Time begins to pass in indeterminate chunks. Small attacks of sleep overtake him. Once he wakes to find an oar sliding out of his hand and through the oarlock. He snatches at it, draws it back up. There is a long confused period during which he tries to find his jacket, only to discover he is wearing it. His hands burn, go numb. He pulls the socks away, the fibers tugging at the raw flesh of his palms. He rows. For a long time he hears the chugging passage of a distant marine engine. It sounds like the *Tarsal*, but possibly he only imagines it.

And then at last the night begins to end. The dawn comes on forever until in the first real daylight he can see a long horizon of green earth. His mother wakes. "Felix," she exclaims, her voice a ruin. But now, so close to rescue, he cannot continue. His hands are sticky, clenched forever around the oars. Empty. Cannot. But there are no boats out that might see them. He shuts his mind to his body and rows on, and his mind goes away, returns, goes away again, returns. His mother's face is drawn and gray. The land grows ever larger at his back. A pillar of white smoke rises from what might be a town. It is surrounded by green forest on both sides, and it is just *there*, wrapped wetly around the back of his head, so it feels, as he pulls, that he is pulling *it* toward *them*. And as he enters the harbor a sensation comes to him, a sensation that he realizes now has been with him for hours, as dawn has come up. After the fury and the homicidal urges, now there is a kind of sorrowful filling, as though a huge fluid sadness is beginning to pour down into him from above. He shuts his eyes. There it comes, the sadness, rushing down into him through his burning shoulders—a heavy final ballasting sorrow that fills him, fills him to the top with the leaden density of water. *This sorrow is a trace*, comes the thought. And then: *This sorrow is a trace of God.* And yes, he sees it now, abruptly; that is what he has been hunting all along, unknowing—the largest and most dangerous of all creatures. He has been hunting for God.

The sand rushes against the bottom of the boat. They are still. He pulls his hands from the oars. They are streaming with blood. It is the last thing he sees before the sky goes white.

4

As it is known that the Martian canals appear to move from place to place depending on the changing seasons, as though the mighty Martian engineers are chasing an ever-dwindling supply of water, it is now necessary to shift and to consider one final part of this enlarging and eventually intersecting story in the person of the former amateur heavyweight contender Edward Howe. Edward, Teddy, the three-time second-place finisher in the City of Providence Young Men's Amateur Boxing Tournament (light-heavyweight division, 1902–1904) and two-time winner of the Rhode Island Strongman Competition (250-pounds-and-over category, 1908–1909), the longtime journeyman fighter and boxing instructor and current fights promoter enjoying a touch of the posh, and also the estranged husband of Isabel Howe, is now, at forty-four years of age, in love with a woman not his wife. Edward happens to live in the city of Boston, a mere twelve minutes on the streetcar line from the brick building of the Harvard College Observatory (though Edward has never been there, does not yet know it exists, any more than it knows he exists), and on the morning Felix DuPrie and his mother are scraping up on the beach, Edward Howe is decidedly not enjoying himself, because he has a hangover that has to all available evidence left something dangling inside his throat, a sort of slick sack of evil like a failing organ. He is afraid to move too quickly in any direction in case this causes the sack to rupture and spill whatever awfulness is inside it. This gruesome artifact was made at Jerry Fitzsimmons's table from the raw material of gin and oysters, but overnight it has changed into something else.

"Hell of a peach," he mutters to Louise, the housekeeper and cook, in the kitchen.

She assesses him from under her gray curls. "You'll want some eggs, Mr. Howe."

"Christ, no."

"Porridge!" she cries. "Liver for the blood!"

He puts an imploring hand out. There is sun from somewhere and he wishes there weren't. "Where's Mary?"

"Who?"

"Please," he says. "When did she go?"

Louise relents. "Eight. She's got a head start on you, Mr. Howe."

He calculates his next move. He will need something absorptive and plant-based and brown. "Make me some toast," he orders, finally, turning to the sofa. Undressed he is a huge, broad-throated, hammy giant, strapped with sagging muscle. The glass in the parlor cabinet shivers as he stumps past to lower himself to the plush of the chaise longue.

In a minute Louise enters with the coffeepot. Her gray outfit crackles with starching. "Met her going out as I was coming in."

"How'd she look?"

"She seemed very *interested* in something. Wouldn't talk to *me*, of course."

He sets the coffee cup on his chest, where it spreads a medallion of heat. Everywhere he sees evidence of Mary, her discarded blue shoes set at a right angle to each other, her shapeless hat tented on the post of a chair, her gray sweater mounded on the tabletop. He shoves himself up and allows his brains to settle before he sips his coffee. A girlish cup with a bony handle, it is a tiny thing in his broad paw. He sets it down. It clicks on the table.

Oh, Mary.

He has known her eight months, and the thought of her still strikes a blow at his soft old battler's heart. After his wife, Isabel, left him for Hardeur of Hardeur Hats a year ago, he nearly lost himself; Edward was entirely outclassed and there followed a welcome period of self-dismantlement in having so convincingly scotched his own life, during which he did a good deal of drinking and prowling around and waking up at noon with the windows wide open and snow in the ashtrays.

But then came Mary, who appeared at his office looking for work as a secretary, and his life resumed; and now it is better than it has ever been. What she sees in him, he can only guess. He is surely no great catch by anyone's reasonable measure. But now that he has her—and this is one thing he's sure of—he will never let her go. He stirs, clutching his spinning head. He crosses the room, picks up her sweater, and brings it to his nose to inhale. He cradles it back to the chaise longue with him and lays it generously over his face, and when he hears Louise enter again to refill his coffee he says, into the gray muffled Maryness, "Maybe I will have some eggs after all," and Louise scoffs and repairs to the kitchen: *men.* They do like their beauties.

Mary, for her part, has gone off early to the flower market, not that this is a habit of hers, but this morning (at quarter past five) she was jerked from sleep like a fish being hooked. Beside her Edward was giving off his vapor of onions and liquor and a single branch of the bay tree was etching something in shadow on the blind. She crept out to the front room and dozed sort of in the armchair with a blanket on her lap watching the sky come alight. The apartment is on the second story so there is a little height to the view and it gave her a nice feeling of being hidden in the summer trees. Then she dressed and tugged at her hair and wrapped herself in a raincoat and on the way out encountered Louise, with whom she never stood a fair chance anyway.

The streetcar was half-full. At the little flower market in the square under the corrugated stalls the tulips were out. She had left the house with only four dollars but for that she was able to get two dozen white tulips, so fresh their stems squeaked. They filled a box a yard long and a foot deep. This was a serious transaction and took some time to enact, the old woman's hunt for the box, the admiring onlookers, her own muffled polite pride that she had a place to put these, a home to take them home to. The box was awkward and heavy in two arms like a giant tuna, and when she arrived at the carstop she noted with sudden sadness that she had forgotten to hold back money for her return fare. She would have to do better than this. She considered just climbing aboard and asking for someone to pay her fare but she was in the mode of *improving* herself so she decided to walk instead. She would make it a lesson to herself. She hoisted the box to her shoulder. The apartment house was only nine blocks away so it was not so bad and as she walked she changed shoulders at the end of each block. A smudge was developing like an epaulet on both shoulders of her raincoat but it was due for a cleaning anyhow.

Only now when she is two blocks from the apartment does it occur to her that she is a strange sight. As a rule she does not like to be looked at at all, which is difficult because she is quite the beauty. There are periods when it doesn't seem to matter much, when she can act almost naturally despite everything, and Teddy would say that those are the times when she is most herself: a kidder, a live wire, a spark. But in fact her normal way of being is to feel that she has grown a single enormous tusk about six feet long not quite out of the top of her head but rather around to the back slightly, and also that a horrible sort of withered-up tiny man, a three-foot spy, a dried-up mummified jockey, is riding on the tusk, clinging to it and watching her from his perch above and behind her. She understands she is imagining it. But she has the urge, very strong, to dig constantly at the back of her head, to get at the root of the tusk. She does not like to touch it, but she also feels that if she digs deep enough she might remove the whole thing cleanly, although she has also gathered that it is attached in some important way to the bone of her head. The tusk is about four inches thick where it joins to her skull. It is gray, and along the way up it is ridged and mottled, and at the ridges pieces flake and peel off as they would from an old toenail, and sometimes she will reach up to dislodge an unusually large or disturbing piece. At its base the tusk is thick and woody, while the thin rounded tip is newer and more sensitive. She ducks her head going through doorways, and sometimes without thinking of it she shakes her head in an effort to dislodge the rider, like a moose that has gone through a clothesline. She can surprise the rider sometimes but he never falls, although occasionally she can make him shift his weight, and then she has to lean to accommodate him, which causes her to stagger a little. She has never seen the man, of course; he does not appear in mirrors; and he never comes down. It is the rule that he is not allowed to come down, only to observe her without comment from above and behind, to ride along silently, indifferently, her permanent burden.

Now, none of it is true. She knows this. Dr. Miller and the others instructed her on all this during her three months in the asylum at Belmont, where she received the diagnosis of Involuted Paranoia of Kleist. For twelve weeks she delivered urine into a paper cup and produced bowel movements into the upside-down paper hat, she was subjected to weeks of immersion baths and basket weaving, and she suffered the dog-taste of paraldehyde and dear Dr. Miller with his giant blond-tufted fingers and whomping books and reciting "The Cowboy Story" to him, and crazy Mrs. Donovan at the grille feeding the birds through the wire and afterward the old woman sleeping peacefully in the hot wrap and her wet sheets going *spat-spat* in the blue light.

And poor Hollis, her loyal, exhausted brother, having to see her there.

She suffered it all, the shame and embarrassment of it, and at least came away knowing it wasn't *real*. It was the product of her mind and not true. But they hadn't cured it or made it go away.

Still, Mary mostly knows how to get along in the world in spite of things. She hides it all well. Teddy has no idea of any of this. To be fair, he does not have much idea of much, but Mary is fond of huge mournful Teddy without exactly loving him; he has been good to her, first as her employer and now as whatever he is, and she does not want to make him sad by going back into the hospital. This is why she wants the flowers, so she might make him happy, now, when it is still possible, and this is why she is hurrying back, now, across the sidewalk, with the box on her shoulder, not looking down at her shadow, which shows nothing, only her own plain form without a tusk, not looking at it because to look at it would be to confirm again how wrong she is about herself, how she cannot tell what is true about anything; she cannot even stand to wear a regulation hat like everyone else. What is she good for.

Yet. She slows. She goes normally up the walk and into the lobby. She climbs the rubber treads past the brass planter and opens their door, 2A. She is the picture of original beauty. "Hello, Teddy," she says. "I couldn't sleep, so I thought I'd get you a little something."

"Mare."

"Cheer the place up a little." She tips the box down as she would a swaddling babe. Then she carries it in and slides it along the kitchen table for Louise to trouble with. And she goes off to wash and dress. She feels Edward's big steps along the hall and takes comfort in them, his size anyway.

But it is labor for her, every minute of it; she is strung out like a tension cable. And despite Teddy's attentions she is not getting better; she is getting worse.

Out at Belmont in Dr. Miller's cabinet there is a thick case file on Mary Hempstead, a complete history. In all probability Dr. Miller still thinks of her fondly, once in a while, when he is not prying Christmas ornaments out of the mouths of his patients or instructing them on the way to sit up straight despite hearing a voice warning them about the ax. For Mary is memorable. A very pretty girl, all right, and troubled. For our purposes the file begins in April of 1927 when she was all of twenty-two and her parents died within six weeks of each other, her mother finally succumbing to the cancer that had been eating at her for a year. Then her father, distracted, still using the present tense to describe his wife, cut his fingernails too short and gave himself a blood infection and died wearing the same suit six days later, rigid and staring, his teeth clamped on a leather strap. Suddenly she was alone in the world except for her brother, Hollis, who traveled back to Scranton from Massachusetts to stand with her twice, his coat dark as a magician's cloak, stood with her through the embarassing keening of their parents' friends, all seemingly fat and healthy as ponies; and then her brother packed a trunk and bought her a train ticket and extracted her firmly from their little coal-stained city.

"Just for a while," he said, on the train to Boston, "until you feel like yourself again."

"A likely story," she scoffed.

At the end of the journey was a large, pretty, shingled house on a great lawn, an hour from Boston, by what seemed to her the sea. Not her brother's house, of course; he only lived there under some arrangement with his friend Scotty MacAllister. "Are you sure this is all right?" she asked, parting the lace curtains that looked out on the great lawn.

"Trust me," he smiled. "Scotty's a push."

She knew her brother was a queer so she had some sense of how things were, and she was still young enough to think it lent her some distinction to have a brother of that sort; it gave her interest. In the MacAllisters' house she had a room upstairs at the end of a white sun-beamed corridor. For the first few days here at Seahome, during which she was let mostly alone, she was still awakened early by the unaccustomed sound of the water; stirring, she would leave the silent house and step barefoot across the grass to the rock wall that held back the tide, and turning back to the vast white shape of the house, she would look up at her own bedroom window as though to catch herself there. As though she herself could be, in an echo of her sudden displacement, duplicated. She was weirdly convinced of the possibility of it, though it was plainly not possible.

She wondered at this, and in fact she was beginning to lose her mind; but as it was the first time it had ever happened, she did not recognize the symptoms of it. Instead she felt herself to be held within the thrall of a mysterious suggestibility. The air beyond the lawn was filled with a yellow light at sunset, a light so palpable it seemed to be always on the verge of coalescing into something material. The two cinnamon Airedales, Reggie and Cal, began to seem on the cusp of some transformation, their sinuous bodies seeming almost, but not quite, to trace a meaningful pattern. It was here in the MacAllisters' house that the tusk first appeared, a soft nub which then grew longer and longer, and then she imagined a dried-up man riding on it like a fireman on a pole, regarding her indifferently. He resembled the gnomes in the book of Brothers Grimm she and Hollis had shared as children, his face sepia and fissured, his failed body swaddled in rags, and at first it seemed she was only pretending to herself, that she could stop whenever she liked, that she was in some way reaching for some familiar figure in her childhood in an effort to gain some solace. As though she could just as well have imagined the Tin Woodsman. She spent sessions staring into the empty gold-leaf mirror in the MacAllisters' upper hall, tutoring herself against what seemed to her strange impositions from someone else's mind, as though these visions were being carried on radio waves into her brain. If they were from outside, this meant that they were not really there; but in another sense this meant they *were*, if only temporarily. The man, the tusk. Even if they came from elsewhere. She stared at her reflection. *Yes,* she decided, *there in a sense.* (Blue sky in the mirror, visible through the upper parts of the seaside windows.) For a time—a few weeks, perhaps—it seemed she could sense the tusk and the dried-up man coming and going, waxing in strength before waning again, just as though they were a signal carried up the coast from the WBZ studios, *The Hart Carrigan Hour,* sometimes very solid and definite and other times just a ghost, the faintest hint of a shape in the air above her. But as the weeks passed the tusk and the man grew more definite and began to be with her all the time, so that even at the moment of waking, before she even knew where she was in the world (a white room, a seaside murmur), she could feel the tusk resting against the sheets and pillows and could sense the little man clinging to it, himself asleep like a monkey wrapped around a branch. And with a great effort she could make it vanish; with a concentrated push of her mind she could stand unburdened and slip a dress on over her head without feeling the impossible strangeness of it. But finally she found she could not, with any amount of effort, make any of it go away no matter what she did, and she felt a growing panic, as though she had discovered a growth but was afraid to tell the doctor; and from then on a little shriveled man was always riding on a tusk that grew from the back of her head.

Watch her come into a room and toss her head, she looked to everyone's eyes like a regular pretty girl but she knew better.

And so the weeks passed for her, and she was just able to keep going along, the thing on her head growing woody and dense, and the man rustling as he shifted position, and all the time she felt an accumulating oddness and strain as she pretended nothing was wrong. *Stupid.* If only she could *stop it.* Because at the same time here was the beautiful, faultless house, and Hollis happier than she had ever seen him. He was tanned from spending his afternoons painting; after some casual mention of the matter Scotty had given Hollis an easel and a series of stretched canvases and his first box of oils, and Hollis had put up the easel at the edge of the lawn and had since been painting, over and over again, with the avid eye that longing imparted, the clambering endless white of the giant Mac-Allister house, with its black shutters and massive chimneys. "Don't look," he would protest, "I'm terrible."

"Not terrible," she consoled him, "just learning."

"Shows what you know," he said.

Anyway she liked watching her brother there in his whites, the straw hat beside him on the lawn and the palette crooked in the corner of his elbow, cloud-shadows skating toward him across the grass. He was a boy from Scranton made good. A sort of jaunty what-the-hell that reminded her of themselves as children. It gave her a little hope, despite everything. If her brother could make such a catch as Scotty, possibly she could too. Scotty supplied them with a car and suggested they make use of Boston,

as they were so close. And admissions to the museums. And tickets to the
Symphony Orchestra. Scotty came along as a companion, languid and
bloodless, his tie worn loose and his brilliantined hair rigid with the
marks of the comb in it, the white scalp shining sickly through.

And what a dangerous joy it seemed to duck her tusk through the
front doors of Symphony Hall and to enter the cavernous decorated lobby
and mount the carpeted stairs and settle into their loge, where she had the
feeling of being seated out on the bowsprit of a ship. It was a creeping
strangeness to be surrounded by the thousand other black figures, perch-
ing above and around them like buzzards, Scotty lifting his hand in faint
greeting again and again; then came the pleasure of the isolating dark
descending, and the ceremony the musicians made of their own stiff-
necked appearance.

It was still impossible to play Schumann or Brahms, they were too
German, and even the great Germans who could not be blamed for being
German were, it was felt, somewhat suspect, as though concealed within
their sublime gigantism were the seeds of a dangerous bombast. It was
Holst on the program: *The Planets*. "But *isn't* he German?" asked Hollis.

"English, actually," drawled Scotty.

The boys had arranged themselves bonelessly over the red velvet as
though trying to appear to be only two sets of good clothes, unsupported
by any flesh; she could not do that. No, she sat upright. Waited.

There came a moment of perfect soundlessness as the conductor raised
his baton.

And then oh, how unprepared she was for it! The massive assault of
Mars, the Bringer of War, the tympanist attacking his kettle. She was
pinned to the velvet seat. And then followed painfully ethereal Venus, as
though skeins of silk were being drawn through the air; and skittering
Mercury, like water on a hot stove. All of it struck her as almost unbearably palpable, as the music ballooned from the stage like a second, richer
atmosphere—but it was the effortless majesty of Jupiter that brought her
hand to her lips and started the tears. That grandeur! That overpower-
ing excellence! And when the lights came up there was a rising wave of
applause, nothing out of the ordinary as she would come to learn, but it
seemed to her that nobody in the auditorium wanted to stop applauding,
and from her seat she could feel the waves of sound compressing the air
around her, as dense and palpable as the music had seemed just a minute

before, and as unapologetically joyful. At last the sound began to diminish, the first few people could be seen turning to their neighbors, and slowly the sound of applause, as blurred and impersonal as a waterfall, was replaced by a thousand conversations. How could she have lived this long and not felt *this* thing? How, when it was so evidently essential?

And the tusk and the rider, when she stood, had vanished under the spell of the music. How *strange* she felt without them, how light and *simple* . . .

And they remained absent on the dark drive home, and superstitiously she did not want to go up to bed; instead she stayed downstairs and installed herself in old Mr. MacAllister's octagonal room, across the carpet from the old man who sat beneath his cone of yellow electric light, where he was at work on the new Wharton. The dogs looked up when Mary entered and exhaled heavily as they put their heads down again on their paws, sighing themselves back to sleep. The night beyond the windows was utterly black, and this antique room, with its smell of leather and woodsmoke and dogs, was the only place in the world she wished to be; there was too much beauty in the world—no, there was simply *too much* of the world to let herself vanish into madness, as she at last suspected was in danger of happening—*no*, she would not go without a fight. She would sit on the old man's sofa wrapped in a wool blanket, her feet tucked under her, and refuse to succumb; hear her brother wandering his insinuating way through the upper corridors; and that ringing music that had floated her away and healed her would go on ringing in her mind— those hard tyrannical harmonies—oh, they would sound and sound and sound and sound . . .

But it didn't last. The tusk and rider returned the next morning. And she managed as well as she could, but she could no longer fight her descending strangeness. And other people began to notice it—there had been parties, and people wondering who she was and looking at her from across the room.

Looking at her as if they knew! Whispering behind their hands!

And all the men unable to stop staring.

And then a few weeks later she tried to cut the tusk off with a grapefruit spoon, and there was all that blood, and Hollis wrapped her head in a towel and whisked her out to Belmont, one more thing Scotty provided them, and Hollis moved to a green-walled apartment in the city in order to be nearby. And in three months, no, Belmont and Dr. Miller hadn't cured her; but they had calmed her down. Given her some perspective. Taught her how to be sanely crazy. And it had been good to be out of sight for a while. And then around Thanksgiving of 1927 they let her out, and she moved in with Hollis for a while and then found the job with Teddy and moved in with him, because she had been enough of a burden to her brother, and at least Teddy was getting something out of the deal in exchange for keeping her.

She is a good lay, if nothing else. She figures it is something. Not everyone is.

Now in the summer of 1928 her brother still lives in town, with Scotty, in the same green apartment. When she goes to see him he is at his easel on the screened-in porch drawing with a black crayon. In the summer heat he is wearing an undershirt and dungarees and no shoes, his blobby shoulders smacked with moles, and Scotty is in the kitchen turning toast over the burners and making coffee. They are a fine queer couple, Scotty wearing a blue apron over his brown silk pajamas with a cigarette in his lips. "Darling," Holly croons from his stool.

"Hello, Holly, you old bum. You look pretty hung."

He rolls his eyes at her. "Party last night," he says. "That bunch."

"They're yours too now," Scotty calls. "Don't think you can stick me with them."

"Charlie Chambers and everyone," Mary guesses.

"Charlie's got a setup at the moment," her brother says. "This big scenic apartment and nobody in it. Sister's gone off to Arizona or somewhere getting married to someone."

"Dick Morrow," Scotty supplies.

She ducks her head and carries the tusk around to inspect his drawing. She sees a pretty girl with her head back. "Why, that's *me*, Holly!" she says.

"It's supposed to be, anyway."

"But it is!" She chucks him on the shoulder. "That's not bad!"

He suppresses a smile. "I thank you. And Weber's, for making it easy to steal supplies." He eyes her, checks his drawing, rubs something out with his wet thumbprint. It seems as though he sees something unusual in her, for he asks, too casually, "You're all right?"

"Holding my own," she answers.

He does not quite believe her. "Treating you all right, I hope."

She goes to the edge of the porch, staring down at the garbage cans and the concrete pad below. The ivy is turning dull with the onset of summer. There is a brown mangy dog or something crouching behind the garbage cans, it looks like; black turds dot the little scrap of lawn. "Actually I wanted to suggest that I think it's about time you should meet him," she says.

"All right."

"You could get all duded up and impress him."

He grimaces, indicates the paint in his nails.

"Don't you have a file? All the best girls have *files*, Holly. No, the truth is, I want him to know I have at least *somebody* behind me. I mean, he won't scare."

"Holly wouldn't scare a Girl Guide," Scotty says.

She smirks at Scotty and says, "No, I just want to give him the idea there's somebody paying attention. I think it's time."

Her brother calculates the truth of this, then leans forward, removes his cardholder from a back pocket, and extracts one for her. "I have a card now."

She whistles. "Whew! My own brother!" It looks nice: navy-blue lettering on pale ivory card, a silver border.

HOLLIS HEMPSTEAD

Portraits—Landscapes

SPECIAL COMMISSIONS

She leers out from under her eyebrows; it is her patented sort of catsy look, but he is not the best target. "You're not suddenly making any sort of living at this, are you?"

"I am wide open for business."

"Isn't that the truth."

"Such dirty talk," he says, gently. "No, actually—Scotty paid for them."
Scotty raises a faint hand in acknowledgment.

"Aren't you generous," she calls. She bats a pack of cigarettes toward herself and lights one. "No, but *Special Commissions*, Holly, it *does* sound sort of dirty, doesn't it? I mean what else *can* it mean? There are commissions, and then there are the *special* ones. And especially when you put it in the little teeny type, you know, it's just sort of dirtier. Why didn't you just say *Nudes*?"

"In Boston," he smirks. He works for another minute, glancing at her as she smokes. "Do this," he says, and lifts his chin. She does. The tusk nearly tips her backward; the rider makes his shifting adjustment. To balance it all she sticks the cigarette between her lips as though she is her brother's corny moll. While she is holding the pose he asks, "Do you want to marry him?"

"Oh, well," she admits, "I think *he* wants to marry *me*." She plucks out the cigarette. "Once the wife's out of the way."

Her brother is pretending to be neutral on this score, but he can't look at her.

"All right," Hollis decides. "I'll come see him."

The honest truth is she doesn't want to marry anyone. She couldn't make anyone take care of her—never again. She is going to lose her mind again, she knows, and it just isn't fair to make anyone come along for the ride. "Attaboy, Holly," she says. "I just wouldn't want him to think I'm all on my own in the world. He's such a sentimental old bum, you know." She drops her chin, hands the card back. "It would make him too sad."

Meanwhile, Edward is enjoying the stormy summer. He is working long hours, but there is Mary in the outer office to make it all fine. A bolt of lightning kills a Gerenuk antelope in the Franklin Park Zoo, and there is a front-page story about it in the *Globe*. It is a rare beast from darkest Africa and about as hardy looking as a folding chair, but if Edward had been the deer's press agent he would have been proud of the work. He chucks the paper on a stool. He catches Mary's quick voice on the telephone and feels a gust of contentment. The only sour note is that he cannot marry her, because he still has a wife, at least in name; although in fact, as he has come to see, he has never really had a wife at all.

But now he is feeling a revival. Old things that died long ago have been coming back to life. Long ago he had been a happy man, an admirer of Teddy Roosevelt, had worn old boots and slapped his pals howdy, had imagined himself running for selectman or something more, feeling he was in possession of a dumb straight-ahead affection for all his friends and for the public at large, a grand and agreeably stupid feeling that seemed to be his natural way. He looked the part, but more than this, he felt it *suited*. Big fella, big heart. It got him in trouble sometimes, for example in the ring; when any sort of emotion got the best of him he would overswing, making a bid to win the fight with one punch. He would open up on the right side, and anyone who knew the book on him would be waiting for it, and that would be that. If he could have stopped doing it, he would have. But he understood it to be an aspect of his character, and anyway it displayed his natural self—and a good self it was on balance, a man suffering from no hesitation and prone to big declarations of passion, with a bounty of feeling he harbored for individuals and for whole races of humanity. That's who he was once, most fundamentally, and it's who he feels himself becoming again with Mary.

For now he is aware of what he has been missing all these years: the joy of life. Just life, that's all it is. Frankie serves them coffee in the mornings when they arrive together off the streetcar and step into Vernon's for some breakfast before work. Tomato-on-rye at lunch. Mary kids him and feeds him lines, and he detects the admiring glances of every other man in the place. There is a brother somewhere, or so the story goes, but Mary is reluctant to produce him so maybe he's just a figure she feels she needs, a source of possible threat. She is no shrinking violet, either; together they sit in the fourth row at the Palace or the Foster-Wilde Hall out of range of the flying blood and sweat but close enough to see everything, and Mary tucks herself into his arm but never turns away; she loves watching the big fellows go after it hard, and in the car going home she is definitely hot to trot, while Isabel had always turned up her nose at the whole business. "Come on, Teddy," she will say, putting a hand on his leg.

And they go to the movies and sit in the dark and laugh together; she has a heartbreaking *hee* of a laugh that he could listen to all day. And on Saturday mornings they lie in the sun in the apartment garden with dark glasses on and read the newspapers with a pitcher of orange juice between them. And airplanes pass overhead, and they watch them go, wondering who the lucky stiff is to fly away like that. And Edward's heart feels full, it feels *packed,* as though more blood is suddenly reaching it than before; he feels a richness there now, a beautiful glory. He can't believe his good fortune.

And then a man comes to see him in his offices, with a froggy, loose-lipped mouth, his eyes half-lidded, wearing a silver suit and a red tie, carrying the air of an established gent. He is squat, powerfully constructed, an inch under six feet, a year or two short of thirty.

"Mr. Howe?" the man ventures. "I'm Hollis."

It takes Edward a long moment to place the name. He doesn't know any Hollis, and the man from Guarantee, who is expected in ten minutes to talk about insuring their fighters, is called Mr. Farber. When he gets it, his surprise is too great to mask. "The brother!" he exclaims, delighted. "Sit!"

"I beg your pardon; you were expecting someone else."

"I thought you were a figment!"

Hollis Hempstead looks down at himself with pretend concern as he settles in. "Sometimes I don't feel all there," he admits. "I wonder some-times if it's worth getting out of bed at *all* some days."

Now he notices the man has the mincing air of a fairy, and Edward recoils a little. "Sure," he says.

"Mary tells me all about you; I hope you don't mind my dropping in to see for myself. She let me in. I like your view." Hollis nods appreciatively at the potted palms, the brass cigar lighter, the brass lamp. He seems to fix each of these in his memory before he says, "Very comfortable. I'd imag-ined something more rough-and-tumble."

"We don't let the hard boys up here," he says, and hears the double meaning too late. For a second it occurs to Edward that Mary has hired someone and put him up to an impersonation, some flamer she dug up from somewhere as a joke on him. It would be her style. But no, there is a strong resemblance once you look for it. Only what is smooth and shapely in Mary is froggy and out-turned in the brother—the liquid lips, the pro-tuberant eyes, the heavy shock of black wiggly hair. He feels a surge of pity for Mary, having a queer for a brother, and in its wake, wanting to do right by her, he offers her brother cigars.

"Thank you." Hollis selects one and accepts the cigar cutter and executes a brisk snip. He tosses his tip into the cuspidor and half stands again to receive the flame from Edward's lighter.

"What line are you in?" Edward asks.

Hollis winces at this. "For the moment I work in an artists' supply shop."

He thinks carefully before he says, "Honest work."

The brother works his cigar and says, "Let me say before you decide to take my head off for butting in where I'm not wanted—you make my sister very happy."

"She makes me happy as well."

"If you're wondering where I stand, I can tell you I don't mind any of it. In fact I'm here to let you know I encourage it."

Edward notices now that he is straightening the files on his desk. He steeples his fingers. "I guess you wish it was otherwise."

The brother lifts his cigar in salute, surrender. "In a perfect world," he concedes. "But that's not what we've got. Not even close."

"You ought to know I've asked her to marry me, after my divorce."

"Yes, she mentioned. Your wife left you for—a hat designer?"

"That's right." He flushes hotly. "Some story, I guess."

"Remarkable," Hollis says faintly, though his attention seems to be drifting. His glance strays over Edward's shoulder. "That's you?"

Edward turns around, examines the photograph. Midswing he wears an expression of strange neutrality, all feeling wiped from his face. Only a faint stare of concentration shows. "Years ago," he admits.

The brother eyes it for another moment. "If you're half that much now, you'll do, won't you."

"I can still stand up, if that's what you came here to see about."

"Partly," Hollis admits. "She hasn't had the easiest time of it," he says now, choosing his words.

"Girls don't, these days."

"Possibly you know our parents both died within a few weeks of each other, last year, in Scranton. I was already established out here, and Mary came to live with me."

"She told me."

Hollis calculates, presses on. "Our parents left us a little money. Not much, I'll tell you. The only thing Dad ever owned that ever came to anything was a half share in a shoe store, and it burned down a year before they passed. Fortunately he had been keeping up the insurance."

"We do all right here," Edward offers. "I can give her what she needs."

"I just wonder if you've quite figured out what she's about, Mr. Howe."

"Why don't you just let me and her talk about that," he says.

"Well—why don't you sort of ask her what I mean," Hollis says. "She's by far the strongest person I know, Mr. Howe, but she has her vulnerabilities."

"Don't we all."

The brother gives him a faint acknowledging smile, then reaches into his inner pocket and withdraws a card. He takes a pencil from the desk, writes a telephone number on the reverse, and hands it across to Edward. "I'm sorry for your divorce," the man says.

"That's a little over the line, pal."

The brother rises, extends his hand. "If for some reason you need me, please let me know. I'm happy to drop everything for her sake, no questions asked. Call me if you like." He lifts a hand in salute, then exits through the outer office. Edward waits, frozen, hoping to hear the exchange between Mary and her brother, but at the last moment Edward sighs and in that instant loses the two words that the man utters, though he catches the tone—friendly, but with a note of warning.

"I will," she says, in reply.

A moment later she appears at his doorway. She looks at him from under her eyebrows, the look that opens the veins to that rich object in the center of his chest; but she is different now. She is, unmistakably, a sister. Her hair is two firm braids along the sides of her head, and in her eyes lives a look of tender worry. As though she is keeping something from him that would hurt him to know.

"My two protectors," she tells him.

Be careful, she has been warned.

5

Clyde's root cellar will be twenty-four feet long and eight feet wide and seven feet deep. It will take him a couple weeks of solid work, he figures, but he has the time. So he sets out the boundary stakes in the side yard. He inflates the tire on the wheelbarrow. The digging goes easy for three feet and then a band of clay comes up and it becomes slow going. His boots grow caked with mud and the edge of the spade grows dull, so in the evenings he sharpens it with a file and a rough slurry of Carborundum.

"You ought to get yourself a steam shovel," Roy says.

"Well if you got one," Clyde says.

In the evenings he is joined by Roy and once in a while even their father, who can't stand to see a job done without him, even a job he thinks is for the birds. "He won't pay you numbskulls to do it," his father notes. But he joins in anyway. They slice into the packed clay with their shovels and picks. They do not say much as they take turns muscling the wheelbarrow up the bowing planks. They are all tidy workers and the corners are square and the walls true. When it grows too dark they bring lanterns from the barn and place them on the soil so their shadows stagger across the walls. The mosquitoes find them and the bats swoop overhead and the stars come out over the prairie above the cottonwoods. And there is the Milky Way. The lights go out in the house and they are still laboring to the sounds of the horses, the frogs plonking in the culvert. Three Tombaughs at work without complaint.

———————

Well, Clyde likes the work—it is uncomplicated. It is a relief from the rest of his life, which seems complicated. The complication arises from who he is. He does not always feel the oldest but he does seem to everyone—to himself, too—distinct from his two younger brothers. He is the sourpuss, the one not satisfied with things. Moping around all day he can appear younger than he really is. To counteract this he will sometimes wear a tie when he does not have to. But he is lousy at this too. His collar is rolled, and he is always having to hunt for clean cuffs. (While he is digging, though he does not know this, his four remaining cuffs are in a round pasteboard box in the middle drawer of his desk, under the sloping pile of *Popular Mechanics,* each issue of which he keeps, as he keeps most things that suggest he is destined for someplace else. He has read them all front to back.) Clyde holds the opinion that he got the worst of the family's move west, which came about when his father saw a chance in Kansas. You can make a better living here as a tenant farmer than in Streator, and Clyde knows it. Land is cheaper and more productive besides.

Still, he blames his father for stranding him here. He is alone and considers himself trapped, and it is convenient to blame someone. Having entered as a junior into the high school's tumble of constantly shifting allegiances, he was never entirely accepted as one of *them.* He joined the track team hoping to make friends. To his surprise he turned out to be a decent miler even after a bout of the whoop. But he was an outsider and remained mostly friendless, and since graduation he has just tried to make the best of things. He has worked the farm and hired himself out to the Steffens and to anyone else who needed him. For six months he was secretly, shamefully in love with Lily Gooden, the daughter of the Steffens' hired man, Jim Gooden, eventually working up the nerve to ask her to see a movie with him, but she declined.

"You're a nice boy," she told him, "but you don't seem like you know very much about the world."

A month later she was engaged to Lance Usterhall, a hired man on another farm a few miles down the line.

This was how he began making his own telescopes, because of Lily's rebuff and because of a magazine article he read about how it wasn't that hard, but also because in the middle of Pawnee County, way the hell out on Route 11F, two miles from the intersection with Route 82, a good six, almost seven miles from downtown Burdett, which itself is not exactly Chicago, there is just damn-all else to do.

In the cool, nearly motionless air of the completed root cellar, the Foucault knife-edge test works perfectly. You punch a nail hole in a coffee can and drop a candle in so a pinhole of light comes out. This is your star. Then you set the glass disk in the brace on the wall exactly twenty-two feet eight inches away, where it will catch the pinhole light, and then you go back and crouch down behind both the coffee can and also behind a razor blade you have cemented to a brick. You put one eye blind behind the brick and let the other eye peek out just along the knife's edge, and you look down the root cellar at the glass disk as it attempts to resolve the pinprick star, and in the still air you see that the glass is humpy and mottled with dozens of shadows. But that is all right. Because if you can see them, you can get rid of them.

The final stage—the one that follows now—is a long series of tiny fussy fixes. Every shadow represents a minute irregular rise on the disk's otherwise perfect surface. You cannot mark the glass with a pencil because it will cause a scratch, so you go up to it steadily where it awaits in its brace, fixing your eyes on your spot, and give a quick wipe or two with the polishing pad. Then you go back and look again to see if anything has changed. He is cautious, and often he will polish down one irregularity only to divide it into two sections of slightly different heights, and he dreads overpolishing, which will create a tiny trough in the mirror, at which point he would be forced to go back out to the grinding post and make up a lap of pitch and smooth down the rest of the mirror to match the area of depression. So he is very slow. When he grows wary of the power of the polishing pad he dips his thumb into water into which he has stirred a dusting of #303 emery and polishes the mirror in spots with just his damp thumb: one, two, gentle strokes, after which he goes back behind the razor and checks it again.

It takes two weeks to get it right. But the progress is steady and he loses himself in it until at last in the cool root cellar he sees no shadows, just an illuminated disk of perfect regularity: a bright featureless sheen of silvery light. And when he puts the Tolles eyepiece to his eye he sees only an unshadowed spot about the size of a dime, and wherever he aims the eye-piece across the mirror he sees only that same bright flawless coin. Then he sits down and opens a jar of pickled beets and draws a red hunk out, dripping, with his fingers and lies down chewing on the concrete floor.

See, pop, that's how you go and succeed at something.

He can bring it with him to Lawrence. Take some girl out into the fields and from there he figures it is a piece of cake. Show Roy how it is done. The next day he bolts the mirror into a shipping crate so it can travel untouched by anything. It stands up from the bottom of the crate like a big blue toadstool. He bangs the crate around until he is sure it is impervious to even the worst mishandling, then he writes FRAGILE on the top of the crate and all four sides with a gray oil crayon and drives down to Burdett with it beside him on the passenger seat and mails it off to Wichita, where Napoleon Carreau will complete the final step of silvering. He counts out the money for the freight and nods at Mac and out of satisfaction slaps the wooden post office counter. Well, he feels like a man at the moment anyway. Such a pretty thing, on its way.

Then it is time to harvest the wheat. A traveling outfit cuts the wheat along Route 11 for a price (ten cents an acre), and then it is the farmer's job to thresh it all where it lies. When the wheat is dry his father tows the thresher to the cut fields. A crew of five other farmers pitch in, as the Tombaughs will pitch in for them in turn. Taar Olefssen and his sullen downy-haired son Per, and Carroll Cartwright, a bachelor making do, and the Swenson brothers, two bald giants in overalls and undershirts. And Clyde and his father and Roy. The steam tractor provides the power for the great whirring thresher belts while you rake the cut wheat and gather it into your arms and throw it into the thesher mouth to be separated, grain from chaff. After an hour of standing beside the roaring machines, gathering the cut wheat into your arms, bending and standing, raking and kneeling, you stop hearing the engine, you stop thinking of hearing as something you do, and then all at once the noise emerges again into your consciousness full of its many constituent parts, a rumble and a liquid pounding and a million high whinnying sounds from the belts and other things besides. You feel it in your sternum in a strangely personal way.

The wheat in his arms is fresh and springy. If you leave your rake in one place too long, the grasshoppers will crawl onto the handle and start gnawing at the sweaty wood. If you upturn a damp patch, out comes a cloud of long-legged Dutch flies, so wispy and transparent they are hardly visible, nip-ends of thread and knotted Cellophane. Clyde likes the feel of an armload of wheat, its intershifting heft. You bring it to the gaping square mouth of the thresher and set it sliding down the chute. A moment's pause, then the whirring, and a moment later a trickle of grain pebbles into the wagon bed, and the straw is rushed air-fluttery out the hayer onto the stack.

Because it is the last time he will have to do this work, he almost enjoys it this year. He was never meant to be down on the farm, he thinks now with satisfaction. He misses that woppy gangster jingle leaking over the eastern horizon, Chicago a blur of light in the sky, when you could tune the radio and hear the Ben Morrison Orchestra tootling away in the Stansfield Hotel. Now he'll go to Lawrence and walk among the brick campus buildings and eye the girls and make his mark. Meanwhile more than a hundred miles away Napoleon Carreau applies black iron oxide, stannic oxide, silver nitrate, potassium hydroxide, and ammonium nitrate, swirling them around, sponging them off again, silvering this farmboy's excellent mirror.

While he waits for his mirror to be returned, he builds the housing for the telescope. Simple stuff. The ten-minute drive south to Burdett for supplies takes him past a dozen tenanted farms. It is flat here, almost exactly flat. A mile from town the first shabby houses appear: hard-packed yards under the sunstruck vacancy. Laundry plunging on the lines. A girl runs a wild circle around a fresh stump while her brother looks on from where he sits atop it like a cat, full of opinion but saying nothing. Then he comes to the railroad tracks and the tiny depot, where the baggage cart stands casting its shadow on the unpopulated platform.

The dirt road turns to brick. Now the houses are separated from one another by fences, and the shade of the elms reaches deep into the green yards. Here is the Lutheran Church, blazing white in the sun. Paint is peeling, as it always is, from the sign in the churchyard, and in his mind Clyde scrapes it away once and for all. Main Street is a row of low shop-fronts. At the far end of Main Street stands the Masonic Hall, three stories of concrete, the flag flying. Clyde parks in front of Zeebe's Hardware. He sets his hat on his head and ducks into the store. It is cooler inside, the fans turning up near the ceiling.

"Another one, Clyde," says Bill Zeebe.

"Looks like it," he says.

But a good one this time.

He buys a ninety-inch length of galvanized steel pipe, ten inches in diameter, a few screws, some more Carborundum. At home, from the side panel of a dead 1910 Buick (the landlord's ancient barnbound car, slowly being cannibalized for this and other purposes), he cuts twin strips of iron and bends them into hoops to encircle the pipe. He builds an iron mount-ing from the innards of an old cream separator, using the universal hinge of the baffle joint to construct a sturdy rotating pivot. The Tolles objective is mounted in an hour and the focusing mechanism he has in place by the next night, and then he is ready.

Roy comes back on Saturday nights and climbs into bed and lies unsleeping for long minutes, humming satisfied in his little bed. He has news he wishes to spill. But Clyde is feeling onto something himself, so he sort of goes ahead and lets Roy stew in his own juices.

When the mirror finally comes back from Carreau he unlatches the lid and peeks in.

The mirror is perfect. Brilliant silver, smoother than anything he has ever seen.

He walks to the porch and, holding it by its edge, lifts it up to the sun. A faint gray disk of light shows through, a ghost sun.

With shaking hands he goes around the house to the barn and bolts the mirror into the steel housing. Then he sets up the tripod in the yard and screws the telescope down and swings the telescope at the horizon. He stands on tiptoe to see into the objective.

He turns the focus knob.

A bright circle of wavering heat sharpens to perfection. The telephone poles show exact at two miles. He counts the hard black birds on the wire. And the green glass of the insulation knobs.

Yes, indeedy.

His heart is flopping in his chest. He's done it, goddamn it.

That night, as is his custom before going out to view, he lies down in a dark room for an hour to gain his night vision. His bedroom is good enough. Not entirely pitch-black but all right. The white curtain drifts in the breeze. He sets his head on the pillow. The slanting beadboard ceiling comes down to an imaginary meeting with the floor somewhere behind his head. He is always reaching for that point in his mind; somewhere behind the little wall there is a perfect point that does not exist. Extending lines to the horizon, intersections. Someone shouts in the reaches of the downstairs. A sing-song apology from little Charlie is followed by silence. Later Roy starts up a chant on the stairs.

Ratty, stinko, crocko, boiled—

Charlie answers:

Lousy, high-hat, blotto, spoiled!

When he can see the gleam of the blue dish on his dresser Clyde finds a pencil and his drawing board with its clipped papers. Then he calls out, his face at the crack of the door, "Lights!"

"All right, Clyde," his mother calls up.

After a minute he steps out into the dark corridor. He feels for the railing.

"Don't kill yourself," Roy suggests.

His family is waiting in the dark at the bottom of the stairs. He leads them through the dark kitchen, the glassware jingling. He pushes open the screen door into the vast dark prairie night. He knows it is a good mirror, but his breath is short. Something still might be wrong. In a moment he finds Jupiter with his naked eye, high in the west, and aims the telescope that way.

A black field. No, a dozen stars, faint and faraway. Shining like pinpricks.

A glow—he nudges the telescope southwest. And Jupiter swings into view.

When you have seen Jupiter in photographs, you have seen it in shades of gray. Light gray and dark gray and middling grays, with the Great Red Spot a small gray blemish. With his two previous telescopes he managed to resolve a blurry golden-orange smudge of light, but that was all. So when he sees it now—a brilliant bright orange globe—it is breathtaking. Even across the 400 million miles of empty space the planet projects its grandeur. An enormous world, hanging in the interplanetary sunlight. King of the universe.

He is transfixed.

The Great Red Spot stands dead center.

After a long minute he stands. "Well, that's all right."

His father bends and after a moment lets out a low whistle and says, "Not bad."

"Not bad," Clyde agrees.

His mother, leaning in, says, "My goodness, Clyde," and his brother Roy says, "You dumb old clodhopper," but will not leave the eyepiece. By the time little fly-haired Charlie has had his turn, the planet has nearly dropped out of the field of view. He pivots the telescope gently down. Then the family steps back and filters toward the house, and Clyde takes a pencil from his inner pocket and begins to draw.

His life, as it was meant to go.

He draws for six successive nights and on each night he watches until the features on Jupiter's surface have moved. Jupiter has only a nine-hour day, so after three hours the Great Red Spot has traveled considerably, while the other bands, peach and ochre and cardinal red, make similar eastward motions, the swirls and irregularities passing repeatedly across the surface of the planet, each band appearing to be tendriled into the bands beside it, and—though this is at the limits of his vision—seeming to tug or hinder the bands above and below it, so the whole swirling mass interferes with itself. One part influencing all the others. It appeals. He draws this effect as well as he can, as the summer air, itself swirling in its massed miles above the farmhouse, produces its blurring and obliterating effects, the planet sometimes smeared clean of any features and becoming only an undifferentiated orange disk, sometimes swelling to three times its real size. Twice over the week the swift bright granulated trace of a meteorite flashes in his field of vision, the eddying pools of ignited nickel glowing, then diminishing, but remaining visible, in the way fireworks do, for a long moment, before fading out entirely.

For a little while he forgets himself. What a relief it is.

The weather holds. August skies. The oats are nearly ripe, and the Kansas nights are vast and full of crickets. The moon is scalding white through the 9-inch: craggy cliffs and scooping craters, the shadows broken. It is a world entire. Fly there on a giant moth and meet an ivory princess.

"Say, Roy," he whispers. They are on the porch roof, where Roy is sneaking cigarettes. "You can come up and see me in Lawrence if you want."

Roy smokes. "Show you a thing or two, you mean."

"If you like."

Roy exhales peaceably. "That Lily Gooden wasn't no good for you anyway. All you'd end up would be son-in-law to a hired man. Think how much you'd kick then."

Roy knows him pretty well, Clyde supposes. He will miss that, anyway. From the rooftop he can see in the starry darkness the telescope on its tripod in the farmyard. Beyond that the barn and the fields of good wheat and oats and inside it all a sort of heartbeat, a fine strong pulse of water and soil and sturdy growth. A little stirring of the air and he smells the horses and the wellhead and the chickens and the tomatoes and his mind reaches out to the big old Kansas emptiness and all right he will miss it all, a little.

He asks his brother for a cigarette and Roy cries a little in false alarm and sends one over with the matches. "My big brother," Roy exclaims quietly. And the brothers smoke while below Kelly beats her tail in the glossy grass.

The next night a haze moves in and settles, promising rain and heavy weather for the next day. The moon blurs. He fits the Bakelite cover to the open end of the telescope and gives the tripod a good shake. Sturdy. The next morning he stands out on the porch and watches a storm rise up out of the west. After climbing to a good height, the storm stands on the far horizon, in no hurry. It is a big thunderhead, full of lightning and rain, but nothing out of the ordinary. Still, he is wary. By the time he has finished his morning chores the wind is up and the oats are tossing beyond the fence. Hunched against the rain he unbolts the mirror from the tube and covers it with a polishing cloth and hurries inside. Upstairs he stows the mirror in its box for safekeeping while the sky darkens and the rain increases.

The hail starts just after noon. The porch roof begins to rattle and ping with tiny white hailstones, no bigger than pea gravel, springing and dashing all over the yard, ricocheting off the polishing stand and the well handle and the telescope housing, a faint white curtain. There is a smell of sudden winter, and then some quality in the air shifts and the noise becomes a massive, thundering attack; the hailstones grow to the size of marbles and larger and pelt down, burying themselves into the moist soil of the garden and hammering the beans from their vines. A minute later when the storm has abated, the farmyard is snow-white and beyond the fence the field of oats is battered down flat.

In a second he is out the back door and across the sliding, melting mass underfoot. The oats are a disaster. The stalks are bent and broken, the seedheads have been torn from the shafts, and the whole field is a sodden ruin.

His college money, destroyed.

Desolate, he turns back to the house. His parents are standing on the porch. His father puts on his hat and picks his way slowly across the yard. The urge rises in Clyde to knock his father down. Instead he heads off into the icy field, his father calling after him. Already the air is clearing. The smell of frozen winter. The crunching of the pellets underfoot. A white and empty world. The surface of another planet, not your own.

6

With Lowell's *Memoirs on a Trans-Neptunian Planet* on his lap and a pencil in his teeth, Alan Barber sits on the chaise longue in the shady screened porch off the second story of the Main Building. When he hears a noise in the hall he tucks the *Memoir* under the other papers on his lap, but it is not Dick, only Mrs. Fox making the daily rounds.

"His laundry bill," she says, brandishing an envelope.

"I shudder to think."

"He's not up here. He's not anywhere."

"Check the comparator."

"He's *not* at the comparator," Mrs. Fox says. She is a poodle-headed number in a long blue dress and gold-rimmed glasses on her nose. "What happens is these outfits end up billing the director's office, and then it ends up on my spindle." She wags the envelope at him. "He's your friend."

He leans forward and plucks the bill from her.

"It's always the rich ones," she observes.

Back at the Harvard College Observatory most of the brute calculation is done by the computers in the computer room, largely girls who have a math degree from Radcliffe and who aren't yet married and distractible. The feeling is girls have a capacity for the dull labor and that it is the men who have access to flights of insight. The girls will somewhat bristle at this proposition, but it is the understanding. So Lowell's numbers will have been long ago backed up by someone in the computer room, where Florence herself now works; and this gives Alan a certain feeling of satisfaction, of connection, he has a reason to talk to Florence again while he is in pursuit of this silly project. It is the sort of project perhaps that he is best suited for in the world: he is out on his own but with a romantic star to follow.

Of course he has not always been in love, or whatever it is, with Florence. There were a few girls in high school and then at Indiana University Alan had a girl named Olive Harper, pretty, brown-haired, willing to listen as he described the newly discovered outward-rushing nature of the universe, the fact that the universe not only was vastly larger than had been previously thought but was moving away from itself at titanic speeds, expanding at hundreds of miles per second in places. "Expanding into *what*?" Olive asked, acutely, and four months later he made his proposal with his heart thudding, and she smiled happily while absorbing it as she would have a gust of wind, shutting her eyes as though to protect herself until it passed.

She returned from Cincinnati to tell him that her father would not allow it. Alan was poor, his prospects doubtful. He was surprised by her refusal, as he had not expected Olive, who could be moved by a Doppler shift, to show this easy obedience to her father, a real estate man whom Alan had never met. But the matter was closed, and they did not see each other again except in halfhearted, friendly passing. It was wounding, and seemed to make Olive at once smaller, less of a person at liberty in the world, and larger, attached in a permanent way to a complicated system of obligation to which Alan had been denied admittance.

Alan himself, an only child, was raised without a father (dead of pneumonia when Alan was three). He did not really feel the lack as a boy and in fact would have resented any intrusion into what seemed, to him, the pleasant life that he and his mother had arranged. He made every effort to be a good boy as he understood it, to work hard and not get into scrapes and not want things he couldn't have. Their town, Belleville, was a brick prettiness of four thousand people situated on a forested shoulder above the Ohio River; across the water was the panhandle of West Virginia, and coal barges were a constant traffic. In Belleville his mother taught piano at the Bains Academy, a school for adults who wanted to further themselves: music, history, languages, the basics of biology and physics, fundamental and advanced accountancy, and shooting. (Manwerth Bains was good with a rifle.) When Alan was a boy and finished with his own day at school, he would walk the two blocks to the dark yellow stone building that had been formerly a county orphanage. He did his schoolwork at a vacant desk and roamed the mostly empty halls, now and then lingering outside a doorway where someone was giving a lecture on the history of France. His mother taught piano in the evenings but spent her days as the Bains Academy secretary, answering mail and writing dunning letters to the school's unpaid accounts, the pleats of her leg-of-mutton sleeves coming unpressed in the humidity.

The building was nearly a hundred years old and had seen its share of suffering. Sitting alone upstairs at an overlarge desk studying his McGuffey and staring across the room at the map of Africa, he would sense it. As a half orphan he supposed he found some fellow-feeling in the ghosts that drifted here down the parqueted hallway where the ancient nails were always rising up black as burned-out matchsticks. Each nail a parentless child, he imagined, snugging them back into place with the heel of his shoe: *You stay there.* Then up from below would come his mother's voice, singing just for the pure lungwork and joy of it, and it would draw him down to the door of the music room, hat in his pocket, the steel cables of the piano twanging in the old cabinet, his mother's hard shoe going athump. Standing there he would be flushed with a sweating love for his mother which had to it an element of physical delectation, he wanted to climb into her lap (he was of course too old for this) and to put his flesh on her flesh, he wanted to be taken up into her somehow, and while he understood this was wrong it had a shameful intestinal urgency to it, stirring something low in his groin that had never been named in his hearing. It was a lurid, helpless feeling but one he could not resist when he heard her there, sounding the rhythm with her foot and pounding out the octaves. Then one afternoon when he was seven and outside, he found that the motion of the rope swing suspended from one of the elms was matching itself to the song that played in his head, and that even as the swing slowed and he covered less and less of the scrubbed-out dirt underfoot he could keep up the same pace as he sang. Galileo had discovered this, the isochronous nature of the pendulum, in 1581, but for Alan this was his first mathematical experience. He would later know that music is enacted mathematics, that each proceeds by relating one thing to another, translating a small notion into a larger corollary, and that each relies on the workings of an internal synchrony that moves along in time, as it were, proposing and solving, proposing and solving, until the matter comes to resolution. His mother would lead him to all this, eventually, but at the time he was satisfied to keep on humming in his mind, his small body kept very still for the purposes of experimental integrity, while diminishing sections of the packed, root-humped dirt moved past beneath him at ever-slower speed. It struck him as meaningful, though he could not have said how.

At any rate he had uncovered something. Using the books everywhere in the Bains Academy (his mother tugging them out of high shelves), he mastered trigonometry by nine. At fourteen, on a hunting trip into the back basement realms of the Belleville Library, he discovered *On the Calculation of Orbital Ephemerides*. It was his first book on celestial mechanics, and he sat there in the single ladder-backed chair beneath the high mud-spattered window and began to read. The Newtonian operations of the physical universe were knowable—the real forces by which the earth was swept around the sun, and the moon kept lashed to the earth like a dinghy, and the other planets kept in orbit on their invisible leashes. It was here that he first learned that the planets interfered with one another, that they swept by and gave each other gentle tugs from across the interplanetary darkness in the same way he might rush by Harold Alter on the street and call his name and cause him to look up. Through the long winter of 1919 he sat at his ink-blackened desk in his slope-ceilinged bedroom and figured. It was possible to take the heliocentric ecliptic coordinates of a body and translate its position into the *geocentric* ecliptic coordinate system—with just a few trigonometric jugglings—which gave you a body's position relative to the earth (in fact, its position relative to the *center* of the earth); further juggling would give you the body's position in the equatorial topocentric coordinate system—allowing you to use your position on the *surface* of the earth as the origin of the three-dimensional graph on which the body's position was plotted; and these tender, elaborate repositionings, as though you were lifting a bird back to its nest, thrilled him with their involved, cascading, ten-page solutions. He founded and was president and often the sole member of the Belleville Senior School Mathematics Club and the Belleville Association of Astronomers, though he had only a little 2-inch telescope bought through a catalog and found the actual viewing of the moon and stars disappointing, as they never matched in power and momentum what they seemed to own on the page. Because of all this and because his father was dead, the Kiwanis put him up for the Southeastern Ohio Regional Scholarship, and he won it, and went off on the train to Bloomington, Indiana. Dutiful, grateful, absorbed, he did not really look up until the summer before his senior year, which was when he met Olive.

The wound she administered to him lingered, during which time Alan finished his degree and, on the strength of his grades and a paper on the orbital mechanics of Phobos, to which Wilbur Cogshall added his name, won admission to the doctoral program at Harvard. He was prepared to be the hick and was not disappointed, though it was in fairness more his area of specialization than anything else that made him an outlier. Already planetary mechanics were seen as old-fashioned, having lost ground to the spectacular discoveries being made in deep space. But he could be stubborn when he needed to be; all those years of solitary study had made him resistant to certain pressures. So along with the other, required work of nebular mapping and spectrographic analysis of the ionized helium in the B stars in the Pickering series and some catch-up work in physics, which he had skimped on at Indiana in favor of courses in kinematics and analytical mechanics and theoretical statics, he managed to get in courses on dynamic astronomy, mostly following Tisserand on planetary perturbations and Newcomb on lunar theory, and on orbital mechanics, following G. W. Hill's work on the nonspherical figure of the earth, and G. H. Darwin on the development of planetary systems as a by-product of tidal friction, and the orbital mechanics behind meteor swarms, and then there was the great mountain of Poincaré's three-volume *Celestial Mechanics,* the steep foothills of which he had explored under Cogshall but which now he began to climb in earnest, mostly alone, not just the horrible three-body problem but the degree to which each orbiting and rotating body acted as a mass of fluid under its own attraction as well. All of which went directly into that seemingly unfillable part of his mind that he had first discovered within himself while swinging back and forth over the dirt. He came to think that maybe this was what Olive had seen, and decided against in him, this strain of youthful inward seriousness unattached to the normal business of the world; and he did feel, very essentially, that he was still the same abstracted boy he had been then, only now needing to shave and buy hair tonic.

It was also possible, of course, that Olive simply saw through his flash and dazzle, such as it was, to some fundamental dishonesty or indecency. For it is true that by now, after four years at Harvard, he is not entirely sure about what a good man is or does. He does not follow any religion so that is out; he suspects being decent partly means you just don't do anyone harm and you act politely in front of people, no matter what you think about them privately, and that you at least consider how you might improve your standing as a citizen, adding something to the pot. There is also an element of self-improvement, you are supposed to work on yourself in some way to better your character as needed. It is not much of a system to go by, and it has become all confused to him lately, for plainly he is good at what he does and he is not doing anyone *harm*, exactly, but surely it is not good to want another man's girl or to allow oneself to suffer these longings all the time. It is not a sign of good character, and he doesn't even fight it that much. Also you do not sense that the room is full of good people when you are all rolling along on homemade gin singing dirty songs, where a girl is getting her tit squeezed for a joke at the doorway and only shrieks and bats at the ape's hand while also smiling at him to mean *later.* If Alan is in with a bad crowd, he is part of the crowd himself; and if he makes any noise about it he'll get the razz himself, so he keeps mum. And that is something you are not supposed to do, keep mum in a bad crowd, you're supposed to stand up.

But it is also true that none of this really bothers him that often, and seen in the right perspective his bunch are not really bad at all, only a little wild sometimes; only when he stops to think about it sometimes he has the feeling that he has come down a long way without really having done much falling. Not so much a fall, then, as a slump. He is not a boy any longer, possibly is all it is. And sure, he has a leg up on a good number of his fellow students; by now he has known more than his share of the cringingly awkward mathematical wizards, Harvard is full of them, breath nasty, eyes agoggle, and certainly he is not difficult to look at or to get along with, and he is not an outright bastard like some of them. But he sometimes suspects he is not really cut out to be part of the world—that he has no real capacity to take from it what everyone else seems to be content with: a reasonable measure of ambition, a moderate draft of nostalgia, a small shot of love. He wants too much, and he is not very good at getting what he wants, because he'll never admit any of it to anyone, and because also he suspects his own desires don't do him much credit. So what a serious private fellow this all makes him, finally.

Only a motley crew of mostly country-raised boys full of their own ambition have provided anything resembling friends at Harvard; but they are far-flung now and most of them gone for good, including the man who shared his apartment, Gerald MacAvoy, gone last year to a position at Yerkes Observatory. And while he knows about Bohr and of course is current on Einstein, it is not this work that fires his imagination and he finds the math unsatisfying, all the irreducible quantum uncertainties remaining like an irritant in his vision. It is possible that he is missing the boat entirely, that he is already removing himself from serious future work, but so be it. This is who he is. The closest thing he has ever had to a companion in Cambridge is Dick, who like Alan was anomalously studying planetary science, once upon a time intending to study the effects of the solar corona on the atmosphere of Mercury; and who from among the other mice picked just the girl Alan would have picked for himself, the blond small pretty computer named Florence, the girl whom Alan had, unknowing, asked to the movies, and she had put her hand on her round soft chin and looked up from her paper and her eyes had flashed and she said, "I'm engaged, actually. But maybe I'm being hasty. What do you think?"

And then Dick had come loping in and introduced them. Dick had gotten her the job in the computer room; she had just finished her degree in math at Radcliffe. Those few interrupted words between them had been the extent of the pass, and in the years since he has seen Florence everywhere, including in her cube-root-minus sort of bathing suit, but in the way of such things the strangeness of that first moment never entirely went away, and really Alan still feels as though he is waiting for a chance to talk to her again, to answer the question he had not had—had never had—a chance to answer.

It is a long trip from Boston and it is hard to keep yourself in any sort of shape on a train, but Florence manages. A fresh white dress to arrive in, obviously saved for days, and it is not her looks, not exactly, that are so appealing—something instead about her stance, her expression, the good playful set to her jaw and a liveliness in her eyes as she pivots at the hips, gripping the handle of her yellow valise, surveying the platform. A look of patient good humor, as though listening to a child tell a joke. She has a strong, small-breasted body and fine legs that show beneath the pleated skirt. Her blond hair is bobbed under her round yellow hat. Her eyebrows are pale and her nose is flattened a little on the end, as though someone has pressed a thumb to it.

She steps down the metal stairs and comes across the bricks to greet Dick. They kiss. Then she turns to Alan.

"Big bad Barbie," she says.

"Hello, Florrie."

She extends two long white hands to take his. "One more mile on that thing and I'd have thrown myself off the back end."

"There's a line in that," he says, "only it's not fit for mixed company."

"Who is," she sighs. Then she indicates the pile of seven yellow suitcases the porter has taken down. "Someone had better tip that poor man."

"Florrie likes her things," Dick says.

She gives Dick a secret hard look, and, receiving it, Dick propels himself forward to attend to the porter. She turns to Alan. "Sort of desolate out here, but I bet the seeing's something else."

"It's all right," Alan says, "but it just got a hell of a lot better."

"That's not a bad line," she returns, "but it's nothing special."

They watch Dick from afar, his frame bent in an attitude that seems predatory, as though he is about to suck the blood from the porter's neck. Then Alan risks a glance at her. She is eyeing him coolly.

"More of a front end man myself," he says.

"Is that what you are?" She takes his arm and pulls him closer. Her arm is warm, and muscular from tennis. "You're not making him do *all* the work, are you?"

"He's about a mile ahead of me on every count that counts."

"Well, he doesn't look so good. Is he drinking?"

"When he can get it regular like."

"*Oh.*" She sighs. Then: "But *you're* looking fine, anyhow."

"You too."

"Poor Dickie." She grasps his arm closer. Blood goes thudding up his throat.

After Dick directs the luggage to the Monte Vista, he comes loping back with a sly grin and says, "Let's go get the car out, what do you say?"

"Oh," Florrie says, brightening, "I forgot about the car."

They walk out into the blazing midday sun. Heat slams down everywhere. The car, which Dick had shipped out and which has gone entirely unused since, is kept in a barn a block away, just into Mexicantown. The barn is a dark sweet-smelling cave, and the car is backed up against the far wall, under a tarp. "Heave-ho," says Dick, and he and Alan both grip a corner of the tarp and fold it back from the grille. The chrome comes visible and the little silver trophy of the hood ornament, and then, as hay dust billows up around them, the rest of the car is revealed, low and sleek, a Stutz BB four-seater. Alan's instinct is to stand back and take a long look at this beautiful cream-yellow machine (it is new this year, after last year's Cadillac), but neither Dick nor Florence will do anything of the kind. Instead Dick takes the key from his pocket, and the three of them get in, Alan in the rear. The seats are brown leather, very soft. Well, he will feel them.

"Show you the sights." Dick presses the ignition button. "Such as they is, anyway."

They roll out into the daylight, and Florence sneezes once, at which sound Alan's silly heart leaps.

They roll out past the Black Cat and the Monte Vista and the Orpheum. Alan and Dick know it all backward and forward, and don't have much to say about it. It is a little brick frontier outpost with wooden sidewalks, but humble enough to count for something, as Alan sees it now through Florence's eyes; it is an adventure worth counting. Dick steers the mighty car to the edge of town and stomps on the accelerator. Florence gives a yelp and claps her hand to her hat. The Stutz roars along into the dry, empty, hilly territory north of Flagstaff. Scrubby pine and pink thistle grow in the sunny pastures, where a few dusty cattle drift. Pebbles clatter violently against the undercarriage. When Alan turns he sees a wake of dust plumed behind. The road is lined with a wire fence and they are coming up fast on a shambling wreck of a lumber truck. Without a pause Dick sails them past and as they rocket by Alan hears a shout from the tanned Mexicanos within. Or Indians possibly. Under the buffeting wind Florence shouts a question about the Grand Canyon. "Is it really worth it?" Dick sends her a sheepish grin that takes in Alan. They haven't been yet.

"Well, we should all go!" she shouts. "You could come with us."

It is not a real invitation, though it seems too precious to turn aside. But he must. "Fat chance," Alan manages, after a swift silence.

Serenely she turns to Dick. "What'd you do to him, Dickie? He used to be sort of fun."

"Altitude poisoning."

"Isn't there a cure?"

Dick says, "Not for that one."

In a little while Dick knocks the car onto a connecting road and they make a long square return to Flagstaff. Back in town they find Santa Fe Avenue and follow it into the woods. They ride to the top of Mars Hill with Dick wrestling the Bearcat around the sharp turns and winding the huge motor through the gears until they pass the iron gate that marks the start of the property. Then he stomps on the gas again and they go bolting into the empty dirt lot in front of the Main Building, where he skids to a sideswiping stop and kills the engine.

"Christ, I love this car," Dick pronounces.

He sits quiet for a moment, hands braced on the wheel. Then he yanks his handkerchief out and wipes at the shiny walnut of the dash.

Florence steps onto the dirt. She whacks at her front to clear the dust. She is a pioneer girl just down off the wagon train and ready to make camp. "So I bet that's the big old Clark," she points.

Alan joins her. "That's right."

"It looks like a pilgrim's hat. What's that?"

"The 42-inch."

"Handsome, I guess. Sort of sunk in." In fact it looks like a giant silver blister outfitted with a doorway. "And this must be headquarters or something." She puts her hands on her hips and leans back to take in the Main Building. "Pretty nice. You're billeted here?"

He nods. "That's my room right up there."

She scuffs at the dirt with her toe and plucks a pebble up and plinks it neatly off the glass. She grins, pleased with her aim. "Oh, and the famous Baronial *Mansion*!" She takes his arm and strides with him across the lot under the pines. He is dragged along and it is sport for her, but what else is he going to do? She smells of floral soap and wiped-away sweat. A week on the train.

She peers through the front door. "It does go on in there." She gives the door a shake. "Ooh, not fair. A girl could get curious."

"Slipher says there's a little nest of good vintages in there somewhere."

"And you haven't even *tried*," she scolds.

"Slipher won't give up the key."

She rattles the door again. "Just like Lowells to have all this and keep it to themselves. I mean, you'd think she *owned* the place."

Slipher has heard the commotion of the car and comes squinting out into the day. "That's him," Alan whispers into her sweet little ear, "now you're going to get it." They go toward him across the gravel arm-in-arm; then she tugs herself loose from Alan and thrusts a hand to Slipher at a chopping angle. Every bit of this is familiar to him, and precious. "Dr. Slipher!" she exclaims. "An honor."

"This is Florence Chambers," Alan offers.

She sends him a winning smile and tucks her hair behind each ear. "Nice place you've got here."

The director is pleased at this. "Surely nothing compared to Oak Ridge."

"I wouldn't know," Florence declaims, "they won't let me near it."

They collect Dick, and together they all enter the Main Building at the library doors. They walk the creaking halls and after Slipher waves them on, they go up and inspect the living quarters. Alan grins helplessly as Florence slings her head around his bedroom doorway and says, "Needs a *woman's* touch, doesn't it, Barbie?" Back downstairs she peers through the eyepiece of the comparator and steps back respectfully without a word. It is a nice piece of equipment; the latest thing. Then they head outside and hike around the hilltop. It is strange and thrilling to have Florence here, and he has to work to keep the joy out of his voice when they enter the big dark barn of the Clark observatory with the giant telescope hanging in midair as though cradled in drydock. She slaps the cool barrel of the big instrument and, later, of the blunt stubby 42-inch.

Up on the far rise they pause to watch Sykes on his scaffold, hammering his guts out as always building the new Planet X observatory.

"Hello, Mr. Sykes," Alan calls.

Sykes peers down, nails in his mouth beneath his bristly mustache. "Mr. Barber."

"Coming along?"

"On schedule," he answers, "at least on *my* end. Don't ask me about the guts of it, that's Dr. Slipher's lookout."

"It'll be a 13-inch triplet," Dick tells Florence.

"Fancy that," she says.

"Finest instrument on the face of the earth!" Sykes calls, and plucks out a nail. "For this line of work, anyhow."

"Oh, brother," Florence whispers, as they head downhill again, "they really *mean* it, don't they?"

"It's Lowell's pet project," he answers, feeling a twinge of disloyalty. "They sort of have to mean it."

"Bunch of loonies," Dick mutters, "if you ask me."

They explore the rest of the hilltop, beating through the wildflower meadows and padding down the deer trails. As they walk Florence leans on their elbows without discrimination and at one point takes Alan's hand while she works a rock out of her shoe. Alan is careful not to meet Dick's eye during this operation, and he feels mildly put out that she would play so free with him as this. She must know what it does to him. At the same time he is grateful for it and wishes Dick were elsewhere. All this happens just under the surface while the grasshoppers fling themselves out of the weeds. It is hot, and after a half hour Florence is flagging and sweating freely. At the car again, she extends a hand to him. "Well," she exhales, "more tomorrow, Barbie. Thank you for the little tour."

"One of our many services."

"You must let me know about those *others*," she says. Her knees reveal themselves as she lowers herself to the Stutz, and she places her hands on them out of modesty. Then Dick starts the car. "See you tomorrow, old man," Dick calls, tolerantly, and turns the big polished wheel. Alan steps out of the way. It is just Dick's sort of play, giving Florrie a little string and tugging her back. The mean pleasure of this is sitting high in his face, and Florence is very straight in her seat, a good girl, happy to be mastered as they roll unhurriedly away. Two white-suited upright figures, like angels sliding away in the giant yellow car. Alan watches them go with a stupid pain.

He is in the library when he hears footsteps in the corridor. He closes *Memoir*, slides it beneath his papers, and pulls the *Astronomical Bulletin* in front of him. It is only Slipher, who has come to read the newspaper. But Slipher is not fooled; he recognizes the volume immediately. "*Oh*," he comments, sliding it out with his fingertips. "Well, *that's* interesting."

"Yes, sir."

The director tosses his paper down and whumps into a chair and draws consideringly on his Lucky Strike. "You know we never found anything there."

"I know."

"Solving residuals." Slipher sighs. "A sucker's game, if you ask me.

Look at Pickering, for example. He's never stopped running the numbers, and look where it's got him. I don't suppose you put much stock in Bode's Law, either."

"No. It's a fantasy."

"Yes," Slipher agrees. "Percy followed it for a while until he saw the same thing. He was always looking for a shortcut, of course. Residuals being the most plausible shortcut to simply *finding* the thing on a plate somewhere. A ten-year shortcut, as it turned out. He just didn't quite live long enough to see the comparator invented. If he had, he'd never have—" Slipher gestures dismissively at the *Memoir*. But he offers, in exchange: "Actually you remind me of him, you know. A little."

"Thank you, sir."

Slipher rolls his ash, smiling. "That's what you think." He takes up the paper. "So he's off with this *girl*."

"That's the idea."

"And she's really a computer for Shapley?" Slipher turns this over. "Sort of a pretty one. And she came all this way by herself for Morrow."

"Of all people."

"I guess if a girl can fly across the Atlantic." Slipher shakes out the *Republic*. "You'll sing at their wedding."

"Not if I can help it."

Slipher only eyes him sidelong with what looks like complicit amusement. A whisker of fellow feeling comes Alan's way across the table. Meanwhile Dick is down there with Florence on a bed in the Monte Vista. He pictures the shades drawn, the tower of yellow cases in the corner. He feels Slipher's affectionate attention lingering on him; but it feels like a claim, and like any claim he wants to resist it. He would rather be where Dick is.

"I guess it'll be a pretty big affair," Alan says.

"Oh," Slipher gusts, "they usually are, back there. The five-dollar dinner and the tower of champagne cocktails and," he waves, "all that. No sane person would ever stand for it."

They sit in silence for a minute.

Slipher whips back his paper. "Look, how would you like to eat with me and Mrs. Slipher tonight? You look like you could use a square meal. One that comes in solid form, I mean. Emma and I would be happy to have you."

"Well," he says, his resistance crumbling, "thank you."

"Don't mention it." Slipher disappears again. "Take your mind off the girl."

"I haven't got any interest in the girl."

"If you say so, Mr. Barber."

"Well, gee," he flushes.

The Sliphers live in an unpainted one-story shingled house at the edge of one of the meadows, past the Clark dome and the barn. At the suggested hour Alan sets out along the trail through the wildflowers. The sun is slanting hard in his eyes, and he pauses at the barn to watch Jennings milking Venus into a tin pail. Her enclosure is moist and trodden and smells pleasantly of cow. Jennings is fifty and nearly mute but hugely strong, as square as though cut from granite. Alan watches him milk Venus for a minute in silence, then elbows up from the fence and goes on. At the Sliphers' he knocks on the screen door. The house is low-ceilinged and informal with a piano along the wall and dried statice in vases and an oval-framed portrait of the couple as newlyweds in Indiana. Mrs. Slipher is smartly turned out in low heels and a blue print dress with a scalloped lace collar and short gray hair. "V.M. is on the veran*dah*," she tells him. "Would you like some fruit juice?"

"Thank you," he says. He is shown through the kitchen onto an area of back decking, where Slipher sits with his feet up on a rail and a tidy arrangement of flask and ice beside him on a wicker table. "Sir," Alan says.

With his highball glass Slipher indicates the chair beside him. "I'd ask you to join me, but I suppose you opted for the juice."

"Wouldn't hurt to mix, I hope."

"Never done it myself," Slipher says, "but it might not kill you outright."

The view is enormous. To the south is sprawled the vast Martian land-scape, the brown lowlands lifting heroically into the famous orange pla-teaus of Sedona. Mrs. Slipher brings him a glass of apricot juice and an empty glass too. He uses Slipher's chrome tongs and makes himself a rus-tic sort of Tropicana. "Pretty nice back here."

"In the summer it's not too bad. Winter comes, though." There is another wildflower meadow in front of them and pine trees here and there and the smell of warmed grass. Nothing of the observatory is visible from here except the white monument of Lowell's tomb. "Forty thousand dollars,"

Slipher says, lifting his glass that way. "While she was nickel and diming us to death, she spent forty thousand dollars building that thing. Constance Lowell, I mean. The Mad Queen of Mars Hill. Baroness of the B.M. All the while pretending she was blind."

"Truly?"

"Truly." Slipher lifts his glass, and his eyes flutter closed. "Like this. Her particular affectation, Mr. Barber. The widow Lowell walks around like this all day feeling the edges of things. When anybody's *watching,* anyhow. In fact she can see perfectly well."

"Some fun," he laughs.

"From here she's not too bad, if you can manage to ignore the mail," Slipher agrees. "From up close, she's Hell in a fur coat and crazy as a polecat."

"Not a bad match," Alan suggests, feeling it might be all right, "for the man himself."

"Well," Slipher demurs, "only in a way. Certainly Percy had his peculiarities. But he was always a decent man. Whereas they don't come meaner than Constance Lowell, if you want my opinion. But no, the *irony* is the thing, I think. Widow of a great astronomer pretending to blindness. Wouldn't you like to get *that* one under analysis. Which reminds me." Slipher sets his drink down. "One moment."

Slipher disappears inside, then a minute later returns with a cardboard box. Lifting the lid, he reveals a neat stack of old ledgers with marbled covers. "You know what *these* are?"

"Your daily diaries, sir."

"Better." He grins. "Percy's. And not diaries—his notebooks. This is most of what he used, Mr. Barber, to arrive at the figures he arrived at in *Memoir.*"

"Really."

"They're yours to borrow, if you like." Slipher hands him one. "For what they're worth."

Alan opens the ledger. A long fall of regression analysis in a hasty, penciled hand. He feels a little chill of anticipation.

"Thank you," he says.

"That's what you think," Slipher answers.

They eat on the porch after some rearrangement of the furniture. Mrs. Slipher is used to hosting the occasional summer staffer, and she has seen her share of dutiful young men from Harvard. Over the chicken and a cabbage salad she politely avoids watching him drink his Tropicana, and when the time comes she offers the water pitcher without a word. She has heard that he sings, but she also manages to worm out of him that he is something of a piano player. "Now!" she cries, setting her hands down firmly, "you're not getting out of here without playing us something." He objects, but in fact it has been a while and he misses it. The piano in the parlor is an Orson, strained by the desert air but not unplayably out of tune. He whisks out imaginary coattails and adjusts his imaginary monocle and riffs through the music on the cabinet front. It is sappy stuff from Mrs. Slipher's girlhood, and he thinks to try "O Avalon," or something he remembers of Barbecue Bob's:

> Lemme in Charlie it's only me
> Gimme a pint of that Tan-que-ree!

But there is the box of ledgers, and there is Slipher standing in the slanting sun, so instead he blows out from memory the twenty-four bars of the Fugue in D major, stomping on the bass and doing the fancy rapid-fire arpeggios with the right hand while grinning like a chimpanzee. The Orson twangs. J. S. Bach is just this side of jazz when heard from a certain angle but Mrs. Slipher does not seem quite in that line so he moderates into the slow Prelude in E-flat minor which makes for a somber and querying contrast. He plays its stately old harmonies while she seats herself and listens. When he finishes, the little house is silent. Through the screen door comes the far-off grinding of Jennings taking the Model-A truck out on some evening errand and the two-note sundown pipings of the black-capped chickadees.

"Well," Mrs. Slipher stirs, "that was a treat, Mr. Barber."

"My mother," he explains. He feels he has shown off. But the Bach has put him in a masterly mood, and his apology is halfhearted. Slipher's look now is private and faintly grateful, as though Alan has done him a secret good turn.

With Lampland at the 20-inch photographing the spectra of Saturn's moons (Mimas and Enceladas) and Dick Morrow gone for the night with

Florence, Slipher invites Alan to join him in the 42-inch dome. This is a welcome break from the endless Variable Atlas exposures, and he has never worked the big 42. The passage into the dome is a staircase down as though into a pyramid, and then it is a great open space inside, with a subterranean feel. As in the Clark dome, it is nearly pitch-black here with only a few dim red lights to see by. The 42-inch is an old instrument—it has been around since 1909—but still brutally powerful with its giant mirror and especially good for planetary survey work as it collects a lot of light quickly. It is stubby and broad and supported in a massive steel harness. Also like the Clark, it is so perfectly balanced a man can stand flat-footed and with one hand pivot its huge bulk on its multiple axes. Slipher's observation of the North Polar Cap of Mars continues. "You can find him for me," Slipher offers, and Alan checks the charts. This dome is moved electrically, so he lifts the heavy gray switchbox from its place on the cement floor and depresses the black button that sends the big hemicircle shuddering around above them to the proper position. Then he directs the telescope at the hot red spark of Mars using the little aiming scopes aligned along the barrel of the 42. He turns the gears that lock the telescope to the tracking motors, then loads a plate into the spectroscope and checks his watch by the low red light. Then he bends to catch a glimpse of the planet itself through the main scope. The detail is good, a wavering red-brown disk the size of a nickel, three dark slashes in the northern hemisphere and a white blur at the pole. By photographing it, week after week, year after year, you could build up a fairly complete picture of the Martian atmosphere, the weather systems, and thereby arrive at a convincing idea of what it would be like to live there. *Impossible* is the consensus. Although you don't really say such a thing aloud at Lowell.

The ember of Slipher's cigarette glows. There is a certain feel to the overnight work in an observatory, always dependent on the company. With Dick it is quick and professional with a contemptuous undertone, as though the two of them might make a break for it at any moment. Slipher treats the observatory as his living room, sitting mostly in silence and gouging at his pipe with the end of a wire, his legs crossed at the ankle showing the tops of his boots. The director lets Alan keep his eye at the objective to be sure the driving motors don't slip, and fills the observatory with the sweet smell of blended perique, and naps a little when no one is officially looking.

When the exposure is done Alan checks that the plate is secure in its holder and, standing on tiptoes, lifts it out, holder and all. Feeling for the four thumbscrews, he transfers the plate to a lead box and sets the open holder ready beside the box of unexposed plates.

"Shall we go again, sir?" he asks in the direction of Slipher's armchair.

Slipher offers a little laugh. "No need to be such a sop. Take a minute and look at some of the nebulae with this big beauty. Take a peek at the Sombrero. Eleven hundred kilometers a second. One of my old pride-and-joys, you know."

"Yes, sir."

He checks the charts again and moves the roof; then gently he heaves against the massive telescope and slowly it begins to glide up to the zenith to Virgo. He puts his eye to the objective again. The Sombrero stands like a painting, nearly edge-on, with a dark dust lane and substantial central bulge. It is very beautiful and still hard to credit as containing billions of stars on its own. "There's some nice scenery just north of there, too," Slipher mentions. "*Very* deep-field things. I spent a lot of time just learning my way around, you know, when I was doing the spectrum survey for Hubble. Just a little north and east of there you'll see three spirals together, equally spaced."

Alan presses on the barrel of the 42 again, and the stars swim down. He searches for the spirals but sees nothing, only a flickering series of stars, blue and red. He is so lousy with the equipment. Dick has him well beat on this score. After another minute of nudging the 42 around he sighs; it is hopeless. He is about to apologize for it when he sees—what?—a white smudge. There is a moment when nothing quite makes sense. It is a defect in the lens. Then he thinks he has done something terrible to the 42, and now he has to tell Slipher. Then all at once he understands. He lifts his head and with a tremor that he cannot disguise says, "Sir?"

Slipher looks up at the unusual sound of Alan's voice.

The words catch in his throat. He takes a breath.

He'll be damned if that isn't a little bit of a comet.

He says, "Sir, I think you should come take a look at this."

7

From his position on his left side Felix can see, in the immediate foreground, grains of sand clotted wetly like sugar, most of them a transparent sort of white and others gray, others black and infinitesimally glistening. He can hear the stirring of water. He can also hear a heavy, troubled snorting, which, after a muddied procedure within his mind, he understands to be the sound of his mother's breathing.

They are alive, together, on the shore.

Far off in the direction he is facing, perhaps a mile away, is a village.

With great effort he lifts his head.

"Mama," he says.

She sleeps on, unmoving.

He shuts his eyes again. The motion of the dinghy remains in all his cells, a poison waited to be excreted. The heaving sea. The stars. The leaden pressure of sorrow. *God*, he thinks, and to stop this line he wrenches himself upright. From the direction of the village a black-robed figure is approaching, the hem of his cassock swinging around his ankles.

A priest.

A prickling, uncanny feeling enters Felix's bones.

It takes an hour to walk the distance across the yielding sand, the priest between them, offering them each an elbow. His name, they make out, is

Xavier. Eroded bits of shell are intermixed with the sand and press against the bare soles of Felix's feet. At the village there is a wooden wharf, and Xavier's gray church is a squatting frog of stone on the riverbank. Xavier leads Felix and his mother to a bedroom, eases them gently down, and, after a moment's hesitation, leaves them alone.

A boy brings water, food, a change of clothes.

Sometime later Felix wakes in darkness. He has heard a noise. Where is he? The ship is still. Immobilized by pain, he remembers. The loss is too huge to grasp.

His mother is breathing softly in the other bed.

Silence.

His shoulders, one giant knot of pain.

Where is the *Tarsal* now? He has left *Gentlemen of Effort* bookmarked on his bedside table. The potatoes are happy in their dark dry barrel, vibrating along with the engine and not yet missing him; and now entombed in the perfect darkness of this stone chamber in this fortuitous church he thinks of all his tools, the carefully amassed collection of picks and brushes and crates of plaster-of-paris and canvas wraps for cast making, and the tidy tents ordered by mail from Indiana, teak boards and canvas walls and each with a stained pine floor that unfurled like a rolltop desk. And—oh, devastating to think of—the books, and his notes are gone too, the sheaves of them pinned together in a paperboard portfolio where he has even begun to practice his drafting! Little crosshatched pencil sketches of fruit! Leads shaved with his pocketknife! Gone, gone!

Then abruptly he hears again the noise that must have awoken him: the desperate sobbing of a man from far off, somewhere in the stone chambers of the church. He sits up, fighting the pain. Creeps to the door. Puts his ear to it. Puts his hand to the knob. But as he does the crying stops. He waits there, poised, his whole body alert.

Nothing. Silence.

Spooked, he returns to bed. He listens, staring at the dark ceiling.

In the blue light of morning they are walked down to the wharf. Xavier gives instructions to a fishing boat's captain; the two men have what seems a heated discussion in which they are passionately agreeing with each other. Felix becomes unsure of the protocol; he has no money, surely everyone understands that. He tells the priest he will send some when he can. To Felix's surprise the priest begins to laugh and embraces him roughly there on the wharf, grasping his shoulders painfully and imploring him. He speaks thickly over his gums: "Chetumal," he exclaims. "Chetumal!" Felix can only nod and attempt to repeat this mysterious word and offer again his assurances while his mother looks on skeptically.

Then Felix and his mother step onto the swaying vessel and the boat is under way, not out to sea but making a smooth roundabout, Xavier's exuberantly waving figure diminishing behind them as they now steer inland, up a green river, a huge grin the last thing Felix sees as they speed up the middle of the silent, green-shrouded stream. In a moment the town is gone.

"I *will* send him some money," Felix says.

"You had better send him something," his mother tells him, "or he'll hunt you down and kiss you to death."

She takes off her bandanna and runs a hand thoughtfully across her hair.

"I'm sorry I lost your boat," she says.

"It's all right."

They stand together at the stern, watching the brown river unzip itself. A mingled stink of jungle and ocean envelops them. And engine smoke. Then with a resigned sigh his mother tosses the filthy bandanna into the water, a red scrap swirling away across the surface. It is not like his mother to do such a thing, and Felix at once perceives some meaning in it. The rope slips, and there he is, adrift in the vast ocean. Of course she would fling herself over, to join him in their common death.

In a moment the bandanna is gone. He puts out his hand to his mother. She handles it gently, aware of his injuries.

From Mexico City Felix notifies John Reynolds, the manager of the house in Indian Head, that they have lost the *Tarsal*; his wire is intentionally brief, only asking Reynolds to send on clothes and other necessities, leaving out any details of the mishap. There is another wire to send to Gustav

Isenbright of the same character. No one need know, Felix decides, exactly how it all happened; but as he does in fact file official reports stating the truth, he imagines that some reasonably intact version of the story will eventually make its way back to his chums. The Lucky Dupe. The Dumb-Lucky Dupe.

Humiliating, yes. But more than this he notes how few people would have really cared if he had indeed vanished at sea.

They are few days recovering in the Mexican capitol. He buys some snakeskin boots. In the white-carpeted hotel suite, he eats mostly silent meals with his mother.

"Excellent coffee," he observes.

"Yes," his mama agrees.

Then comes the trip by train through Mexico on the NRM, the brown scrubby vastness; he stares at the winding electric brightness of a river—a clump of green trees—the red-tiled roofs of a remote village. And then they are into Arizona and the true desert, the empty plain of the high country. And the canyons. They are still mostly silent, as though nothing more ever needs to be said between them; they have survived something terrific, and what is left to discuss? "Why, what a beautiful color," his mother remarks once, peering out intently at the orange earth. "Have you *ever* seen so perfect a color?"

It is only orange to him—red-brown-orange.

"Lovely," he agrees, a hand on her back.

She is warm and frail.

Then the arrival in the mountain town, where Lowell Observatory is visible as an array of white wooden structures on top of the highest peak. And then the hot spicy Arizona air—they inhale it as they step down from the train, carrying nothing at all—which seems the first breath of a new life.

It is a truism that you do not know what you are capable of until you are asked to reach beyond what you feel is possible. In terms of magnetism, *the human body is capable of a million million wonders, so long as sufficient concentrated energy is supplied.* Perhaps his energies have been too disparately spent until now. Felix anyway takes immediately to Arizona; he feels reborn. Part of this is no doubt due to having survived something so terrible; and part he attributes to the desert air, the sparkling stars. And part he assigns to the fact that no one knows them here aside from William Willoughby, Isenbright's local man. No matter that a week after their arrival they are still eating only at the Frontiersman, nor that their only furniture in the house Willoughby has rented for their use remains a pair of white iron beds which appear to have come from an orphanage, nor that Felix has yet to visit the site of his future dig while Willoughby makes certain mysterious arrangements. While for official purposes they are still waiting for word of the *Tarsal,* Felix figures it is gone for good; indeed he almost hopes never to hear of it again, as though such comforts, such ease of appointment, would threaten to unbalance the new sense of what he might be able to accomplish on his own terms.

He is no fool, he knows he is still a rich man; but he doesn't feel rich at the moment, and he rather likes it. Less to live up to, is possibly the point. Certainly—*less.*

Having never lived in such a small house before, Felix finds himself coming upon his mother when he least expects it, coming out of the toilet or facing each other down what seems a very narrow hallway.

"Why, Felix," she says one day, "if I didn't know better, I'd say you're growing a *beard.*" She grabs his chin and tips it into the light. "You're going to end up looking like my father. I suppose there are worse fates. But they don't make any of those marvelous old barbers' products they used to, you know." She releases him. "You're going to try to be a cowboy, all of a sudden."

"One more or less has the manner thrust upon one, I would say." His present clothes are all from Babbitt's, so he does look like something of a dude.

"Who would have imagined it?"

"Yes, mama." He kisses the top of her head, which is warm and slightly sour-smelling, and pats her shoulder and makes his way past her in the hall. He has not forgiven her, exactly, but it seems the force of all that sorrow in the dinghy, and in the church, has diluted his anger, so that now to his surprise he feels it evaporating, as it were, into the dry lightness of the desert air.

———

Downtown is the brick warehouse that Willoughby has arranged to rent where they will have the dig headquarters. It is all brick and pillars and unswept floor, but Willoughby has claimed it is suitable, and you don't lightly question what Willoughby says. A tall slat-ribbed cowboy in a black suit and a wedged-on Stetson, Willoughby is an old hand; it was he who first suspected the Morrison Formation extended this far south, and he who tipped off Isenbright in Washington. Whether Willoughby has got any of the money Felix paid Isenbright is not known to Felix, but Willoughby does not seem the type to go unrewarded. His fingernails are rimmed with red dirt, and the creases in his face appear permanently floured with it.

When it is at last time to visit the dig site Willoughby reaches into a desk drawer and hands over a folded brown lunchbag to Felix. "Something you might need."

Felix unpleats the top of the bag. There is a blue-steel revolver nestled within. A little wisp of excitement goes through him as he breaks the barrel and sights down it, then breaks the chamber and spins. Six brass cartridges.

"For protection," Willoughby tells him.

"From whom?"

Willoughby grins, showing irregular teeth. "That all depends," he says.

The drive to the dig site is ten minutes south over a jarring washboard road. The disreputable pines stand in isolated groups as though making plans against the others. There is a wire fence suggesting rangeland, but this peters out soon enough. Felix had a cushion-ride Amplex back in Maryland, along with an eight-seater Victoria and a nice old steam-powered Oldsmobile from his father's day and a 1927 Cadillac, but none of them would last an hour on these roads. There is dust in his teeth and a dry feeling in his nostrils. He wiggles a handkerchief from his back pocket and honks out a few brown beauties and weighs the gun in his lap. Depends on what? he wonders. But he will find out soon enough, he supposes. For now he feels it is largely enough to be alive and undrowned, and no water in any direction, in the middle of all this.

At last Willoughby pulls up at the top of a slope of earth. It slides away westward for a few hundred yards to end at a dry gulch. To the north rises a hundred feet of brown bluff, layered black and tan like a Lady Baltimore cake. To the south is a group of boulders.

"Well." Willoughby gestures. "What you paid for."

"The most expensive real estate I've bought in a while."

Willoughby works out a cigarette and lights it. "Sure," he says, "but you can't beat the company."

They head off down the slope. It is steeper than it appears in places, but Felix's snakeskin boots (acquired in Mexico for the equivalent of ten dollars) provide good traction. After a minute Willoughby says, "Let me start you right over there."

There is a brown lump nudging out of the earth. Sitting in the dumb emptiness, it seems a very small and lonely thing. Willoughby goes down on his haunches and Felix crouches beside him. Before them is a rounded knob, about the size of a loaf of bread. Willoughby props his cigarette in the corner of his mouth and extracts from an inner pocket a small hard-bristled brush and a long sharp implement like a lobster pick. "Now," he says, "what do we have here, we wonder."

It is a question, but Felix hasn't the first idea.

"Well, what we have here," Willoughby provides, "is a suspicious lump. Smooth slope, a rock standing out in the middle of it, ought really to be down *there*, should have rolled away. So what the hell's it still doing up here? Well, it deserves a little looksee, don't it. Here. See what it is."

Felix takes the brush and makes a few delicate passes.

"Go on. It ain't about to bite."

He stabs a little with the ends of the bristles, then exchanges the brush for the pick. After a minute the brown crust begins to crumble. The friable stone comes away like a stiff batter coating, and in a minute he reaches a thumbprint's worth of true stone underneath. A hard blue-gray. He puts a finger to its smoothness.

"What is it?"

"Well," Willoughby says, "hard to say. Might be a snail or a clam or a twinkle-toed unicorn. But I do know who the neighbors are. Down here." Willoughby thumps his hat on and throws his cigarette away and motions him down the hill to another gray mound. He crouches, claws away at the soil with his hands, and reveals a gray hump, a double-lobed roundness like a stony brain. "This here's the big fella. Big beautiful Steg. Goes up that way. I sort of explored it a couple months ago just to see how it looked. He's on his back. Head uphill, tail downhill. That's a right knee, so his left is downslope." He takes a few steps down the hill and begins brushing at the soil with his hands.

After a moment a second gray stone emerges.

"There you go." Willoughby squints up at him. "My advice is, you don't touch this one till you get a little field time under your belt."

They face each other in the great vacancy of the windy slope.

"All right," Felix says. "What's the gun for?"

"Sure." Willoughby squints. "So you've got staked out these four hundred acres for yourself, from ridgeline to ridgeline. There—to there. Got a two-year lease from Dundee Timber Company at two dollars an acre, which buys us mineral rights excluding oil, coal, gas, and anything else you could reasonably make a buck on aside from artifactual remains. It's ours, but that don't mean there won't be poachers. Everybody knows we're here, which means you've got to keep an eye out." Willoughby reaches into the back of his waistband and pulls out a massive black pistol. "Left yours in the car, I noticed."

"Yes."

"Don't do that," Willoughby advises. "You never know. My men are all trustworthy. They come with me wherever I go. They were at Bone Cabin Quarry with me and Isenbright. They were at Meadow Farm. They were at Edgewood. They do what they're told. They can do everything. I got a Mexican watchman who ran with Zapata; he can shoot your eye out from a hundred yards. I got a cook. I got everybody. We've been doing this for a long time. What you *don't* want around, sir, is your local curiosity seeker. Also your people who come up off the street looking for a little job of work. That's the people who see you as a mark. You especially. You give off a real nice smell of easy money, if you don't mind my saying."

"It's money," he says, "but it isn't easy."

"Sir, I believe you. I mean no disrespect. Also what your local people are inclined to do, is they're inclined to come on out and take a little souvenir for themselves. They take a little tooth or a little claw or something else. They don't even think of it as stealing. They don't understand that the less complete your specimen, sir, the less it's worth."

"I see."

Willoughby replaces the gun and extracts another cigarette. "And then there are just your usual bad folks," he says, "who might take an interest in

us, one way or another, for one reason or another. For which, sir, the boys
and I are well prepared."

"Pack of Boy Scouts, I guess."

He grins again. "They'll be down from Wyoming at the end of the
summer," Willoughby promises, "and you can decide for yourself what to
call them."

The warehouse has three beadboarded rooms in the front with a telephone and a desk and a set of empty bookshelves. The windows are dusty
and flyspecked. The single wooden chair (made by the Johnson Chair
Company of Chicago, Illinois) creaks and squeals on its black iron spring.
But it is enough. There is a makeshift kitchen in one corner and a rough
bathroom. Telegrams can be sent from three doors down at the newspaper
office. It is from here that Felix does what he can to put his life back in
order after the loss of the *Tarsal*. He writes to the insurance company. He
sends away for more picks, brushes, plaster. Willoughby directs him to a
barn, where Felix finds some secondhand materials Isenbright sent on
from Wyoming: sleeping cots, a crate of blunted chisels, maps, sketching
materials. It is not much but it is a token, and Felix stands in the hay-
smelling interior wrenching open the crates with a grateful heart. He is
a sucker for the decent gesture. And a week later when the new expedition
tents arrive by train, Felix pries open the long crates with a crowbar and
wrestles one out and, over the course of a few hours, erects it in the back
yard, to air it out, he tells himself, but also simply to see what it looks like.
When he is finished he is satisfied; it is the first thing he has really built
himself from start to finish, and lo and behold it doesn't fall down on top
of him. In fact it is a trim little pleasing thing. The side panels can be
rolled up with a cord; there is a strap to hang a lantern from. The jointed
floors are springy. On some instinct he coaxes his mother by the hand
into the back yard to look at it.

"It's like a little boat," he observes.

"Oof. Don't let me near it, then," she says. But he takes her elbow and
escorts her into the yard and into the tent's canvas interior. The light is
warm and diffuse. The floors smell of their new varnish. Possibly he takes
her here out of a forgiving impulse, as though the tent is a big breezy con-

fessional. But she immediately becomes stiff and guarded, suspecting a ploy. Her eyes dart helplessly into the corners as though in search of escape. "I'm *sorry*, Felix," she says.

"Oh, it's all right, mama," he tells her.

"Oh, Felix, don't be ridiculous," she says, "of course it's not all right."

"It is," he says.

"You were going away from me, and I didn't think for a second."

By now they have said it all a dozen times, out loud and otherwise; they understand each other, but where is there to go from here? Maybe they don't need to go anywhere. "That's my mama. Beauty and brains."

"Neither one," she insists, "as you very well know. I didn't mean it about the beard, by the way. It looks just fine."

"Rough and ready."

"Let me see your hands."

He offers them forward. They are still raw, shedding skin, no longer blistered from the hours of rowing but still injured. "I ain't no cowboy, mama."

"No," she says, taking them up gently, "you're Felix DuPrie, of DuPrie and Son. For better and for worse." Now she meets his eye. She appears still weak from their ordeal; or some underlying weakness has been laid plain. Now, a rasp in her voice, she says, "I *heard* you, dear."

Heard him.

"Oh, *crying*, sweetheart," she whispers, "in that church."

"That wasn't me."

She holds his gaze. A flicker of doubt crosses her face. "Well it certainly wasn't *me*," she says.

The hair rises on the back of his neck.

"Oh, Felix, of course it was you. Who else could it have been?"

Abruptly he reaches out and places his hand on her mouth to stop her. Shakes his head infinitesimally. No, it is mad. But if he is hunting God, no one must speak of it.

So it is that the next afternoon Felix takes the Ford Tudor that Willoughby acquired for his use and drives out himself to the hillside, lays the gun on the dirt, and begins scraping away at the gray fossil assigned to him. His land, after all. He feels a sudden need to be here, to be in the field, as it were, stalking his game. At least getting a sense of the country. He feels uneasily that he is trespassing; that he is creeping across the surface of a sleeping giant. That the sun behind him is an eye on his back. Arizona is one quiet spot. When you are out like this on your own, it is even quieter. You start to move a little less abruptly. You listen to the wind and the minute scrabbling fall of pebbles from a bluff nearby. He is on his knees, the tools on the earth before him. And something appeals in the *skrik-skrik-skrik* of the metal tool on the stone. They are a penitent's duties. A vanishing into the sandstone. The sun bakes his back. God a sorrowing God: that blunt pressure from the Other Side only His frustrated efforts to enter the world again. God a lost God, wandered off, crying, out of contact with His world. The brown grains fleck away, giving up the ancient gray bone. Felix goes at this for a long hour, then another. The sun, the buffeting wind, the silver sparkle of the sandstone. He is on the track, all right. Of what, he still cannot say; of something. So hours later when the two figures appear at the top of the hill and call out in his direction, he himself is lost to everything; he does not know where he is or who, and a stroke of some mysterious emptiness pistons through him and he stands, electric, absent, waiting, his afternoon shadow elongated to the east, his soul flattened on the rock, and his heart filling slowly with dread, excitement, as the twin figures in white descend, hand-in-hand, upon him.

8

Suddenly, near the end of July, to Edward's great surprise, long after he has stopped hoping for such a thing, Isabel agrees to divorce him. Once she agrees to do it the matter proceeds with startling swiftness. They meet in her lawyer's office, six blocks from the syndicate.

She has always been a handsome, well-organized, well-constructed woman. Even as a girl, she aimed to present an air of effortless imperium. Now that she is forty-two, she has grown into herself and the performance is convincing. Her hair is dark and her manner superior. The hat is new. A Hardeur, Edward cannot help noticing, with the trademark blue silk band. She stands when he enters the room and performs a tiny, almost invisible two-step, in which she brings her heels together and locks her knees in order to straighten her spine. It is his lot as her husband to know that she was taught this by a nanny named Miss Minnie Minch, but what is he ever to do with this kind of information? He cannot remark on it, or else be thought to be making a jibe, and no amount of protest on his part will convince her otherwise; and he cannot tell anyone else either, for what would anyone care?

They touch hands and sit down across a polished table from each other, with their lawyers beside them.

They agreed to terms through the mail, and Edward took the forms sheepishly from Mary's hand and signed them. ("The most worn-out stunt in the book is sleeping with your secretary," Mary told him.) But they will end the marriage here, in person. Edward has insisted on it: no last-minute tricks.

"Edward," his wife pronounces.

"Isabel."

"You're looking just fine."

"Thank you," he says.

Together they listen to the sound of papers being sorted.

"So are you," he says.

If he says anything else at all, he will never stop.

A minute later the last paper is in front of him, awaiting his signature.

There is only one first marriage, and for all the death that had entered this one, it had once been alive, and anyhow it is the nature of things to appear most valuable in the instant just before they are destroyed. But he takes up the pen.

Isabel's signature is there above the blank that waits for him.

"You know I'm seeing someone," he says.

She delivers a hooded, blinking nod. "Yes," she answers.

The lawyers exchange a glance. When the husbands have been deserted, they tend to pull this.

"We're planning on getting married."

"Congratulations."

"She's my secretary."

"I know who she is."

The pen, a hefty Pearl, lies balanced across his fat index finger.

"Do you mind me asking, Edward, if you're very sure of your plans with her?"

He looks up. "I am."

"Do you know her history?"

"Yes."

"Are you sure you know it all?"

"I know what I need to know."

She raises her imperial chin to him. "Do you know, Edward, that she was in the asylum?"

"Yes," he says. Before a single thought can cross his mind, he bends to the paper and inscribes his name.

"You didn't know," she says.

"I did," he says. This is true, in its own way; now that she has said it, he feels that he has known it all along, but managed to keep it a secret from himself.

"You didn't. Oh, poor Edward," says Isabel. She means it, he can see that, too; and that is not the way he wanted to finish it, not at all. He stands from the table blindly, turns to the door, makes his way into the street.

Of course he knew, of course he did.

But why on earth can he never admit to himself the truth of things until it is too late? He comes to a group of businessmen in the middle of the sidewalk, and he pushes his way through in growing fury. One of them shouts at his receding back. At this, Edward turns and advances. He lifts his fist and with a single driving downward punch he knocks the man out cold. Motionless on the sidewalk with his hat upside down six feet away, the man is, to Edward, just the start of something even larger.

He reaches down and takes the hat with him. A Cranewell, he notes. Expensive.

Now, he thinks, he can marry his darling. And everything will be all right. That old instinct in him rises up, that impulse to win the fight in one punch—and he can't help it, he will go for the big kill. It is another mistake, as he will soon discover, but after all it is his mistake; it is what makes him Teddy.

In his new resoluteness he decides to take her into the country, on a drive. He has work to do out there anyhow; Fitzsimmons keeps a training camp in the woods north of Pineville, hilly country good for conditioning. In the ditches, red-winged blackbirds are clinging to the reeds. Before she was just some kind of a wonderful girl, and now, as they drive, he looks her over with a new eye. Crazy. It does explain certain things, most of all her being with him in the first place. He watches out for signs of it but beside him on the seat she appears the same as always, one hell of a gorgeous creature and a live wire besides. And she likes the drive. "We should get out of the city more, Teddy," she tells him, her white bare feet on the dash.

There is something called the Nature Cure, he recalls dimly, from somewhere. It is why all the nuthouses have the big grounds in the first place. "Sure, Mare," he tells her. "Any time you like."

They are still a half mile from the camp itself when they see the fighter Coughlin and Joe Hass on the road ahead. Coughlin is unmistakable: all in gray and his boots laced up his ankles. Beside him on a bicycle is the old trainer Hass. A dried-up number in a black suit and tie, Hass steers the black bicycle wavering back and forth over the dirt.

When they pull up alongside Coughlin shoots Edward a look of pure malevolence. But he looks fine, red in the face and dark around the eyes and his ginger hair plastered to his temples. They are sweating him, all right. "How's he feeling?" Teddy calls.

Hass pronounces, "He feels like hell as usual. He don't never feel no good." The old man grabs the door of the Buick and allows himself to be pulled along at two miles an hour. His face fills Mary's window, but out of politeness Hass will not notice her in Edward's presence. "He hates my guts and your guts and everybody's guts."

"What's he at?"

"One thirty-six and a quarter. We'll keep him a little under for the next week and then let him come back."

"I hear we've got a line on Schlemmle."

"Schlemmle," Hass drawls, disgusted. "He's a pancake."

"It's what we've got," Edward says. "It's a start, you know." It is true there is not much to promote in the way of Coughlin versus Schlemmle. The tired old angles present themselves. The Micks and the Huns. Et cetera. But Hass seems agitated; he wants something more.

"This kid," he says now under his breath. "He's a piece of work. You wonder how the hell a kid gets made that way sometimes."

"They're all like that."

"Nn, something new," Hass insists. "Son of a bitch's got an iron claw for a heart. You try to talk to him, he'd just as soon kill you. Makes me nervous. You never used to see that. A kid'd talk to you at least. Now I don't know."

"He's tough. We could build that up."

"It'll show, too," Hass agrees. "We're lucky we got him when we did. Did a service for the public good. Make him out"—Hass is mooning now—"like a gangster type. Like a kid Capone."

"Kid Capone," Edward repeats. "Well, I don't know as the real article'd quite like that."

"Also, thing is, that's not quite it; Capone's got a kind of woppy style to him. A kind of tone at least. This kid's not about tone. More just crazy. Crazy Kid Coughlin."

"Not that," Edward says, suddenly hotly ashamed. "I don't like that."

"All right. You're the boss. But he *is* crazy." Hass taps three times on the metal of the door. This is his way of saying that maybe they have something; but he does not want to jinx it by saying so. The old man lets go of the door now and for the first time looks at Mary. "Miss," he nods, and Mary snorts once, in dismissal and in something strangely like pleasure. And Edward would say something; but of course he can't let on that he knows.

She is curious to see it, but the camp turns out to be just a farmhouse along the road. There is a well for fresh water and chickens for a plentiful supply of eggs. Teddy parks the car and stands stretching while the boy named Coughlin comes shuffling up and falls into a sullen walk on his way to the barn, where the ring is. Hass leans the bicycle against the fence and gestures to Teddy, and together they all follow. The ring is elevated about a foot and made with simple wood posts and blond rope. She tips the tusk and tastes the hay dust and an ancient hint of machine oil, and the rider sways above her. Coughlin is stripping off his sweat clothes, revealing a torso of taut glistening muscle. It is strange to have a girl here, she senses at once, so she ducks back out into the daylight. She leans against the fender of Edward's big Buick and after a minute comes the repeated explosive sound of leather gloves hitting a bag.

She crosses the yard with the idea she will sit on the long screened-in porch and wait for Teddy. Pines overhang the yard, so no grass grows. The feeling is of a shadowy secret place under the trees. She likes driving with Teddy, likes the feeling of traveling, the courtly way he has of resisting himself as they drive along, so she is feeling all right. But on the porch the single chair's cushion is gray with what looks like mildew. She passes into the house instead. The house is dim, quiet. Evidently no one is about. The housekeeper is in town, or there is none. Maybe boxers are like sailors and tend to their own cooking and mending. A carpet runs the length of the central hall.

"Hello," she calls, quietly.

When no one answers she takes a step and then another into the house. There are doors off the hall, and Mary passes the open doorways. A sitting room and a dining room.

Then through a door she glimpses, or more senses, the shape of someone stretched out on a sofa, asleep. He is a small man in the dark, turned away from the door, wearing gray—he is no more than a suggestion of a presence. He does not move. She watches for a minute but sees no hint of breathing until all at once, to her horror, she sees him stirring in his heap of rags, lifting a long bony hand into view.

The hand wavers, stretches, its sharp fingers quivering.

She feels the rider shifting on her tusk, his interest caught, a dog sniffing the air, so she hurries along. This thing on the sofa, this little man, must be some *other* rider, she thinks, a free rider that Teddy has neglected to warn her about. Possibly it is the case that when you are a boxer and you are in the ring your rider consents to come down for a while, possibly you can make an agreement with your rider that way. And this would mean that *everyone else* has a rider too, that she has never known about this, that Dr. Miller hadn't told her this because he hadn't wanted her to know. That she is not crazy after all but only—

Nonsense.

Scolding herself, she tiptoes through the house to the back. The kitchen is very cool with soft wood countertops and a dull metal sink, where a rag hangs square over the faucet. A blue bowl holds glossy pink apples on the worn table. From here she passes out into the yard. There is a garden: autumn greens in tidy rows, the last beans on wooden stakes. Onions and beets and potatoes. Someone is growing squash, or it is growing on its own a distance away in the grass. There are raspberry canes, done for the year. It is very peaceful.

She walks a little way into the pines. When she is sure she is alone, and that there is no one to see her, she chooses a tree and begins to scrape the tusk against the bark, working its ridgy roughness down; it will come back again, she feels, but this is what she wants now. The rider swings and clambers out of the way as she scrapes, and the flakes fall around her; she kicks the soft pine needles over them.

When she is done she wipes the tusk on the leaves of a thick low shrub and walks quickly down the path again. She passes through the gate and closes it behind her, then goes through the garden and into the kitchen.

There is a feeling of newness and rawness, a scab pulled away just too soon, a sensation of a barely contained lymphatic oozing. But also of relief. Down the central corridor she goes. She hurries past the room where the sleeping man was, but he is not there. The heap of rags has vanished, and the sofa is unmussed. When they are in the car and heading back up to the city again, she asks Edward about the camp, about who lives there. Just Hass and Coughlin, he tells her.

"Nobody else?"

"They've got a cook," he tells her.

She can hardly bear to ask it, but she does: "An old man?"

"No, some girl from town." Guessing, he assures her, "It's on the up-and-up."

On a sudden impulse she looks into the back seat. It is empty. Nobody is riding along with them. "Just—they're very tidy," she mentions, recovering herself. "Like sailors."

He pulls the car over by a swampy declination in the road. They are alone under the blue Indian summer sky. In the car he turns to her with a look of terrible fright in his eyes. She is sure he is about to tell her the truth about the little man, but instead he asks her, stammering, to marry him. In her relief she nods. A minute later, after he has kissed her and the car is under way again, she understands that she is in fact disappointed. She feels she was on the verge of some disclosure, some real truth about the world. But in fact she is just alone in her madness. It is not something she can tell him about; he is too desperate, too fragile; and she will not subject him to what it would require.

Their engagement party is held on a Friday night in July. Everyone is there; they take over Vernon's for the night and lay it on. He puts tulips everywhere—white tulips, fleshy and faintly stinking. Fitzsimmons and everyone else, even the brother Hollis, gliding in with his silver suit and a bright red tie and a hat with a matching ribbon. Edward's father, his chair tipped back, regards the proceedings from the rear wall, drinking and presiding in the way noble men from small towns can do. They all drink together, and Edward in his drunkenness can tell himself that it doesn't matter, that things will be all right; he stands on a chair and toasts the room and wins the crowd's fond laughter while Mary merely watches him with a look of cool worry. He is a tragic figure, is he not? Doomed to love the women who cannot quite love him in return. When he watches her from his high perch, he feels that old glory opening in his heart, but now he suspects it when before he did not. And it is mixed, too, with a measure of pity—for her, for himself.

The next morning he is hung over again. The bed is empty. He comes out in his robe again, and takes the coffee that Louise offers, and lies on the sofa again watching the ceiling, and looks into the next room to see Mary's shoes at a right angle to each other at the dining room table again. But something is not right about it, he senses. With his new knowledge he feels that something in the room is not right. He stands, unsteadily, and goes to the table. On the polished tabletop he sees her hairpins are arrayed in a design.

An alphabet, but not of this world. A message from another dimension.

With his heart pounding he races through the apartment, but it is empty of her. With a frightened rage building in him he storms back to the front room and sweeps the hairpins from the table, and immediately regrets it, and goes down on his knees to gather them up again, to reassemble them into their otherworldly code; and this is how Louise finds him, crying.

"Did you see her?"

"Only the back of her," Louise says.

"Which way did she go?"

"Oh," she warns, "it was hours ago."

"Which way?"

"Out, Mr. Howe. Just . . ." She lifts a hand.

"Did she say anything?'

Louise shakes her head minutely.

He steps out into the day in his pajamas and looks up and down the sidewalk. It is empty in both directions and offers no clues. He can rush off chasing her, he supposes, but it would not make much sense. He turns and storms back into the house and along the hall to the study. There are several places she might go, and if he alerts someone at each place there is a good chance she will turn up.

Vernon's is one. The office is another. And her brother's place, wherever that is.

He picks up the telephone. Frankie will look out for her at the restaurant, he says, and Dobson will keep an eye out at the office. With this settled, he reaches into his billfold.

He still has the man's card. He turns it over. On the back, the scribbled number: MA5-1342.

And he hears Hollis's voice in his ear. *If for some reason you need me, please let me know. Call me, if you like.*

But also: *Be careful.*

He does not trust Hollis. But he has no choice. He takes the earpiece from the stalk and speaks into the telephone again. It is his own damn fault for getting mixed up with a nutter, he knows, but he has never felt a pain like this before, never, nothing even approached it with Isabel and now he knows what people mean when they say drippy things like *she took a piece of my heart* because that is exactly what it feels like, all right; it feels like a section of his chest has been cut out and is yet somehow still attached to him, wandering around loose in the world, sending back a sorrowing ache. And this is why, when Hollis picks up, Edward tells him everything.

For Mary—well, the effect of all those people looking at her in Vernon's is too much to stand. Everyone raises their glasses to her, and Edward's benevolent possessive gaze sits on her like a wet shawl. It is as though the pressure of their looking is enough to make the thing visible, to bring the tusk and the rider fully into the world—as though they have the power—

That night she does not sleep because she cannot find a comfortable position with the tusk, and the rider will not stop shifting and turning, tugging on the tusk until she develops a headache of such cavernous throbbing that she gives up after a while and goes out again to her chair.

She should never have *agreed.*

It wasn't *fair* of her. But no matter what she does now, it will be unfair.

She resists until dawn. The dining table with its great brown sadnesses all glowing and polished. She will leave him a note, but *secret,* a secret note that no one but he will be able to decode, and she puts it there on the tabletop where he will see it, and finally she takes some of the tulips from the vases around the room and stuffs them under her coat and steps out into the gray predawn. No one is awake. She walks to the end of the block and waits for the early streetcar and stands in the cool morning for a long time as the rider shifts and shimmies overhead. At last the car appears at the far end of the street, and it comes up and she ducks her head and boards. She lowers herself into the cane seat feeling the woolly thickness of her Steener coat and the tulips under it and on her head the blue felt hat with its black metal berries on wire stems, pushed forward of course on her head, and her puckery knees just showing beneath the hem of her dress and her black shoes with the Cuban heels driving her ankles up and even as she sits there lending a shape to the musculature of her calves, and the tulips squeaking under her coat and slipping out to the floor, and the wheels bang along the rails and send jarring reports up through the floor of the car while a blurry fatigue begins to infiltrate her mind, a spongy abandoned feeling behind her sternum. The moon is still up in the trees, and the lights are on down the length of the car and wrap in amber light the porcelain pull-stops overhead, and the green bamboo handgrips that hang like wooden teardrops down the length of the rail, which is chrome, and which takes the little light and polishes it and sends it back; and the floor underfoot is sandy with old footprints, and here and there the floorboards have been nicked and gnawed away so that splintery parts offer themselves to your toe, to worry idly as you sit observing the stupid old streets of Boston wheel by, one brick avenue after another, lined with autos. And with this sort of mumbling going on in her mind, she reaches up to feel the tusk on the back of her head and finds it is still there.

When she puts her hand down, she feels that something is wrong. She does not know what it is until she senses without turning her head that someone has appeared on the empty seat beside her. No one has boarded the car, but someone is next to her.

She will not turn her head. She will not look. But he is there, she is sure of it. He is looking at her. Staring. From the corner of her eye she can sense his wizened face directed at her, waiting.

Interested in her.

He is not supposed to come down from the tusk.

She will simply not turn to look at him.

She will not.

Then, she cannot help it—

His puckered, flaking face has a deep vertical seam down the middle of it, and his teeth are grotesquely jutting, sharp, disintegrating, made of the same flaky stuff that the tusk is made of, and in his eyes is a look of fascinated malevolence. *Watching her. Wanting something.* It is too late; all those stares at Vernon's have done their work. She cowers back against the window, unable to look away. Oh, where is Hollis? She will have to make it to her brother!

He opens his terrible mouth to speak.

"No," she gasps.

"Mary Bone," he says.

9

Thursday night becomes Friday morning, and Dick does not return Friday night as promised, and is missing all day Saturday, and does not finally appear until at eight o'clock Saturday night, drunk, on a horse, an hour before sunset, looming out of the trees like a centaur. He finds Alan sitting on the steps of the Main Building. "Well hello, old man," says Dick, from the height of his horse, "I hope you haven't been waiting for me all this time."

"Not me," he answers. "But some others, maybe."

Dick swings down effortfully. "I meant to call, but I kept being detained by forces beyond my ken. Hell to pay with Slipher, I guess."

"I don't know. I think he's just wondering where you got to."

Dick tucks the reins under an arm and removes his hat and swats it on his leg, then snugs it back on his tall head with a grimace. "Well, we got a little out of hand, frankly. In point of fact the old girl also sort of cracked up the Stutz. A tragedy beyond mortal compare. One wheel gone and the two of us breathing our last in the desert emptiness. But we got a lift in the end. Anyway, hence the rented horse."

"Wait till it gets a whiff of you."

"Her name is Victoria," he says grandly. "And we offered her a snoot, but she is abstemious. But we had reason to celebrate. We are now man and wife."

"Are you?" He feels a sick twinge deep in his groin. "That was speedy of you."

"When we cracked up the car we just happened to come across a strange desert clergyman who is also a prospector. Charged me five American dollars to betroth myself to her forever, which is five dollars pure outlay. She offered to go Dutch, but I told her there's a limit to how modern a man I am."

"Venus will take it hard."

"As well as a few other parties, I guess," Dick says, not meeting Alan's eye.

He stands up and extends his hand. "No, congratulations, Dick," he says. "That's fine. She's a super girl."

Dick shakes his hand, still avoiding his gaze, then sniffs violently and hands him the reins and rushes past him through the double doors into the library, the incendiary smell of liquor on him. Married. No, he was not expecting that. When Dick returns a few minutes later, he flings his arms open and cries, "Now! Now it is time to go say good-bye to the wife, and you are invited." He takes the reins from Alan and with one heavy lunge is in the saddle. "She's booked on the midnight train. I'm telling you, in his position I would've sacked me. Come on up and sit next to me, you big beautiful hunk of man."

"No thanks."

"It's all right, Barbie. I got you permission. He knows who's to blame. Me again as usual." He leans down, extends a hand. "Turn around and put your foot there, darling, and I'll hoist you up. Watch your skirts."

It is another claim on him and he wants to resist it; but he takes Dick's hand and with a swinging lift he finds himself deposited on the animal's bare back. He grasps Dick around the waist. It is an intimate gesture, and they both feel it as such, and in the shadow of it Dick's voice moderates. "She wanted to say good-bye to you, that's all."

"She did?"

"And time's awastin."

"You're really married?" But he hears the pathetic twinge in his voice and stops.

"Sure." Dick snorts, starts the horse moving. "I guess I know what's good for me."

So he will have to wait to tell Florence—he will have to wait for just the right moment. The last thirty-six hours have been full of the novel details of submitting, via telegram, the position of the cometary object now beyond the orbit of Saturn and inbound, thereby staking his claim as its first observer; then reconfirming its position the following night; then calculating the trajectory of its shallow parabolic dive, discovering that it will cross Earth's orbit on April 27; and sitting for long minutes just looking admiringly at the tiny faint smudge it produced as it shed its ice crystals at the approximate rate of one milligram per $10^6 cm^3$ in the immense interplanetary vacuum; and finally hitting, while sharpening his pencil, on the perfect name. Astronomers will refer to it as 1928—VII. But the full official name, the name that will stand for as long as the comet survives its peregrinations through the solar system, is 1928—VII—Florence. He laughed aloud when he thought of it first, and then he figured, Well, why not. It is not a gift to her out of the purity of his heart; it is not really the act of a decent man. He has designs, of course; and when he is able to pin himself down about the matter for long enough, he can see that he also means it as a sort of declaration—the message being that no matter that Dick is rich and he is not, no matter that Dick has known her forever and he has not, he loves her and that is that. If it should serve to work her loose from him, all the better.

But now she is married, and this complicates things. He is not sure how exactly. You have to play things by ear sometimes. Down in town they stomp into the Monte Vista and Dick calls her name, and she emerges from the sitting room through the beaded curtain, her face softened by the lamplight, her hair turning a little dark in the red light and her skin very bronzed. She is only twenty-four and is the obvious prize among the many women who work as computers, and she is frankly brilliant and now she is marrying Dick Morrow. Well, it is the way things work, isn't it. The rich get richer. As she steps through the curtain her hair is caught in a tangle of beads, and for a moment she stands with her head tilted backward, her hand at work loosing herself, a patient self-mocking look in her eyes. She meets his gaze and returns it for a long, heart-shattering moment. Then she is free. "Barbie," she says. "You've heard."

"Meet my wife," says Dick. "Or maybe you're already acquainted."

"Mrs. Morrow," Alan says.

"Ooh," she grimaces, "doesn't that send shivers up your interior?"

"There's a line in that, too," he tells her. "But I'll keep it to myself."

They begin to drink at once. They patrol the downtown for an hour, consider seeing *Street Angel* at the Orpheum, but Florrie wants to walk. "Ants in my pants," she says, and Dick says "Some ants," and she swats at him with feeling. They strike out for the edge of town. The night-blooming flowers come open in the fenceyards. Bats go rustling overhead. They walk out past the smaller of the two sawmills, iron ramps and chimneys, heaps of wood chips and stacked bright lumber in metal straps. Then they are beyond the town and into the desert.

The sky is filled with stars. His unaided eyes cannot see 1928—VII—Florence, but he can look in its direction anyway. When an hour or so has passed they are still wandering in the darkness, breathing the good air and tromping around being best of pals as it seems they must show themselves to be. Alan is pregnant with his news, but the time isn't right; he can see that Dick and Florence have done something they consider a little dangerous, and in the aftermath of it they are full of something themselves. "Ooh, my *parents*," Florence croons, holding her head with two hands as they tromp along. "They're going to murder me."

"Worse yet," Dick says, "they'll close the tap."

"They'd never dare," she scowls.

"We should not underestimate the importance of ceremony," Dick says, "in the tribal customs."

"Mama has a dress—" She lets out a whoop of despair and amazement.

Dick says, "We can break it to them slowlike. Wear the damn dress. Why, they don't even have to know if we don't tell anyone."

"Sure. The Liddys did it," Alan says. "What's his name, Mac Macklin and Asta White. Married twice. Once by law and once for show."

"Oh, but I also just want to *rub* it in. Even *Charlie*," she growls, "I even want my *lazy brother* to hate me."

"He won't hate you," Alan assures her. "Although he does like a nice party. He'll think you've cheated him out of one."

Florence groans. But she means, Alan estimates coolly, only about half of all this. The other half is the half that allowed her to get the position in the computer room in the first place, that doesn't care everyone thinks it is a strange thing for a girl of her sort to do. She takes some pride, as Alan knows by now, in being *hard to evaluate*. Even the girls who take Dos Passos to the Charles to read in lawn chairs while tapping their cigarettes into the grass don't know what to make of her. Last August when the uproar over Sacco and Vanzetti was everywhere there had been excitement in the computer room after Florrie had managed to get arrested; as she told the story later in fact she had been arrested three days running, each time very politely, and every day she had been bailed out by one or another of the angels who hovered over that episode, then turned out with her papers onto the street with all the others of her bunch to stand around, humiliated. "And then we all went home and had our cake and tea," she minced.

And even after all this her family is used to her, and very fond of her. So her despair now is mostly a show: a guilty relishing of her own small bravery.

He starts refusing the flask when it comes his way, and he figures he will be presentable by midnight. Dick, however, is a loss. By the time they turn back toward town, he can hardly walk. "My god," Dick groans, after he has vomited onto the road, "what'd that man put in that?"

Still there is no danger of Florence missing her train until Dick announces that he needs to lie down. In the faint light that reaches them from the outskirts of town he can be seen getting down on one knee. He supports himself with his right hand for a moment, as though in a football stance, then with a careful self-preserving motion he rolls onto his side and begins to breathe heavily through his mouth.

"Oh, hell," says Florence.

They stand over him for a moment.

"Dickie!"

She prods him with a toe.

She sighs. "Down for the count."

Now is his chance, very plainly his last chance ever.

"Quite a honeymoon," he says.

She turns to him. In the darkness her face is only a pale oval marked with a pattern of dark smudges, a blurred, reduced idea of a face, but it still does the trick. "I am actually sort of frightened, Barbie," she says. "I don't know if we did the right thing. It seems sort of selfish suddenly. I mean we could have waited. *I* could have . . ."

"It'll be all right," he tells her. Then, daring: "You're super."

"I just . . ." She nods, a quick pretty flurry. "I know we'll be all right."

"Anyway," he says, "I got you something." He orients her in the correct direction and moves himself up behind her and, extending an arm out over her shoulder, aims her gaze at the right part of the sky. "Distance at perihelion, .339, eccentricity .84, longitude of ascending node, 334.7, argument of latitude 185, inclination of orbit 11.9."

"You *didn't*."

"Just a little cometary body," he says.

"You *didn't!*"

"Know what I named it?"

She inhales suddenly. "Oh, no, Barbie."

"I named it Florence."

She turns and faces him. "*Barbie*." Her tone is so dark, so scolding, that he fears at once that he has made a terrible mistake. It is far too much, he sees, suddenly. He has been a fool. But then she leans forward to kiss him. She takes his face in her two hands and delivers to him a long, serious, drunken kiss, full of meaning.

"Florrie," he gasps.

"My dear, stupid Barbie," she laughs. "But I have a *train* to catch, sweetheart."

Patting his cheek, she goes to rouse Dick, and a minute later they have all set off again to the station, and it is as though nothing happened.

At the station the yellow suitcases are arranged in a diminishing row on the baggage cart. At the sight of them his heart sinks. She is going. She is married. She is rich. Well, so much for all that. Feeling himself a man of great resolve and clarity, he kisses her chastely on the cheek. But then she leans into his ear. "April 27," she whispers, her voice hard and cunning.

"Gee," he only manages, in a hot whisper, "you're a hell of a girl." She has calculated the orbit in her head between the road and the station, drunk as she is. It took him an hour, dead sober, at the library table.

When he pulls back she won't meet his eye, so he says only, "Safe trip," and swallowing hard he claps Dick on the shoulder and starts off for the top of the hill.

He has almost reached the top when he hears the train thundering in from the west. He turns to watch it approach, a long line of lights drawn across the darkness of the desert. It stops at the station, pauses for less than a minute, then begins its eastward journey again. He makes himself observe the whole operation. He continues up to the Main Building and sits on the steps again, waiting for Dick. But he can only stand this for so long, and he goes to set up the night's first plate at the Clark, alone.

It is an hour later when Dick has still not appeared beside him that he begins to get a queer feeling. Following his nose Alan leaves the Clark in its gigantic sling and tromps across the dark meadow under the stars to the Main Building. With only the low nighttime illumination to guide him, he goes to the second floor and goes down the hall and ducks his head into Dick's room and flips the lights. In the sudden glare he sees the room is empty, stripped, the bed pulled out from the wall, the sheets balled up. Dick is gone.

It is an act of such absoluteness, such negligent and majestic totality, that he has to admire it. She never said a word. Neither did he. The goddamned rich. They do put on a hell of a show.

They wait for word, but two days pass, and nothing comes. Then a week, and another, and really it is chastening. A rich bastard, a little lazy possibly, but he knows his rights, and he has rounded up his girl and taken her away.

Not his girl, Alan reminds himself: his wife.

No letters, no wires, no telephone calls. Dick and Florrie have vanished.

For a while it is definitely awkward around the observatory; Alan gets the sense of a practical joke having gone badly, unfortunately awry. He is embarrassed, all right; indeed they all have reasons for feeling sheepish: Alan for having named the thing after Florence in the first place, Slipher for having allowed it, Lampland for not kicking up more of a fuss when he got wind of Alan's intention. They face one another in the halls, stiff and contrite.

"I guess he really didn't like you horning in," Lampland opines one morning, over the sports pages.

Alan can only grimace. "Go figure."

"On the other hand," Slipher remarks, "maybe he's paying Barber back enough, trying to stick him with the Planet X hunt on his own." The director shakes out his own section of newspaper. "I never got the sense Morrow was too keen on the idea, anyway."

"No," Alan says.

"Two hundred photographs of the ecliptic, a few years at the Bosch on your own—fitting punishment, you might say."

"Just about," Alan manages.

"Of course we *will* have to get you *someone*," Slipher considers. "Although *who*, is the question. No one back in Cambridge really wants any part of us. I've got *my* duties. Maybe *you'd* like to pair up with Mr. Barber, Carl. Really I think you two would make a wonderful couple on the comparator."

"Not unless you'd like to see me shoot myself, V.M.," Lampland answers. "Or Barber," he adds.

By now Alan is blushing red as a beet. A silence fills the library.

"Well," Slipher sighs, finally taking pity, "we'll find someone somewhere."

"Better be someone cheap," Lampland's lilting voice rises from behind the *Sun-Democrat*.

"Cheap," Slipher repeats, wearily. "We're used to that, I guess."

"Oh *my* yes," Lampland agrees.

It is awful, all right. Dick has done the running off, which was bad, all right, but Alan did the chasing. And what would he have done, were he in Dick's shoes? The same thing, likely.

So in an effort to make it up somehow Alan pitches in extra where he can. He helps Sykes cut some wood. He drives some nails on the 13-inch dome. He walks to town for the mail when the truck is out. He spends his nights at the Clark and his days at the comparator. Also with some idea of preserving his young man's dignity, he makes a single run into Mexican-town on the hunt for liquor during which he walks the hot dusty streets for an hour, sloping past tin-roofed shanties and once daring to knock on a likely screen door, but he is lousy at this sort of operation, and his heart isn't in it, and finally he mounts the rise and climbs back over the tracks and into town again empty-handed. If he wants it he can ask around, but he doesn't mind going dry for a while. He is back alone at the Clark most nights, and the work that Dick has left to him is tedious stuff: night after night, when the weather is decent, he is at work on the Variable Atlas Survey: ninety-minute exposures of the northern sky, one plate after another. But he accepts the penitent's duties, and anyway the great Clark dome is his for the summer, and alone he spiders himself up the ladder and hauls the giant shuddering roof around. He peeks at his comet Florence. It is a handsome thing with a little silver tail, nothing spectacular, but he has a founder's pride in it and in watching it grow. On cloudy nights or during lunations he develops plates in the darkroom down the hall from the vault, swishing the developer across the heavy glass and sliding the finished plates from the rack into their gray paper envelopes. Lord of the manor, he is, with no one to suggest otherwise. Leaning back from the comparator and pressing his palms over his burning eyes, he will drift, a little blind himself, past Lampland's door and all the other doors down the length of the quiet green corridor, where Lowell himself walked, a madman with a mad wife, dreaming of Barsoom.

And he manages to spend time with the notebooks, too. While he does, he cannot help it, he thinks of Florence. Sure, she can see him there in his tweed coat and white shirt and dusty chestnut boots. The lamp of Saturn sends down its facets of amber. The fireplace exhales a dry gust of charcoal. And any moment she will enter at the double doors and make some fine remark. As in, "Aren't you a picture of duty?"

Who on earth thinks this way? He is such a patsy.

But he will pass the summer like this as the weeks wheel by, taking his spare hours to the library, where he slides the tip of his pencil along old sheets of paper on the hunt for Lowell's mistakes. It is very slow going (he will barely make a dent in the notebooks before the end of the summer, he can see), and there aren't many mistakes to be found, and those he does find don't matter. Lowell is a leggy, erratic thinker, it soon becomes obvious—enthusiastic, emphatic in his crossings out, leaping from page to page, dropping one line and picking up another, solving simultaneous analytical equations on alternating pages, as agile in the field of pure statistical mathematics as he is in the field of higher-order orbital mechanics (whereas for Alan the derivation of linear least squares is far from second nature; he will have to study this in depth when he returns to Cambridge)—and running all along, all through these pages, is the constant hum of a determined mind. You do not solve a decade's worth of least squares residuals without displaying a certain focused mania. All your madmen need it.

Well, he will be equal to it. He gots his own mania, don't he? In the morning mirror he shaves with care. Combs down those leaping eyebrows. Whaps the dust out of those trousers. Gets a decent crease in the trouser leg with the Hotpoint electrical iron. Observe, please, the rakish open Arrow collar. See him hold his jaw to the light. Await the arrival of Florrie. Continue till dark. Do his duty. Discover a planet, that's all he has to do.

10

It is hard, for a while, to get up in the morning. Clyde wakes at eight, the damp sheet tangled around his ankles. The white lace curtain hangs motionless, and from the farmyard comes the sound of cicadas. Someone, Roy most likely, is chopping weeds in the garden, the hoe producing a soft *chup, chup* in the soil. Roy showing him that life goes on. Like it or not.

Now that college at Lawrence is out of the question, he has nowhere else to go. He has no offers in hand, unless he counts the endless rows of advertisements in the back of his magazines.

HELP WANTED

MEN—Experience unnecessary; travel; make secret investigations; reports; salaries; expenses. Write American Foreign Detective Inst., 303, St. Louis, Mo.

OBTAIN Employment! 70 Jobs offered one person! Get work you want, quickly, anywhere. Complete information, 50 cents. Money promptly returned if wanted. Better Yourself! New Idea Service, Box 39-D, Station K, New York.

STEAMSHIP Positions—Men—Women. Good pay. See the world Free. Experience unnecessary. Send self-addressed envelope for list. Box 122-Z, Mount Vernon, N.Y.

BE A Secret Service Man! $5.00 covers year's membership, official detective journal, button and credentials. Continental Secret Service System, Box 81K, Waukegan, Illinois.

Or unless he considers the sound of the distant train, itself a sort of advertisement, running at midnight through western Kansas, westbound to Santa Fe and California, carrying its sleeping passengers wherever the hell they're going.

For a while Clyde sits and sends away for anything free. Steamship positions, why not? His mother's secretary, with its fold-down front and slots where you can stow your envelopes and clippings, sits in the corner of the dining room. He uses up all the envelopes sending away for these booklets and secret guides. "I'll get more," he says.

"When you're in town," she answers.

He buys them, twenty count, bound around with a paper strap. They hang in his pocket as he sits in the Bijou, feet up on the plush, watching meaty old George Bancroft make it with Betty Compson and her funny lip. *Are you gonna let me have a good time in my own quiet way,* he snarls, *or do I have to take this place apart?*

After the oats dry they plow them under with the harrow. This takes a whole day and he hates every minute of it, the sky a stupid blue overhead and the blackbirds flinging themselves up from the earth, and after they have done this they plant a crop of autumn wheat with the idea of salvaging at least something. The seeds go glissading into the sowing tank and swirl around, and with his father at the wheel Clyde sits astride the metal funnel watching its slowly circling paddle, and every few minutes he wrestles a sack of seed from the trailer onto his lap and slices the top with his jackknife and pours the contents down between his knees, the sack losing its shifting heft until it is just an emptied canvas skin, which he then tosses back into the trailer as it jounces and rattles along behind the tractor. By lunchtime he is covered with wheat dust, as though he has been lightly floured. His mother brings them lunch at the wire, and they eat together on the soil sitting in the shade of the tractor; bread, butter still cold from the icebox, oven fried chicken with its skin done to crackling, hardboiled eggs already peeled and sliding against one another in the white china bowl with blue ivy trailing around its edges, potato salad with celery, bean salad, cucumber pickles, blueberry pie, cold water—two great jugs of it—and a sloshing cylinder of coffee.

"And this," his mother says, pulling a letter from her pocket. "From Wichita."

Clyde's heart leaps a little, but he will not show it, not in front of his father. "I paid him," he insists. He takes the envelope and works a floured nail under the flap. "I paid him up front."

His father, his mouth full, peers at him keenly.

The letter is typed, the lines widely spaced on the wind-rattling page. The mirror Clyde sent for silvering, Carreau has written, it had *such* a good figure. It was nearly flawless, in fact, without a doubt easily the best he'd ever seen on a handmade 9-inch. But how had he solved the Foucault knife-edge problem? Had he finally dug the root cellar to dampen circulating air currents? At any rate it was very extraordinary and quite promising in such a young man on his own. And, as he would have an opening at his firm in Wichita within the year, was Clyde interested in taking a position as assistant grinder?

"He wants to give me a job." Clyde slips the letter into the back pocket of his trousers. "Sometime before 1930."

"Why, Clyde, that's wonderful!" his mother beams.

"Sure."

"Bench work," his father puts in now, his mouth full. "Watch out for bench work."

Clyde considers his father for a long minute before he says, "I'll take any goddamned thing."

In his room at the Wichita Hotel for Men he sets his suitcase on the bed, and in the mirror he is surprised to see that he does not look any different. The knots in his shoes are still tight, and his necktie remains where he left it after lunch, snugged up neatly beneath the cellulose collar that has preserved its shape all afternoon, through Great Bend and Sterling and Hutchinson, all along the Arkansas River, as the sun sank through the sky, good faithful collar that it is, the last one.

He does not want to eat before dark, sensing that it is a provincial thing to do. It seems to him a real man of the world would have something more to do in his room after arriving in the big city. Well, he can think of a thing or two. He doesn't do that and instead stands at the window for a minute looking at the streetcars until finally he just gets bored and without exactly noticing it he is out in the hall again with his hat jammed on. Downstairs at the cigar stand he buys a newspaper, which he tucks under his arm without looking at it. Then it is a sort of prison-yard walk across the echoing lobby into the restaurant.

The other solitary diners, all men, look up as he enters, then look down again.

He is shown to a table, and, speaking so quietly the waiter has to bend down to hear him, he orders a hot roast beef sandwich with gravy. "And a vegetable, sir?" the waiter asks.

"No. And coffee."

He waits for the waiter to press the vegetable on him, as his mother would, but he only closes his booklet and walks away across the carpet.

Clyde, proud of himself for having it, opens his newspaper.

He reads that Lonnie Cummings was elected president of the Oaklawn High School senior class and "Moon" Mullen was named yell leader. And that Elizabeth Larcey was appointed class reporter.

And that Roy Grace, Sedgwick County engineer, was seriously injured when a car passing near where he was standing just north of the city limits broke a spring and veered into a ditch. The driver of the car was L. R. Ross, a worker who lives in the tourist park east of the city.

Then Clyde has his coffee in front of him. He sips at it. Through the plate-glass windows he watches another streetcar trundle by. No one is watching him. No one in Burdett knows exactly where he is at that exact moment. He feels a shiver of homesickness and then another shiver of capability. Who the hell cares if anyone knows where he is or isn't? He could stand it, if he had to.

Carreau's outfit is in a single-story brick building near the edge of the city, a twenty-minute walk from the Hotel for Men, past the bus depot and some warehouses. As Clyde picks his way across the pocked gravel parking lot the next morning, he catches the stench from a grocer's loading dock. Carreau's door is painted a bright red with a single brass mail slot.

Clyde knocks once, his heart beating hard. His new life awaits him here, possibly. He finds he cannot much imagine it. He turns the knob and enters.

Inside, he has the impression of a large, cluttered space, full of rows of tables and equipment stands. Workbenches line the walls beneath the glass-block windows. Brass-housed optical equipment sits dismantled on what appear to be a series of white-sheeted platforms. There is the familiar bloody smell of iron sesquioxide and waterlogged emery, and he can hear, from somewhere, the breathy roar of a welding torch. Carreau comes forward through the pillars, white jacket, swept-aside sheaf of black hair, tiny spectacles perched on the big French nose.

"It must be the famous Mr. Clyde Tombaugh," Carreau pronounces. "We meet at last. The boy who makes his own mirrors!" He extends a hand. "Very pleased finally to make your acquaintance."

They shake. "Mr. Carreau."

"So now you see where your nice mirrors all have traveled to. So *fine*, that last one," Carreau murmurs, remembering. "You finally found a cellar, it would seem."

"I couldn't stand it any longer, I guess," he admits, "not finishing them."

"Yes. You know we could have finished them for you, for a price."

Clyde does not know what to do with this, only shrugs and buries his hands in his pockets. "I guess that would have defeated the purpose of making them, partly," he offers.

Carreau peers at him strangely and says, "Well, yes, and of course a cellar is pretty good for your purposes, but here we have the basement, which is *two* stories belowground, over there," he indicates a flight of stairs disappearing into the floor, "with a cumulative variable temperature of less than one degree per hour, and this is before the regulators are turned on. In fact we are so exact that when Mr. Bundt comes down he stands behind a glass wall so he does not ruin all my hard work. But," Carreau nods, "I don't have to tell you very much about hard work."

Clyde accepts the compliment, if that's what it is, in silence. He has the strange feeling of being boxed in, suddenly, even as for the next half hour he follows Carreau slowly around the shop. They begin in the optics corner, where the speculae are cut from heavy sheets of plate glass using a giant jigsaw; they move on to the grinding bench, where Henry Bundt labors in his buttoned vest; then to René Poule in his gloves at the silvering table, above which the brown bottles of nitrate of silver and tartaric acid and caustic potash are lined along a black shelf. Around a corner, in the instrument shop, is where the telescope housings are welded, finding scopes fitted, mountings bolted.

It is work, all right. And he can do it. In particular he covets the sturdy, tidy grinding table, not a wobbling oil drum but a hefty butcher block; and the beautifully arranged canisters of Carborundum, and the swift confidence with which Henry Bundt addresses his glass. But is this all he wants from life? Is this all that awaits him? Will he never go to college, ever?

"Well, that's it, you know," Carreau finishes. "Henry wants to move to Florida next year, but he has to sell his house before he goes. Henry, you want to go to Florida!"

"I will die," announces Mr. Bundt, in his buttoned black vest, "if I have to withstand many more winters here."

"He will die! So he says. So I say, okay, I have this young guy Tombaugh who can do it, I'll ask him what he thinks. So, you can have the job if you want to have it. I don't have anybody else to hire. I can put out advertisements, but, you know, this isn't just lifting a box. I need a man like you."

"Thank you, sir."

"So, you want it?"

Clyde puts his hands in his pockets. "I don't know."

"You don't say yes, you don't say no."

There in the middle of the floor, with everyone listening, he has to say yes, of course. But he can't. Not yet. Maybe this is what it really means to be a man: to see your only option, to hate it, and still to be bound to it. As his father is.

But he can't. "Not yet," he says.

"Not yet. Oh, well, okay. But you know, Clyde"—Carreau's voice grows mild, dangerous—"you can tell me to go to hell if you want, but honestly, let me number these things. One. You are twenty-two years old. Two. You are living on your farm with your mother and father. You are not married. You have no job except, what you say, working on the farm—you know, what else do you want? I say this to you because I am older, I don't care what anybody thinks about me, you know."

Clyde steps toward the door, his face burning. No one has looked up, but everyone can hear.

"I make you angry, I don't really mean to, but you could have this job! I could use you! And you come all this way to see us! I mean, really, I don't understand it. What do you think is going to happen? Do you think something is going to come down out of the blue to you, because you're standing around waiting for it?"

"No." He crosses his arms over his chest. "Just"—he shrugs, gesturing with his shoulders, trying for nonchalance, for the faint *not caring*, that he felt a wisp of in the restaurant—"just, you know, watch out for bench work, I guess."

"Watch out for bench work?"

Clyde nods.

"Watch out for bench work." Carreau fixes him with a pained, insulted, mystified look. Then the man softens. Turns his hands up. "Okay, so watch out for it. Okay. You can tell me later what you want to do."

"Pleased to have met you," Clyde says.

Carreau smiles formally. He steps forward, reaches out, and shakes Clyde's hand. "Good-bye, Mr. Tombaugh," he says, "and best of luck."

He follows a roundabout path back toward the Hotel for Men. He passes a dozen boardinghouses. And residential hotels. And wood-frame houses divided into apartments. A thousand places to live if you are a man on your own. Standing on the sidewalk, he studies these places boldly. The beat-down lawns, the unpainted fences, the bottles lined up in the windows. It can be his life, if he agrees to it.

And what other life is there?

He has plenty of time to kill before his train, so he stalks these streets for an hour, kicking stones to the gutters. He walks the acreage like a farmer, his hat back. Replays the conversation in his mind. Measures himself against—what? Who the hell is he? And what the hell else *does* he want?

Back in Burdett no one asks about his trip. His family will let him break the news if he has any. He will hold it. Until he can't stand it any more. There is a pile of mail on his dresser, envelopes he opens without hope. This is what you get when you send away for the steamship brochure: you get a flimsy two-page stapled circular he would not have picked up off the ground. The official detective journal is made of gray paper and sewn with string, and the little tin button has a blurry stamp of a sheriff's star on it;

it would not fool a little girl. What embarrassing stuff it is. Ashamed, he sweeps it all together and sets it on Charlie's pillow for his delight.

Summer swells, fattens. His mother, increasingly pregnant, puts up tomatoes in the steaming kitchen. She attacks the garden with the hoe, chopping yellowed stems into the soil. In September Roy travels to the high school in Larned—the school in Burdett has closed over the summer, for lack of attendance—and returns late in the afternoon, stomping and singing:

> Ho ho ho! We fight and play
> for the dear old Larned Braves!

With his father Clyde plows the stubble fields under. The weather continues bright, cruelly sunny. The pumpkins are already heavy on the vine when in early September Maggie finally manages to push her failing stall all the way off its anchoring. Clyde finds her nosing guiltily through the sweet winter hay at the back of the barn. Rather than repair the stall, Clyde decides to pull it all apart and build it again with new wood. So one by one he pries away the ruined old planks, infused with Maggie's pissy smell and threaded with her stiff hairs. He levers himself with his boot against the uprights while Maggie looks on from the pasture, canny and defiant. He piles the splintered boards onto the dirt of the farmyard.

Maggie puts her head over the wire fence.

"Some help you are!" he shouts.

But she huffs, scorning him. His girl. Well, his only one. He is standing by his beautiful 9-inch, watching Maggie's brown coat rolling glossy in the sunlight, when he is struck with an idea. He snaps the latches and slides the mirror from its barrel housing. It flashes blue-gray, and he can see his face in its slight concavity, upside down, as in the bowl of a spoon. He carries the mirror by its handle to the pile of boards, then aims the disk at the sun, angling it so that a bright spot, about as big as a grapefruit, falls across the grass. He steers the spot across the grass and into the heap of timber. In a moment the boards begin to smolder.

Simple: he will burn down the yard. The barn. Burn down the fucking house, with his family inside. Burn it all. *Tear this place apart.*

He lets this ugly thought surge through him completely. The timbers smoke. This is the mysterious thing: that he can be so full of fury at his life, so ready to destroy it all, when no one is really to blame.

After a minute, with the boards fully caught, he goes off to the pump to fill a bucket. His father never mentions it, only the next day hands him a rake to gather the potash for the next spring's garden. The great blue sky yawns open above him. The smell of autumn cools the wind. His leaning shadow hovers on the floating ashes.

That night he sits at the kitchen table. Filled with a steady, undramatic desperation, he composes a letter.

Dear Sir, he writes, What would you advise a young man with this set of accomplishments to do? A lens maker, a technician, an amateur astronomer, with an offer in hand but a year away, without hope of college in the near future—what opportunities do you see? He writes to the bottom of the page, examines it skeptically, his blue handwriting almost girlish in its conscientious tidiness, then makes a good fair copy and roots around in his mother's writing desk for an envelope. He has used them all up again, and he can find only a large one. It will look silly with just the single sheet of paper inside, so he goes upstairs and brings down his observational drawings of Jupiter. He writes a second sheet explaining when he made them and how and with what instrument. Then he clips it all together and slides the papers inside. He affixes the glue and winds the string around the two tin pivots with their red paper disks and gums some postage on and sets it out in the box addressed to MR. V. SLIPHER, DIRECTOR, LOWELL OBSERVATORY, FLAGSTAFF, ARIZONA.

In the morning Mike Landry comes along in his truck and takes it away. Clyde finds that he hopes for nothing. It is just sick how easily that hopelessness settles onto him—pressing down on him from the sky, from everywhere.

Just sick.

11

They arrive on the Denver train, a mob of them in black jackets, their sun-tanned faces bulging over their ties, resembling a crew of sailors or a troupe of acrobats in mufti as they march in loose companionship across the platform. Italians, half of them, the others a mix of Irish and American mongrel, fat and lean, short and tall. One Mexican who must be the watchman. One tall yellow Negro with a cruel and skeptical squint. Felix shakes their hands as Willoughby recites their names: Mann, Maxwell, Boccioni, Musolino, Girimonti, Telesio—he will learn them all eventually. Their hands are callused. They size him up, the money man. What they see Felix doesn't know. It is his first crew. He only ever set foot in his father's factories as a favored son, a figure of fond ridicule in his polished shoes.

"They pay for their own lodgings," Willoughby tells him. "I've got them two houses in Mexicantown."

"They live together?"

"Always do."

The eleven men are to be paid $15 a week and are to be on the slope, which is now called Lightning Creek, six days a week from dawn until sunset. Willoughby has an apartment to himself and draws $30 a week. The Mexican night watchman with his bandolier and drooping mustache is paid $10 a week, as is the cook, the Negro. The total comes to $215 per week for manpower. Then there is $4 a week to rent his own house and $5 a week for the warehouse. And the lease payment to Dundee Timber comes to $800 a year. Altogether close to $10,000 annually, assuming a forty-week season.

It will furthermore be Felix's duty to arrange for all these payments and also to keep the outfit in supplies. This means additional outlay for pails of plaster and burlap squares and empty sugar sacks, and shipping crates to get the stuff back to town, and some means of conveyance to get it back, and beef and potatoes and bread and bacon for Frank to build the lunches with and firewood and coffee and barrels of water, and aside from the few favorite tools the men have brought with them and the items Isenbright spared him, he will need to provide all the incidental things required at a dig, pencils and tablets of graphing paper, replacement picks and scours and brushes, and boxes or crates to contain all these materials at the site, and every few weeks there will need to be a garbage run unless he plans on setting up an incinerator, which people are known to do, as usually it's cheaper in the long run if the dig is to be open more than a year or two. "Plus," Willoughby enumerates, sitting on a crate in the warehouse, "once we begin getting things out of the ground, you've got your shipping costs to Washington, if that's where they're going, and you'll want to provide yourself some insurance on the shipments. Or otherwise you'll have to find a place to keep everything around here."

It is not the money but the arranging of everything that daunts him. He creaks back in the chair. "The hell," he says.

"It's a business, all right."

When Willoughby is gone Felix sorts through a few papers and whaps open the check ledger and goes about it for half an hour. Through the flyspecked window he watches a boxy white mutt explore the weedy yard. He ought to hire a girl, is his impulse. But he wants to be really in charge of something for once. He is more than thirty years old, if just barely more than a boy at heart, and he has never run a single thing. He imagines it can't be that hard once you get the hang of it. Friends of his from Dartmouth are at this moment in Mexico working for State and finding oil in Texas and writing plays and what-the-hell, and they are no crew of particular brains as he happens to know.

The empty floor of the warehouse behind him, its scattering of straw. He leaves the desk, searches out a broom.

In charge. But also the apprentice. Once the action starts at Lightning Creek, Willoughby instructs him on some new tools. The first is a serrated metal scraper like a grapefruit spoon. "Now with this item you don't want to have a whole lot of business with the fossil itself," Willoughby instructs, crouching beside him in the dirt. "You can do a fair bit of damage before you know it. When you get down close to something, you can use either the pick or the brush, or this." The second tool, wood, like a blunt leadless pencil.

"You've got to be joking."

"No, sir," Willoughby acknowledges, "I wish there was, but it ain't no faster way."

He makes some progress on his little gray lump the first week; then he is given a chisel and a wooden doll's shovel with which to move a little soil, and he continues with some faster results. The Smith & Wesson is pinned now in a holster on his hip. Hot as hell out here with the sun on him. The tents whomp in the little breeze while Frank boils potatoes and cooks up stews and loads their canteens with ice in the ease of the tents' shade. Meanwhile if anyone has found the *Tarsal*, they are keeping mum. He has left a ghostly part of himself aboard the *Tarsal*, and even on his knees in a bone pit on the plateau of the Arizona desert he can sense that absent portion of himself still out there, afloat, waiting to be rescued.

There are tracks in the morning of snakes and mice, and he contends with the occasional crouching spider who glares at him with red eyes. Go your way, little spider. Meantime most of the crew is two hundred yards downhill going after the big treasure, the Steg. They have a practiced way with the picks and brushes. Along the lip of the pit stands a row of slurping plaster pails and a fuzzy stack of burlap squares and a mousy heap of the empty sugar bags. Already they are harvesting. Felix graduates to a few more tools: a chisel, a collapsible forester's spade, a steel brush. He is a tidy worker as though to make up for his laxity at the desk. He kites a whisk broom without permission to swish the loose sand away. His little spot. As he digs out whatever it is he makes a hollow around it, and when he has uncovered a good twelve inches of bone Willoughby decides he is working on a Camptosaurus, a modest, light-footed plant eater. "Going by the shape of that right there. This is your femur, Mr. DuPrie. Fortunately a nice easy place to start. Nice big bone. Down another six inches you'll hit the pelvis, if we're lucky." He steps three feet up the slope. "And under here you've likely got the skull."

"How's the work?"

"Well, it's pretty nice," Willoughby admits. "You got a nice touch." But he is happy about something else: "You know what a Camptosaurus means here? I mean in combination with the Steg?"

"No."

Willoughby sniffs, cocks his hat back. "Means this here is a part of the Morrison Formation, no doubt about it."

"That's what you thought."

"Yessir." Willoughby shoots him a cowboy grin. "Damned if I didn't."

He continues. He acquires an affection for the creature, like an anatomist training on a cadaver. The pelvis is intact, an arrowy thing like you'd find in a turkey. The ribs have retained their limber delicacy. One shows a puncture that could only have come from a predator's fang. After painstakingly drilling out the stone, he inserts his pinky finger into this old wound eternally unhealed. Fellow beast. He thinks of the countless animals he has eaten at a thousand decorated tables, sawing into them without a thought. So. Countless deaths to make a life. And these creatures, dreamed up aeons ago, out of God's great brain, and set out in grazing herds for a million generations only to be crushed in the enormous dry compress of time. There is no evidence of Mercy in the sandy rock. The rock itself is a giant brain, he thinks, riddled with faults and crevices; the whole hard desert a brain, a humpy maze of gullies and dry washes and tendriled emptiness. In the heat he pours the canteen empty over his head. At least he is not back at that creaky desk and the flyspecked window and the unshipped crates containing the pieces of the Steg set neatly down the brick wall. He can sell it all to Isenbright back at the Smithsonian if he wants to, but he isn't sure he does. He doesn't need the dough, anyway. Also it turns out to be a hell of a hassle to arrange for space on the train. He has to set it all up with the station agent, who wants to know weight and value and size, and that means lugging the whole load down to the depot and then back again because it's too much to keep down there and he just hasn't bothered yet. Everyone gets paid and so far they haven't run out of anything, but that is as far as Felix has managed. His desk is a confirmed disaster, but he doesn't think of it. Now and then one of Willoughby's blue-shirted men will drift up the slope with a sandwich in his hand and stand, observing, at the edge of Felix's little hole. They have rarely had a money man on site before and never one who spent a month digging.

"That skull ain't half bad," one of the men offers—Bryce, a burr-haired tough with a smashed nose—after staring down into the pit for a minute or two.

"Not half," Felix allows. "Except here." The back of the skull has been crushed to a jumble of tiny fragments.

Bryce crouches, swipes his hat off his head. "Yeah, that's a bugger. You want to just leave it like that. Otherwise take you a week to get it all out, and plus you got to chart the whole damn thing. Just cut it out rough." He spits an olive pit into the dirt. "You work too fine, maybe."

"Well, I guess I don't mind it."

Bryce considers him. "Kind of lonely out this way."

"I just go where the man sends me."

"Sure," Bryce says, "you'll get your long pants one of these days."

"I guess you don't mind me paying your salary."

Now Bryce stands. "You know what I'd do, sir, if I had your dough? I'd get the hell out of that hole you're in and go to some nice place that's far, far away."

"I've been to a few places like that."

"I bet you have. I guess that means you know everything."

"No," Felix answers, "I guess I don't."

"Sure. There's all kinds of things you don't know, ain't there, Mr. DuPrie?"

Now Felix stands too. "Why don't you go on back to work, Mr. Bryce."

Bryce stares hotly, caught up in some passion. Then he relaxes. "Aw, nuts," he mutters, "it ain't your fault." Bryce turns away across the slope. On his way he kicks a stone away with idle violence, and when he arrives at the main site he slaps his hat on again and lowers himself with care into the Stegosaurus pit.

No one looks Felix's way.

It is not the last incident. From across the slope Felix has heard angry shouting. Willoughby, red-faced, hurls a chunk of stone downhill in fury while his workmen, including Bryce, bitter and grim, stare elsewhere. At him, some of them. Meanwhile half an adult Ankylosaurus awaits removal, all spines and spikes; in the flood-catch gully two men are lifting from the matrix a tumbled wash of mismatched parts: the skull of a Barosaurus, the willowy shinbone of an Othnielosaurus, what appear to be parts of at least a dozen different Elaphrosauri. Enough to keep them all occupied for a year at least, and all Morrison Formation creatures, to a beast. So why the fuss?

Well, they know he is a rich man. And here he is doing their work. Maybe that's all it is. The rude discovery that the rich can be good for something. His mother knows the Chamberses, of course, and the Morrows, and is pleased to hear that he married them to each other using his old commission from the Living Church of Mind.

"Was it a *real* wedding, Felix?" she asks, wrapped in a blanket near the fireplace.

"Yes, mama, legal and binding. Aren't you warm?"

Her eyes flash, offended, ignoring him. "Small world, I guess, I knew Dick Morrow's *grandmother*. About a million years ago. She used to come down to see us at Trelawney. She was always very funny to all of us because she pretended she didn't know how she'd gotten there, you know... 'Well, we've had our fortune since time immemorial.' When her own father had been the one who found all that coal. She just went ahead and *pretended*." And she gestures faintly, lifting her fingers from the wool.

As for Felix, he hadn't known either of them but he hadn't minded, after they had found him in the desert that day, driving them back to town in the Ford Tudor and dropping them at the hotel and then, as a further service, agreeing to marry them. Evidently they had been planning something of the sort for a good while; they had all the official papers filled out, and they had done the blood tests and were ready to do business; all they needed was his signature. He had been still tingling with strangeness from their sudden appearance like two white and terrible angels and had also felt they had done him a good turn of some kind by getting him off the desert when they did. As though something had been about to strike from behind the sun. After he pronounced the words in city hall with the hotel clerk as the witness, he shook their hands and said, "Congratulations."

"Thank you," the girl said. "You have no idea the ordeal you've saved us from."

"I think I might have some idea," Felix said. "I've been to a few of those fancy getups."

"Not like *this* one, I wager," the fellow Morrow chortles. "Now, what do we owe you, friend?"

"Usually the fee is five American dollars," he said. He was DuPrie, he told them. They didn't catch at the name, and it felt peculiar to have become so swiftly invisible; on the other hand, no one would think to put DuPrie and Son together with Felix as he appeared to them, especially as he took their money and folded it into his hat. But there was another reason he didn't expect to be recognized. He didn't know Dick Morrow, but he does know the type. There is a clannishness to the Boston bunch. Nothing they need to learn from someone who isn't their own. They have got it all figured up there.

Sure, he thinks now, watching Bryce climb down into the pit. And he knows a gang when he sees one, doesn't he. Boccioni, Musolino, Girimonti, Telesio. Something afoot he hasn't been told.

12

Now that Mary has run away from Teddy and come back to Hollis, she is worse off than ever; at parties when she is feeling her best she can manage a few smart remarks from the corner of a sofa, but mostly she is watchful and quiet. Hollis will glance over and see her working her lips together, engaged deep in some interior argument, and he will cringe and feel a wave of shame and sorrow. He is all she has in the world, and he is not doing her much good. The Bostonians have seen their share of family oddballs, everyone has someone stowed away somewhere; but it is made more difficult when you are not one of them, and when you can't seat your sister at a table with her back to a window or to an open doorway without worrying what she's likely to do. It is lucky, Hollis thinks, that she is such a good-looking girl. You can account for a certain amount of strange-ness that way and have it seem half-charming. "No!" she will cry, scooting around the table, "I'm going to sit *here*." And everyone does a do-si-do to accommodate her, Mary Hempstead, the strange pretty quiet girl from Scranton who runs with the MacAllisters and their lot.

And of course Mary feels her strangeness too. She tries not to pick at her tusk when people are looking, and she can disguise her urge some-times as an airy overhead gesture, but the bad ones in the bunch are ready to pounce on anything funny. "What're you, tuning a guitar up there?" a wiseacre once asked.

"Who are you, Segovia?" she shot back.

At least the rider is gone; he stayed behind when she made it off the streetcar and has not returned. And while this is in some ways an improvement, she is always on the lookout for him now; she worries he might come up from behind a chair, or he might be folded up in a cupboard or slipped down between the sheets like a lost nightgown. In conversation she is distracted; she is listening for the sound he will make as he comes up, a dead leaf rustling.

Meanwhile there are endless ranks of dumb fellows who try to put the rush on her and who she turns aside. They are a bad bunch, mostly. Not a decent man among them, no one half as good as Teddy. At someone's big apartment Charlie Chambers leans over with his long frame and says, "You ought to think about ditching that brother and his ladyfriend once in a while and try a night out with the boys."

"Maybe I will sometime," she says, "if you know of any."

"Oh, you'd like me," Charlie croons. He has a yellow face and a disturbing angular set of teeth; you can hear the gums smacking as he smiles. "You could come places with me you've never seen before. You don't need these two girlies."

"But I like these girlies." She lifts an arm over Holly's shoulder. "Maybe you should try them out sometime, Charlie. You look like the type."

"These two chickens couldn't make me with a kit," he says.

"That's a good line, Charlie," she offers. "I guess you have to use it a lot."

He flashes his chompers. He is by no means the only one; they are a dime a dozen, Harvard boys some of them but also the anciently rich, the heirs to textile factories and sons of old professors, and those who simply have money as a sort of aspect of their character, it seems. And distantly she recognizes the unfairness: that she should be here now when she is least able to shine. Even the few nice fellows with good manners—well, they're made soft by money, too soft to take her on; and they wouldn't want her anyway, not after they knew.

(She reaches up to pluck at the tusk and forces her arm down again.)

It is a long autumn, and now and then she thinks of Teddy and his green apartment and the outdoor chairs where the orange leaves are no doubt falling in the courtyard and where by now he is likely entertaining another girl. For a few days Mary considers what it would be like to go back to him, but she has done him very wrong, she knows this, and anyway if she were to return she would be stared at just as much as she is stared at here, for being Teddy's lost sweetheart. So it is impossible.

Instead, she stays. She gets off her lines as she is able, and remains at home when she can; she wraps herself in Holly's robe and smokes on the screened-in porch and reads his magazines and assures herself all the doors are locked, and she will lay herself in the bath and try to regulate the temperature to exactly blood warmth as the nurses did for her at Belmont, working the taps with her long pretty toes. She considers putting herself in a hot wrap, but she is not sure how to do it and doesn't want to ask Holly for that kind of help. And she stares into the mirror, too, as training; she forces herself to look at the nothingness that is there. Still there, despite all the evidence of her mind.

Nothingness, but with a definite *outline*. An absence defined.

And then one day she is in the corridor at one of these parties when she hears two girls whispering in a paneled alcove, a pearly light from the sconce shining on their gray silk dresses:

"Everyone's taking bets," one says, "on who'll make her first."

"I'd take one on who'll make her last," says the other. "Once that type goes, they don't stop."

And she just knows they are talking about her; it is the sort of thing you hear all over, and of course she had enough of this in high school; but it especially rankles here under these fine high ceilings and the plaster God's Eye medallions. It is just so stupid and small, as though who you've slept with is the most serious matter in the world, when Mary knows firsthand it is hardly anything. And she has not slept with that many anyhow, and only Teddy since she came to Boston. She puts her head in and says, "You would know, dears—which one has the longest johnson?"

"Leslie Granger," says the first of them without blinking, a blond girl with the blunt head of a snapping turtle. "But everyone says it's always sort of half-floppy."

"Maybe with you it is," Mary answers. "You know you're supposed to act at least a little bit interested."

The blonde smiles wanly. "You can't fool us. Everyone knows what you are."

"What am I?"

The girl settles herself on her hips. She is uncomfortable for a moment before she pronounces, reluctantly, "Well, you're not all there, are you?"

Mary does not know how to respond; it is something she has never really imagined being said to her. *Not all there.* That's it exactly, somehow. "Am I?" she asks.

The brunette puts in sharply, "You think Scotty doesn't tell us everything? You're the one who cut herself open with a spoon."

She feels herself go scarlet. She has no line she can deliver in response, so she turns, poised, upright, into the big room and finds her brother in conversation.

"Holly," she manages, and jerks her head, wildly, at the door.

"Instantly, dear?" he asks.

And she can only stare. Everyone knows; she can hardly stand it another second, the *looks . . .*

He sighs, rises, and takes her arm. "A minute," he apologizes, bowing in a half circle.

Outside on the sidewalk he is sagging, defeated. "Mare," he exhales. And also the look, unexpected, of something like anger in his eye.

She says, "They're talking about me, Holly. I'm not just imagining it, they really are; they're talking about—" And she shakes her head, meaning, *what I did.*

He is still holding his drink. "Well," he says, toasting her, as it begins to rain, "what the hell do you think? They talk about everybody. You're in the club, I guess that means."

"But they don't *know* anything," she insists. "They don't know the first thing about me."

"I'd say," Holly answers coolly, over his drink, "they know the only thing they think they need to know."

But she is frightened by his calm, and all at once, with a terrible passion, she misses home, misses Scranton, before any of these horrible things happened—the long fence against the back yard, the sooty coal-field air and the midnight crashing of the trains along Holloway Street, and the trucks barreling along the highway. And her poor parents—Mama! Papa!

She is so sad, so lonely. Under the weight of it she leans into her big broad brother, all she has in the world. He is surprised, still holding his glass; then he relents. "Oh, *Mare.*" He breathes, sadly, into her hair, as the rain increases. "It's all right."

But now there is a feeling like the one she had in the MacAllisters' house as she cut into herself, only more frightening, as it seems a deeper fracture; it is as though some wall deep inside her comes down and there is a cavern revealed and a wind comes from it, just emptiness comes breathing through her, and this is what she says: "He's going to get me again, isn't he, Holly? He's going to find me again, and then he's going to get inside of me and start being the bones of me; that's what he wants, he wants to be the bones of me again, he's tired of being on the outside and he wants a way *in*."

It is nonsense as it comes out of her mouth, part of her knows it; it is only the underground wind speaking through the voice of her. But it's also correct, it's the honest truth, and she didn't know it until this very moment, as though saying it has made it true. The boneman will hunt her down and become her bones. This is the truth of the underground. And *this* has never happened before, this nonsensical talk, and it is as though she has let herself roll a foot down a hill and grabbed something to stop her progress; but the hill is still there tugging at her, and if she lets go she will roll again. So she stands in the middle of the sidewalk and holds him close, his fat back, all of him; she needs a good man like Holly even if he's hardly good any more, even if she's driving him to be just as lousy as the rest of them. And that wind, pressing up against the bottom of her heart.

Hollis is indeed now, in the fall of 1928, at a loss with his sister; and the worst part of this, the part for which he blames himself most severely, is that all along he has done so little to help her. He cannot claim ignorance, only—well, what must it be? Uncaring, could it be that? Surely he has not been her best protector. Even going all the way back to last year, when they had first come to Boston and she had cut herself and she was first in the asylum—well, you couldn't blame anyone for not catching it the *first* time, surely, but he *had* been warned, advised as to the best course of action, yes, as soon as she had gone into Belmont. As the next of kin Hollis had been asked to consult with Dr. Miller, so, still ashamed at what his sister had done, avoiding Scotty's gently appalled inquiries, and with little aftershocks of horror going through him at the memory of all the blood she had managed to lose into the towel (it had become actually *heavy* with blood), he had taken himself out on the car to find this Dr. Miller, eventually being shown through the pillared common room, past the hanging plants and pianos and upholstered divans, following a blue-uniformed nurse ("bluebirds," they were evidently called) down a corridor and through a locked door and finally into Dr. Miller's dim spare office, where a few ghouls went slanting past in the halls outside and carts were pushed jingling past the door. Ivy rustled around the edges of the window, which was glowing like a portal to the upper world.

Dr. Miller was bluff, grainy-tan, yellow fur tufting from his cuffs, a fullback's bulk behind his tweed. He wanted to explain things: how long she might be locked away, as far as anyone could guess; what exactly had happened. "My belief, Mr. Hempstead," Dr. Miller offered, "is that she was very, very good, for a very long time, at existing from day to day. Likely she was suffering in some fashion even before your parents died, before she left Scranton to live with you here. But she finally reached a point where she couldn't stand it any longer, and the pressures she had been feeling all along, whatever they consisted of"—Dr. Miller produced a blossom with his gesturing hands—"could no longer be controlled. And so she did this."

"But why . . ." he whispered. "What made her . . ."

"Hurt herself?"

Hollis blurted, "Try to *kill* herself," then swallowed a sob.

Dr. Miller shook his head gently, kindly. "It's only been a week, so we can't know for sure. She's hardly said a word to me. But if you want to know what I think, I don't think that's what she was doing, Mr. Hempstead." Dr. Miller fixed him with a meaningful stare. "I don't think she was trying to kill herself at all."

"Well." The blood; the grapefruit spoon sliding through her fingers. "That's an interesting theory you've got there, doc," he managed.

"And I may be wrong, of course. I am, more often than I'd like to be. But in my experience suicides cut themselves where they can see the blood. Where they know there's blood to be had. The wrists, of course, but also the arms. And it's a strange fact that if someone's near a mirror they're more likely to try for their throat, because they can see it." He pressed two fingertips to the hollow beneath his larynx. "But I think she had some other sort of idea."

"Just a fun afternoon, I guess."

Miller was unperturbed. An irresistible calm emanated from the man, from his big hands, the sandy planes of his face; *Chief,* one of the nurses had called him. "Some kinds of wounds aren't attempts at suicide. Some we see as evidence that someone's trying to *fix* something. Certain compulsives, for example, sometimes try to amputate a finger or a thumb or a toe. Then we see the marks here, or here, right at the joint—or in the same places on the foot. Or if they want to try to take off part of an arm, we see them here." He rested the two fingers on his elbow. "But I don't really know what *this* means yet." He put the fingers on the back of his head. "I don't know exactly what she's trying to do *there.* What I would guess is that she was trying to get rid of something. But what?"

"Beats me."

"Exactly right. There's nothing there to get rid of. So what *I* think is she has a delusion that something is there that isn't really there. She won't talk about it with us, at least not yet. But that's what I think. How does that sound to you?"

"That would make her very crazy," he said.

"Well, hypothetically, that would give us a diagnosis of Involution Paranoia of Kleist. Which is no crazier than being generally neurasthenic or having a compulsion neurosis or an undifferentiated fixation hysteria, of which Kleist is a particular brand. So, no, it doesn't make her very crazy."

"Just crazy enough."

"Yes, I would say just crazy enough." Miller lunged up from his chair and tugged out a whomping green book. His aspect became canny, unserious. He was a hell of a handsome man, actually. "Now, this is all sort of boilerplate stuff in the books, Mr. Hempstead, so we'd best take it with a grain of salt, but it gets you the general idea. It's the same thing as if you ever took a biology class and you look at the drawing of the frog and then you look at the frog in front of you and you say, 'Well, my frog don't look like that frog.' Okay." He jabbed his finger onto the page, squinting at the tiny type. "First, who the hell is Kleist? The answer is, I don't know. A German fellow, I guess; maybe we don't have to hold that against him any more. Second, *involution,* what's that mean to us? Essentially it means private and self-contained. The delusion refers to itself and does not tend to be ramified in the rest of the world. So you're not involved, for example. I mean there's nothing *you* do that confirms what she's convinced of."

"I noticed she was sort of strange, that's all."

"It's got nothing to do with you, Mr. Hempstead. Except she does rely on you to show her what's real. She relies on people, I mean."

"She's always been very social."

"Yes, she's that way here, too. She's very successful in the wards, and well liked. Not everyone is. She's taken to the craftwork, which will be important for her in the future; she'll always want to have something to do. She's bright. but she's not pushy. People like her."

"She's pretty."

"Yes." Miller blinked neutrally. "That also makes a difference how people are treated. Here and elsewhere. Most of the patients want to be her friend. It is a sort of schoolyard environment. So is everywhere else, come to that." He studied the book again. "So, *involuted*, meaning private. Next, *paranoia*, here clinically meaning simply a delusion. 'Beginning: sometimes in close connection in time with the menarche.' That doesn't hold up so good, I bet."

He blushed, appalled. "I think she was a bit of an early bloomer."

"Okay, strike one. 'Occurrence, ninety percent in women, seventy percent living alone at the time of onset, often in connection with family trauma or disturbance.' Closer to the mark there, of course."

"Yes."

"Three. 'Symptoms: misinterpretations, illusions, peculiar sensations, peculiar disturbances of thought.' She more or less admits to these already, you'll be interested to know, although she hasn't told us any specifics yet. And the kicker: 'Psychasthenic symptoms happen with a clear mind, with the patient fully recognizing their abnormal nature.' That means you feel something strange and you know it's strange but you're still convinced it's true." Miller squinted up from his book. "I think that's your sister," he said.

At the word *sister* his eyes suddenly filled. Their canvas wigwam in the back yard, the deep personal shade inside. His Mary. "When can she come out?"

"We'll let her out when we don't think she's going to hurt herself, but it won't mean she's all better. I won't lie to you, Mr. Hempstead, Kleist is pretty serious business. She's got to see someone."

"Can she come here?"

"No. I'm a purely inside man. You're not married?"

"No."

"I was going to suggest your wife ask around. But well, look, there's plenty of places she can go. You don't have to come to a place like this. I'm happy to give you a list of doctors I can recommend."

"All right."

"One thing you can be sure about with Kleist. It's pretty bad in the beginning. But unless you really go after it, it always gets worse." He whumped the book closed again. "Also, for what it's worth, we often have on WBZ in the common room, and she seems to like listening to the music. Her knitting and her music. *And*"—Miller leveled a long flat finger at him—"*seeing someone.*"

But Hollis had not done that. He had gone to get her after three months in Belmont and just installed her with them in the apartment in the city, and from there she had washed up with Edward Howe, and then Hollis had visited the man's office and had forced him, essentially, into asking Mary to be his wife; and that had evidently sent her over the edge. And the morning after the engagement party, when Hollis hung up after his conversation with Edward Howe, Hollis feared he had made a terrible mistake by interfering; he stood frozen in the apartment, wearing Scotty's robe, forehead in his hand—

What a stupid meddling queer he was, what a stupid fat faggot—

He suspected she would come to him, so he went down to the street to await her. It was only a few minutes when he saw her a block away, shuffling strangely along. She was hatless and looked very large under her coat. When she finally spotted him there she began to run, and the coat opened and flowers came falling out, two or three, more, a dozen, but she paid them no attention and the flowers seemed, comically, to keep falling, as though she were helplessly producing them from the folds of her clothes as she hurled herself forward past the other apartment houses, terrified. He stood back as she dashed past him and ducked inside. He picked up the tulips as he climbed the stairs, and by the time he reached the apartment himself she had locked herself in the bathroom and the shower was running and the overcoat was sprawled on the floor. He knelt. The coat was cashmere, light as an elf's cloak. He lifted it gently and shook it to dislodge the remaining tulips, which plopped to the floor. Some product of her madness, she would not want to see them again. So he swept the flowers into a heap with the edge of a *Harper's Bazaar*, then took them all to the window and with regret heaved them out.

She was in the shower long enough to make him wonder if he should break down the door. But finally she reappeared wrapped in Scotty's blue robe, and she looked all right. "How are you feeling?" he asked, a safe opener.

"I just wrote myself a little pardon out of that joint, that's all," she told him. "I'm not trying to be alarming."

"He called, you know. Your big protector."

"I'm not doing it. I'm not marrying him."

Cautiously Hollis offered, "He sounded all shook up."

She faced him down. "Well, I ran off, Holly. And now nobody's going to want me. Look at me."

"You look all right."

"He's chasing me. I left him on the car."

"Who's chasing you, Mare? Howe?"

"Oh, no, no," she insisted, "it's nobody, nobody, nobody. *Please* don't worry. I'm sorry, Holly, I'm really sorry. I know I'm a pain. But I'll be all right if you just let me stay here a little while. Nobody knows I'm here. Nobody followed me. I won't bother you two, really, I promise I won't."

So he should have done something then, of course. All of it so long ago, now. He should have gone back to Miller to get those names. But he hadn't. He couldn't ask Scotty to foot the bill again. Scotty would have done it without a whimper, but it was asking too much. And, after she came to stay, she managed to come along to parties, and to survive, so instead of solving the problem they had muddled along, and muddled along, and now it is too late, and here they are standing in the cold rain that has begun on the sidewalk outside the roaring party, and she is in his arms and talking nonsense. *The bones of me.* What can she mean?

"All right, Mare." He sighs, tossing his glass into the bushes. He separates from her, looks her in the eye. A little clear rivulet is snaking down her neck. Gently he removes the handkerchief from his breast pocket and dabs at her neck, its lovely, perfect length. "We'll be all right."

"So what are you going to do, then?"

They are in bed that night, he and Scotty, rain tapping the windows. "You want me to turn her out?" Hollis replies.

Scotty will let this one pass for the time being. "You should go see that fighter of hers. See if he'll take her back after all this time."

"No."

Scotty rolls over to face him, grinning, his long hair flopping. "What if he knows gangsters and so on? I wouldn't be surprised if he's hunting her down right now."

"No," Hollis says, "he's not quite like that." Then: "She'll be all right."

Through the window they can see, blocks away over the fences and the rooftops, a rusting derelict of some industrial purpose, lit up tonight—a part of a gantry, perhaps, standing up hugely like a hangman's scaffold. A place to hang giants from. It is the only grand thing to be seen anywhere; their apartment is small and modest, and in it Hollis is living a modest life, at least when they are home from the parties. It suits him. And possibly this further explains his reluctance to go to greater lengths for Mary; he wants his own regular life, and this is it. A feeble excuse. But certainly he doesn't want to endanger anything. As it is, Scotty's continued devotion makes no sense to Hollis; when he looks in the mirror he sees nothing remarkable, his old livery droopy face and beneath it the pouchy, slumpy torso, the swinging purple cock, the diminishing legs. Hollis knows he is not a catch, he has continued to work at Weber's, stealing paints as needed, and when they roll home from parties Scotty has posed for paintings, casting arch looks over his shoulder, his white flesh glowing in the dim when he dares to remove his shirt. "Oooh, hurry," he cries, "I'm *going* all *icy!*"—vamping for Hollis, who has been pressed by Scotty's enthusiasm into an ever-more-serious version of himself, extending his lower lip and stabbing at his work with the same old embarrassed obligingness. The rich boy's mascot painter. But something is there. Those clouds out on that lawn.

And they have gone to the movies like a couple of old chums, Mary along as well, to see *The Circus* and *The Docks of New York* (twice, because Hollis does like George Bancroft, actually), and *The Farmer's Wife, Gentlemen Prefer Blondes, Our Dancing Daughters, West of Zanzibar.* Before the showing of *The Singing Fool* they sat with their feet up on the velvet in the Royal Brougham Cinema and watched, with slightly drunk rapture, something called *Steamboat Willie,* featuring a drawn mouse who picks up girl mice by their underpants and throws cats overboard and chokes ducks to make them squawk and yanks on piglets' tails and presses the sow's tits like an accordion's keys to play "Turkey in the Straw." There is an uproar in the theater. This is one straight-ahead son of a bitch of a mouse, anyway. And then it was only the other day, during *The Guns of Mexico*, that Hollis began to feel a thrill of something new. Something in the sky reaching huge and pale above the soldiers—the rocky desolation—the great fields unrolling beneath their boots—entranced him. California light, he supposed. Something giant, on the other side of the country. Away from it all. Something that stirred him. Stirs him still, as he lies here.

Of course she is not all right. Will not be.

Scotty says, "I've never heard of a fighter who wasn't tied up with gangsters," and kisses him behind the ear and swings up out of bed. He pads out in his second-best robe (maroon) and begins to make his midnight coffee. He will be up reading magazines and making phone calls until dawn, when he will sleep a little bit. In another minute Hollis himself is wrapped in his socks and pajamas and slippers. He looks in on Mary sleeping, then wraps the old car blanket around his shoulders as he goes out to the back porch. It is very cold, and the screens are jeweled with rain. He turns on the electric light and sits in front of his big square of blank newsprint. California light. The sky is as difficult to capture as the sea at Seahome, isn't it, it is as changeable and detailed, and furthermore the sky has to contain a kind of *movement*, as something is always going from one side to the other in the sky, there has to be a sort of *notional story*, there has to be—he drags a pencil left-to-right—a sort of *direction*, there are currents in the *blue*, never mind the clouds there is a current in the *blue* as well.

He draws an ochre line below to mean the earth.

Scotty comes in and sets a cup of coffee on the little rickety paint-stained table. "Pretty," he says.

Hollis untacks the paper and hands it to him, and Scotty makes a little simpering bow and withdraws.

He tacks up another square and makes another try at Mary. He is still mostly lousy at people; he hasn't got the sort of craggy perfect materiality of, say, an N. C. Wyeth. He would like his people to look like that. Mostly, if anything, they end up being sort of blobby and Bentonish, everyone with that sort of fat-titty roundness, Scotty and himself and Mr. MacAllister and even the goddamned dogs and the house at Seahome, fat as though inflated. But Mary is good practice, as her face is so regular, her eyes so strangely large and mobile, her posture so arch and pained. Her face is complicated without being difficult.

That long neck, that rivulet running down it.

In one of his stolen booklets there is a chapter on portrait techniques, which he will study on the can or in bed or as now when he is a little uncertain where to begin. Tonight his attention is particularly caught.

HOW TO PAINT A HEAD

The head is notably mobile. Like an ornament on a newel post it rests on the atlas vertebrae, which in turn sit upon the cervical vertebrae at the top of the spine. The design of this joint provides for ease of movement, from side to side and up and down. The joint is maneouvered principally by means of the two sternomastoid muscles. These muscles are anchored just behind the ears (see fig.3). In their progress toward their conjunction at the clavicle these muscles wrap around the neck in a more or less graceful line. It is important that the portraitist come to see the head and neck not as separate but as joined in tandem. The head is only rarely drawn to convincing degree without at least some suggestion of the neck below, as its weight and density are best demonstrated through effects on the neck, spine, and shoulders. Note that a figure may be effectively captured through the set of a head alone.

And he does see how this is true. He reaches around to feel the back of his own head. Taps his cigarette into the saucer on the floor.

He rips this passage out carefully and tacks it to the top of his easel, then sits there in front of the blank sheet of newsprint. He sees his breath in the air and his skin has contracted everywhere, but sensing he is on the track of something he takes the pencil from his teeth, and, fondling the contours of his head with one hand, he makes a sketch on the paper with the other. It is not too bad, although a little cockeyed. He slashes a line through it and tries again.

Fat-titty, big fat faggot faggoty cocksucker Holly . . .

Fat-foggity, fag-figgity, frog-faggoty Holly . . .

He goes at this for a little while until the sheet is full of heads and necks. Then he hears a banging in the back yard. He goes to the screen and peers down. One of the trash cans has been overturned, probably by a raccoon. Lidless, the can is rolling along the concrete pad at the stunned pace of a man who has had his hat socked off. Hollis puts the pencil in his teeth and goes down to retrieve it. The rain is steady. The yard is empty. He takes the trash can in one hand and hauls it back to where it was and puts the lid back on. He inhales the cold air and stares into the cornered darkness, listening. No fighters anywhere.

Well, Howe would come barging in the front door, wouldn't he?

After a minute he decides to hell with it and stumps back inside. At his easel again he sees it immediately, that Miller was right, that Mary is indeed carrying something on the back of her head, and that it is something very long and counterbalancing, that this is what she has been doing, this is why she carries her head at such an angle.

A shiver.

He paws through his papers until he finds the old picture of her with the cigarette. His best of her, the one with the most sort of humor and life.

He is sure of it. Something large, something long.

A giant hat.

A tree.

He reaches out with the tip of his pencil and draws a long wavery line from the back of her head.

A pole.

A bone.

He claps his hand to his mouth. Another chill. She is a creature. A speared beast on a skewer. A monster. His poor brave sissy.

13

Upon his return to Cambridge Alan finds his mailbox full—stuffed with reprints of Cecilia Payne's *On the Absolute Magnitudes of the Class M Stars* and Willem Luyten's *The Proper Motions of 1,800 Stars in the Large Magellanic Cloud*, and Harlow Shapley's first installment of the massive survey *Studies of the Galactic Center*, these sober and impressive things suggesting Harvard College Observatory's ever-growing attention to matters well beyond the solar system. These sleek booklets are layered in among the rest of his summer's more mundane mail, which includes: many discardable announcements of talks long since given; the registration slip listing the last course he is required to undertake at Harvard, Nebular Analysis, filled in with Mrs. Albert's scrolling hand; a starched letter from his mother in Belleville which has lain there all summer (he was given the contents again when she realized her mistake), and which seems, in its stiff white Easter dress of an envelope, to be marooned in springtime, as though to touch it would be to launch it in an instant five months forward in time; and, right on top, a fresh folded-over invitation to Mr. and Mrs. Richard Morrow's apartment, for a party celebrating their marriage.

The rumor is neither Dick nor Florence will be returning to the Brick Building until January. The program seems plain: wait for him to clear out. Let him stew in his own humiliation, everyone talking about him behind his back. You can't just go naming a comet after Dick Morrow's girl and get away with it.

Well, imagine what they'd do to him in their own house. So the invitation seems a sort of dare.

He stumps into the computer room. Six girls, all of them on the decent side, though nobody like Florence.

"Say, Barbie," says Nell.

"Say, Nellie."

"You going to name one after me next, Barbie?"

"What've you got on offer?" he says.

Nell is the new ringleader now that Florence is gone. They are a funny crew, the computers, at least one Lesbo he knows of and another who is said to be double-gated; he is wary of these girls, not knowing quite how to play them. Nell is okay, blond but with a strange unbalanced face, all her features crowded in the middle and around them a flat white expanse of cheek and forehead and chin. Still, when she smiles the effect is somehow appealing. "Poor Barbie," Nell croons, "all fallen off his horse."

He sinks into a chair. "I ran along as far as I could, but those two can get up some respectable speed."

She pouts. "Mean old Florrie." Her hair is lustrous from a recent application of Golden Glint. She spies the invitation in his hand. "Ooh. You're going, I hope."

"Who, me?"

"Oh, you wouldn't miss it," Nell scoffs. "Which is why we wouldn't either."

The Lesbo leans over and says, "We are hoping for some fireworks, Barbie."

Nell says, "Actually we're hoping *very much* for some fireworks, Barbie."

"I ain't going."

Nell says, "You are going if we have to roll you up in a carpet."

"Then you'll have to dance with me."

"Oh, I'd do that." She smiles. "Anyway, they put on a good party."

"We'll show her what she's missing. Me and you and the whole roomful all together, we'll show her. Clothing checked at the door."

"Oh, well, look, Barbie, this is how you get into these jams in the first place; you get everyone all hot and *interested*." Nell laces a strand of her hair behind her ear. She is conscious of her strange face, of his eyes on it as he rearranges her features. "So the pipe is you're really leaving, I guess," she says. "Which is awful of you. Mean old *Barbie*."

"Get your fill now, while tickets are still to be had."

"Sure. That's nice for you, I guess. You know they've got me doing Pickering's work again. It won't go away, even though he's *absolutely a madman*." She tips her paper toward him. Ranks of residual calculations, much like his own, creep patiently down the page. "Please tell me he's going to give it up one of these days."

He knows the computers are the central exchange for information; say something here and it is eighteen miles down the wire in ten seconds. "Planet O."

"Among other things. Planet O at the moment. But at the same time I'm also supposed to be looking for Planet P. Florrie's *supposed* to be doing it but you ran her out, so here's all that right here; in case you wanted to be of some use to somebody, *you* could do this one. You know what we think about Planet P? Planet P is forty times bigger than Jupiter and 145 astronomical units from the sun. Make me laugh. And this is what I do all day, Barbie."

"You're a sweetheart. He means it, anyway."

This is not quite gossip, but it is close, and her eyes fire. "He's a pain in my rear," she says.

"You could work for me instead," he says, and for an instant means it. But no, he will keep his work on the residuals quiet. Not to be thought a madman himself.

She examines him. What does he mean, anyway? She can guess, maybe. But now he is getting up again, and she accepts this, too, as only her due. "Any time you ask, Barbie," she agrees, sadly, and in saying this releases him. She is tired of being funned with. It is her face; no one cares enough to take her seriously.

Nell is right. They know how to throw a party. They always have. And he will not turn away the chance to see Florence again, no matter what they intend to do to him. So he takes the brush to his gray suit and polishes his boots, and on the appointed day a week later he skiffs up the marble steps to the Morrows' door, which is propped open, the fanlight glowing over-head. Guarding the vestibule like an armored beast is a hefty brass-collared telescope, a 10-inch Brashear aimed out the door on its wooden tripod. Someone has glued a giant winking paper eye, complete with lashes like the Pinkertons', to the lens cap.

Music from down the hall, the hot burble of a big crowd.

At the apartment door he finds Dick leaning against the jamb as though he's waiting for him. "Say, old man," Dick exhales. He is drunk as hell and slams a hand down on his shoulder, then leans against the wall again. "I'll be damned you came to our little party."

"Say, Dick."

"You are some, some piece of work, Barbie. You are some other sort of creature, pal. You got some nerve. How's the old grandmas out there, any-way? You miss me?"

"It wasn't the same without you, Dick."

"That's what I thought. And now you come here and you think you can get a drink off me for nothing. After what you did."

"I just had a little idea, I guess, Dick, if you'd give me a chance to apologize I'd do it."

"I hope so. That's the worst idea any man's ever had about another man's girl. Everybody looks like a big old chump, you know, you most of all."

"It was stupid," he says, "and I'm sorry."

"You're damned right it was. And you sure as hell are. You are one sorry son of a bitch, Barbie. Whatever you think you end up getting up to out there, you are one sorry deluded son of a bitch."

"All right."

"I didn't even want to invite you, that's how far that goes. But Florrie wanted to, she thought you'd find out and you'd get sore. I said sore. What's sore. Who cares sore, what he's got is a bad idea about everything. Well, here you are. Welcome to my house, you son of a bitch." He elbows off the wall and comes forward again. He towers over him now, an inch away. "You'd better fucking well behave yourself."

"Oh, Dickie," Florence says, appearing behind her husband. "Knock it off, would you."

"Sure," Dick says, "I'll knock something off, anyway."

"Hello, Florrie." She is tanned, pretty, her eyes alight. A comet, that's what she is. "Awfully nice to see you again."

"Hello, Barbie, you old bum. See the trouble you've caused."

"I told him I was sorry."

"Gang up on me, you two, see what I knock off then," Dick spits, and passes into the big riotous apartment.

"You're looking fine," he says.

"I have some things to say to you myself," she tells him.

"In that case," he says, "I bet I could use a drink."

"It may not hurt," she says.

He senses an air of waiting scandal as he and Florrie enter together while Dick beelines away into the crowd. But the rooms are full and the gramophone is blaring and a whole mass of folks are dancing, and it turns out you can avoid making a scene if you want. The mob from HCO is all there, among a million others. Here in a corner are the girls from the computer room, including Nell; she squeezes her knees together and sends him a little wave; he could definitely make her if it comes to it. And the other computers have all brought their gentlemen friends, and here are a dozen or so of his fellow students, the tweedy bunch of bores and their various attachables, and a little circle of Divinities who hang around the astronomers sometimes like a choir of doubters. And on the sofa here is Charlie Chambers, Florrie's brother, and Charlie's girl Merna, and here is some flop-haired, languid boy named Scotty, and blond Barbara, and hazel-eyed Hazel, and a dark toadish man everyone calls Hemp, looking as though he is infinitely tired of everything. And next to him, a stunner named Mary who looks as though she's about to bolt the place.

"Hello," Alan says, to all of them.

"Charlie's friends," Florence mutters. She takes him off to the drinks, where she assembles him a gin and tonic.

"Well, cheers," he hollers, above the noise.

"Cheers to you."

"It's good to see you, Florence," he offers.

"All right, if you want it fast, you'll get it. So plainly I gave you the wrong idea about me somewhere along the line." She pushes a piece of hair behind her ear. "Somewhere along the line I sent you the wrong signals, and for all that I'm sorry. And I'm sorry I kissed you like that out there, it wasn't my place to do it, and it didn't mean anything past it was exciting and sweet to have you name something after me. I didn't expect it and it was a surprise, and I do *like* you, you know, when you behave yourself." She prods him with her sharp forefinger. "But listen, Barbie, it actually wasn't fair of you to do it in the first place. Dick's right. Naming the thing after me, Barbie, you just didn't have the right to do that."

"I did that?"

"I'm not kidding around, Barbie. People *talk*. You know, they really do talk. You don't know what that does to a girl. Let alone her marriage. Or you do, which is worse. Think of poor Dickie, if you don't care what it does to me."

"Poor Dickie, all right."

"Oh, you're an idiot. He has every right to be steamed at you, but he's not, really. He just feels like he has to pretend, for dignity's sake."

"He seems pretty steamed to me."

"You haven't seen him really angry," Florence tells him. "He just doesn't like being made to look a fool. Nobody does, do they?"

"Why'd you run away, then?" he finds himself asking. "Made *me* look like a fool, all right."

"We didn't run away, Barbie," she tells him, "we went on our honeymoon."

"Without a word. I was sitting there waiting for him for a week. We all were."

"That bunch." She rolls her eyes. "They were lucky to have him as long as they did." Then she amends: "You too. Honestly, Barbie, what a pack of clowns. I should be as angry at them as anyone. I can't believe they let you name it after me in the first place."

"Slipher didn't like the idea too well."

"But he didn't stop you, did he?" Her eyes fire. "That should give you an idea of the sort of crew they are, Barbie; they just don't know how to do things the usual way. They don't have any idea of how the forms of things are supposed to be. They never did because they never had to because Lowell didn't either. But there are *reasons* most people behave the usual way, even the rich ones, because it's all for the best in the end."

"That's funny coming from you."

"But there are *limits*, Barbie. I guess that's why you liked it out there so much; you don't care about the limits. You just want to do whatever the hell you please. You want to be a Lowell, is what you want."

"Well," he says, downing his drink, and making to go, "I guess that'll do."

"No, no, Barbie," she whispers, gripping his arm, "then they'll think we've fought and make a big story out of it. That'll just make it worse. Just don't look so *serious* around me. That's the big giveaway, Barbie, you don't laugh about it enough. It's like you don't know how to have any fun. You've got to show a little more gas, even when you don't feel it." She shakes him a little. "Come on, you can do it."

He gives her a forced smile. "How's that?"

"Lousy. You look like an orangutan. But you can be my friend again, just as long as you keep it right there and don't try to advance it."

The fire in the grate settles. The party roars around them. He peers through the crowd for Nell, who is looking better and better.

"You're really going back out there?" she asks.

"Yes."

"Not for long, I hope."

"It's a staff position. I'll just carry their water for a few years."

"You like that stuff."

"You're starting to sound like Shapley."

"It *is* second-rate, though, Barbie. You don't deny it. They're a million years behind everyone."

"I'll get to do what I want. They won't let me mention planets around here."

"Well, you're ridiculous; you could talk your way on at Oak Ridge and look at Mars all night. Unlike me. The best I could ever do is end up in charge of the computer room. But you could get all the time you wanted. Shapley'd do *that* for you, anyway. Then you could stay and we could be friendly, you know."

"I don't think Shapley's interested in cutting me any favors. I was supposed to go to Arizona to shake the planetary bug. Like a case of TB." There is a sudden moment when he sees her as a colleague, only, and in that moment he feels a peculiar, unexpected settling, as though a swirling flock of birds had all come to rest in a tree at once. "And besides," he ventures, "it's not Mars I want to look at."

"Oh, you're joking."

"Well," he says.

"Please tell me you're joking, Barbie. You can't really think there's anything. Or you *do*."

Lowell's loony search, and his own. But he will say no more. The mockery would be too much to bear, and surely she would feel obliged to deliver it. He looks into the fire. The embers pulse with heat. "I like it out there, anyway. You should come. I mean—both of you."

She huffs. Planet X, of all the crazy things. He is reduced in her eyes; all at once it seems nothing remains to pass between them. She takes his glass. "You're really ridiculous, Barbie," she tells him, sadly, without heat.

"I'm not," he tries now, unable to help himself. "I'm really not. You could come on out sometime, couldn't you? I'd promise not to make a pass."

"Oh," she sighs, "*that'll* do, I think."

This weariness. What was there all along. She is not really enjoying herself, perhaps, not really enjoying anything. She cannot be who she wants to be, so nothing will ever be quite right for her; nothing will really answer. And he senses that it will cost him, too, for causing her to expose herself this way. On some cue they both look across the room. The man called Hemp is watching them curiously. Alan takes Florence's arm and leads her into the mob and goes, himself, to sit at the piano. It is a big lovely machine, dark and shining. He lifts the cover and plunks the keys. Amid all the other noise a gorgeous mood comes welling up. Chastening. Not a chance in hell.

This life she has. It isn't bad, at that.

He cracks his knuckles for show. Then he puts down a few bars of nothing in particular, just to get the beauty.

How terribly he has missed the piano, he realizes. The record comes to an end, and over the sound of the party Florence calls, "Play dem bones, Mr. Barber."

"Yes, Miz Morrow, I shorely will," he says. Remembers to smile. Some gas. Another walking flourish. Then, with what little syncopation he can muster in his black mood, he falls down jolting into the first ragged bars of "Lonesome Joe," an amateur's staggering introduction but not too bad. He keeps at "Lonesome Joe" until it begins to repeat and then steps up into "Ain't My Lady," which seems the natural thing, and gets about half-way through this when he hears a bar of "Evangeline Rag" taking shape in his right hand and goes off with it for a while, and by this time people have mostly stopped listening again and are sort of dancing or milling around anyway, arguing about *The Cock-Eyed World* and *The Mysterious Dr. Fu Manchu,* how they hate it when everyone has to stop and stand around talking, how it ruins all the good chase scenes, and with the air of a host Charlie Chambers comes staggering over, another tall Yankee with his sister's blond green-eyed looks. He delivers a great tall tumbler of Scotch and says, "Not bad, boyo," and Alan reaches up and takes the glass with his left hand and does a sketch of "O Margaret" with his right, all of this in some way serving somewhat to pacify himself, and even, it seems, to argue for his presence there; he is an uncertain friend, all right, but one who can play a damned all right rag for a white man. Later, after the tumbler is filled again, and a long time passes during which he is simply making music for himself, Florence comes to sit beside him, rustling her skirts and joining in halfway through "Happy Harriet," nothing special but she can keep up all right, Dick slanting by in the middle distance not watching, and he feels the keen, unstoppable loss of her, her long thigh incidentally against his own as he works the pedal and their occasional touching of hands, crossing over when she reaches for the bass notes of the chorus. She is showing him, he thinks. How they might be, as friends. But also what he is going to miss by going away to pursue his stupid hope.

Hours later when he emerges onto the sidewalk with everyone else, there is a man beside him whom he recognizes, the one called Hemp, short for Hempstead—they all have these goddamned names.

"Some show," Hempstead tells him, handing over a cigarette.

"Some show, some damned show. That's what they're good at, isn't it?"

"That is it exactly," Hempstead says.

"Well, I guess I got what's coming." He leans into the match and straightens again. Well, he is pretty well soused at this juncture, and why the hell not? The end of an era. It is still a warm night, now just spitting rain. There is a bunch off to see *Bulldog Drummond*, but not Florrie or Dick, who will stay behind. He waves up at her standing under the fanlight, seeing them off. "Some damned show, all right. There she is. Blow her a kiss. Good-bye, you beautiful brilliant girl of a thing."

"You're shouting," Hempstead tells him. They are suddenly alone on the sidewalk.

"Oh," he answers. "Where's your girl?"

"I haven't got a girl."

"You *had* one," Alan points out, "but I know that story."

"We want a drink," Hempstead decides.

It is the start of a long night, but he wakes up more or less whole on a strange sofa in a strange apartment. There is rain against the windows, and the flop-haired boyo MacAllister from last night is in a maroon robe at the stove Alan can see from where he lies. He has a head and there is some pressure behind the eyes, but the good stuff doesn't do the same damage as the stuff he is used to. He sits up.

The room does a little quarter turn but not too bad.

Florrie. In the fanlight, waving. The number 313 in purple glass above her head.

"Mr. Barber," Hempstead says from the breakfast table. He is eating a chocolate cake from a white plate and drinking coffee.

"Hempstead," he says. You end up in the oddest places. This little setup and his socks still on. He shoves the little plaid blanket aside. The apartment smells of coffee and cigarettes and paint. He hoists up and makes his rolling way to the can, where he lets fly for a little while. He needs a shave, but who wouldn't and otherwise he appears unharmed. He has his billfold in his back pocket even. He smacks some water on himself and comes out and sits down at the breakfast table. "I guess we missed the movies."

"We did." Hempstead eyes him. "Cake?"

He takes a cigarette from the man's case. "Not for me."

"Coffee?"

"In a couple of shakes." He takes in the apartment. A sort of hideout with a countertop radio and a stack of newspapers and some bananas in a bowl and a vase of dried flowers.

His class, anyway.

Hempstead says, "Some night for you, I understand. According to Scotty, anyway."

He eyes the smeary trails of the cake on Hempstead's plate. "You know everything there is to know about everything, I guess."

MacAllister turns and gives him a sweet smile. "We do get evah so tahed of our own little scandals; sometimes we have to go importin' one or two."

"Sure." He is not up to this at the moment. "Well, I encourage you to keep your nose in your own bag for a while."

MacAllister laughs a little and turns an egg, and Hempstead regards

Alan through one eye, rolls the cigarette on the edge of his saucer. "You're funny. You didn't see what she was about at all."

"I saw it, all right."

"No, you didn't," Hempstead pronounces.

"You're queers, actually," Alan realizes. "I'll be damned. Both of you are queers."

Hempstead's expression shifts as a definitely queer Chinesey thing happens along the folds of his eyes. "That's right," he says.

Alan is about to get the hell out when the stunner from last night appears from the second bedroom. She wears a gray dress whose top black button she is doing up as she emerges. There is a skirt which falls to below the knee, but in a way that gives an impression of knee and everything else above it. Seeing Alan there, she reaches up to touch her hair, then quickly pulls her hand down again with a strict look of self-discipline. She is a very pretty girl, and a moment later it is evident that she is in fact a true beauty, her milk-white skin flushed across the cheeks with red, her eyes blue and lively, and her lips a pink double bow.

"Alan Barber," says Hempstead, "you remember my sister Mary."

"I thought you were with him."

"Well, in one way," she says. "I never thought of trying the other way. Are you hungry?"

"All of a sudden," he says.

"Why not take me out somewhere," she says.

"Well," he says, "I can't think of a reason at the moment, but if you give me a few years, maybe I'll come up with one."

She sighs. She has heard everything, has she not. "But I'm hungry now, Jim."

"It's Alan."

"I know, Jim."

"All right."

He has a coat around here somewhere.

"Silence from the great astronomer," MacAllister comments from the kitchen.

Churchbells sound across the chill morning and he is hoping for a chummy little walk, but two doors down this girl pushes open a door and sits at a little white table and hands him a menu. He is finding it hard to look at her. Like peering into the sun.

"Do you always look like that?" she asks him.

"From now on, maybe," he says. "Like what?"

"Like you're about to jump across the table at someone."

She is so pretty it is embarrassing to be seen in her presence. Everyone knows what you're after. All the heads turn, and he detects a lively attention being paid to her. To him, too, by association. "I don't know," he admits. "I don't think so."

"It's not a bad look," she says, "as long as you don't mind sitting across from Machine Gun McGurn."

"Sure. Well, truth is, McGurn and me go way back. It was him and me hit Frankie Yale last summer. Pow pow pow. What I wouldn't give for a clear shot at Bugs Moran."

"Old Bugs has it coming."

"I'll get the dirty double-crosser, I swear it."

The coffee appears.

"Cheers," she says. "I guess that was some night for you."

"You too, eh? I plead the Fifth, Your Honor. A fifth and a pint and a few bottles of beer and about eleven million cigarettes. And all you got out of it was *Bulldog Drummond* and a ride on the number 11 car."

"As far as you know, that's all I got. I like Ronald Coleman, anyway."

"I bet he'd like you."

"I bet he would, given the chance. But I heard a few stories about you last night."

"Me and McGurn," he says, "we go way back."

"That's some piece of real estate McGurn's walking around in."

"If she ever spends any time on her feet," he says.

"Now," she says, "that's not a nice thing to say about your ladyfriend."

"If she was my ladyfriend, I wouldn't be saying it."

"If she was your ladyfriend," this girl says, "you'd shut up and like it."

"Is that how it goes around here."

"As far as it goes at all," she says. Then she laughs once and sends him a big toothy grin and tosses her head in annoyed grievance at something and says, "What in sam hell are you up to, Jim?"

"Who says I'm up to anything?"

"You are, though." She grants him, then, a real look at her, unshielded.

She sits still, that's all it is, and meets his gaze. A long moment of it, and it knocks him out. "You know what you looked like last night, Jim," she now says kindly, "following along after her."

"I hate to hear it."

"No," she says, "you looked awfully good to me. In that bunch. You looked like you didn't belong there at all. You looked like a trustworthy person there who'd got himself into a bad crowd and was just figuring he wanted the hell out of it."

He flushes hot to the roots of his hair. He likes this description. Something to live up to. "Takes one to know one," he ventures.

She doesn't buck at this as he feared but instead lifts her coffee and peeks at him over the rim. She smiles as if she sees right through him. And oh, he is a dead man. "You've got that right, at least," she says.

14

Clyde watches his brother undress. A bruise purples Roy's left rib cage, and he is stiff. "I guess he got you," Clyde comments.

"Didn't nobody get me." Roy grimaces. "This is what we call a wound of love, big brother."

"That's where somebody punched the hell out of you."

"Kicked, actually." Roy turns silently and shows Clyde the meat of his throat. A scalloped line of hickeys droops like a necklace. "That's Martha Beale for you right there," he says.

"That's you with the end of a vacuum pump."

Roy only grins.

"She'll get you," Clyde says, "and then you'll be sorry. You won't leave here till you're in a box."

"You're the one talking about leaving all the time."

Clyde puts his hands behind his head. The ceiling still angles to that invisible point of intersection behind his head, and he still reaches for it. "I *am* leaving," he says.

"Sure. Whyn't you go to Wichita then, you dumb hick."

"Why don't you mind your own business."

"It's business of mine," Roy counters, "if you sit around here and take up all my air that I could be breathing clean if you didn't sit here and breathe it first."

The October wind rattles the window. They have it stuffed with newspaper so it doesn't *tump* back and forth all day, but the newspaper can only do so much.

"Who are the Beales, anyway?"

"Aw, nobody. She's fourteen," Roy says, excusing him. "Did you hear the one about the fast couple?"

"Probably."

Roy flops onto his bed, puts himself up on an elbow, and recites: "She offered her honor, he honored her offer, and all night long it was on her and off her."

His mother still stumps around in the kitchen, wheezing, the apron rising over her enlarging stomach. She is not going to press Clyde about his plans, and they can pretty well feed him and he is handy around the place, so he earns his keep. But there is no hiding that he wants to be elsewhere. No one asks about Wichita. He can be a stubborn son of a bitch when he wants to be; his father's son, all right. He spends his nights at the telescope, staring at the million stars of the Milky Way, the tilted spinning beauty of Andromeda. If he had a bigger mirror, he could see even more. But he is not about to start another telescope. He hasn't got the heart for it. He hasn't got the heart for much.

"Richard has been asking," his father mentions, sidling up to him in the darkness, "when you're going to send him that."

"I told him I'm not," Clyde says.

"He'll pay, Clyde." His father works loose a little slug and spits into the lawn. "The hell, it's a way to make a little something."

It is a roundabout way his father has of sounding him out. Asking about Carreau. But it is delicious to sink like this—to feel defeat oozing up around him—to root himself in place. Despite what he tells Roy, he suspects he will die in that bed with the ceiling sloping behind his head and the window rattling.

"You could make him another one at least."

"Maybe."

"You ought to," his father concludes. "You said you would."

But he plain can't face the grinding post. He descends into the root cellar and stares without interest at the coffee can, the candle, the bracket on the wall, all the equipment for the Foucault knife-edge test. It is cool in here and comfortable, and he has the idea that he might move in forever and eat what people bring him and lie in a heap of blankets and never see the sun again. Instead he takes an old apple crate and loads it with the labeled paper packets of Carborundum, the packets of Wellsworth emery, the cannister of Snow's grafting wax, the cannister of Archangel commercial-grade pitch. It takes three minutes and then he carries the crate into the dark back corner of the barn, where the cats piss and have their kittens, and sets it on a hay bale. Perverse, to do this without emotion. To demonstrate something—what?—to his father.

That he doesn't expect a goddamned thing from the world either.

In town he slopes along with his hands in his pockets, observing the little wood-sided downtown with a lifer's resignation. He gets his hair cut with his glasses in his lap and the brush whisking at his ears, and when he can see again he looks like a prisoner in a camp, shorn and starving.

The freight train goes by at a thousand miles an hour, shivering the sidewalk underfoot. When it finally blasts away he watches the rust-red caboose go and the little iron railing where it would be possible to stand and regard the world as it slips away from you.

He spends his dimes at the Bijou. He has a seat, six down on the left on the aisle, that he thinks of as his own.

Autumn comes on cold. He stuffs his socks with rags, and buttons himself into his barn jacket, and spends a day with his father draining gasoline from the tractor and the harvester. The gas is pink, and when he pours it from the gas can into the big gasoline drum he feels the fluid unreeling in his hands in a strangely biological way, as though he is bleeding himself.

Still, he attends to Maggie. He palms the currycomb and chuffs it down her side. As though he is simple, he spends half a day laying out the entirety of her tack and addressing it with neats-foot oil. With a toothpick he scours out the snaffle bit and puts it up for the winter. He takes out her winter hackamore and gives it a going-over until it is brown and shining and the nose band is soft and floppy as a noodle. When he is done he hangs this on a nail. Her stall remains unfinished, but she doesn't seem to mind it coming up only to her shoulder, so maybe he will leave it that way. She can lean out and watch him anyhow and fill the barn with her horsey breath, her eyes inquiring from his hands to his face, her long pretty eyelashes batting.

"If only you knew," he tells her.

One day he walks out into the farmyard and down the driveway to the mailbox. Inside he finds his new *Popular Science Monthly* and a letter from his cousins in Illinois. And another letter. He expects it is a response from one of his sad old mailings—something from the American Amateur Detective Association or the National Boy Astronomers' League. But it is a letter from Lowell Observatory, in Arizona.

With shaking hands he rips it open.

October 1, 1928
Dear Mr. Tombaugh,

   Dr. Lampland and I have read your letter with interest and we have admired your drawings, particularly the Jupiter sample of July 7. Your letter arrives at an opportune time as we happen to have a position open at the moment for a man able to operate a new photographic telescope in collaboration with another staff member.

   Would you be so kind as to answer some questions we have. What components of the 9-inch reflector did you fashion *yourself*, and for what parts did you need professional assistance? Further, what sort of observation training have you had? Have you ever made long-period photographic exposures of Solar System bodies, or stellar bodies? Also, what is your physical health? Especially, would you be able to withstand long, cold nights in a mountaintop observatory?

   We would welcome a reply at your earliest convenience.

Yours sincerely,
V. M. Slipher, Director
Lowell Observatory

A joke. It has to be. Carreau. His father. He reads it again, standing. He checks the envelope. It is postmarked Arizona. He lifts the letter itself into the light. There is a watermark. The blue letterhead of Lowell Observatory.

This, he thinks, is what he has been waiting for. *This*. Out of the fucking blue.

Full of snarling triumph, he goes charging up to the house.

15

Boccioni, Musolino, Girimonti, Telesio. Gaetano, Galeni. Bryce, Mann, Maxwell, Frank the Negro, Madero the Mexican. And Willoughby makes twelve. The names on his payroll book.

"Well, I haven't any idea," his mother tells him. "You can't expect me to recognize any of these."

"You read the papers."

"Well! But all those wop names sound the same to me, Felix." She is in a wicker chair on the front porch beneath a row of spinning ferns. "Torrio and Colosimo and all those people. The one who used to know some Italians was your father. I mean just to talk to, at the machines."

"Say, that's an idea. He didn't ever mention anything?"

His mama puzzles. "You mean, did your father ever mention that his friend Dr. Isenbright was in the habit of hiring gangsters?"

"I suppose," he says.

She tugs at at her sleeves, considering. "Well, no, Felix, of course not. On the other hand, your father knew a lot of different people. And he didn't tell me absolutely everything. *One* thing you learn, Felix, is the minute you start doing something that's not just enjoying a dinner party, you can end up talking to a *very* wide range of people."

He considers this; it feels obscurely like an insult, but he lets it lie. "I don't know if I can ask Willoughby about it outright."

"What if, Felix," she says patiently, "they're only just men?"

"What if they're running booze?"

"Oh, well, in that case I think you'd know it," she says, closing her eyes. "If that's all you're worried about. I think you'd smell it on them."

Still, he wonders if he's stumbled onto something. Whether this crew is something more than what they appear to be. He tugs down the books he managed to replace and rifles the indexes in search of clues. You are not about to find gold in this part of Arizona. Nor diamonds. A reasonably intact Stegosaurus can bring upward of ten thousand dollars, which is riches enough, he supposes. Nearly enough to break even over a year. Maybe that is all they are after. And maybe they are not above taking a few choice bits for their own profit. There is no doubt they are experts. The fossils continue to come up out of the earth, and cased in burlap and padded with straw the specimens in their crates continue to accumulate in the warehouse. The crates go all the way down the wall now, heavily numbered in black. Each giant armored fin, veined and textured like a skeletonized leaf, gets its own box, like a piece of Meissen.

The Camptosaurus is here in boxes too, those parts that aren't still in the ground. He is about halfway through excavating it—he is slow, but he feels a tender need to remove the most possible stone from the fossil. His results are nice. And he likes the look of what he does, the gray bone varied in its mineralization, a subtle rainbow of slate and brown and black.

He sets the books aside on the floor. What if they're only just men?

He will entertain anything, possibly, to distract him from the responsibilities that are mounting. Now and then he manages to pay some bills, but his desk is becoming a weather system of its own, a tempest heavy with obligation. He is surprised to discover an outfit will send you more plaster even when you haven't paid for the last two shipments. Well, it has its hooks in you. And he is good for it, of course; the name DuPrie puts others at ease. Others, anyway, if not Felix himself.

But money. An analyst would have some fun with him now, not paying his bills like this. All his father's money lying virtually untouched in its humiliating vastness. And during the fall of 1928 the DuPrie fortune grows faster than it ever has, funds managed from Wall Street and harnessed—even as the spiral of margin buying expands—to oil and coal and manufacturing. The hardheaded money men his father trusted are evidently not the sort to be swayed by the lure of easy profit. And it is easier to be cautious when you have so much to start with. As always, want breeds risk and loss. But in the able hands of Carrier, York, and DuBray, the DuPrie fortune sails on heavy with the following wind.

He gets himself a horse: Sissie. She is a sweet bay roan with black eyes and arrows just above her knees. Willoughby's horse is a bay silver named Picobel, and once the weather cools off some they ride out the six miles together to the site on what Willoughby calls their hay burners. It is not much slower than driving, and Felix has always liked setting up in a saddle. Sissie likes the center of the road, and he has to wrestle her out of it when a car comes grinding past in the dust. The Italians in their suits and hats gaze soberly at him. Dark beards already at this hour.

On the slope Willoughby lends him a man to finish the Camptosaurus. Gaetano. At first Felix is a little protective, but Gaetano is far better than he and faster. They pass two mostly silent weeks dislodging the last few dozen bones from the matrix, pausing for water and to smoke and to watch the October clouds climb up the plateau. For once the sun is not a killer, and the windborne smells are modulating into something richer, a dark dusty Côte du Rhône with a note of wet rock in it. Fall in Arizona. Gaetano is a roll-gaited heavy with hair on his arms and heroic eyebrows and folded sleeves and a fat neck. He looks as if he could easily be on the lam from some shady business in Chicago. But he knows his way around a bone pit. Once the fossils are free, they wrap them as usual and set them on the lip to dry.

"All right, then," Felix says.

"Not-a too bad," Gaetano allows.

When his pal Cam is done they shovel the upturned soil back into the pit. Then Felix slings his tools and follows Gaetano downhill toward the flood catch. From across the slope at the Steg pit Willoughby props his foot on a box and sucks on a cigarette and gives him a half wave. Graduation day. His back hurts. His hands are thick with calluses. Soil is embedded in the creases of his palms where the new skin joins the old. As he has seen Gaetano do, he spits into his hands, rubs them together. Then he kneels to the earth with his tap hammer and his #1 chisel and begins to work.

Possibly it is work that he has never really understood—its dailiness and demands and its dependable mild spectrum of success and disappointment. He has been reading some more, and this season of study has filled in some of the gaps in his knowledge. From what he can tell it will take another year of steady work at least, during which they will pull out at least a dozen more indicator species, to really prove the case that they are uncovering the southernmost extension of the Morrison Formation. But a year is nothing, really. From his reading he knows that a man can spend eight years in Mongolia kneeling on the nasty gray sand and bitten on the back of the neck by giant Mongolian armory flies and facing, month after month, the squinty brown Oriental faces of his local crew, then account for his time in three inconsequential papers totaling thirty-one pages. And of course he could be back in Maryland staring out at the ivy or sitting at his table at the Staunton ordering the crab bisque and the champagne and generally waiting for the days to pass.

A week after he follows Gaetano across the slope, he understands he might spend two years on the flood catch alone. The fossils are black with absorbed iron and gleam up out of the stone like fish out of milk. But the tumbled field is at least twenty yards on a side and at least two hundred yards long, and no one knows how far down it goes. His meticulous finework is now an asset. You think you are going to be studying fossils, but in fact you end up knowing mostly stone, how it is denser in some places and soft in others and how there are streaks and seams and where it is brittle or glassy. That desert mind. It is not alive, but it has the character of a living thing, the variation.

And there are surprises. Gaetano grunts, beckons. "Mister. Here. See this. You get a spot like-a this around here"—he gestures at the stone with his pick—"you see how the stone, it's a little shiny, you know, a little *tough*-a, so you have to really *go* like *this* to take it off. This is called silicification," he pronounces, proudly. "And now and-a then, in a place like-a this, you get *this*. Look. You know what this is?"

Gaetano indicates a crushed ellipsoid, its surface a web of cracks, about the size of a baseball.

"An egg," Felix suggests.

"Sure, an egg. Good-a guess. But-a guess again."

"A skull."

"Hey, that's-a right. It's a little skull of-a somebody. Sort of-a junk. Too cracked up to tell who it is. But-a look. You get a skull like-a this right here, in this silica mix, and sometimes . . ." Gaetano looks both ways, then casually lifts the tiny #8 chisel from Felix's belt and with a smart tap from his own hammer drives the blade into the skull. "Ah," he says, "presto."

The skull has cracked in two, the larger half coming free. The interior surface is lined with purple quartz crystals.

"What is it?"

"A geode-a." Gaetano smiles.

"In a skull."

"A beautiful thing-a."

"Yes." It *is* remarkable, as though the creature's glinting sharp thoughts had somehow become fossilized. Felix turns it in the light. Sparkling. He hands it back.

"No, no—for-a you, boss." Gaetano gestures bashfully. "For-a good-a luck."

Well, he is proud of this. *Boss*. Sure, he can see it. He wants his mother to see it, too. He presents her the beautiful skull with the geodes shining inside, and she admires it, setting it on her dresser-top; on the strength of this, he cajoles her to come see the works before they close for the winter. He wants her to see the new Felix, the one who might actually manage to make a go of it. "You can sit in the car the whole time, mama," he says.

She is shrugging her outfit together and sliding into a fox coat. She faces him from under a close-fitting hat.

"Lead the way, cowboy," she says.

In the plain Tudor she sits upright, rather small, and observes the town rolling past. She is game, of course; she is game for most things. But in the light she does not look entirely well. Possibly it is only unease at being taken so totally in hand by her formerly wayward son. What will he get her into next? But she too has some access to daring, does she not? In her bandanna on the back deck of the *Tarsal* reading mystery novels and sneaking his cigarettes—that was also his mother. And after, in the little stone church at the mouth of the Mexican river, stunned from fright and shame. More likely there is some recalibration occurring, he thinks. It has taken her some time to fit herself back together, all the new pieces. Possibly she is only still reassembling herself.

At the dig she climbs down. Seen through her eyes, it is a grubby unpleasant place. "Well, I knew you got *dirty*," she says.

"This is how."

She clamps a hand to her hat as a dusty wind climbs the slope. "You're going to introduce me to all these people. I know Mr. Willoughby."

Having his mother on the site produces a jovial atmosphere. She is short and obviously of a certain type, with the metal grapes on her hat and her fur and her city shoes. It is a comedy. The Italians are exemplary at this sort of thing, grinning and swiping their hands elaborately on their trousers before offering to shake. Sour Bryce is stiff and contrite and assists her down into the flood catch, where he is at work uncovering the two front toes of a hysilophodont. It is funny to see his mother in the pit, slightly alarmed and her head very nearly at ground level. She takes a little turn with the pick, then hands it politely back.

His mama, disappearing into the earth.

They are halfway back to town when she mentions a place called Bel-Aire. He has heard of it, a rich women's resort clinic. "Oh, you know," she breezes, "I've been meaning to stop by for a long time. Donald Yost's boy is in charge of it, and I really should go see him."

She has such a casual air that he is instantly on his guard. "You never mentioned it before."

"Oh, don't panic," she scolds. "Honestly, Felix, it's just a social call."

"Where is it?"

"Five miles," she points immediately, "down that road."

When the white-shingled bulk of Bel-Aire appears before them on a far rise it is a fantasy in white, a massive seaside cottage on a green lawn, set on a tawny bluff. "You won't remember Mr. Yost the elder," his mother says.

"No."

"He used to come around when you were quite young, before they moved west. You used to like his mustache. I haven't seen the *son* since he was—well, very small. But evidently he's very accomplished now."

"This is all his?"

"This is all his."

"You've been planning this," he guesses.

"No," she pronounces evenly, watching Bel-Aire approach as though it were an unfamiliar dog, "not this."

The building is two stories, shambling, shingled, its many windows glinting. The dirt road climbs, twists, and ends on a pavement lot. A double garage with two empty bays, and a set of white-steps with a white wooden railing. Also visible from here, above them on the second story, are eight barred windows.

His mother sees them too.

At the door he depresses a buzzer. For a moment the only sound is the ticking of the Ford in the drive. Then a nurse swims into view. She is a pretty blonde governed by competence. At the mention of Dr. Yost's name as a friend, the nurse beckons them gladly inside. A smell of rosewater, a distant sense of a conversational murmur from another room. Really a charming place. The sun falls through the puttied windows with a blank entirety. The patients or inmates or residents sit in groups playing cards down the length of a glassed-in porch. Slow fans paddle the sun-warmed air. The view from the windows is immense. The gorge and the orange canyonland collapse massively in the blue-shadowed south.

Dr. Yost is a long-boned man about forty with the insouciant presentation of a collegiate rower. As though to age himself he smokes a pipe, which he works like a prop while squinting through the smoke. "Larry," Felix's mother coos, fondly. "You're really here."

He spreads his arms. "Dad wouldn't have me, so I had to make my own way."

"Who would have you, is the real question. My son, Felix."

"Mr. DuPrie."

"Dr. Yost."

The doctor looks him over. "You're the dinosaur man, that's who you are."

"That's right."

"Damned mess you're making of the desert, I guess."

"I guess that's right."

"Finding anything?"

"Oh—" He faces suddenly the expert's difficulty in the face of polite amateur interest. "Well, a few nice things."

Yost turns to Felix's mother. "You're looking fine."

She says, "Well enough. But pardon me, am I mistaken, or did I see something that looked like a Debberson out there?"

"One of the cousins. Margaret. Called Mitts. Among other things."

"Oh, I know Mitts, all right. They always were a rough bunch."

"Soft as a petal now. Trip her with a teaspoon, and she'd never get up again."

"And what a relief for everyone."

"Oh, well, she's pretty quiet." Yost draws on his pipe, producing a comical pop. "You'd give her a run for it, anyhow. Say, you know who else is here is Tunny Childs."

"I knew her daughter a hundred years ago."

"Well, that's about right. Tunny Childs is about two hundred fifty years old, and from what we're able to tell she thinks she's in Morocco."

"Not a bad place to die."

"Not if we can help it," says Yost. "We think of it as a pretty nice place to be while you're alive."

Some signaling richness has entered Yost's tone. There is history here that Felix does not know—will never know. "Your mother was a dear friend of mine, Larry," his mother says.

Yost blinks once, in gratitude. "She often spoke fondly of you, ma'am."

Yost takes them around. Ancient Mitts Debberson flashes her empty gums and grasps Felix's mother's two hands in hers. A few of the other women are familiar through one connection or another. To Felix they are names from childhood and the ancient ailing aunts of a certain outlying, expeditionary branch of their tribe, the ones who went in for ranching or whose railroad interests or mineral concerns took them west of necessity, to Colorado and California. This is their local encampment, their moon colony, high on a cliff overseen by the trusty Dr. Yost. There is a flurry of chickeny gossip, and Felix's mother strides along in her fur, pointing him out and mocking his beard. Proud of him, in fact. The dinosaur man is what he is.

Outside, the lawn drops away to the rim of the canyon, fenced off. "So no one tries to go out the back door," Yost tells them. On the edge of the canyon the light is clean and spare. Where the lawn pillows up to a rise, they all stand together in the wind that climbs out of the gorge. The air is cool, as though it has brought up with it the shadows of the canyon floor. His mother squints in the high illumination.

"Well, it's very nice, Larry," she admits.

"We make it so everyone can enjoy themselves."

"Do you ever come to town?"

"For you, I might," says the doctor. "Or you can come visit us sometime."

She puts a hand on his forearm in acknowledgment, in farewell. Back in the Ford she returns a strand of hair to its place behind her ear. "Well, it was worth looking at, at any rate," she says. "Otherwise I would have wondered."

"Wondered what, mama?" Felix asks, his voice unsteady.

She only sighs. "But it's very *windy* up here, isn't it," she murmurs.

And as they drive away they see the door open onto the lawn. Three women in white gowns come stepping down onto the grass, attended by three nurses. Something in their aspect tells Felix they are madwomen, and a current of fear shivers through him. His mother is transfixed. Drifting there on the grass, the madwomen have the appearance of daylight ghosts. The unmoored dead. Her mother turns back around, silent. Faces the windshield with a shamed look in her eye. As though she has only just escaped in time.

Not this.

Then what?

16

He takes her into his dim, dirty bedroom. She tips off her shoes and climbs into his bed, her gray dress still on.

"Come on, Jim," she says.

He undresses to his shorts and climbs in. The sheets are cold and smelly. Beneath the mounded quilts he shivers and pulls himself beside her. She sits up, maneuvers her dress over her hips, then rolls it over her head and tosses it across the room. Next she unhooks her brassiere and thumbs the straps down and sends him a look down the slope of her arm.

Everything she does sets off flowering explosions of lust and of something else within him, *gratitude*, that he should get to see this.

He is hard as a dowel and desperate at once to have her on her back and also simultaneously to not move at all, to do nothing but lie beside her and watch her undress, her small round breasts come free, her throat come into the light, her stomach. Some more maneuvering beneath the sheets, and she extracts a tangle of garters and underthings and tosses them away. "*Harvard*," she states, pleased to say it aloud. "I've never slept with anyone from Harvard before. You don't look like the Harvard type, anyway. Do you eat baked beans on a Saturday night? Do you regularly read the *Transcript*? Do you support the Symphony? Do you demonstrate sufficient-unto-thyself-is-the-dignity-thereof?"

"Not really," he says.

"Maybe that's the best type, the not really type. Jeez, you're fast off the mark." She puts a hand on him, gripping. "Feel that. Say something, Jimbo."

He can't, that's all.

He has been with one other girl—not Olive but a girl named Catherine, who had very kindly broken him in after Olive had turned him aside. It had been hurried, and she had seen it as a duty, he suspected, not to him but to some ghost in her own past; she had a sweet rounded abdomen and pretty auburn hair, but she was plainly only using him to demonstrate something. He had not complained; but this, with Mary, this joy, is new.

Later, sometime in the afternoon, he wakes. She is awake beside him, smoking with an ashtray on her stomach and reading a week-old newspaper. He feels the stubble on his chin. He no doubt stinks to heaven, but she hands him the cigarette and he takes a draw and hands it back. Even just this. A car starts up below the window, two hard cranks and the engine caught, the door whapping shut.

"You *do* read the *Transcript*," she says.

"I got to blend in."

She grins. "Don't let them see this place then."

"I paid the extra fifty cents a week for the window with glass in it," he says.

"I knew you were fancy." She passes him the cigarette again. "You know what else I knew you were, Jim?"

"A beast in the sack."

"No. You're a softie," she smiles.

"Is that so."

She examines the ceiling. She is a sweetheart who has been in a dozen beds at least, he estimates. "I like it," she says. "It's been a while since I've seen a real softie up close."

"I'm biting down so hard on a line I'm getting a headache."

"Well gee, Jim," she drawls, "what kind of girl do you think I am?"

"You can't be any kind of girl," he says, "if there ain't no others like you."

This pleases her. "Softie," she pronounces.

"Don't make me," he says.

"Did you really name a comet after her?"

"Oh," he says, "you heard that, too."

She gets up on one elbow. "That's one for the books."

"Look," he says, "who are you exactly, anyway?"

"Mary Hempstead," she says, "no middle name, no middle initial."

"Pure and simple Mary."

She grins again but lets it go. She has other business. "What'd she say when you did it?"

"I missed my play," he admits. "She'd just married. I told her it was a present."

"Some stunt. I bet that made you a lot of friends."

"I'm still counting them up."

"She's not about to forget it, either."

"Every six hundred years it comes back around," he says. "Maybe by then she'll give it up."

"I know that type," she warns. "They don't like being funned with."

"I didn't mean it as fun," he says. "I thought I had a chance."

"What do you do when it's a sure thing, I'd like to know."

"I don't know," he says, "I've never had the opportunity present itself."

"It don't just present itself, Jim," she says. "You gots to goes and *does* it."

"How come I haven't seen you before?" he asks. "Where've you been, anyway?"

"Oh, that's not really my bunch. Holly's the one. Scotty's his ticket. I'm just along for the ride these days."

"In between horses," he suggests.

"Who you calling a jockey," she says.

"They don't mind him? I mean, the—?" he tips his wrist.

"Not that bunch. Everybody's got one or two in their back pocket they can bring out as an example. They're up on all the latest psychiatry. Everyone's a *little* bit of an introvert, Jim, didn't you know? Except maybe you and me."

"Even Ronald Coleman."

"Ronald Coleman can run me over in a tractor if he likes," she says. "I like Ronald Coleman just fine. A comet, boy!"

"Where do you live, anyway?"

"Oh, you know," she says, "here and there, wherever I happen to wake up. No, I live with Holly and Scotty."

"All the time?"

"Now *I'm* getting a headache," she says.

"Okay," he says, "I can stand a little mystery."

"*You.* You're moving to Arizona."

A truck bumps down the cobbles outside, and he reaches for her cigarette, takes the last drag, and extinguishes it on the saucer on her chest.

"Come with me," he says.

She barks a laugh. "*That* was fast. I believe that one just set an air speed record, Jim."

"I promise only poverty and long hours, but you can have as much of those as you like." He is giddy, nearly giggling. "You'd like it out there, you know, trees, mountains, deserts, no more *stiffs.*"

"Sure," she says carefully. "Go for the company, stay for the scenery."

"Who you calling scenic?"

"Sure. Actually you're not half bad," she tells him, "at least when you're not pretending to be Tarzan or something. You do a thing when you look in the mirror. You should have seen yourself preening in the pier glass." She thrusts her chin up. Arches her head in a strange way that seems to be an imitation of him. Looks at him in sudden shy appeal. Does he like her? She has her antics, and you have to follow; do you like that? And such are the things that make a man go weak in the knees forever. And everything else drops away, doesn't it. And already he is thinking, *How can I make this last.*

There is a note in his mailbox to see Shapley, so he goes. In his square blue uncarpeted office the director of the Harvard College Observatory is at his desk looking over a manuscript, slowly manipulating a yellow pencil so that first its eraser end, and then its sharp point, meet the paper. "Barber," he states.

"I can come back later."

"No," Shapley murmurs, not looking up, "I want to talk to you." Harlow Shapley is a trim figure of forty-three in a tan summer suit puckered at the shoulders. His sandy hair is razor-cut over his ears, giving him a scalded, monkish look. A gray globe of the cratered moon stands on the windowsill, and the desk is cluttered with piled-up papers and a seamed Harvard telephone directory and the black flower of a telephone, the patent-black bakelite worn to matte on the stem where the director has gripped it during his six years at his post.

Finally Shapley slides the papers away. "Just wanted to give you my congratulations, in person this time. You don't deserve it, but sometimes it's better to be lucky than good, I think is how it goes. Sit."

"Thank you."

"I'm not sure Florence deserves the honor either, just between you and me, but maybe you know what you're doing."

"It was a wedding present."

"If you say so. I was sorry to hear about that, actually; once they get married they're usually no use to me. I guess you weren't too happy about it either, is the idea I get around here."

"Not really."

Shapley sends him a friendly grimace. "Well, she's fairly brilliant, I'll give her that. Look, but I wanted to ask you what the hell happened to Dick Morrow out there."

"He got married, sir."

"And chucked it all."

He feels an urge to stomp on Dick, but some remnant of loyalty prevents him. "Once she showed up I guess he felt like he had to show her a good time. I don't know, sir."

Shapley takes this in, hand cupping his chin. "Did he tell you he was going?"

"No. He just got on the train with her. He'd cleaned out his room. I mean she came out with a big shipment of things, so I suppose she had it all figured out from the beginning. Maybe they both did. I don't know. It wasn't as though he was ever all that hot to take me into his confidence."

"Where the hell'd they go?"

"Mexico, everybody says. But we never even got a cable."

"Well, he's got more guts than brains, I guess. And more money than guts. But I could use her."

"She's back in town."

"Well, she hasn't shown up *here*." Shapley sighs, his nose almost buried in his palm. "Well, Slipher likes you, I guess. He's an old granny, but he did some good work in his day."

"Yes, sir."

"You really want to go back out there for good?"

"Yes, sir. I was hoping the work I do out there would be sufficient—I mean, the photographic search is one element, but also really looking back into Newcomb, and combined with a survey of the orbits of the long-period asteroids—"

Shapley waves this away. "We'll work all that out, Barber. We'll give you a degree one way or another; that's not what I'm concerned about." He rearranges himself forward in his rigid chair, discomfort appearing on his puffy features. "I just mean you won't be doing yourself any favors by attaching yourself to that outfit for the long term. Or us. We're trying to build ourselves a little reputation around here."

"Yes, sir, I know how you feel about them."

"V.M.'s doing what he thinks best, but it's frankly a subpar shop out there, which I suppose you have occasion to know by now. That said, it might be just the sort of place that suits you."

He flushes. "I think I can do good work there, sir."

"I'm sure Pickering feels the same way about what he's doing. I'm sure he felt the same way when he announced he'd found grasshopper swarms on the moon."

"I'm sure he did, sir." And how interesting, how welcome, he finds Shapley's rebuke—how it stirs something protective in him. He has the urge to guard Mary from this, whatever this is. From this version of him that Shapley sees. "But honestly I'd say the comparison's grossly unfair, sir. I'm not out there chasing ghosts. I'm just going to be taking pictures."

"Plenty of them, it sounds like."

"I don't mind."

Shapley considers. "Well, no, of course you're right, you're not Pickering. I suppose if you've got a genius for *anything*, Barber, I would say it's the genius for going on after everyone else throws in the towel. At least no one can fault your work ethic, can they? And that's all right; we need that kind of man. Just like we need those girls out in the computer rooms. Someone's got to do that kind of thing. It all adds up, in the end, doesn't it? And the Lowells will absolutely adore you, I imagine. I hear Abbott Lowell himself is partly paying for that new astrograph."

The president of Harvard. "I hadn't heard that, sir."

"Oh, yes. Never mind Constance, she's bad enough. But they're *all* determined to get themselves a planet." Shapley grins. "And here you are stepping up and volunteering to find one for them."

"Not for *them*, exactly," he says.

"That's what you think. I mean frankly, and I don't mind you repeating this, it's all just perfectly nuts to me. And Slipher's idea is he's going to find Planet X and save poor Percy's reputation. Well, he's got this loyalty to Percy that's sort of strange, if you ask me, given the sort of damage the man managed to do, to himself as well as others. Even V.M. used to do good work but now—planets! Comets! The period of Miranda!" Shapley throws up his hands. "My god, what are we supposed to *do* with it? What the hell's it all *for*? Unless the Lowells are all planning an expedition."

"Not that I'm aware of, sir."

"Might do us a world of good," Shapley murmurs, "if they *all* flew to the moon." Then he pauses, changes tack. "So you'll have heard I've put Dr. Payne on the Nebular Atlas Survey, which she now hates me for."

"Yes, sir."

"Well, I'm going to put you on with her. Short term at least, but I'm willing to go medium-long term. If you wanted to stay around here I could put you together for—say two years? She'd be good for you. Put you through your paces. You two could complain about me in harmony. Publish handsomely and on a regular basis, too. We're running another one of her bulletins this month. That could be you."

"I'd much rather go to Arizona, sir."

"You really would?"

"Yes."

"It's a dead end, you know."

"Not to me, sir."

"Slipher's not a young man any longer."

"No, sir."

"This has very little to do with you personally, by the way. Only, you're one of ours, and you've got our name draped all over you, and it bothers me that you're taking our name and sort of wasting yourself like this."

"You know *you* suggested me out there in the first place, Dr. Shapley."

"And you didn't find it somewhat—unbearably second-rate? A little less than what you might have expected? I mean you do have *some* talent."

He is glad to hear this, anyway. "It's what I want to do, sir."

Shapley shrugs. "Well, here's my guess: you'll last five years out there, and then you'll end up as a schoolteacher somewhere. It's not a bad life, I guess, although I can think of better ones." Shapley steeples his fingers and presses them against his lips. "She's married to him, you know. I don't know what kind of deal you two struck up out there, but it can't lead anywhere happy. Not that it's any of my concern."

He can only nod at this.

"What's the period?"

"It'll cross in April."

"You didn't want to name it after your mother or someone? Or me, maybe? There's a thought. I could use a thing like that once in a while."

"It was a—gesture. I wouldn't do it now."

"Sort of overreacted, is that what it was?"

"Yes, sir."

"None of my business, of course, except it sort of is, you know. And now you'll forget about her."

He smiles. "Yes, sir."

"You seem pretty sure. Well, the girls are all talking about it. You sure you don't want to stay and see what turns up here? One of them might take pity on you."

"I want to go back, sir."

"Fell in love with Slipher, did you? I didn't know he still had it in him."

"I've already been running a few residuals again," he admits now, edging close to the truth, "with some of the newer observations."

Shapley rears back and guffaws: "Residuals! Oh, no, Barber."

"Yes, sir."

Shapley gapes. "You *are* chasing ghosts."

"It's a problem I'm interested in solving, that's all," he says. "They've got to come from somewhere."

"*Maybe* they do," Shapley warns. "Well, so he *has* got his hooks in you. That old goat." But the director is looking at him almost admiringly—you can get away with foolishness, maybe, if the gesture is grand enough. "All right, then, Mr. Barber, you go right ahead with your residuals. But until January I'm putting you with Dr. Payne. She's actually up to something useful. And when you get back out to Flagstaff say howdy to those old aunties for me. You can tell them you heard it from me, they're all a bunch of goddamned loonies. You included."

Dismissed, then, with a laugh and a shrug. And now everyone will think he's a nutter, not just Florence and Dick. But if Lowell stood it, so can he. It is only until January. He can bear anything for four months. "Thank you, sir," he says, and turns on his heel.

When he reports to Cecilia Payne the next day, he is prepared for the worst. She is only twenty-eight, but to Alan as he has passed her in the halls she has always looked about forty, a tall, mannish Englishwoman with an air of the country horsewoman. By now she has been either principal or secondary author on forty-eight papers, a truly disheartening number, most of these appearing in the Harvard College Observatory *Circular* but others in *Science Monthly* and *Popular Astronomy*. She is, in addition, the author of the very first Harvard Observatory monograph, *Stellar Atmospheres*, the work that earned her a Ph.D. from Radcliffe at the age of twenty-five.

Alan is not that good a match for her, as he well knows, knocking at her open door at the end of an untraveled hall on the fifth floor; certainly she is badly underemployed in the work of mapping the galactic center—at this juncture meaning the tedious work of poring over plates in search of uncataloged nebulae—and she broadcasts, in the small, oak-paneled room where she has been assigned this task, a sardonic air of blunted aspiration. "Well, Mr. Barber," she says, in greeting, from behind her lightbox. "Welcome to my little kingdom."

"Dr. Payne."

"I hear you've been shackled to me."

"Looks that way."

They are so far removed from the bustle of the sixth floor that their meeting seems almost illicit. Using the sole of her brown buckled shoe, she nudges out the chair opposite. "You sit there. I don't know what you've done to deserve this, but I hope it was worth it. And congratulations, by the way."

"Thank you."

She fingers the jeweler's loupe on a string around her neck. "*Romantic*, you. *Silly*. What were you *thinking?*"

"I bet you can guess what I was thinking."

She flicks her eyebrow and shows him a notably straight row of top teeth. "Yes, I bet I can," she says. She wears a brown tweed suit and a brown flimsy neck-scarf and no jewelry aside from a slim wristwatch that encircles her considerable forearm, and she has the round benign face of a Gibson girl, not considered pretty any more but handsome in a hazel-eyed, out-of-fashion way. She is what Florence could be, possibly, if she did not have all her family watching over her shoulder constantly, wondering what on earth a girl like her was doing. Dr. Payne is unmarried, no Lesbian as far as Alan knows but also no one is after her, not because she is not pretty enough but because she is too unaccountable: a girl astrophysicist. Who would dare to take that on? But she does not seem to care much for all that, or at least she has dignity enough to pretend not to. With two flat palms she passes to him an exposed spectrographic plate, a negative sprinkled with dozens of tiny spectra. "Do you know what I'm doing in here?"

"Yes."

"Do you pity me?"

"A little bit," he says.

"Good. You know what *that* is, of course."

"I'd say that looks like a little patch around Rho Ophiuchi."

"Very good. You will notice we have some spectra to count."

"A few," he says.

"Okay." She gestures for the return of the plate. "God bless the band-pass filter. Have you studied Zeeman yet?"

"No."

"The Stark effect?"

"No," he says. "I'm supposed to be taking Nebular Analysis this term."

She gives him a small, purse-lipped grimace. "Aren't you funny. I don't know whether to laugh or cry. This is it. I'm your instructor." She gestures, including in her sweep the tiny entirety of the windowless room, the careful stacks of spectrographic plates in their soft lead casings on the side table, the single globe light suspended on its brass pole from the distant ceiling. "We two smashing persons are it."

"Oh," he says.

"Yes! We catalog the nebulae, Mr. Barber, and together we map the galactic core. I know you can't think of anything more rewarding. Do you know what this is?"

"A knitting needle."

"Yes. This is what we use to count with. We tink. Like this." She taps the needle against the glass. "Tink! It helps you keep count, I've found, if you tink every time you make an entry. And it goes *much* faster if one of us is tinking and charting and the other of us is taking down the catalog. I would like to propose that, for the first week or so, until you're up to speed, I do the tinking and you do the cataloging. Also, we don't have a lightbox for you in here yet."

"All right."

"Good." She wearily hands across the table a worn leather-bound journal, halfway filled. "Just take down what I tell you."

"Is that it?"

"For now." She smiles ruefully. "Isn't it *fun*?"

It is more or less impossible to talk during such a procedure, and in the long hours at the table with Cecilia Payne during this first week, worn out from nights with Mary and dozily attending to the distant grind of the elevator and with the slow, irregular tinking coming from across the table, he finds, to his surprise, some of his old *sean nós* rising up in him, the strange old Irish songs that his mother now and then urged on him as a child and which, after the Easter Revolution, she dropped forever. They were all in Irish and so he has forgotten their lyrics, never knowing their meaning in the first place, except remembering that you faced the corner with the listener behind you and you sang fiercely to the witches and the invisible ancients, nasal and glottal and thumping down on the meaningless consonants, and while it seemed a sort of game there was also a sober exactness expected of him. He has not thought of these songs since he was a boy, but now the tunes come back, one after the other, raw excursions through the minor scales. As he inscribes each entry while Payne makes her minute crosshatches on the chart of the sky, Alan entertains these songs silently, with long hesitations, finding his way through the old elaborations and tonal fractures as though exploring catacombs left to long neglect. It is a solace, working as a sort of corrective to the treatment he continues to receive from Shapley: offhand half waves and a hurried, hunched retreat, as though wishing to avoid an awkward scene. The result being Alan feels he has been busted a rank or two.

"Like to sing, do you?" comments Cecilia Payne, on the fifth day.

She has stopped, the knitting needle suspended above the plate.

"My mother," he admits. He has been humming aloud, obviously. "I'm sorry, I'm bothering you."

"I was thinking we might bring a radio in, but you'll do for now,

I guess." She resumes her tinking. "When I was a girl we had a little tiny eighteenth-century pipe organ in the parlor, and do you know what we used to sing? Doxology! 'O Sanctissima'! 'The Galway Piper'! 'The British Grenadiers'!"

"I know those."

She arrests again. "Oh, you don't, though."

He sings: "Of all the world's brave heroes there's none that can compare, with a tow-row-row-row-row-row, to the British Grenadiers!"

"Well, that's the one," she says. She is pensive for a moment. "Do you know," she pronounces, finally, "I used to think it was a song about a bridge that deer liked going over. The Bridge of Grenna Deers. My father used to sing that."

"My mother," he answers. "Once in a while. When she wasn't full of nationalism."

"Oh?"

"Well, not really. She didn't have much use for Ireland once she left."

"Is she alive?"

"Yes."

"Your father?"

"No," he says. "He died when I was young."

"Mine too," she says. "Do you remember him at all?"

"No."

"Nor I mine, not really. Aside from the singing." She resumes her work. After another long minute she says, shyly into her plate, "I must say, Mr. Barber, you *can* carry a tune."

There is a little pleasure in getting her to blush. And the work is steady, sure, and earns him the favor of Shapley while he does it. So it is another alternate life, maybe, that he is not living—the safe path, where all his future would be assured. Over the course of the next few weeks, Payne guides him through the subtleties of the Zeeman effect, and the Stark effect, and soon he is given his own plate to work on, and his own jeweler's loupe and knitting needle, and his own chart of the sky where he must pencil in the locations of the nebulae, deciding which ones are really globular clusters, which ones are clouds of gas ghosted with doubly ionized oxygen—showing the forbidden bands at 495.9 and 500.7—and which are in fact deep-field uncataloged extragalactics. He is the first to catalog these very distant galaxies, and someday someone will go after them for Cepheids to determine their distances.

But not him, and not now. This safe life is not for him. He has bigger, wilder game in mind.

In his off hours he buys a radio and he cleans his rooms up a little bit, and Mary moves some clothes in and a little sort of dop kit. She brings her knitting bag and wears a pair of heartbreaking eyeglasses down on her nose like a librarian. She is deadly at any speed then. They listen to the Bees-Knees broadcasting from the Statler Hotel, WBZA, 250 watts of power at 242 meters, Leo Reisman and the Hotel Brunswick Orchestra announced by EFA and AGS, and Thornton Burgess and the Radio Nature League. They catch the news. In November Hoover beats the pants off Al Smith except in Massachusetts and Dixieland, to no one's surprise. That lucky stiff Charles Lindbergh is flying around in Mexico on a fishing trip with his new wife. "I bet *she'll* catch something, all right," Mary deadpans. They are in bed when word comes over that Amelia Earhart has broken off her engagement to Sam Chapman. Earhart is a local girl these days and you see Chapman in the papers, and here is another Boston hand, Admiral Byrd, broadcasting from Antarctica and the Ross Ice Shelf, and here you are with this girl while the snow swirls at the window and you look over every iridescent black hair of her eyebrows and every powdered rise of pink flesh and you don't move if you can help it. Byrd is a tough son of a gun, all right, with the high Brahmin voice. Naked, they listen to him shouting up from the bottom of the globe. Now that it is nearly summer down there, he is making incursions inland for the purposes of photography and geographic exploration, and next year sometime he will try to fly over the pole. You feel the world encompassed in this way. You live on a planet. The bedside Crosley model has a maple lattice cutout of a sunset across the leonine-tan speaker fabric, which you can watch thrumming as the sound comes out.

As they spend these weeks in bed he learns, from Mary, about Edward Howe and her own broken-off engagement, and about living out at Seahome at the MacAllisters', and about her and Hollis and the deaths of their parents. And even after all of it there remains a certain spaciousness to her history. But he doesn't press it. Boyfriends and so on, he senses, and something more serious, a marriage maybe quickly annulled, something that gives the telling an arranged sort of storybook quality. Certain things left unsaid.

But he leaves some things unsaid too, doesn't he? He tells her about Florrie and Dick and Arizona, about Slipher and Lampland and the cow Venus and about Flagstaff and the sawmills and the old Clark dome, rotating on its Model-T tires. But he doesn't mention a word about Planet X. Because if *Mary* scorns him the way Florence and Shapley have done, he will just have to jump off the goddamned Broadway Bridge.

So they are each, it seems, keeping something from the other. As he shaves he considers the interesting, dangerous truth of this. What remains to be discovered. In the little bathroom the green tile turns his reflection a sickly bilious shade, but otherwise he looks pretty fucking hearty. And even with the space between them she seems to agree to come with him on the train to Arizona. Or at least when he continues to mention the idea she talks as though she wouldn't mind coming along. Her eyes flash, and she tips her head speculatively. He talks it up, yet at the same time he doesn't quite believe it. She has her own reasons for wanting out of this town, she cracks. And he doesn't find that too hard to believe.

"But I want Holly to come too," she says.

"Sure," he says, "only I wonder whose berth he sleeps in."

"You tell me, sailor."

Since that morning he has barely seen the man—once, standing in the apartment while Mary packed a few things, again at his shop, Weber's, dropping in with Mary for a visit. "You sure he wants to?"

"He's got *his* own reasons. Anyway, we like to stay together." There it is again, that cagey note, the half truth. "He and Scotty," she adds, "want to see the West. So maybe we'll all go together."

"Ain't that a pretty picture."

"Maybe it bothers you, the idea of two fellows."

"Well, it should," he says.

"You're just a little old schoolboy," she tells him. She goes on with her knitting. "Of all the fellows I could have ended up with, I end up with you."

End up with; he thinks about this phrase. He likes it very much. Already the night at Florrie's apartment seems a million years ago, something buried in the earth and fossilized.

And meanwhile he is at work on the residuals.

After Dr. Payne has released him for the afternoon he will spend a few hours in his little windowless office on the fifth floor, with its black gooseneck desk lamp and its heavenly smell of scalded dust, Lowell's box of notebooks in the corner. He has at least glanced at all of them by now, ordering them as he can. The crimson covers seem to date from one era, from 1902 to 1905, and the emerald covers are from another, 1909 and later, and he finds a handful of undated grays and blacks, and buried at the bottom of the box are loose notes in a feminine hand, some long-ago girl in the computer room putting her oar in. Altogether these papers represent Lowell's efforts to describe the vastly proliferating, interacting influences among the planets.

> Jupiter's effect on Saturn, Uranus, Neptune, and Planet X;
> Saturn's effect on Jupiter, Uranus, Neptune, and Planet X;
> Uranus' effect on Jupiter, Saturn, Neptune, and Planet X;
> Neptune's effect on Jupiter, Saturn, Uranus, and Planet X; and
> Planet X's influence on Jupiter, Saturn, Uranus, and Neptune.

Lowell's work has continued to show itself to be full of leaps and gaps, and Alan suspects there are several missing notebooks; but so far as he can see, and as far as it appears to matter, the work is accurate.

But there is some judgment called for as well, and it's here that Alan sees some room for correction. In a normative calculation of least squares your model assumes that data errors occur at random and at a steady rate, with the task of the regression analysis being to smooth away these randomly distributed errors and to arrive at a most probable true value, in this case a true value for these several orbits. From this value the work is to determine whether this corrected true orbit makes any sense given all the other influences upon it—that is, whether what one sees can be accounted for by all the known perturbative influences.

But this method means that the observations of Jupiter as conducted in 1754 are considered as accurate as observations taken in 1900. This is what Lowell appears to have assumed, at any rate, no doubt for the sake of ease of calculation.

However: you go upstairs to the library and come down with Stanley's

Saturn tables from 1814, and they are now known to be full of error. And here they are, plugged in blandly as though they are just fine. Whereas the Yashita Uranus tables from 1880 are much closer to the observed values. You do want a large data sample; the larger your sample, the more accurate your final value will be, as a rule. And you also want observations over as long a period as possible. But it begins to seem foolhardy to enter the Stanley values, say, without somehow accounting for their known errors. A few of these old atlases have seen corrected editions published, but many have not. On the other hand, correcting one of these atlases would be the work of a year at least.

So you begin to see why the man might have been a little erratic in his hunting. What the hell do you decide is reliable?

But he pushes on. He transcribes and, when it is not too much trouble, carefully adjusts the data he enters, using a series of his own notebooks; then, feeling the pages are too *small* to contain everything—maybe this was Lowell's problem also, he thinks—he visits the grocer and returns with a roll of butcher paper so he can work in larger falls, like the painter of a vast cyclorama, his calculations becoming as wide and as tall as the page of a newspaper, the meat of the side of his hand acquiring a slick gray coat of polished graphite. Over the course of an hour he will follow Lowell through his linear least squares as he arrives at a corrected value for x, the result being the likely mean motion of Neptune in degrees per day as observed in Paris in 1865. Rounding it to the fifth decimal place—$0°\ 03'\ 14.99287''$—he can then introduce this value into the computations involving Neptune's calculated *true* longitude, the running state of which larger equation he keeps current along the bottom of the paper, the result after a few days of labor being a set of reasonably accurate values for Neptune's calculated true longitudal position observed over the course of a month in 1865, which value he then introduces into a different, related equation whose running state he keeps current along the *top* of the paper and whose ultimate value will be introduced as one part of the totally separate orbital work that awaits him at the end of it all, and whose solution will be a simple set of coordinates, where Planet X should be.

He keeps a vacuum flask of coffee on hand.

He will not get through the notebooks before he leaves for Arizona. He may barely finish half of them. But he *is* getting a good head start, anyway, Shapley be damned. He is getting a fair education in certain statistical methods, if nothing else, but already the work he has done—unless he is badly mistaken—has narrowed the possible search zone to a narrow strip: seven degrees on either side of the line of ecliptic, at a longitude somewhere between 240° and 310°—or 60° and 130°, depending on how the solution is oriented. He has a long way to go; but it is something. So maybe Shapley is right—that his talent is to go on after everyone else would have given up. But maybe it is just what this project needs, after all.

Anyhow it is all going along, slowly but without a hitch, until one day when Dr. Payne asks him to bring up a set of plates from the stacks. He hefts up the leather plate satchel and rides the elevator to the basement to get a set of plates from Serpens, and as he is searching for them he spots a yellow slip in an odd place, high up on a shelf, in the ancient Draper plates of Gemini. No one bothers with those any longer; they are too old to be of much interest. But Gemini.

Who?

Then he suddenly knows.

Florrie.

He takes the paper down. There is her signature.

He turns and looks down the row. Yellow slips every so often, as though she knows just what she is looking for, and just where.

A sickly chill goes through him.

He has not considered what she would be like as a rival. An enemy. For an hour he stalks the plate library, his hands shaking and a fluttering dread in his gut. He notes all the plates she has checked out; without further study he can only determine that all of them are along the ecliptic—and therefore potential Planet X plates. When he returns to Payne's office she says, "Did you slip out for a few, Mr. Barber? You look absolutely poisoned." But he can't joke, not yet. He settles unhumming into his chair.

It's not *fair,* that's all.

You can't ridicule him and then go hunting for Planet X yourself, Florrie. It's just not right.

In the apartment that night he considers not telling Mary, but he blurts it all out at once. He sinks into the hard desk chair and tells her everything, and she flumps her knitting into her lap and says, "Really, Jim, there's another planet?"

"That's what we think."

"What's it called?" she asks.

"Nothing yet," he says. "Lowell called it Planet X."

She laughs. It is such a schoolboy thing, you can see it in her eyes. Not scorn but a kind of amazed delight, that respectable people would take such a thing seriously. "Where is it?"

"We don't know exactly. Pretty far out."

"The planets are," she recites, "Mercury Venus Earth Mars Jupiter Saturn Uranus Neptune—*Planet X*. I can name the Galilean satellites, too."

He smiles, despite himself. "That's my girl," he says.

She takes this in; something about it has struck her, plainly. She knits, loops, her own needles clacking. Finally she asks, "So is anything living on it?"

"No. No, it's too far out."

She eyes him speculatively. "Nothing at all?"

"No."

"How do you know it exists?" she asks, reasonably. "Maybe you're only making it up."

So, generally at first and then in more detail, he begins describing it all: the complex laws of orbital resonance suggesting there's one more planet remaining to be found; the invisible gravitational influences drawing objects across empty space. And the madness of it, the fact that most people think it's a crock.

And she follows, all right, putting in a comment here and there, asking for a clarification. Finally she says, "Anyone else in the world, and I'd say you were kidding me. Trying to tell me a good story to keep me around."

"I would," he says.

"Well, but you said *she* doesn't take it seriously."

"She does now, I guess. I let it slip."

"At that party," Mary guesses.

"Goddamn my mouth."

Mary looks into the air, divining something. "No," she announces, "she doesn't actually care, Jim. That's my guess. She probably doesn't really think anything's there either. It's just that she wants you to see you can't go dropping her. That's the lesson she wants to impress on you.

See what happens when you drop her, she comes *after* you. She'll show *you*."

"She might," he says. "That's the problem."

"Oh, don't let her get you down, Jim. Not *her*." She grins brazenly, a look of challenge in her eye. Very slowly and nonchalantly she pushes a strap off her shoulder and gives him the killer look. "I know, Jim," she whispers, comically, "you could find it for *me*."

Of course this is the idea. But to have it said aloud seems the worst possible bad luck. Some things should stay secret until they're accomplished. "I'll name it after your brother," he says, going to her. Full of gratitude, again—this time because she doesn't think he's a goddamned loony.

"Planet Holly," she answers, putting down her knitting.

"That beautiful big hunk of a man," he says.

"That's you, Jim," she corrects, as he climbs on top of her.

It is not long after this that he finds another note in his mailbox, this one an invitation to meet Roger Putnam, the executor of the Lowell estate. The meeting has been long proposed, but together with the discovery of Florrie's yellow slips and after suffering Shapley's dressing-down he begins to feel that the weather is up. He has gone along anonymously enough until now, but no longer. Putnam's stationery is creamy white with a blue heading, and as Alan walks the long polished halls with the man's note in his jacket, his boot heels tocking, peering in the vacant, tiered auditoriums and passing out into the November chill under the leafless elm trees, he has the creeping sense that he is being watched.

On the appointed day he rings at the entrance to the Colonial Club. A subterranean pool of dread knocks within him as he waits in the red entryway for Putnam to appear from behind the walnut door. But when he does he is disarming, a bluff corn-fed ape stuffed into a gray suit, his blue necktie strangling him. "Mr. Barber." Putnam shakes his hand. "Good to lay eyes on you. Old V.M. talks you up impressively. From Ohio."

"Yes, sir."

"But our common alma mater Harvard. And Indiana before that. With Cogshall?"

"Yes, sir."

"Right. Well, come on in. Sorry to drag you away from things for this;

V.M. wanted us to meet, and I thought it made sense too." Putnam beckons him back into the club, down a long maroon carpet, under the walnut copings. He huffs through his nose: "You know you and I are both in the same business, more or less. Did my mechanical engineering work at MIT, graduated Harvard with a degree in mathematics, for all the good it's done me. Counting other people's money is what I've been up to lately. I suppose you know all the history, Mr. Barber."

"A little. Dr. Slipher's given me a version of it."

"I mean all about the will."

"Some of it, sir."

Putnam swings, takes him in with a squint. "So you know the dear widow Constance and Harcort Amory were the original executors. And Connie had the idea she was going to fight for every nickel she could get. After what we all thought was a generous settlement. Lifetime residence at Concord House, of course, here in Boston. Lifetime residence at the observatory when she visited. One hundred fifty thousand dollars lump sum and half Percy's property and a nice healthy income. With all the rest, more than two million dollars, going to the observatory. Well, it seemed fair to everyone but Connie. I don't suppose you give a damn about all this."

"I'd like to know it, sir," he says. "It gives you the lay of the land."

"I suppose it does. And you could stop with the goddamned sir business, Barber, I'm not anybody's boss. Not yours, anyway." He leads them into a side room: tall windows, maroon velvet drapes, a fire rustling in the grate. "You want a drink or something? Scotch they have."

"Thank you."

Putnam picks up a telephone and barks the order, then directs them into two armchairs and says, confidentially, "Well, old Amory was a good man, you know, old Uncle Percy's cousin and roommate and all that, but he couldn't stand up to Connie. She wanted him to resign as executor, and so he did. And then the next person in line for her to take down was my brother George. And George is no dummy, he wanted no part of Connie, so he was happy to keep well out of it. Finally she settled on poor old Guy Lowell, who was old Uncle Percy's *third* cousin, far enough down the line as to be possibly a little easier to bend. Stop me when this gets too sort of Caesarean for you."

"It's just the names," he says, "they keep turning up."

"We do have a sort of wagon circle, don't we? Well, you stick to the old stuff. No one's claiming any imagination in all this."

"Guy Lowell," Alan says, "the executor."

"You are following. Guy Lowell, the executor. What Connie wanted, of course, was to fight old Percy's wishes all the way down the line. Too much money was going to the observatory, she thought. That ought to be *her* money. But Guy wasn't as much of a patsy as she had hoped. He fought her like hell. I won't go into all the shenanigans, but they were outlandish and endlessly creative, and she made herself very much unpopular. She cut everyone's salary out there, for one thing."

"She didn't."

"Old V.M. didn't tell you this. Of course. He wouldn't. A gentleman to the end. She cut his salary while building that ridiculous marble temple to house Percy's poor harassed bones. Brought all her friends out there every year to overrun the place and expect everyone to wait on her, hand and foot. I used to spend a fair amount of time out there, in fact." Putnam turns a little shy. "Bit of an amateur astronomer myself, in fact."

"Oh," Alan says.

"But nothing like you, Mr. Barber."

"Well." He blushes, looks away. Manages, finally, "I'm sure that's not true."

But Putnam is only aiming a look of amused Brahmin incredulity at him. The drinks come borne by a gent in tails and white gloves, and Putnam lifts his glass to Barber. "Over the teeth, et cetera. Anyhow, we suffered Connie because we had to; she had her lifetime rights out there, after all. We went back and forth and back and forth, and speaking personally I've heard more about the judges in Coconino County, Arizona, than I ever care to. But we finally won, three years ago. Old Guy came through. But by then, with both sides suing and countersuing for nearly a decade, we'd spent more than a million dollars." He swallows. "In legal fees, I mean."

"Holy moses."

"Jarndyce and Jarndyce hasn't got a thing on us. And in the meantime poor old V.M. and Carl Lampland were stuck. No money to build new equipment. No money to update what they had. No money to hire new staff. And you know what I wanted them to do."

"No, sir."

"I wanted them to find that goddamned Planet X."

"*You* did." So Slipher was right, he thinks. They all want a planet for themselves.

Putnam grins. "*I* did. Percy's old goose chase. V.M.'s, I think, always been a skeptic, though he keeps pretty mum. I don't know what Lampland thinks. He's got his own projects, atmospheric spectography, you know. So in the meantime while Guy was at work on Connie I got onto Uncle Abbott to shake some money out of his own tree to buy us a new telescope to give us a real shot at it."

"You mean Uncle Abbott Lawrence Lowell."

"Yes, I'm sorry."

"You mean the president of Harvard," Alan supplies.

"The very one. Although I only got ten thousand out of him."

He makes a show of surprise. "The whole family's in on it."

"Think of it as a sort of memorial fund for Percy, really. I mean you think that's real money, but in fact it's not that much when you're considering what we've put together. And still we're cutting corners. Why do you think we're having Mr. Sykes build the mounting? Why do you think V.M.'s designed the telescope itself? Because we're doing this on the cheap, still. We're *still* trying to get our hands on the money in accordance with our settlement with Connie. It's all too complicated. And Clark and Sons already botched one of the mirrors, you know, ground the goddamned thing too thin. That was V.M.'s fault, I think, but anyway we ate that one, too. To the tune of six thousand dollars." Putnam drinks. "That one *I* paid for."

"*You* did."

"Well, poor old Guy died last year, you know, and I took over. Which is why we've got this all coming together now, finally, sort of staggering along, I guess, but it's almost there, isn't it? How do you like the comparator, anyway?"

He offers a hard grin. "It's nice. I mean, it's an instrument of torture, frankly, but it works just fine."

"I should hope so. That cost a pretty penny, too. A thousand even. Well, I tell you all this just to give you the background. Ideally you won't give a damn about any of this. Just keep your head down and *hunt*. Speaking of which, Barber, I heard about our friend Morrow."

"Right," Alan says. "Well, I'm sorry about that."

Putnam lunges back in his chair, adjusting his waistband. "So Dick Morrow used to be the kid down the street from us who'd build his own bicycle. Sort of a mechanical genius when you get down to it. He built a little man who could walk around under his own power when he was eleven or twelve or something. Ran on electricity. I always figured he'd get into engineering or something, but I guess his mind took a different turn. Surprised he ran off like that."

"I was too."

"Some stunt you pulled, though, wasn't it?" Putnam presents a tight-lipped little smile. "That's some moxie."

"Well," he admits, "pretty stupid, I suppose."

"I'll say. Well, I know Florrie, too, of course. A little bit, anyway. So, you know, maybe you'd better just forget about her."

"Yes," he says, "sir."

Putnam smiles tolerantly at this. He picks at the knot of his necktie and raises his glass again. "Pleased to meet you, anyway, Mr. Barber."

"You too, Mr. Putnam."

"You're going back in a month or so, I guess."

"That's right."

"Cold as hell there in the winter, up that high, be advised. But the viewing's good. Might just find old Planet X, after all. That'd get their attention."

It would indeed. He sets his drink on the spindle table between them. If the man knows Florrie, knows everyone Florrie knows, anything Alan says in this room will eventually find its way to her. But this is all even larger than he has quite understood before. And more people are invested than he has quite imagined. He has the unwelcome feeling of being not only observed but guided along. And used.

Putnam says, "Now, I'm right, you never knew Betty Williams or J. K. McDonald."

"No."

"Percy's old computers, you know. They were before your time. Nor have you come across Wrexie Leonard."

"No."

A foxy look crosses Putnam's features. "His secretary. There's a story there, mind you. And Ross and Greene, of course. You know they spent— well, they spent a lot of time looking for it."

"Yes, I've read their logs."

"Ross and Greene were, when they cared to be, a thorough pair of doughty gentlemen. Otherwise they were lazy bums. But who can blame them, with Percy sending them all over hell and gone. Have you looked at their plates?" Putnam stirs. "Boggles the mind. Five thousand stars a plate pair. Dozens of plate pairs. And never mind what it'll look like with the Lundin."

"Seventeen-inch plates, too."

"Yes. Massive starfields. *Fifty* thousand stars a plate pair. Extraordinary resolution." Putnam sighs. "Hell of a task. Forget looking for a needle in a haystack. More like a pebble on a beach. But V.M. tells me you're on Percy's trail a little bit."

"Just a little bit," he says, "when I get a little spare time."

"You're not by some mischance following Pickering, are you?"

"Speaking frankly, Mr. Putnam, I think Pickering is more or less a lunatic."

"Yes. Not a happy story. Good. Well, look, we're trying to get you someone to work with out there. V.M.'s apparently got a sort of line on someone to help you with the blinking. He knows you're not really too happy about that sort of slogging side of it, and I don't blame you. You don't think *Morrow's* at all interested, do you, after all this?"

"No. I don't think he really ever wanted to do it in the first place."

"No. Well, too bad. Too bad you ran him off, for that matter, we might have talked him around. To be completely honest with you about the money for a moment, the situation is this: we've all more or less put up really as much as we can *justify*, given everyone's expectations. The instruments have just been *much* more expensive than we thought. Morrow was paid for already in a sense, you see—a trained man and so forth. But we'll try to scratch up enough to get you someone who can be of *some* help, anyway. An assistant of some kind. But. Be that as it may." Putnam lifts his drink and proposes, in a mild, querying tone: "To Planet X?"

He lifts his glass and drinks. The leathery, peaty, Lowellian excellence to the whiskey sets him back a little. "To Planet X," he says.

And now the real business: Putnam sniffs, looks into the fire. "So. I also wanted to ask you one more thing, Mr. Barber, more or less in confidence."

"Mr. Putnam."

"I wanted to ask you honestly, now, *honestly*, what you think our odds are. Or, no, not exactly," Putnam corrects himself, "no, what I really want to know, is what you think the odds are that such a thing exists in the first place."

"You're asking *me*?"

"Yes," Putnam says.

"I think there's a planet out there."

"Yes, all right, I know that's the official line, isn't it? But I want to know *actually*. I don't quite have the math you've got. I can follow Percy a little way down the road, but I can't go as far as you can. You can be honest, if you've got your doubts. I won't tell anyone where I heard it. I won't give you the sack. I *can't*, as far as I know."

"You want my honest opinion."

"I do indeed."

Pressed, he says, "I think there is something."

"The residuals," Putnam says.

"They have to come from somewhere," he answers.

Putnam sighs and stares into the fire again, considering. "Now that we're right on the edge of this whole thing, I guess I begin to wonder whether he was really as mad as everyone says."

"I don't think so," he says. "At least not on this score. Anyway, you've got the money laid out already, don't you? There's no point not going ahead. And I work cheap."

Putnam smiles faintly. "In that case, Mr. Barber, here's what I want you to do for me."

"All right. I think I can guess."

"Yes. I want you to find it for me, please," Putnam says quietly. "For me and for Percy of course. And for Uncle Abbott and poor Guy and for V.M. and Lampland, and for terrible old Constance, too, for what that's worth. We've sunk plenty into this project, and we're prepared to sink a little more. But you're our man, Barber. And we need you to find it."

Another claim; stupid, how he resents this as well, when really he should be grateful. "Yes, sir," he says.

"Put us on the map, wouldn't it? Just as much as finding life on Mars would, if you ask me. More so." Putnam shoots him a canny glance. "I never bought into *that* one, anyway. I always thought Venus was the more likely target. Warmer down there. Sort of stuffy and humid under all those clouds, junglelike, you know. Sort of Tarzan country. You haven't wandered into any, you know, Arizona caves or anything?" Putnam waggles his eyebrows above his glass. "That'd solve all our problems in a jiffy, wouldn't it? Discovering the portal to another world. Nobody'd call us crackpot after that." He knocks back the rest of his drink. "Now, I think we should go see Constance."

"Now?"

"Well, why the hell not?" Putnam slaps his thighs. "You're presentable enough. You can talk to her about least squares, you know, whatever it is you think she'll be interested in. The truth is, one doesn't do much talking in Connie's presence. More like the artful nod. The respectful *hmn*. The speechless *appreciating*." Putnam rises. "And don't worry. She hasn't killed anyone yet."

They are in the car for five minutes before it pulls up before a great Beacon Street mansion: brownstone, four stories, an iron railing around the grounds. "Don't be afraid," Putnam says, pressing him up the walk. The front door is opened by a butler, not the first Alan has ever seen but easily the tallest. They are shown to a drawing room, done in the height of taste circa 1908, with Japanned screens and an oriental swag over the back of two low-slung black-upholstered chairs and enameled pots arranged on teak sidetables, and a swaying forest of palms obscuring the light from the high front windows. His heart is beating despite himself, and he wipes his palms on his handkerchief. "No hope of a drink here, I guess," he says.

"Dry as the Sahara," Putnam returns.

"You'll do most of the talking," he says.

"Oh, no!" Putnam reels. "She'll want you on your own. I'm just here as your escort to the keep."

"The dark queen."

"Oh, well, she can be all right." Putnam crosses his legs nervously and arranges the fabric swagged over the sofa. "It's just good manners, Barber, that's all. You don't have to have a fit about it."

"I'm not going to have a fit," he says. Five years and a schoolteacher somewhere. Not the worst fate indeed. On a ranch with Mary, under the spinning stars. Away from all this bunch and what they want from you. He twirls his hat in his hands.

Poor hat, it never meant to get in this deep.

After a minute of debating with himself Putnam offers, finally, "Ah, Barber, *one* thing I should mention, she might appear to be having a little

trouble with her *eyes*. But in fact she can probably see you." Putnam tugs
at his tie. "At least a little bit."

"Slipher told me."

"Ah," Putnam says, "good. Then—" Putnam flashes him a warning
signal as a maid enters, at which Alan stands, leaving his hat on the sofa,
and follows her out of the drawing room, back into the palatial caverns of
the house. He keeps his eyes straight but cannot avoid seeing two Rem-
brandts hung across from each other and what looks like an Aubusson
tapestry featuring the progress of one very sedate and green-tinged sheep-
shearing and some blue silk chairs and a row of ebony-inlaid side tables
and a Steinway grand, alone on its ballroom parquet.

At last the maid stops at a polished red door. She knocks hard three
times, then enters. Beyond, an immense, darkened chamber. The windows are heavily draped. Far off, a single electric lamp burns orange on a
fringed table. Everywhere in their teak cradles are enormous Renaissance
globes, six feet across at least and so massive and dark with antiquity that
they seem not globes at all but shrunken, wizened planets, dried and preserved in the vast mansion of some celestial collector. At the far end of
this room is Constance, sitting alone on a cushioned chair. Her hands are
in her lap, and she is smaller and more demure than he expected. As far as
he can see, she is wearing a black dress of some fancy provenance, full of
lace and bows, black on black on black, and a black cap with a black veil.
He crosses and sits opposite her on a hard upholstered chair. She does not
look up but keeps her eyes closed and her face aimed at the ornamental
carpet between them as the maid retreats.

"Ma'am," he says.

Her voice is slight, firm: "You're named Barber."

"Alan Barber, ma'am."

"Are you related to the Barbers, formerly of New Land?"

"No, ma'am. My family's from Ohio."

"Ohio!" She settles. "*Good* for you. You've been at Harvard how long?"

"Four years, ma'am."

"Are you studying astronomy?"

"Yes."

She sits, waiting. There is a great silence.

"From a mathematical angle, mostly," he adds.

This does not impress. "Percy was a mathematician, of course. Very brilliant. First in the class of 1874. Dr. Peirce said he'd never seen anyone like him. And he would know."

"Peirce was brilliant."

"He was. Although you couldn't have known him, of course, you're much too young. I come out to Observation Hill every year, usually in the spring before it gets too hot. Percy spent a good deal of his life there, and I like to go and talk to him. It really seems to me that he's still out there, you know. Sometimes I think I'd like to live there year-round, but the weather's not very nice in the winter and all my friends are here. They'd come see me once or twice, but the novelty of that sort of thing wears off pretty quickly. You'll live in the Main Building?"

"I don't know," he says.

"Do you have a family?"

"No," he says.

"Good."

"The blink comparator works very well," he sallies, into another quiet.

"Which is what?"

"The blink comparator is a machine," he says, "we'll be using to compare pictures of the sky to one another to see if we can see anything moving."

"Oh," she says. "Well if it's a machine doing it, what are *you* going to be doing?"

"You still have to be the one to see it. I mean, you sit there and look through an eyepiece while the machine works."

"I suppose that cost a good deal of money."

"I don't know," he manages.

"I see. And this is your task."

"I'm afraid so."

"You make it sound pretty dismal."

"No, ma'am, it's not dismal."

"You're not married?"

"No."

"Are you engaged?"

"No."

"Well, then you shouldn't care what your life is like that much. When we come out you may have to give up your room and live in town. Sometimes I have people with me, and I like them to be comfortable."

"The B.M.'s pretty big."

She stirs, producing a rustling from somewhere in the bower of lace and crinoline. "That's not what it's called; it's called Hollyhock House. I don't care what you call it among yourselves, but that's not what it's really called. I don't suppose you know what *B.M.* also stands for—bowel *movement.*"

"Yes, ma'am. Baronial Mansion, I meant."

"That was Percy's name for it, not mine. He thought it was funny. I guess you think it's sort of funny to call it that. Have you been inside?"

"It's kept locked."

"Well, it's a dear old place. You can just get it ready for me. Just a minute." She rises, feels her way across the back of her chair and walks vaguely to a cherrywood secretary. She works open a drawer, fumbles inside, and returns. "Here's the key. You can clean it up a little bit before I get there. I'll send a letter ahead of time. Mr. Slipher ignores all my letters except the ones that have to do with money, and when I get there the place is always a ruin. Last time I got there there was an owl in the chimney. How tall are you?"

"About five feet eight inches tall."

"You're not a tall man."

"Not particularly."

"What do you look like?"

"Irish," he says, helplessly. "Black Irish."

"You'll fit into the little spaces," she says. "So you're the one who's going to find Planet X, I understand."

He pockets the key. "That's the idea."

"It's going to be named Lowell," she says. "That's what Percy wanted, and everyone I've talked to thinks it's the most wonderful name for a planet. The Lowells deserve a planet, after everything they've done for this state, not to mention this country. I'm sure you agree."

"Well," he says, "it's a little out of the main line of names."

"But those are *old* planets, you see. This one's *new.* One of my friends wants to call it Americus, but I think that's just ridiculous."

"Actually it's the discoverer who gets to name it," he tells her.

"Why, but Percy's the one who *discovered* it," she says, serenely. "It just hasn't been *seen* yet."

He has nothing to say to this.

Hearing this final silence, she decides to dismiss him. "It was thoughtful of you to come." She reaches into a little clasp purse and removes a silver dollar. "And this," she says, "is for you."

There is no avoiding it; he takes it. Suddenly he cannot wait to be gone—away from all these people. Dick and Florrie and breezy Putnam and this old horror too. He'll pack his things and take his new girl to Arizona and show them how it's done. And who really deserves it, after all. Walk back in here with a planet of his own called Mariana.

"Thank you *very* much, ma'am," he says, rising. He will remember this loathing. Stoke it carefully. Fuel. Fire. "I expect you'll be hearing from me very soon."

17

Clyde writes back immediately, assuring Slipher of his absolute suited-
ness. He is the man for the job! He sends the letter from Napoleon Carreau as proof of his capabilities. He sends the notebook containing the
remainder of his Jupiter drawings, and two photographs of himself taken
the previous fall, bundled up in sweaters so as to appear slightly larger
than he really is. At the last minute he includes his track medal in the
envelope as well, which means waiting at the mailbox for Mike Landry to
hand him sufficient postage.

Four days later a telegram arrives inviting him to come to Flagstaff in
January, on a trial basis, and asking if the 9-inch was capable of resolving
the new object in Virgo? As he reads it standing in the front hall, with the
radiator clanking to life beside him, Clyde is overtaken by a spasm of
pure joy.

Because he is going to Arizona.

Suddenly impervious, he finishes work on Maggie's stable, whistling
beside his silent father as he whangs the eightpenny nails in. On the first
night of decent viewing he takes Roy and Charlie out to look at Virgo, and
after ten minutes he finds the tiny white smudge of a new comet, still way
out near Jupiter, and for the first time in his life he feels the thrill of being
an insider, of knowing more than other people. It is as though a door has
opened in the world, as though some magic now connects him to the rest
of everything. A few days later a fat envelope arrives from Flagstaff, full of

Lowell Observatory publications, and he is able to face their terrifying opacity with something like courage. Dr. Slipher knows he has not been to college, so how can he expect him to make anything of *The Chemistry of the Sun in Long-Period Oscillatory Spectroscopy*? Or to make use of the physics in *Seasonal Variation of Martian Surface Temperature*?

"Some reading," his father observes. But Clyde is able to shrug and say "Ain't it, though," without drawing either of them into a tussle. He is proud of this, and also proud of the final version of his letter to Napoleon Carreau, a short calm note, empty of the wild, adolescent rancor of the early drafts, informing Carreau only that he is taking a position at Lowell Observatory, in Arizona.

And that he wishes Henry Bundt well, in his travels to Florida.

In an attempt to be not just plumb ignorant, he goes off to the library and studies what he can. There isn't much available. It is all old and meant for schoolkids, and half of it he himself checked out years ago in his first years in Kansas. He makes some sense of the idea of retrograde motion, and he manages a halfhearted stab at some trigonometry, but it is a tangle to him. Still, he can justify it; he can make a good picture of himself here in this country town. It is a rainy fall and the world stays green a long time, and it is all right to be holed up here with bootprints everywhere on the library linoleum. It is how his life is supposed to go, he thinks to himself, satisfied, as his bicycle gets wetter and wetter against the wall outside. Without noticing it, he draws himself up into the chair, where he idly chews the fringe of his scarf. Something about it recalls him to that previous version of himself, that old version that was near enough to Chicago to hear it on the radio. The idea that your longing had a power to it, had the power to make things really happen. Wish it hard enough, and it will come true. Sure, Roy would have some fun with him. But it strikes him now that this is not kid stuff, after all.

For example, look at Polly there with her elbows on the counter, watching the door, wishing with all her heart for the fellow who'll never come in. And still she watches.

In the darkening afternoon the girls go by in their Cuban heels, on their way to the drugstore, swaddled in their coats against the rain. He exits and stands for a minute on the sacred spot where Lily turned him down, feeling high and nobly above it all, so much that he figures something of it must show. But when he unleans his bicycle the passing girls still don't pay him any mind.

Well, he's changed, all right. They just can't see it yet.

The weather turns for good on November 21, the day before Thanksgiving. From his bedroom window Clyde wakes to see the fields covered in a rime of frost. Dark snow-clouds climb the western horizon. He dresses and bolts his breakfast and wraps himself in his winter jacket.

When he has finished his chores he goes to Maggie, who is snorting with pleasure at the cold air. She tosses her head in greeting and comes to the rail.

"Your kind of day, girl," he tells her. She produces an emphatic *huff* from the bottom of her throat.

He saddles her and leads her into the farmyard. At the grinding post he mounts to the saddle and, snapping the reins, urges her forward into the pasture. When he turns her north into the fields she does a little approving two-step. The soil is stiff and cloddy, and Maggie picks her way carefully along. She has always been a good cold-weather mare and now she thrusts her big nostrils to the wind, flaring. The wind smells of snow and whistles around Clyde's ears. He turns his earflaps down and tugs his scarf tighter. He urges Maggie toward the fence line, and she breaks into a little trot and, with a dainty flip of her back legs, lifts them both over the wire. Now they are on the Steffens' farm.

Lily, too, will hear of him.

They are nearly to the windbreak when the snow begins. Tiny flakes driven before the storm settle unmelting into the hard furrows. He guides Maggie into the trees. The cottonwoods produce their oceanic whoosh. The brittle fallen leaves crunch under Maggie's hooves. It will not be a serious storm, but it will drop some snow, all right. He can feel the temperature plunging. In a few minutes he will start back, for Maggie's sake; but for now they can stand and watch.

The wind stirs the branches clacking overhead. Maggie sighs with satisfaction, her great sides rising and falling. The white snow falls in tumbling gusts now, swirling across the fields. The sun is a bright coin behind the clouds. Far off, the other windbreaks stand brown and empty.

It is not until they are halfway home across the fields, having leaped the wire again, when he begins to feel it. A hot fullness in the back of his throat. He is getting sick, he thinks—but no, and then it is on him, in a rush, he is sobbing, violent racking cries he is powerless to stop. He drops the reins, leans forward onto Maggie's neck, crying desperately. Maggie stops, listens, then continues toward the barn.

By the time they return to her new stall, he will be all right again. But for now, he can't help it. It is the sight of it—the sight of his white house standing trim against the gray sky, at the edge of the whitening earth, that allows him, finally, to understand it. The root cellar with its humped roof of earth. The porch where he lay with Roy and smoked his cigarettes and felt the heart of Kansas beating. It is home, and as such it constitutes half of everything he knows about the world so far, and he is leaving it. At last, at last—and what beautiful sorrow he feels now, what terrible exquisite happiness. The red stain of the iron sesquioxide, slowly erased by the snow.

18

With the others Felix spends a week breaking camp. They shovel sifted dirt into the unfinished excavation pits to protect the fossils from the weather. They break down the tents. With Bryce he sharpens six dozen chisels against the wobbling grindstone. Then they wrap the chisels together by size in extra burlap squares and tuck the bundles into a crate. Huddled around the oil incinerator they scrutinize two hundred brushes of all grades and toss all but twenty into the fire. The cold begins to come on seriously, and the wind has a bitter edge. He distributes envelopes with the final week's pay and a good bonus, and the men shake his hand and the Italians make a quick sort of comic bow. Now that he is a man with a mother they respect him more but with a flavor of friendly mockery. In town the Italians put on their traveling suits and pack their suitcases and walk over the tracks to reach the brick depot, where they stand like black bowling pins under the electric lights, and then the train takes them away to pursue their mysterious programs elsewhere. By the middle of December the slope is desolate. The gouges in the earth fill with snow. The ugly heaps on the hillside resemble new graves. Willoughby rides out with him in the mornings, the two of them wrapped to the eyes against the wind. There is a feeling their presence discourages pickers. This is doubtful to Felix, but it is a good ride anyway. The air smells of the top of the sky, like permanent clarity. Blue sky above the orange vacancy, with clouds in ribbons to the horizon. Sissie billows white from her nostrils.

"Well, look, now that they're all gone," Willoughby says one morning.

They stop in the lee of an outcropping, and Willoughby extracts a prospecting map with his gloved hands. There is a line traced through the contours. "About four miles, if you're game."

"*X* marks the spot," Felix says.

"It's a spot, all right," Willoughby says.

"What is it?"

"Well," Willoughby says, "it's worth the trip, anyway."

They ride the four miles into the scrub. No roads, no fences, only the stunted pines and the halfhearted cacti now dusted with snow. In the deep distance plateaus lift square to the sky like machine-cut shadows. It is a perfect loneliness. He considers that it is probably too much for a white man to bear. Walk around in too much space without enclosure, and suddenly God is ghosting over the ravines. And the spook comes down out of the sky. All the great religions began in the desert, and this is why; the mind attunes itself to this mystical frequency. The ocean a desert of a sort as well.

The path takes them down a gradual slope of about two miles; then the terrain changes and they are in a section of little dry canyons. The rock is mostly gray here, with only a few bands of orange. The walls are tufted with growth. The canyons twist and turn, and the wind is absent. They remove their scarves. In the sudden quiet as they go along, Willoughby says, "You know what this here used to be?"

"No."

"Village of people called Sinaguas. Look up there." He follows Willoughby's pointing finger. He sees nothing at first. Then he notices dozens—no, hundreds of shallow caves dug into the walls, nearly hidden by the scrub. A secret city. The cave ceilings are black with ancient smoke. They ride on another hundred yards until Willoughby pulls them up at a flat stone face. It is covered all over with petroglyphs, a scribbled dreamscape of many-jointed creatures and stickmen with moon-circle heads and some that seem expressions of pure geometry, triangles and zigzags. There is a million-footed centipede right-angled along a maze of gridded pathways. It is like a treasure map drawn by a madman; the treasure is everywhere.

"Some people would pay good money for that," Willoughby says. "But it's a crime to take it down. I mean an actual crime."

He guesses: "You're not telling the crew about this."

"About what?"

"This." He gestures, at the canyons, the caves, the petroglyphs.

"Well, it ain't really in their line," Willoughby says.

Alone in the silent canyon Felix feels free to ask, "They're gangsters, aren't they?"

"Oh, gangsters!" Willoughby's long seamed face folds, amused, and he resettles his hat. "Well, I guess they're *wops*, if that's what you mean. Plasterers, masons. Calabrians. They all got mothers and sisters. Mann I got off a sidewalk doing three-card monte. Maxwell's got a degree in animal husbandry. Bryce used to be in the merchant marines."

"But they wouldn't like you taking a little something extra for yourself."

Willoughby gives him a pained look. "You've got the wrong idea, Mr. DuPrie. This is just a sort of side interest of mine."

"All right."

"I wouldn't ever consider desecrating a place like this. That's bad magic. I mean aside from being disrespectful. Pardon me for saying such a thing, but I hope you wouldn't ever think about it."

"No," he says, "I'm right with you, as a matter of fact."

"Truly, I hope."

"On my honor," Felix says.

Willoughby dismounts in one smooth motion and loops Picobel's reins around a stunted juniper. "In that case, I invite you to come on," he says, "because this is worth seeing."

They climb a narrow ancient path up the nearly vertical cliff face. The path is a foot across at its widest and turns to follow the shape of the rock. They climb in silence, passing more dug-out shelters. In one he sees the remains of a new cookfire and a litter of tin cans with their tops knived open. Then there is a point at which the path ends, and they have to lean across a yard or so of open air to gain the next section. The horses are a long way down, but there is no question of not continuing. After this there are more shelters but no more litter.

"Just a little ways more," Willoughby says.

Felix is no longer looking much down or up for that matter when they come to the last stop, another shallow cave shelter seemingly no different from the others. The ceiling is four feet high or so, and they crouch to enter it. Even in the cold it smells damp, a rich smokey scent of ancient charcoal and baked stone. When you touch the ceiling, your fingertips come away greasy black. You look out the entrance and over the canyons, you can see how it is really just one canyon that snakes away and doubles back, the whole arrangement when seen from above stuffed with brushy growth, junipers and pines frosted with snow. The earth in the cave is smooth, powdery, clings to his boots, his knees, his hands.

"High-rise living," Felix says.

"Ain't it."

They squat together, observing the view. It is a peaceful, domestic feeling, this human-scale setup out here in the canyons. Even the absence of people is comforting; it is like an empty house left for them to explore. He is reminded of the giant house back in Indian Head, the maids' unpapered gray rooms, the basement and its pillars, the grease-smelling workroom off the garage where Buckley kept a canvas cot tucked behind the barrel of motor oil . . .

"I guess I wouldn't mind," Felix says.

Willoughby makes a noise of assent and says, "I think this was the witch doctor's place, or what-have-you. If you notice."

Now he indicates something Felix missed, drawings on the floor of the shelter. Really one large drawing. It is less frantic than the one below, covering an area about five feet on a side. A horizon line. A circle mounted centrally: the sun. Rays arrowing from it. Small beasts, horses and buzzards and other things, lizards, insects, set here and there on the earth and in the sky. And one weird central figure with a giant featureless head impaled like a candy apple on a tiny, stick-body. Eyeless, hairless, faceless, stick arms at its sides.

"A conjuring place of some kind, is my guess," Willoughby says. "If they were anything like the Navaho they'd use this drawing as part of their medicine. I mean there's some *story* to it." They are on their knees before it now, Willoughby is indicating with a twig. "So those there are arrows or wind or magic, coming down from that, the sun or the moon or the Spirit, maybe, and here's all the animals in the world standing around. And this big old fellow here is—something."

"Big-Head."

"Big-Head himself. You see him around a fair bit." Willoughby wags the twig. "Up in Bone Cabin Quarry the Utes used to draw him. I don't know what he's supposed to be. It's all *some* sort of story, anyway. Maybe he's the first man in charge of all the animals. Adam or whatnot. And maybe all these little fellows mean something in particular. Each of them with their own sort of place in things. You use them all separately, it's like an apothecary's drawer, you know, take two buffalo and call me in the morning. But I mean who knows really. What the *Navaho* think, now, is that you make a drawing like this and the creatures in it are really *alive*. Not here exactly but in some other place. And what you're doing is, you're opening a hole in this world, and when you sing all the right songs and then sit inside it, then you're *in* the world of the *spirit*, where *this* is all happening all the time, all *this* activity, sort of permanently happening, which is how you get healed. That's the Navaho. I don't know about the Sinagua. I haven't read up on them yet. But I imagine it's much the same. So our witch doctor"—Willoughby surveys the floor—"sort of always had his window open up here. I wonder if he slept on it. Imagine what that does to your dreams."

"You've been coming here," Felix says.

Willoughby says, "Off and on."

"There are no others like this?"

"Not that I've found. Although I haven't explored it all. Maybe you'd like to come along now and then, we can make a thorough catalog."

"I would like that," Felix says.

"All right." Willoughby stirs the hem of his duster along the floor of the cave. "I enjoy the company."

"Sure," Felix agrees.

"I don't mind *talking* this sort of thing, either," Willoughby admits. "I guess you got that by now. Stop me when I start to get on your nerves."

Felix gently touches the figure of Big-Head. You expect some heat out of the rock though it is just an etching. But it is hard to account for the feeling of peace he has suddenly.

"I misfigured you, Will," Felix says.

"People do, Mr. DuPrie." He turns his long seamed face away. "But I don't mind it. It usually leaves me with a little advantage."

There is to be a Christmas party. His mother plans it. The visit to Yost at Bel-Aire has enlivened her, maybe. These others left that life behind, and so can she. She can be an improved western-style DuPrie, that's what. That social urge providing the secret charge. You want to put up a life in opposition to something, in answer, anyway, and it gives you a levering foothold. "We ought to do it *right*," she says. "We can round up those people at the observatory; they seem like they might be interesting to know. The Sliphers and the Lamplands. And there's your Mr. Willoughby. And Larry Yost, I suppose. If he's not already spoken for."

The arrangements are set in motion. They hire a girl, Prudencia. A tree, eleven feet tall and sticky with pitch, is put up in the parlor. Willoughby shoots an antelope. They will eat venison and stewed prunes and some of their chickens. Some cucumbers will be brought in to make a soup and onions up from the cellar and potatoes. They can acquire other things in town, peppermints and chocolates and oranges from Mexico. A few gifts. It is a pared-down Christmas compared to the version they suffered at Indian Head, and through its small preparations he remains touched by that unaccountable peace. He gets his mother two jet earrings at Babbitt's, where he buys his tools. For a long minute he stands at the counter gazing at the earrings' glistening facets against the cotton batting in the box. The machine-cuts, the cunning gold hoop drilled into the material, the minute work on the gold clasp. Only when the clerk says, "Problem, sir?" does he recall himself.

It is as though his whole skin fits him, suddenly.

Then it is Christmas afternoon, and his beard is fluffed and polished with the French soaps and combs his mother has presented to him, and they are standing in the front room looking out the windows waiting for their guests to arrive. The Lowells are in Boston, of course, but with his mother's extensive attachments she can claim some acquaintance with the observatory people. The Lowells, who set things in motion, who urge and create and rule. Gods in their own right, he supposes. Felix dips his nose into his glass and remembers this sort of moment from his earlier life, when everything is ready and he is standing in the center of a room waiting for the door to open. A fire in the fireplace and snowy gusts rattling the windows. He considers the dirt impacted still in the cracks in his hand, and something unshaped rises in him. Not pride, not wonder. Something like satisfaction. "Well, mama," he says, raising his glass. "What a year."

"What a year," she agrees.

"And here we are."

He lets the silence gather. Prudencia in a clean apron comes and goes. His mama is smaller, it seems—shrunk down, maybe with the effort of the party. She doesn't meet his eye.

"Mama," he asks, finally, "did you ever feel anything? When we were—?"

She waits.

"—in the rowboat?" he finishes.

She faces him bravely. "Well, what a funny thing to ask. I felt awful, Felix, of course."

"You didn't feel anything else?"

Unconsciously, her hand rises to one of the new, weirdly blooming patches on her ear. "Well, as long as you're asking, yes, I thought we were going to die. I couldn't look at you because I was afraid of thinking, We're going to die together. My son is going to die. I kept resolving to jump overboard so I wouldn't have to watch you die." She glances around to take in the solid house, lamplit in the evening. "That's what I was thinking."

"You know what I was feeling?"

"What, Felix?"

He wants to mention that sorrow flooding into him from above. He wants to put words, somehow, to the way he is feeling *now*. Instead—the words seem to say themselves—he states, "I wanted to kill you."

"Oh," she says. He seems to have offered it only as a curiosity, a truth that can now be told. It sounds that way to him. But a hard pleased light rises in his mother's eye: the necessary betrayal that makes her son finally whole. The merciful blow. She lifts her glass. "Well, Felix," she answers, as the first guests turn up the walk, "I expect you'll one day get your chance."

19

By going down a few days ahead of time Alan is able to get three tickets for the January 2 train, and while he is at the station he ships out the roll of butcher paper wrapped in a canvas duffel on whose surface he prints LOWELL OBSERVATORY—FLAGSTAFF ARIZ—PROP ALAN BARBER, PHD. This last is a little premature, but it looks fine. "Be there when you arrive, sir," the ticket seller informs him through the brass gate. "Astronomer?"

"About to be," he says.

"Wouldn't mind it myself," the man says, sliding over his claim check, "if I didn't have such a plum right here." It is enough to make him smile; then together with Mary he packs his little room, and when he finishes he has a suitcase in each hand, one for him and one for her. He slings the satchel packed with Lowell's notebooks over his shoulder. She is really coming along. He is full of satisfaction as she takes his arm waiting for the streetcar in the sooty slush. Maybe he is only a means to get out of Massachusetts. But she has insisted on paying her own way, so that isn't right either. Maybe he is nothing more than a convenient trajectory to follow, someone nearby who has a reason to go somewhere else: a plot path she can follow without further explanation. Who cares. She's coming.

He is wadded into his overcoat and wearing the tie that was her Christmas present to him, a blue field dotted with white.

"It's the stars in daytime," she tells him now.

"I like that," he says.

She pats his forearm. "It's good on you."

She pulls his arm closer as the streetcar comes lumbering up.

At the station they look for Hollis in the postholiday hustle, everyone loaded down with not only suitcases but packages tied in string and hatboxes and a swag of extra clothing; they are wearing all their new things, laden and leaning back under the vaulted ceiling. You take this train to Philadelphia so there is a touch of tone to the crowd, some furs and plenty of that high old Boston drawling. They find Hollis at last standing alone, a still dark point in the middle of the swirling. His eyes are red, and his expression is leaden. But he is sturdy there, unregretting. He has tried to persuade Scotty to come along, but without success. Now the idea is that he will spend a little while in Arizona with them before pushing ahead to scout out California. San Francisco is a friendly place, he has heard. It is not officially the end of him and Scotty, but Hollis claims he is ready for a change and Scotty will stay home and get the news from a distance and make his mind up then. So it may as well be the end, in fact.

She leans into her brother, full of sympathy. "He only wanted you for your money, anyway, darling," she says.

"Sure." Hollis picks up his suitcase and his battered case of paints. "Anyway, I've got you."

"Don't you anyway me," she tells him.

It is hard to know where to look with Hollis, you don't want to treat him like a man exactly, but if you treat him like a girl that's sort of worse, so mostly you end up not saying much. Alan doesn't know what exactly has gone on between Hollis and this man Scotty and does not really care to inquire. Only you can't help seeing how Mary relies on her brother—she grips his arm as they walk to the platform, and he does make a plausible figure: sober, dark, reserved. She would not be so brave as to launch herself on this trip without him, that much seems clear.

Because it is cheaper they are all in a three-bunk compartment together and after some minutes of waiting the train is moving across the rail yard and they are away. In the rail yard greasy fists of coal sit like little charred hearts. Mary is knitting and watching the window across from him while Hollis studies a newspaper.

"Poor Teddy," she says, quietly.

Hollis tips down a corner of his *Herald*. Congress has approved the building of the Boulder Dam. "Mare."

They thud away.

She says, "I wasn't nice to him, Holly, no matter what you say. I should have let him know."

"He'd have come after you."

"I would have explained," she says.

"He wouldn't have understood."

"He would. You didn't know him. He wasn't stupid. I just couldn't marry him, that's all."

Alan listens very hard to this. He has never exactly understood brothers and sisters, so he has to figure it all sideways. And part of Mary's untold story is contained in this exchange, too. But there is no more to come, and after a few minutes he pulls his tablets from his satchel as the city drops away entirely. Milford, Uxbridge, across into Connecticut. Across from him Mary is quiet, she knits, she keeps an eye on the scenery. In Philadelphia they change for Chicago. He has traveled this way often enough going home over the holidays, and when he glances up now it will take only a minute to place himself—a stalwart stone house, a hillside enclosing a secrecy of sheep, a red bridge over a frozen river. Madmen's floral hexes on the barns, a wizard's geometry. Pennsylvania, her home state, and she shows a certain fondness. "How about *that* operation," she says.

It is a white house on a frozen pond, a barn, a fence, a doll's dusky paradise at the edge of a slanting grove.

"Say the word," he says.

He works away at his papers. It is like his own sort of knitting, this endless work, regular, easily set down and taken up again. But he has his own pursuer too. Not a boxer but Florrie's terrible yellow slips. The two of them, hunted.

But surely they have escaped. They sit down to dinner in a wintry woodland, chicken and creamed spinach, and afterward the berths have been turned down, and Hollis is on the low berth here and they are snugged in the high berth on the other side. The sheets are cool. Lights play on the ceiling. Bells chime as the train plunges through crossings. Mary rocks in his arms. A sweet elation. And courage. In Chicago they change trains again and begin the angled dive southwest across the continent. Hollis spends his hours in the smoker or the diner, drawing with pencil on a little spiral pad while leaving Alan and Mary to the privacy of the compartment. The light begins to change, the sights from the windows begin to expand, and soon they are in the open emptiness of Iowa, the sun rising and setting over the swelling hills, antelope pouring over wire fences, and men in shabby cars sitting at the crossings, waiting, with a clear patient look in their eyes, for the train to pass.

"Oh," she says, across from him, "it's so enormous."

"You ain't seen nothing yet," he tells her.

The prairie light on her face, you just want to look at her forever. Happiness enough. What is left to accomplish?

Only keeping her, he thinks.

And at this he turns back to his tablets.

It is that evening, after they have just finished dinner, when Hollis looks across the tablecloth for a long, stricken minute, then lifts his hand to his shirtfront as though to steady his heart. Then he excuses himself and goes away down the aisle toward their compartment. This is not unusual, as he likes to gather his things for the evening in the smoker. But the sight of his disappearing back—rounded, burdened, vanishing through the swaying door of the vestibule—stirs something in Alan. A fellow feeling. They are both men in love, he sees. From such a height as he commands, he can admit to such a thing just possibly and not be involved in it. The remains of dinner litter the table. The pleasant burble of dinnertime conversation has mostly ended, and only a few stragglers are still being seated, withered men from the plains states with their chickenish wives as the train rocks along.

"It doesn't mean you *never* want to get married," he suggests.

"No." She sets down her water glass. "Just not to Teddy."

"Sure."

"And not with everyone *looking*."

He says, "I know just the man for the job. We'll find the fellow who married Dick and Florrie. He'll do it in a closet if we want."

"Well," she puts her teeth together, a sort of smile. "Maybe."

"Sure, maybe, all right. That's all right with me. I can live with maybe. Maybe I don't want to do it either."

"Sure," she says.

"Try and catch me, then," he says. He has a whomping hard-on suddenly. That he is daring to suggest such a thing. "Think you've got it all figured, I guess."

"You and me, Jim," she says. "Mexican standoff."

"All right," he says.

She reaches across for his hand. "Deal," she says.

It is silly, but there is absolutely something in this understanding, some agreement that reaches into the future; and suddenly he wants to tell Hollis—well, what, exactly? He wants to show him that everything will be all right. That Mary will be fine with Alan alone, possibly. He doesn't know. He wants that fat queer in his sights, that's all. They go back together to the compartment to find him there, but the compartment is empty. Mary sits, and Alan, grinning, sets off for the smoker. You can find a fellow two ways, see. You can wait for him to come to you, or you can go to him.

The smoker is two cars farther down. It is a fog of cigars and chortling men, their boots unbuttoned. Hollis is not there. The bathrooms are not occupied here, and he gets a couple odd looks for poking around. But there is a third-class car next in line, so possibly he is there, sitting with someone. But he is not; and he is not standing in the next vestibule, smoking alone, and he is not in the next car, or the one after that.

This means he has to be standing on the rear platform.

But Alan is beginning to get that funny sensation again, the one he had when Dick pulled a lam.

He pushes open the door and steps out into the windy dark. The tracks are unspooling their silver in the winter moonlight. But the little platform there is empty.

He is not there.

He is not on the train.

Well, but there are any number of explanations. In some bathroom somewhere grunting at a turd. In someone's compartment, having a time of it. You don't just disappear from a train.

But a dark hollow opens beneath Alan's breastbone. He does not like this. He makes his way back to the compartment. He will have to make some excuse, and she will see right through him. In the compartment he finds the window open. A frigid wind gusts around the little room.

Mary is holding her head nearly upside down out the window—she is holding the glass open above her, her face toward the ceiling—as though she is doing some strange calisthenic. For a moment she remains in that pose, her body contorted backward, her face frozen, her head resting on the sill, while the wind enters in a rush.

Then she releases the glass. It comes slicing down like a guillotine. It grazes the top of her scalp and falls into its housing with a crack, and she gives a tiny frightened cry. She sits up, plucking at the few caught hairs, and gives him a grateful, guilty look, full of mystery, a look that will haunt him for years to come.

"There," she says, her voice hollow, "that should do it."

"Do what?" he manages to ask.

III

A DIVIDED SPHERE
1929

TEN MONTHS LATER

20

Clyde hears Slipher's anxious footsteps scuffing down the hall and then the old man is at the doorway, his voice tight with worry.

"The train's coming, Tombaugh."

He is pretty well settled against the comparator eyepiece cleaning up the final plate in Libra where there is a last flickering something that he skipped over yesterday and that he has now come back to for completeness' sake. He is not quite able to see it directly, but if he looks slightly away it is almost there, all right. Just at the edge of visibility. But he can't look up or he'll lose it. Without moving his head a millimeter he answers, "I'm almost finished here."

Slipher pauses, shuffles away, then returns. "Barber's in the library, in case you need moral support."

"Yes, sir."

Clyde can feel Slipher performing one of his meaningful stares against the back of his head but he is going to get this last suspect if it kills him so he holds the pose until Slipher skiffs off again. You take your grease pencil sharpened to its needle point and lift it trembling into the field of vision where it looms like a great dark spear. Looking slightly away as he has learned to do, he senses the tiny object flickering again, a magnitude 14 at best. It is too faint to be a planet and it isn't moving at all as a planet would, but it may be a distant Cepheid. Or a fault of the plate or an artifact of the differential being a little off-key. Anyway it needs marking if he is going to rest easy. He relaxes his eye and sees without seeing until finally he fixes it and labels it with a question mark. Then he exhales and reaches beneath the machine as though feeling around in its skirts and kills the comparator and the bulb, and as the room falls silent he makes his final notes on the plate envelope:

Plate No. __155__   Series A-9

Name __Δ Libra__   RA = 7 h 15 m 53 s

Remarks _good plate_   DECL.=+22.7

      Exposure = 10:13 — 11:13; net 1 hr.

      13 inch Lawrence Lowell Telescope

      Crane's Hi Speed Plate

      Writing at North end of plate

      Rochinal developer

Date of exposure   _August 19, 1929_

Date of examination   _October 17 1929_

Notes of examination   _see below_   ---

      1. — 10 asteroids "A."

      2. — 10 or 11 variable stars 'V."

      3. — 8 temporary objects "T."

      4. — two doubtful objects "?"

      5. — no comets

C. Tombaugh

Then he swings up the objective and flicks away the brass latches that fasten the 155th plate of the Planet X search. He lifts out the plate, which is warmed from the bulb that has been lit behind it for two hours. And he slides the plate with care into the envelope because he isn't going to be hurried. Once you start to hurry on a project like this, you are asking for trouble. Slipher has gone scuffing up the hall to his office and someone, Mrs. Fox no doubt, is banging around in the kitchen empying the old coffee grounds from the percolator, producing a *gung, gung* as she whacks the big perforated drum against the side of the garbage can.

Plate number 155 whispers snug into its envelope, and he muscles open the file drawer and sets the envelope in place. Then he takes number 154 out of the comparator as well and writes his notes on its envelope and sets it beside its companion in the drawer. This project has a square aspect to it, meaning you can only hope to make this particular approach work if you are entirely square all the time. You can't leave even the smallest suspect unrecorded. This is why he is nearly two months behind in his blinking despite spending what feels like every waking hour at the machine. Two months is as far behind as he can afford to fall. You take a picture of the sky when you are at the ideal angle to see something moving against the background stars—although really it is your own motion on the orbiting earth you are detecting—you are near the sun and whizzing around it like a toy train while somewhere far out beyond the orbit of Neptune there is an as-yet-unseen slow creeping gas giant hiding, and as you swing past on the inside track it will appear to first slow down and then to move backward against the background stars. It will appear to retrograde, and something that is retrograding is in orbit around the sun, and anything he can see that is retrograding beyond the orbit of Neptune is going to be Planet X. So far there have been a few dozen suspects out of the nearly two million stars he has seen, but none that have come through.

He is more tired than he has ever been. And now Mrs. Lowell has arrived.

He gently presses the heavy cabinet drawer shut. He stands, feeling the hours in his back. You cannot in any fashion prepare for this sort of work. On the other hand, he has been preparing for it all his life. Throwing seeds into the earth, each one a speck. Countless multitudes, over which he walks nightly. His field of stars. Among them somewhere a hidden world.

Alan is at the library table with his coffee before him and his cigarette cocked almost at his ear. He is still peforming his immense reduction of the observations, and now the roll of butcher paper has been nearly filled. It is laid across the long library table entirely, covered in its usual arcana.

"Slipher gave you the word," Clyde asks.

Alan sends him an empty look of the kind he has been offering lately.

They are companions in this way, each pushed beyond the edge of exhaustion. Mary's problems and the mystery of the vanished brother. "I hear if you aim a mirror at the old lady," Alan tells him, "you can turn *her* to stone *first*."

"Funny trick."

Alan lifts his coffee cup, cold, and swallows the measure down. "Anything?"

"It was just a Cepheid or something," he answers. "Below 13. No motion."

"You want to show me?"

He shrugs. "It's all back in the drawer. If you want, though."

Alan makes a placid negating gesture. You can see the weariness in his every move. "We need a vacation, Clyde," he sighs.

"Sure. But I'm still too far behind to go anywhere," Clyde says. "That's the problem. If I could just get ahead of myself a week. But I'm going all out just to stay this far behind."

"Like I say you don't have to do them all in order."

"I sure do," he replies. "I'm telling you, that's the last thing I want, is to get a good suspect and then be too far out of opposition to catch it again."

"Those Libra plates are about to kill you, Clyde."

"Libra can kiss my split," he says. "I am officially done with Libra."

"You could have skipped ahead."

"You know I couldn't."

Alan draws at his cigarette. He is considering Clyde, maybe, or maybe he is just going over his own problems. The man has plenty, anyway. He is gray under the eyes, and the hair is fringy over the back of his collar. His complexion is painful in places as though he has shaved with a rasp. Alan senses Clyde's frank examining and suffers it for an instant. Then he lunges forward and stabs the cigarette into his cup and rises. "Anyway, help me clear this stuff, would you?" he asks. "The old lady wouldn't like seeing it all over the place."

They have been waiting for Constance's arrival for months, but now with her presence confirmed there is an air of battle. Upstairs Clyde takes the brush to the shoulders of his jacket, wrestling around to get all the flakey stuff off. He looks the same to himself as he did in the hotel in Wichita and even in the dark glass of the train window as he traveled all night over the wilds of Colorado and New Mexico in January. He goes to the window and sees Slipher appear outside carrying a satchel. Slipher shouts something at Sykes before heading over across the lot to the B.M., where he lets himself in with a key he fishes up from his watch pocket. Then Carl Lampland goes stomping up the path to the B.M. with two gauntlet canvas gloves wagging out of a back pocket.

"Some fuss," Clyde says.

Alan has been changing into a fresh shirt and now pinches his collar together, lifting his chin. "She's Constance Lowell, Clyde, she's going to cause a stir."

"She doesn't even write the checks any more," Clyde says.

Alan shrugs. "Old habits," he says. He yanks the points of his vest and wipes a hand down his face and examines Clyde for faults. "Anyway, it's her house. You still haven't got anything else to put on besides that horrible example. Maybe just one jacket somewhere that doesn't look like a horse blanket."

"No, goddammit. To hell with you."

"What do you do with that ninety dollars a month, anyway? Whores and cigarettes, I guess." Alan puts a soft thumb high on Clyde's cheek, near his eye. "Little brass polish, sonny," he says, smearing it away.

It is embarrassing, his touch, mostly because Clyde is so happy to have it.

"You want to see in that house of hers," Alan suggests.

At the B.M. Mrs. Fox is sweeping pine needles off the porch, and Sykes is making his steady way around addressing the shutters. Alan pulls open the squeaking screen door and lets them in. The spring whaps the door shut behind them. Inside the B.M. is cold, and Clyde can smell the musty cotton inside the rustic sofa cushions and the stink of coal gas as Lampland bangs around in the basement getting the brontosaural furnace to light. Lowell's rifles hang crossed above the stone mantelpiece as in some military insignia.

"Could be bigger, I guess," Clyde says, "if they had another mountain to put it on."

"It does sort of go back," Alan says, gesturing him into the creaking reaches of the old house.

They find Slipher in Lowell's office, where he is hurriedly unloading a box of files onto the broad desk. "She likes to look over the accounts,"

Slipher explains, with a sheepish glance at them. "So we oblige her. It's just easier that way."

"Some office," Clyde says. "You could jump a horse in here."

"Probably been done," Slipher notes, nervously.

"If you count Constance one of the horses," says Alan.

Slipher cracks a smile but says, "You just behave yourself. We've got enough trouble from Boston."

This is true enough. Constance has been making querying noises about who this Tombaugh figure might be, and Roger Putnam and Abbott Lowell have been asking for weekly progress reports; so the feeling is they are really under the gun. And of course they have found nothing. And worse than this, they have been receiving the occasional telegram from Florence Morrow, tidy sets of coordinates offering Alan and Clyde places to look for the planet. No one knows where she is getting these numbers or whether they are hoaxes or only meant to goad them, but they are worrisome as hell. None of them have checked out yet, but she is on their trail, anyway, no doubt about it.

Still. In Clyde's opinion you have to admire Lowell's style. He outfitted himself as the baron of Barsoom. There is a Martian globe, a pleasing orange-red sphere streaked with dark, starry tendrils: the canals. Spin it on its axis and it squeaks, a toy world. The shelves are packed with mathematical books that Alan is giving a once-over. The Oriental yields interestingly underfoot. Creaking leather and good wood everywhere, and a smell of old money. Imagine being Lowell, having Lowell's mad guts, to have dreamed all this up for himself. When he could have sat all his life in Boston. The view here gives you the mountains and the valley and the Martian plateaus beyond.

"Why the hell'd he marry her for, anyway?" he asks, as the question strikes him, "if she's so terrible?"

Slipher and Alan exchange a look.

"Curiouser and curiouser," Alan remarks.

"That," Slipher says, "was Percy's business." Slipher continues laying out his papers. There is one missing, and then he locates it and slips it in among the others. Then he looks up. "But what *I've* always wondered about, Tombaugh," Slipher continues, in his suddenly nervous, avuncular vein, "is where he hid the champagne. Supposedly somewhere in this house is a pretty good cache of bottles saved against the day when they found Planet X. Not that this would mean anything to you, Tombaugh, but Percy had a nose for a decent vintage. None of us have ever been able to turn it up. And we've had some hunts, over the years."

"It's a myth," Alan mutters. "It's not there to be found."

"Dick Morrow would have turned it up already," Clyde guesses.

"Oh, well, as to that," Alan says, "Dick wasn't very particular."

Slipher says, "Well, all your predecessors got fed up eventually, Tombaugh, and went stir crazy and took it out on the B.M. Not that I predict such a thing for you. But if you'd like to take a crack at it in the next few minutes, now's your chance."

"Well, I'm just still standing here wondering why he married her," he says, not to be turned aside. "If everyone knew she was so terrible."

"Well, you wonder away, Tombaugh." Slipher peers into the empty box and, satisfied, folds its flaps down and knocks it flat against his thigh. Then he scowls and says, "I mean hell, *I* don't know, Clyde. But then again I don't know why the hell anybody does anything."

"Especially Lowells," says Alan.

At which Slipher laughs once, mirthlessly. "Lowells included," he concedes.

They do not want to be observed in the B.M. or on the porch, so they all head together back to the steps of the library. The October day is brightening, the gray overcast sliding away in portions. The blue is revealed, and the sun. The round dome of the Main Building casts its oblong shadow on the hard dirt of the parking lot. Presently they hear a grinding noise from the road. The box-backed station wagon noses into view with the shadows of two women visible through the plastic windowpanes. The wagon veers away and parks at the far edge of the lot. The figures stir and climb down, one of them stout in black fur and the other a tall dried-out attendant. They aim themselves directly toward Percival Lowell's tomb.

"The pious widow," Slipher narrates. "And Mrs. Wroth, the faithful widowed friend and amanuensis."

The stout woman who must be Constance Lowell grips Mrs. Wroth's arm. At the tomb Mrs. Lowell goes down on a knee, and even at a hundred yards Clyde detects something of the phony as she flattens a hand over the marble and drops her head. If Roy were here they would cut up a little, but everyone stands in helpless silence in the feeble sun. After a minute Mrs. Wroth takes Mrs. Lowell's elbow and with a key opens the iron grate that stands across the tomb's entrance. The hinges give a hollow shriek, and the two women disappear into the vault together.

"Spooky," Clyde says, to cut the air.

"This is the routine," Slipher explains. "She does all this, then she comes over here to say hello."

Clyde can barely stand it.

Finally he mutters, "Maybe they died in there."

Lampland says mildly, "Show some respect, Tombaugh."

Clyde knocks his boot heels against the library steps.

"Be convenient, anyway," Alan offers.

"That's what I was thinking," Clyde says. "Just slide her right in."

Lampland takes two strides away and goes about the business of lighting a cigarette.

"That's enough," Slipher says gently.

"He's nervous, that's all," Alan says.

"I am not nervous," Clyde returns. But he does wish he were elsewhere, and this feeling only worsens when the two women emerge from the tomb and he is unexpectedly struck by some familiar aspect of their posture; they look tired and the October weeds are brittle against their boots and they go high-stepping slowly through the grass, and he is reminded, suddenly, of his stout mother walking alongside his spindly old aunt Grace, the aunt who in Burdett years ago would visit them for Thanksgiving, bringing green apple pie under a dishcloth and a bucket of bran rice each for the horses which she would feed them against his father's wishes as it contained too much phosphorus. He misses home suddenly and feels something give way. He has not been the most upstanding citizen away from home. Needling an old woman is only the latest example. Some private things he is not too proud of. He has a collection of dirty playing cards, for one. Now he has the urge to spit and stalk away, but he has to await her queenly audience like anyone else. But instead of the women coming toward them as expected, they go directly toward the B.M. and disappear inside without giving the waiting group so much as a glance. They pull the door shut, and all is quiet in the sunny lot.

"Oh, for chrissake," Slipher says.

Lampland chucks his cigarette into the gravel and goes without a word back through the library doors.

Mrs. Fox says, "I'll go see if they need anything in the way of groceries," and plucks up her skirt and steps down into the dirt, her walk animated suddenly by the prospect of new female company.

Clyde figures they are off the hook indefinitely. But half an hour later he is in the darkroom developing the second of the previous night's plates when a knock comes. He opens the door to Alan, who looks weirdly enlivened. "She wants to see us," Alan says.

"All of us?"

"Just you and me."

"What'd I do?"

"Oh, boy," Alan grins, "I can't wait to find out." And Clyde would buck, but Alan's enjoyment pleases him. Clyde shakes off the gauntlets and carries out into the light the new completed plate—Gemini, one of the places the planet has been imagined to be. He sets the precious plate in the rack, then shoots his cuffs and nudges his tie against his throat and, without knowing he is about to do it, lets go a whoop of nervous delight which echoes down the basement corridor. He has a flash of Roy beside him as he and Alan vault the stairs, that old brotherly feeling. The last ten months have been a trial, but now he is feeling something coming free. It cannot get much worse, possibly. Or Constance's visit will be the last straw, and he will finally, mercifully get the sack and be allowed to leave without embarrassment to anyone. Full of bounce, Clyde goes out across the sunny lot with his friend. It is all coming apart, and he is unaccountably full of joy; and neither of them say the name, but they are both thinking of Mary now.

21

Alan pinches out his cigarette and stows it as who knows what the old lady will think of him smoking. Surely she will find something to sweat him about, and he does not look forward to it. No, it is not in the least what he needs at the moment, this sort of command performance.

They are admitted to the B.M. by the sour attendant in blue, who moves with a rustle as though she is stuffed with straw. Mrs. Wroth brings them back into Lowell's office, where Constance fills an armchair by the window. She is as sturdy and corseted as before, in a black crepe dress that gives back in its many rounded parts a shine from the October light. She wears a black velvet hat of the sort his mother used to scoff at in 1916, with the veil forming a sort of upside-down bucket that reaches just to Mrs. Lowell's mouth. The veil is very dark so as to make her eyes impossible to see, but he can sense them on him anyway.

Blind his foot.

Mrs. Lowell occupies the room with a certain amused panache; she is in something of a different element than in the Beacon Street house but the same atmosphere of judgment and censure is evident, somewhat more freely let go. She is holding a set of papers in her lap as though she has just finished consulting them and she is aware of how this must look, it is as though she is daring anyone to point this out. The set of her mouth is somehow the giveaway; it is too challenging.

"Is that you, Mr. Barber?" she asks.

"Why Mrs. Lowell," he answers. "Pleased to see you again. Pleasant trip?"

"Oh, it was awful. I can't *sleep* on a train car. Percy used to work when we would come out together, and of course I can't do that, so I just sit up on cushions and think about things all night and sometimes I have Mrs. Wroth read to me. But you can feel the difference when you get here; the *air* is so *empty,* there's a sort of"—she inhales lustily through her nose— "*possibility* in the air when you get out here. And it smells so wonderful, now; I'm not usually out here in the autumn, and it smells different, doesn't it? And when I'm sitting in this office I can absolutely *feel* Percy here, I can imagine that he's sitting right over there"—she lifts a sturdy finger and aims it with artful imprecision at the baronial desk—"and that I'm sitting here, and that any minute he's going to say, 'Oh, Connie, how about a walk down to the barn?'" She drops her hand. "So yes, anyway, despite the terrible trip I'm *always* happy to be here in *my house.* Every time I get here I think, Now why did I ever leave? And you, Mr. Barber, you've been well?"

"Yes, ma'am, thank you."

"And your work is going accordingly?"

"Yes, ma'am."

"Except of course you haven't found anything yet."

"Not any planets, ma'am."

"Which is the only real objective as far as I know. I want to ask you about that presently, because I have a few questions for you about what's been going on around here. But did you bring the other one?"

Clyde says, "Clyde Tombaugh, ma'am."

Mrs. Lowell faces Clyde and says, "Now, Mr. Tombaugh. How do you do."

"How do you do, ma'am." Beside him Clyde has taken on a strange air, as though he has been called up in front of a class: sheepish, half smiling, fitfully rebellious. "It's a pleasure to meet you and to meet someone who was married to Percival Lowell, who was a personal hero of mine."

Mrs. Lowell grants Clyde a genial smile. "Well, he was one of mine as well, Mr. Tombaugh. You're aware he built this place from nothing, from absolutely nothing. There was *nothing* here when he started, just trees. When I first came here I couldn't believe what it was like, how *much* there was of it. Have you had a chance to explore much?"

"A little, ma'am."

"I imagine you're kept fairly busy."

"Yes," Clyde says. "We're just trying to keep up with ourselves most of the time."

She folds her hands around the sheaf of papers in her lap. "Do you know, you're a very mysterious figure to me, Mr. Tombaugh. You appear out of nowhere in January, and according to Mrs. Wroth you've been on these books ever since at ninety dollars a month, and I don't even really know who you *are*."

"Yes, ma'am."

"You're not one of Shapley's men from Harvard. I asked Roger about you, and he said you weren't one of his at all, he'd never even met you. *He* claims that you hadn't even been to *college*."

Clyde looks about ready to uncork one, but he bears it for now. "Not for lack of trying," he says.

"Don't you think that's very *strange* that you would be hired without a college degree to work at Lowell Observatory?"

"Honestly, ma'am," Clyde says, "I guess I do."

"And what is it you're able to *do* for us, if I may ask, without a college degree? Mr. Barber, is Mr. Tombaugh a sort of handyman?"

"A handyman?" he repeats, full of poison. "Oh, why *no*, ma'am, Clyde isn't a *handyman*."

"Is he a sort of young companion to you, Mr. Barber? I know you're not a married man."

"No, ma'am," he answers. Of course she knows who the hell Clyde is if she's talked to Putnam. Full of stifled rage, he jams his hands in his pockets and comes up against one of Florence's telegrams that he has been carrying around for days. It is the sixth they have received from her since January. As Clyde explains what he is doing and how it all works, Alan slowly wads it in his fist. He knows it by heart; it resembles all the others almost exactly.

> DEAR BARBIE:
>
> LIB 14583 S 0819 STOP
>
> LIB 14330 S 1749 STOP
>
> LIB 15297 S 0822 STOP
>
> —FLORRIE

It is a nightmare, that she would discover it before they do. Every telegram that arrives bears a list like this, a column of coordinates, each set corresponding to an especially interesting anomalous image on an old plate—and who else better to look into these than good old Barbie, who owes her something for having named a comet after her? And what is especially worrisome is that the last set of coordinates on this list exactly corresponds to a magnitude-10 object in Libra which Clyde just a week ago marked first as ? and then as V, variable star, which means Florrie is genuinely on the hunt, all right, and is doing just what Alan feared she would be doing: hunting for possible images of Planet X on the thousands of old Harvard College Observatory plates. He has not answered any of her telegrams, but he fears that eventually he will have to, because it will turn out to be the thing that points them to Planet X.

It is nearly too much. And he's out here, and poor Mary is at her wit's end, and he is faced with the ridiculous figure of Constance.

Clyde comes to the end of his recitation with a little rise onto his tiptoes as he describes the need to take exposures at opposition. It is shoptalk, but Alan sees that Mrs. Lowell has in fact been listening very carefully. She is no stranger to the mechanics of a planetary search, after all. "And is there no one else," she queries Clyde finally, "*assisting* you?"

"Well, Barber here."

"But Mr. Barber, I gathered that you were engaged in an entirely *different* enterprise. From what I gather from V.M. and from Roger, you're still wasting your time trying to correct Percy's math."

"I'm rerunning the residuals," he says.

"So you're not assisting Mr. Tombaugh at all."

"Well, only as he needs it. He's very capable. I'll put my hand in at the comparator now and then when the going gets rough."

"*Rough*," Mrs. Lowell scoffs.

"Tedious, ma'am."

"Tedious! Tedium never kept Percy from anything. I don't know what you expect, but maybe you're used to being treated softly. A little competitive spirit never hurt anyone. A little *fight*." She pushes on: "So you're telling me, Mr. Tombaugh, that you, a high school graduate without a college degree and without any formal education in the field whatsoever, are the sole man in charge of the entire Planet X search, with Mr. Barber putting his oar in as you happen to need it but only occasionally."

"Yes, ma'am."

"And you're operating Abbott's telescope all on your own, without supervision from V.M. or Dr. Lampland or Mr. Barber here or anyone."

Alan can't stand it, it's just too much. "But he doesn't need it, ma'am," he growls. "He's just doing exposures. You don't need a degree to take a photograph."

"It's not a matter of needing a degree precisely, Mr. Barber; it's more a matter of accounting for appearances. I suppose this doesn't make any sense to you as I have a feeling what your position is concerning appearances in general, you don't have much use for them. But consider how it might seem from *my* end." Mrs. Lowell accepts a cup of tea from Mrs. Wroth and sets it gently on her papered lap. "*All* this money, observatory money, not to mention Abbott's money and Roger's money, and not only what's been needed to build the astrograph but also to keep it maintained and to pay you, Mr. Tombaugh, your ninety dollars every month for nearly a year, during which you've found nothing, and to acquire the plates and the developer and everything else, and simply the expenses that are involved in keeping you *around*, Mr. Tombaugh, your mail and your laundry and keeping the upstairs of the Main Building presentable so that it doesn't look like a dormitory as I know it used to when Mr. Ross and Mr. Greene were here, all of that, and all the years that Percy spent looking for the planet, and all the time he spent on his calculations, and the computers who helped him with all of it, all of *their* years, and now that it's all up and running again the whole project is handed off to *you*, Mr. Tombaugh. Of all the people in the world it could be handed to, it is handed to *you*, and no wonder you've come up empty." She tests her tea. "I think you'd have to agree it just looks peculiar."

"You should see Barber's office," Clyde says. "He's been working for months."

"The residuals." Mrs. Lowell sighs. "Well, but that work has been *done*, Mr. Tombaugh. Poor Percy *did* it already. All those *years* he spent at it, and the only thing he lacked was the instruments, and now we've *got* them. I don't see what you hope to discover, Mr. Barber. Surely it's not a shortcut."

He says, uncomfortably, "It's by way of a backup."

"To this one," Mrs. Lowell clarifies.

"Just in case."

"So you too would seem to agree that putting this boy Tombaugh at the head of the whole search is a little peculiar."

"No," he parries. One has to be in the room with Clyde while he sits at the comparator to get a sense of how avidly Clyde goes after the plates, how stupidly, insanely patient he is, how uncomplaining he can be even in the face of a freezing fog that teases a milky veil over the sky and insinuates itself into the greased workings of the 13-inch and into your bones, so that even through the Navaho rugs and the buffalo robe you get a chill down your neck spreading to your core, to the heart of you. He is a hell of a worker is the point. "Of all the people in the world least likely to miss a suspect, Clyde is the one least likely to miss it. But you're talking fifty thousand objects on some of these plates. It's just common sense to give him some backup."

"But what else are we paying you to *do*, Mr. Tombaugh, anything else?" Constance has a lightsome air now. "Is this not to be expected of you, to not *miss* things on all these plates you're exposing?"

"If you could only see what one looks like," Clyde says, "maybe you'd understand."

She answers this with a tiny huff and turns to Alan again. "And all these useless reductions, surely that's not *all* you do. You must have *some* other means of occupying yourself. At a hundred fifty dollars a month you had better have."

"I'm with Dr. Slipher on the Variable Atlas."

"Still," she sighs. "Will it *ever* end."

"It's useful," he says. And it is very tiresome, but it is steady and uneventful and just the thing he needs now, as it leaves him time for the residuals and, more important, to tend to Mary. "And it keeps us in good with Shapley."

"Oh, *Shapley!*" she curses. "Shapley isn't anyone! Shapley's only there by *accident*; that should have been Percy's job, if he'd lived." She heaves another despairing sigh and mutters, "Take all this stuff off of me," and Mrs. Wroth sweeps down and removes her tea and the papers. "Mr. Barber, as you can imagine, the gossip doesn't get to me the way it used to, but I still manage to hear things eventually. I can't let you leave without my asking you about this business with poor Florence *Morrow*. What an outlandish thing for you to do."

He says, "It was a present."

"Roger told me all about it, and I couldn't *believe* it. I thought he was having fun with me. Of course I *know* the Morrows, so you would think I would have heard the story earlier, but somehow I hadn't. I like the Morrows. They're excellent people. The sort of people *Percy* would have liked. Unlike the crew that's evidently taken over out here." She ruffles, settles. "And no *wonder* you haven't found anything yet. It's pretty plain that *you* two don't have the faintest idea what you're *doing.*"

"Brother," Clyde sighs, in the parking lot.

Alan is seething, but he manages a cool tone: "It doesn't mean anything," he assures Clyde. "All she owns is that goddamned house. There's nothing else up here to her name, not even a goddamned stick of *furniture.* She's only here because she's too goddamned crazy to recognize nobody wants her around." He clumps Clyde on the shoulder. "So steady on, Mr. Tombaugh," he says.

And Clyde flushes with pleasure; it is one of the things he does fairly reliably. "Say hello to Mary for me," he says, "and see you after dinner."

It is not until Alan is halfway down the mountain that it occurs to him that Mrs. Lowell may well have known, too, about Florence's telegrams. He is sure they are all in cahoots back there, putting the screws on, and now he wonders whether in fact the old woman has something to do with Florence's constant barrage. Whether she has been put up to it, in order to keep them lashed to the wheel.

A little competitive spirit never hurt anyone indeed.

But he can't keep such a thing in front of him for long. He enters the dig office—the brick warehouse, once a great clutter and now a model of modern business methods thanks to Mary—hoping to discover her here. But it is only a chilly emptiness of bricks and crates. Mary's desk is stacked neatly with papers, but they give no clue as to her whereabouts. Her hat and coat and gloves are gone. So he goes to look for her. She is not in the Black Cat palavering over a cup of coffee with Mrs. DuPrie, as she has been lately sometimes; she is not stumping up and down the aisles of Babbitt's looking for something decent to wear; she is not at home hanging up wash behind the paling fence or stirring the laundry on the back porch with a paddle; she is not in the house sitting by the feeble fireplace warming her pretty knobby toes with her shoes beside the grate. He searches their little house coming across pleasureable evidence of Mary in the sink and the bedroom, but no girl. Then he plunks a chord on the pianola and follows it with a few more just to hear something sort of kindly after the pettiness of Constance. It is only a few days' visit, but he fears he won't be able to contain himself very well; but even this pales next to his concern for Mary, for his need to see her at once. He leans down and pets the cat McGurn, whose black fur is electric and full of dust. The old boy winks up at him peaceably. Alan then goes out the back door and through the wire gate to the alley where he mounts his Omega motorcycle and kicks it to life and heads out through town and out to the dig, where he knows for a certainty she must be. He is driven to be with her, to check on her like this; he cannot help it any more than he can help the beating of his heart. He has no idea how he might make her better, make her way easier. But he is trying, trying, to bring her something like contentment. She is all the world to him, and he knows she is suffering, and he can hardly bear it.

The road is well traveled and the Italian crewmen have left their litter all along it, papers mostly and a few bottles, and things have been blown off the truck as well as it motors along, scraps of canvas and splinters of wood as DuPrie ferries fossils back from the site to the railroad depot, where Mary is their station agent sending all such matters on to Washington. He steers the Omega on its thick tires through the ruts and down the one tricky turn that skirts a steep wash, and finally at the end of the road the dig comes into view. It is always a sight that stirs him, striking some old martial note: tents on a desert hillside and a cluster of men at work. DuPrie is there in his boots, wrestling a crate into the back of a truck with one of the crew, and Willoughby is loping along full of purpose. The Italians in their blue shirts are everywhere, and it takes him a minute to find Mary but he does, crouched in a pit with a chisel in hand, a blue bandanna over her hair and a cigarette burning in a smashed tin can she is using as an ashtray. She has been coming out more often and the crew have accepted her to the point of being able to ignore her. He waddles the bike to a stop and leans down. She is his beauty, all right, and what strength she has he can barely conceive. She has been holding it all at bay for nearly a year.

"Hello there, Jim," she says, wiping dust from her eye. "You look like you've seen a ghost."

"In a way. The old lady's finally come to town."

"Ooh," she croons. She blinks and wipes again, adding a long smear to her cheek. She goes for the cigarette and settles on her haunches like a Chinaman. "How is it up there? All hands on deck, I bet."

"We got a little taste of her."

"You've seen her already?"

"We both did. We got called on the carpet."

She likes this. "Serves you right," she says, "for making it with me on all her various ottomen."

"And there's going to be a dinner tomorrow," he offers. "We might get all dolled up. Like the old days."

She goes on pecking at the rock with the chisel until a smile creeps over her face as she pictures them all there in the B.M. "I hope we covered our tracks all right," she says.

"Yes, ma'am."

"But maybe she can detect us," she says, "using her special powers of apprehension."

"Maybe, Mare," he offers. Possibly this is a nutter's line, or possibly it is only a joke. The two can live fairly close sometimes. And in fact he does worry a little that they have left evidence of their travels in the B.M. He and Mary have roamed the cellar hunting for Lowell's old wine by matchlight, picking over the pharaoh's tomb, opening boxes and reading old mail and seed catalogs, making themselves at home. So maybe he does want to be a Lowell, and Florrie was right, after all. Well, who wouldn't?

There is a shout from down the hill as one of the crew levers a plaster-wrapped bulk from the pit. Mary turns. "They think that's the last of the Steg," she observes. "Just in time to see it, Jim."

A round of applause runs raggedly over the slope, through the tents. Even Frank comes out and slaps his big yellow palms together. Mary climbs up and leads him downhill to see. It is as usual nothing to him, just an ugly white mass on the ruined soil. Mary grips his arm, looks intently into the pit. And sure, he knows what she's looking for, for the bone man, for evidence of him. He knows she can't help it, any more than he can help his rush of ferocious love.

"That's all done," DuPrie calls to her, from across the pit, passing his hand down his beard. "What do you think of that, Mrs. Barber?"

She calls, "A hole now completely safe for human beings."

"Yes, ma'am," he returns.

"No, actually Clyde's the one who should look out," she whispers, leaning into Alan. "You want to tell Clyde he's running into trouble; he's about to run into trouble now that she's here. She knows the whole story, I think. Or she will soon enough."

"Poor Clyde," he sighs, "he really got it in the teeth."

"Maybe he had it coming," she suggests; and there is something new, something hard in her voice, and they stand together at the edge of the pit and watch the Italians come up out of it, birthed from the soil, one after another, and she can't take her eyes away, as she counts them under her breath, watches the hole even after it is empty, until he gently pulls her away.

22

But she is tough as hell. The last ten months have taught her that, at any rate, if she hadn't known it already. Jim drops her at the office to finish the day's work. She washes her face and hands until the water runs clear, and then for each of DuPrie's and the others' little speculative dig notes she rolls a fresh sheet of Premium Bond into the typewriter and whangs out the complete version, as in:

1. See Hauff's related work on Plateosaurus from the Holzmaden shales.
2. Contra. Deperet and Dollo on directional development.
3. With Hauff and Heune this is another instance of losing a trait just before extinction. Therefore Deperet and Dollo are contradicted.
4. Support for a synthetic theory of evolution rather than a progressive.

As she finishes these she hands them over to DuPrie, who rests his spectacles on his nose and nods in agreement, then turns away abstracted to his books. She steps swiftly across the room and with a hard push of her thumb affixes the note to its proper crate with a brass tack; then she comes tocking back and sweeps down into her chair again and settles her fingers on the typewriter keys.

"Next," she orders herself aloud.

When she speaks aloud it is because she is used to having a listener, although the bone man has still not found her, not yet. She left him on the streetcar all those months ago in her rush to Hollis, and she has been with

Hollis and Alan since then and so, possibly, protected. Or possibly the new tusk is hard for him to find; it does not smell the same or it doesn't have the legendary feel of the old one, so he has found someone else to ride along with.

Oh, madness. It is so wearying to *convince* herself all the time. To argue against the evidence of her own mind. Especially when the new tusk is so smooth, fresh, springy, sensitive. It bows and bends. As she sits at the desk she tests it out, sends it whipping from side to side, you can almost hear it cut the air. A weapon, it could be, if she could aim it properly.

DuPrie is not a man who makes passes. They work in silent tandem across the chilly space, she at the typewriter and he redoing his sketches so as to pass his own muster. He is a devil for the drawing, and while not minding others' laxities he holds himself to a higher standard. Never, as he claims, will he draw an apple as perfect as the apple he drew the night before the *Tarsal* was lost. There is a spiritual element to this of some kind, whose mysteries she has not exactly pierced. And like Mary he has his own staring strangenesses too. Now and then he will be seen to subside at his desk with the knife in one hand, paring down his lead, and he will observe the curls of cedar shavings from the drawing pencil with such abstraction that he is surely on that boat again, wherever it is, or in the rowboat heaving through the midnight sea. His attention to detail has something to do with this, some sort of loyalty to lost things is involved, but he is elusive on the topic and appears embarrassed by it so she hasn't really pressed. And if you're rich, who cares what you do, anyway? He has no sexual life whatsoever, it appears, and he is devoted to his sweet, fading mother, who now doesn't much emerge from the house except to put her face out for the sun or, rarely, to accompany through the little town a visitor from the East who has come to see them in their desert encampment. Then the dig office will fill with a proud bustle as women in fantastic hats come sweeping through exclaiming their disbelief. The fashions have moved on subtly, but enough to make Mary feel provincial again, and as the swells come past her desk she finds herself suddenly shy. They take her for a local; they ask about the Canyon train. Every morning at seven o'clock exactly, she tells them. Three dollars round-trip, including a bucket lunch. They don't stare at her horn; they don't stare at all. Only once she overhears a woman say *She ought to be in magazines.*

It is possible that she is slightly less beautiful than she was a year ago. The shadows under her eyes are more insistent, and some firmness has entered her jawline that appears new to her. She keeps waiting for it to go away again, but it doesn't. The blue eyes are still the principal feature, and the body remains trim. Nothing will ever undo her marvelous straight pretty nose. But she has now lived in Arizona for nearly a year, and the sun will take its toll, and the dust, and the labor; she can foresee the crow's feet that will pinch her eyes, and in the seamed and furrowed necks of the Italians she can observe a possible future. She applies cream and scarves and tries to rest up when she can. And added to this is the great strain of trying to keep hold of her sanity; she knows this takes a toll as well. In a strange way it's nice to see she can get older, she can look a little worse-for-wear; it is comforting somehow to her. It is what happens to normal human people; they get older like this, in this comforting normal sort of way.

It has been a long ten months for her, and when she is thinking most clearly she can congratulate herself on how well she has done. At first it was still possible to believe that Hollis had just played some kind of nasty joke and that he would reappear, beat to hell or fucked out but alive and well. In the first few weeks after their arrival in Arizona she sat at DuPrie's desk and wrote letters to everyone she could think of: Scotty and the boys in Boston and at Weber's, and mayors and chiefs of police in Abbyville and Hutchinson and all the other little towns down the line. Additionally she visited the station agent, a blond boy with angry pimples on his neck, and stood there while he telegraphed the description of Hollis down the line. She received a chill from picturing Hollis frozen in a ditch some- where. But she believed him too canny to have met with a foul end. More likely he simply boarded the next train to California, where he has now taken up a new life. She is still angry at him but it doesn't diminish her longing to see him again and the sensation that if he would turn up every- thing would be better.

After her letter campaign she received a few answers back, and every time the Kansas postmark turned up it sent a funny electric charge up her spine. No one had seen him, but everyone promised to keep an eye out. And there is still a sense that if she can only angle her thoughts correctly he will simply appear out of thin air. She has this sort of power, it seems, with her knitting neglected in its basket beside the fireplace. If she sits like this in the front room of their little house as the train goes through at midnight, she can catch the ghost of him on it somehow; she can snare him from the ether as the past of him wheels by. A few times Jim has returned from Mars Hill and found her asleep in her shoes, and she has been wakened by him playing the piano to her.

"Running out again?" he asks.

"Just sitting up for you, Jim," she tells him.

And it still does the trick for her: music. She will sit and listen for as long as he cares to play, and it soothes her, at any rate. It no longer cures her, that is too much to hope for; but it brings her some relief.

When she finishes her night's notes she ducks her tusk under the doorway and passes into the cold. As is her habit, she looks both ways carefully before stepping into the middle of the empty street. It is only three blocks home but she walks in the center of the street the whole way so there are no surprises. She knows the boneman is still hunting her, so she is like a deer there, antlered and wary, her heels loud on the new concrete.

At home Jim has worked up a little dinner for them. Jim is his usual handsome self, his boots unlaced and his jacket slung over the chairback. He has the latest telegram from Florrie smoothed on the table, and she takes it up and examines it. The "Barbie" grates on her as always; it makes claims. "I think Constance knows what Florrie's up to," Jim whispers. "I think she's got it all planned out so Florrie'll get the credit. I wouldn't put it past her."

"That bunch," she says. "But what could she do? All she's got is money."

"I don't know. I've got his journals, so that's not it."

She considers this and what it does to poor Jim. It burdens him. She wishes she could help somehow; but she can't. And now that Mrs. Lowell is here, it is all that much worse. It seems to her the signal of some end, that they have had long enough to work and now they are being relieved, that the next wave is coming. Mrs. Lowell and the boneman, come to take it all back. After they have eaten they go out bundled up and walk arm-in-arm toward the observatory, where they will meet up with Clyde. He is a funny sweet kid, but of course he is from Kansas so it's possible that he might somehow lead the boneman here, and that he has something to do with the whole operation. That Clyde is the *secret key*. You drop one off there, and a few weeks later another one returns, very different but still. It makes you wonder.

The tusk never leaves her now, but she is not sure whether she wants it to go. It is a part of her. Dr. Miller would be disappointed, but look at her springing step as she enters the Main Building with Alan, and as she tips it to and fro, tasting the air; there is a dusty leathery wisdom here, an old protective wizardry permeating the halls. They find Clyde in the basement getting his supplies together for the night at the telescope. He is stuffing the pockets of his tweed jacket with cookies wrapped in napkins. "You heard about my afternoon," he says.

"I guess you've had long enough," she tells Clyde. "Time to let somebody else have a chance."

"Fine by me." Clyde shrugs into his buffalo robe and buttons it to his knees. "She's not out there, is she?"

"Coast is clear," Jim says. "She's in the B.M. spinning her web."

Clyde loops the strap of the plate satchel to his shoulder and slaps it gently and follows them upstairs, like a sophomore in a raccoon coat. They part ways in the upper hall, where he gives her his old fond, loyal look. There is as always something waiting in his expression, in the midway hesitation of his posture. He wants to tell her something; but instead Clyde turns to Jim and says, "Good luck tonight."

"Find it, would you?" Jim answers. "Get her off our backs."

"I'll be damned." Clyde shoulders the door open, and the cold wind enters. "I should have thought of that a while ago."

In the library she arranges herself in front of the fire and reads the newspaper until she almost sleeps, the sidereal clock ticking on the mantel and her good, faithful Jim at work with his pencil and coffee and the long night ahead of him. She is safe here, she intuits; the accumulated strangeness of Percival Lowell in some way inoculates this place to other varieties of peculiarity. She can sleep here, anyway. At some point a blanket settles over her; it is Dr. Slipher arranging one of Mrs. Fox's furs over her sleeping form. They do not know what a fantastic creature she is, what she might be capable of. Drawing signals from the air, she might even be able to find a planet, if anyone asked her to.

She can *feel* it sometimes, as she sweeps the sky. Absent but sending out its signals.

And still, faintly, in her momentary comfort, she knows this is madness, and there is still the sense of clinging desperately to the steep slope of a hill; but there is a growing sense, too, of the deliciousness of her coming fall; of the rightness of it; the glory that will come of it; and what a relief it will be.

23

As for Felix, he returns to the house and picks up the evening mail from the hall table. There is a letter from his mother's dressmaker Polly among all the usual run of business. The house is quiet except for Prudencia in the kitchen. There is no evidence of his mother's having been down that day. But this is not surprising. His mother is shriveling up, as she has been all through 1929. Now a gap has opened between the collar of her bedclothes and her narrowing neck, and her hands shake when she pours out the afternoon tea and carries the saucer and cup to her extended, monkeyish lips. Her eyes swim in a pool of excess liquid, not tears but some thicker fluid, which dries unbecomingly on her drooping lids. Felix mentions none of this. He does not, for official purposes, take notice of his mother's body. And yet he notices; and she observes him noticing, and her jaw firms and she sips defiantly and affects not to care as the tea slops onto her lap. She is old. Dr. Yost visits on occasion and slips out of the house without giving anything away, but Felix is sure she is in a steep decline.

It is terrible to think of. Largely he avoids it.

Still, they have lasted this long. They outlasted first the terrible bitter winter and then the hot dry summer, and they have discovered the pleasures of the in-between seasons, February and now October. "There's a note here saying your dress is ready," he tells her from the doorway.

"Oh!" she starts, and slaps the bed gently. "Well, all right, that's good news. Would you get Prudy up here, I want to go try it on. It's my special occasion dress that didn't fit because I'm shrinking."

He flushes at this and says, "I'll just go get it, mama."

"Well, *you* can't *try it on* for me, I hope," she scolds. "I'd like to see you do that. And Polly's such a useless thing, she'll never come *here*. You just *wait*." Prudencia passes him in the hall, and he changes his own duds and stirs the fire until his mama comes downstairs wearing fur, carrying a ghost of her old bearing. "Now," she says, greeting him.

"That's more like it," he tells her.

She sighs, then draws a long, shuddering breath. "Out we go," she flutes sadly.

She peps up in the October chill. They pass the Pure Food Bakery and the Black Cat, where the observatory people have their midday meal, and the Power Hat Shop ("everything guaranteed a year out of fashion at least," his mother comments), Dr. R. O. Raymond's medical office ("he's a very *very* old man"), and the New York Store ("they have some all right things in the area of household goods and a few clothes"), and the Black Bar ("I think Prudy goes in there sometimes; I believe they serve coloreds").

"Connie Lowell is here," he mentions.

"Oh, I know it," she answers. "I already got the letter in the noon mail. Well, the summons."

"We'll go up together."

"I suppose we must. She's a *very* strange woman, Felix. Ninny Larch spent a weekend with that bunch twenty years ago and she *still* talks about it. You know why they had their honeymoon in a hot air balloon? Because she thought they could really go to the *moon* in one."

"Oh, stop."

"It's quite true. Ninny was *there* at the *wedding*."

They walk along meditatively for a minute, avoiding horse apples.

"Do you know what else the widow Lowell is known for, Felix?" his mother continues. "She is known for being very unforgiving toward people who try to put one over on her. I mean you come to expect a certain amount of chicanery from people when you've got money, but she takes it all very personally. She doesn't like to be *tricked*. In fact I think that's finally what made her fight so hard to keep all of her husband's money. Mr. Slipher thinks it's only greed, you know, but *I* think she felt affronted.

Not only that someone was trying to fleece her, she felt it was as though her husband had played a trick on her, leaving it all to the observatory." She grips his arm as they step up onto the next sidewalk. "Really a double trick, after dying in the first place, then to cheat her out of her inheritance."

He cannot say much about dying without feeling he is entering strange territory; she still remembers his remark from Christmastime.

"It *is* like a trick, isn't it?" she prods. "I mean when somebody goes and dies."

"A disappearing act," he offers.

"Now you see them," she sniffs, satisfied for the moment, "and now you don't."

They enter Miss Polly's, a small brick storefront, where she will run you up something presentable if you don't mind waiting two weeks, and if you don't mind the way she does things, with the in-stitching of an industrial strength, as though you are going to mine gold in the thing. "Take this, for example," his mama says, whisking a sleeve from under her fur in the light of the shop. "You see that. She couldn't do anything like that, how the seam is just invisible there. *That's* from Welch's. But she's all we've got. You're lucky; you can just throw any old thing on, and people think you're a cowboy."

At this dark end of the afternoon the shop is quiet. Bolts of fabric are shelved on one wall. Along another wall stand two long tables overhung with electric lights, where two young women are cutting and sewing, their heavy steel scissors producing a violent slicing sound. "Good afternoon," his mother calls boldly.

Miss Polly—young, fat, hangdog, hair awisp—comes forward reluctantly. "Mrs. DuPrie."

"You have it done, finally."

Miss Polly sighs, turns away with a bovine docility, and returns in a minute with an orange dress and Mary's old scarf that served as the color match. "Oh, where did you get that *scarf*?" his mother had exclaimed months ago. And Mary had snaked the thing off her neck and mentioned Hardeur. "Well, it's *just exactly* the color I've been looking for," his mama had insisted, some turn of flattery or ingratiation. But then she had had the dress made in fact, in just that color orange.

"I don't know what took you so long."

"It's the tricky bits in the back," Polly answers. "We had to take it all apart and put it all back together again. We had it right the first time, but then you wanted it smaller."

"Indeed," his mama returns, "it must have been terrible to have to do some real *fashioning* for once. Felix, would you mind waiting for me just a minute, dear." His mother goes tottering around the counter, and Miss Polly follows her mutely into a dressing area. So it is that Felix sees, for a moment, before the green Silvel curtain swiffs down off its hook, his mother's torso exposed in its complicated trussing, the straps and buckles wound punishingly tight over her narrow frail shoulders, and on her face a hard look of determined indifference as she allows Miss Polly to begin her business. Felix turns away, scalded by the sight and feeling a pulse of helpless love for her, for the woman who tended his scraped knees and listened consideringly by as he explained to her the wonders of astral tele-portation. Love, affection, loyalty, a pure drowning need for her. But alongside this too he gathers the distinct impression that she doesn't much want to be loved right now. That she is up to something else entirely— something that has nothing to do with him.

He has continued the shedding of his former life. To that end, he passed off all the duties of running DuPrie Enterprises entirely to a board of respectable men. While retaining ownership, he freed himself of every responsibility. His various other holdings have been administered by other worthy gentlemen, and going by the figures in the bank accounts he has chosen well. He has not shed the memory of his father apopleptic in bed and speechless, the disfiguring sorrow of paternal disappointment plain in his stricken eye; but he has freed himself of nearly everything else his father attempted to hand on to him. And so he also gave up most of his old clothes (he handed them out to the workmen, who took them rever-ently and salted them away in their trunks to be worn on Sundays and feast days) and put aside whatever old ambitions he still held in the area of discovering anything about the nature of Truth. If there was such a thing, he was not worthy of it. Or he was going about it all wrong somehow. At any rate, he was done with it as a going concern. As for his mother, he is working up to the moment when he can admit she is going to be gone. He faces it as he would a door on the other side of which waits—something. Something, he hopes, rather than nothing.

After they carry the dress home in its flat box and she is in bed again that night, he takes himself back to the office. It is cold in the big warehouse, and he tips some kindling into the stove and whangs the grate to. In his coat and hat and gloves he stands at his desk paging through his drawings. He is critical of his performance but in fact he is not that bad. When the heat is up he sheds the gloves and seats himself and discovers again, despite everything, that sweet area of peaceability has remained behind his shoulders. It is what remains of his old hunt for God, a remnant of God in his body. The peace came to him long ago, in that high cave with Willoughby; it has never exactly left him, though he has otherwise given up his search for anything like Meaning. Possibly it is this feeling that has allowed him to let it go.

Now in the lamplight he allows that peace to snake down his arm and into the pencil and to produce, through the diminishing graphite point, a convincing shadow of bone. He will sit here for a while longer, without really a thought in his mind, and when he is done with the drawings sometime after midnight, he will put them away in a loose folder. By any standard Lightning Creek has been a productive site; Willoughby and his men (and Felix, more and more) have identified fossil traces of forty-one dinosaur species and have removed, along with the Stegosaurus and the Camptosaurus, complete or nearly-complete fossils of six other species. He does not know exactly why it is important to have demonstrated that the Morrison Formation extends this far south, but they have. Isenbright communicates from Washington once in a while, sending them a wire of congratulations or a photograph of their fossils all spruced up and ready for mounting. Felix likes this; he particularly likes having proved himself to a man who knew his father, at least a little bit. But mostly Felix is satisfied just to do his work, to read his books and make a midnight pot of coffee on the stove and drink it off slowly, resting his boots on the iron lip of the cooker and then removing them when they get too hot and start to stink. Much later he will look up from his books and see the street becoming light and not know where the time has gone. Possibly he has slept a little. Anyway it is nearly morning. Swinging over the aeons he has lost an entire night, as though the planet is extracting some tax, some repayment, for his being so sunk in its deep and secret history. As though somewhere some accounting is being kept, so it all comes out to nothing in the end.

Willoughby comes knocking into the office with a scarf over his face and says, "Morning, boss."

"Good morning."

The days when Felix considered the Italians to be gangsters are long past. Only just men. Like Felix himself. They are good and steady workers and have fended off those poachers against whom Willoughby warned him so many months ago. No one has yet fired a shot as far as Felix knows, but there have been some ragged types wheedling in and they have been successfully deflected. A dig attracts all kinds of curiosity seekers, he has found. Most of them harmless.

But it is the Italians he has come to appreciate. Some warmth of culture, some knowing joyousness that he finds appealing, better surely than the stiffs he grew up with. He has actually come to know some of them as they will allow themselves to be known. He is acquainted with Gaetano's small round wife, Maria, who has lately arrived, and the two are keeping house in a cottage in Mexicantown. The skull Gaetano gave him, with its purple geodic crystals, still sits on his mama's dresser. It is good to have these people around, not friends but familiar to him. Willoughby is so familiar to him as to almost defy observation, but in the peculiar light of first morning he looks his age, which is somewhere around fifty. Felix administers the last cup of coffee to Willoughby, who downs it with a powerful grimace.

"You ever made coffee in a paint can?" Willoughby asks, hefting his canvas sling of tools.

He hasn't.

"Might be an improvement," is Willoughby's opinion.

In the morning light he crosses the road and says good-bye to his mama for the day. She is still in bed eyeing the orange dress now on its form at the end of the room. "Kiss me, Felix," she commands, and he brushes her soft furry cheek with his lips.

"You'll be all right for the dinner?" he asks.

"Oh, yes. I wouldn't miss it."

He squeezes her hand. "Don't make trouble while I'm gone," he tells her.

"I've made enough already," she answers, faintly.

He squeezes her hand again, surprised by a wave of sorrow too large to manage gracefully, nothing he wants his mother to see. He swallows and turns and leaves her in the dim room. His mama. Outside he takes himself the two blocks to the stable, where he saddles Sissie for the ride to the dig. She is a good gentle beast, and he pets her glossy neck gratefully. Alongside Willoughby on Picobel they cross the scrubby desert. He is so quiet as to prompt Willoughby to ask, "You all right?"

"I am fine, Will," he answers.

Everyone back home has heard of his shipwreck and his later success on Lightning Creek, and while he is vaguely conscious of himself as a certain, even, *dashing* figure, it does not enter much in his daily consideration of himself. He works all day in the pits, and very truly it is not meant for consumption Back East. So he is surprised to find himself troubled to think of Mrs. Lowell being here, this potent reminder of the life they once had. The *Tarsal* has never been discovered; they have not been back to Maryland; he has come to think of Arizona as a second home. What can be troubling him? Possibly Mrs. Lowell is only a reminder of everything he lost already—and all he is going to lose for good when his mother is no longer there.

But even Mary Barber seemed bothered by Mrs. Lowell; how strange she suddenly became yesterday evening, how still and anxious, full of stern mutterings. It would appear the woman sends off a powerful signal in all directions.

Or possibly, he thinks, kneeing Sissie forward, there is indeed some last bit of accounting left for he himself to do, some last attachment to dissolve; something still unsolved remaining. He worries at it as Sissie carries him along. Imagines Mrs. Lowell on the mountaintop, peering down at them all through one of her husband's old telescopes.

Peculiar thought.

24

With a suspicious heart Clyde heads into the New York Store. He is naturally stingy, and the idea of spending money on clothes is repellent to him. The plaid Prince of Wales is $5.98, and he fingers it thoughtfully.

"*Plaid*, Clyde?" Alan whispers.

He says, "I guess not."

Alan is looking at him worriedly. "No, no, no, Clyde. *No.*"

He says, "Not the thing for dinner at the Lowells, I guess you mean."

"Not unless you're looking to start a fight," Alan tells him.

The plain blue serge is $9.98, three buttons. He picks out a pair of shirts for $1.35 apiece and a wool felt hat for $3.00 and a pair of good leather shoes for $7.75.

"You can borrow a decent tie," Alan says.

Clyde has to swallow hard at the counter before handing over the money. When he unwraps his packages in his room that afternoon, he hangs the suit cautiously in the closet and decides to wear the shoes in order to begin breaking them in. They are stiff as he wedges his feet in, but they do shine. And at least he won't feel like a fool sitting down to eat. He goes squeaking along the corridor and downstairs to start the first of the Taurus plates. He flexes his toes as he puts himself on the stool, and in a moment he finds an asteroid and brings his pencil point up to mark it. This little rock, tumbling on its solitary path. In another year or so he will have marked them all, which will be a hell of an accomplishment all its own. But he means to find Planet X, if it exists (and he has his doubts by now), in no small measure in order to make Alan happy, and he wants to do that for the sake of Mary. He recalls her grip on his arm, and for a while as the stars flicker before him he simply feels that pressure, the exact shape of it.

He knows Mary's secret by now, and it is this that pushes him on as much as anything. He continues blinking as he perches there in his new shoes, holding her heart in his hands. A secret admirer. A secret guardian and protector in brand-new McCanns. Mary will rib him over them, he is sure of it. But he smiles, imagining what she might say.

"You going to see a movie with her, Kansas?" for example.

And anyway, how they shine!

He does all his work without worry, it is by now all second nature to him; but 1929 has been a long year for him, and there have been times when he has considered pitching it all and climbing onto the westbound train for San Francisco himself. None of what he had read in the library in Burdett had mattered, and at first he was deadly homesick all the time. But there was no going home either, not a chance. He had said good-bye to his father by shaking his hand in the morning warmth of the station, but the presence of others restricted what they could say to each other, if they had anything to say to begin with.

"I hope you like it out there," his father said. "You can always come back here if you feel the need. I mean I hope you will."

"I might be back next week," Clyde said. "I don't know exactly what they want me to do, anyway."

"They said a trial period," his father said.

"Sure. But they might just hang me outright," Clyde answered.

"Well," his father countered, plunging his hands into the depths of his overall pockets. They had spoken only a little about it after he had charged into the barn, full of angry triumph, and Clyde had the sense his father was trying to smooth things over between them before he went away. "I'm sure they had their reasons for asking you."

It was as close as they were going to come to making it any good between them. At a loss, they moved to the depot window and stood for a little while naming the people they saw, until the brass collars of the light fixtures began to rattle and they heard the locomotive chuffing at the edge of town. When Clyde stepped aboard he waved good-bye, leaning out as in the movies, one hand on the chrome handle and a boot on the waffled iron step. Inside the train smelled of a recent bacon breakfast and the heated grease that lubricated the couplings. When he found a seat there was his father through the window exactly where he had left him, against a pillar with his hands buried and watching his eldest son go off west. You imagined there was some envy there, but you couldn't see a trace of it. A flick of the eybrows, and the man turned as the train began to move.

Later on Clyde will admit that at this moment he had to fight to keep from crying like a child.

You examine yourself at such a moment to see what you are made of. To speak literally, Clyde darted a hand behind his lapels and tugged out from his pocket a few things to occupy him, including the new issue of *Popular Science* with Wilbur and Orville Wright on the cover ("The true inside story of the FATHERS OF FLIGHT *never before published* begins in this issue") and Dr. Slipher's letter with its envelope, and a timetable of the Santa Fe Railroad, which he now opened in order to keep a record of their punctuality. They were twelve minutes late leaving Larned. They were eleven minutes late leaving Kinsley. They were eleven minutes late arriving at Dodge City but only six minutes late when they left. Then they were in Gray County, and the Arkansas River ran alongside the track, twisting and shining in the sun, and he failed to note whether they were late through Cimarron or Ingalls or Pierceville.

The seat across the aisle was empty except for an abandoned newspaper, the *Chicago Tribune* of January 13, 1929. The old familiar script of the afternoon edition produced in him a friendly jolt of recognition. Wyatt Earp was dead at eighty in a seedy Los Angeles bungalow, of chronic cystitis, whatever that was; it sounded like something interesting you might get from a life of corruption, but the old gunslinger made it to his eightieth year so he must have been doing something right as well.

The seatbacks cast their shifting morning shadows into the aisle, eight triangles that moved in graceful curving unison as the train swung under the winter sun.

Oh, he was happy.

He was not the best son in the world, but then again the old man was not the best father. He sat in light, watching Kansas pass, with the wheels saying *contentedly, contentedly, contentedly.*

And what was it like to see Lowell Observatory for the first time? Like finding the place he was meant to be. That this was his old home and now he had come back to it, his soul feeling the rich vibrations of the return. Slipher took him around first to meet everyone and to see the telescopes. Clyde slapped the freezing barrel of the Clark with his gloved hand and barked aloud with delighted laughter as he tugged it up and around. Then later he stood soberly in the cold staring at the empty barrel of the 13-inch astrograph with his hands in his armpits while Slipher ran through the frightening particulars of astrophotography. He breathed in the piney cold scent of the winter hilltop and looked admiringly over the scenic vista that presented itself from the lookout. It was strange to be up so *high*, and he had the weird conviction of the prairie boy that the mountain might just fall over. But here was Percival Lowell's tomb itself in a snowdrift and the marble stained a little gray in places, and here was even a nice old cow to befriend, named Venus, comfortable in her warm winter barn chewing her hay and accepting the attentions he gave her. "Hello, you pretty old girl," he said.

He thought it was a little strange that no one would tell him what he was there for exactly, and why it would be so important to take these hundreds of pictures of the ecliptic, but he was happy enough just to be in what seemed to him a version of paradise. They gave him a room and a desk, and then Alan Barber knocked on his door, peering skeptically at him. Clyde was setting out his few meager clothes in the dresser and sorrowing a little over his ugly boots. But he forgot all this when he heard that they were looking for Planet X.

"You're kidding me," he said.

Alan Barber stood with his arms folded at Clyde's doorway. "I'll be damned. Slipher didn't even tell you."

"*That's* why we're photographing the ecliptic."

"Photographing, nothing. It's the blinking that'll kill you. You see the comparator?"

"I got a look at it. Dr. Slipher said you'd be training me."

"Some fun. We'll have the whole ecliptic to go through with that thing. Plus twenty degrees on either side, just to be safe."

"Twenty degrees. That's a lot of looking."

Barber said, "You have no idea."

He put this together for a minute. Placing himself. It sounded a little nutty, but on the other hand this was a real observatory and Alan Barber was from Harvard and that was the real-life Vesto Slipher downstairs smoking his pipe. "This is top-secret or something?"

Barber laughed. "Not exactly. But I wouldn't go boasting about it unless you like people measuring you for a wraparound jacket."

"And what're you doing meanwhile?"

"Meanwhile I'm sitting with you for a few weeks, however long it happens to take, getting you up to speed. We'll get going on the 13-inch when it's all assembled; we'll get you up to speed on the comparator, teach you how to develop a plate since you haven't done that at all. Then I've got my own angle."

"Which is what?"

"A regression analysis of orbital residuals using the method of least squares."

"Whistle that five times fast."

"I can go as slow as you like," Barber said.

"That's what they're teaching at Harvard these days."

"Not really," Barber grinned. "That's why I'm out here."

He had been prepared to be made fun of, but actually he sort of liked this Barber, he liked the set of him; he was high-class without putting a number over. "So what the hell'd you pick me for?"

"Oh, I didn't pick you," Barber said. "Slipher did."

"What for?"

"I guess he thinks you work cheap," Barber answered. "And you can evidently aim a telescope."

"I'll be damned."

"I guess that was one lucky letter."

"I'll say. Remind me to play the horses sometime." But he felt a sick little swoop, a return of that feeling as he watched Mike Landry take the letter away. He hated this idea, that life was so goddamned chancy. "Honest to goodness, Planet X?" he asked. "You're not kidding?"

Barber stepped into the room and turned Clyde's other chair around and sat on it backward. He lit a cigarette, offered the pack across to Clyde, who declined. "Lowell spent ten years looking for X out here too, only he didn't have the right equipment. Hadn't been invented yet. Didn't have the comparator. Didn't have the good triplet for broad fields like we're getting. He just couldn't find it."

"Slipher said it was a Brashear lens."

"Brashear lens"—Barber smoked—"by way of Lundin brothers, by way of A. Lawrence Lowell, by way of Joel Metcalf himself."

Clyde reeled a little and tossed his hat on the dresser. "Christ almighty, that'll be the day." He knew he shouldn't be allowed within twenty yards of such a wonder. And on the other hand—let him at it. He went to the window to look at the snowy parking lot. "Brother," he said. "How big is it, supposedly?"

"Not quite the size of Neptune," Barber said. "We think."

"How far out?"

"About 45 AU."

"What's that magnitude, about a 12?"

Barber said, impressed, "You're not all farmboy, anyway."

"Magnitude-12 object, and no idea where it is? At all?" Clyde felt his new stubble. "How long'll that take? About two hundred exposures? Just to take them that's a year right there, even if you've got good skies; you'll want to take double exposures to get the blinking done, and that's a good year all on its own." He gaped. "That's crazy."

Barber laughed and propped his cigarette in the corner of his mouth and stuck out his hand. "Welcome to Lowell Observatory," he said.

He'd never had a hero before exactly, but Barber promised to fit the bill. Sure, the clothes, for one thing, and the pair of battered old Masterpiece boots that even Barber liked to admire, turning his ankle while he sat with his legs crossed at the knee. And that tone, where you pulled on the cigarette and squinted one eye and drawled something good out. Harvard as hell, all right. And he had a girl he was living with and wasn't even married to.

And what a girl. You didn't see this type on the farm, that was for certain. Nor even long ago when he had enjoyed some occasional access to Chicago, where the girls had seemed to him a tribe of exceptionally pretty farmers' daughters who under all their fox and fur were waiting to catch you in some kind of misbehavior, the way they watched you on the streetcar as though you would assault them. This girl wouldn't be surprised if you did, or even especially mind, was the feeling you got; she'd deflect you easily but not hold it against you. A good match for Barber in that way, who had such an excellent unflappable style.

"From *Kansas*," Mary crooned, upon first meeting him. "Now I have some questions for *you*."

"Watch out, Tombaugh," Barber said, "we've got a vested interest."

"You made a telescope," Mary grinned, "and you wrote a *letter*, and now you're *here*. That's some trick."

"Don't ask me," he said. "I wouldn't hire me either."

"Tell me about *Kansas*, though," she insisted, sinking into a chair.

"Her brother," Barber began.

"Oh, *I* can tell it, Jim," she scolded him. And thus under the lamp of Saturn he learned the story of Hollis, in all its strangeness, who he was and how he had disappeared, how they had looked for him and written letters and called everyone, how they had decided just to wait him out, to wait for him to turn up. How they couldn't do anything else, after all.

He would learn the rest of their story later, when it mattered.

He did not really know how to behave around Mary and Barber. It disturbed him, provincially, in a way he didn't much like to admit, that they weren't married yet lived together in their little white house in town. He had heard of such things being done, but he had always assumed you did it secretly and lived ashamed and that the evidence of your misdeeds would show on your face. This was plainly not the truth of it. He wondered briefly if Slipher and Lampland knew, but fortunately he stopped himself before he could ask. He thought of Lily Gooden in her simple blue dress, with its black buttons he had longed to touch, Lily explaining how little he knew of the world and not even deigning to touch his hand in consolation while he stood before her in obvious anguish on the library steps. So he knew some things, but he did not know what to make of a girl with a queer for a brother who had disappeared in the middle of Kansas (he had flushed hot as a boiled beet at the word *queer*), a girl who talked so openly about her wild past full of parties and Canadian whiskey. She and Barber had met at a party in Cambridge, a world so removed from Clyde's experience he felt embarrassed to press for details: what did people drink or what music did they listen to? What did they wear?

He had nothing really to offer in return, or so it seemed to him. But he did know Kansas. So over the next weeks as it became a routine to see her in the evenings as she joined Barber in the library or to take in movies with her and Barber after dinner, he returned the favor by telling her everything about himself. Some favor. And how little he had to offer, he would later think—how little she was satisfied to go on, and what importance she gave to how cold it was in January when her brother had vanished (very), how easy it was to find a house to take you in (very easy), or how hard it was to find work (not too hard if you didn't care what you did). Had he really been paying attention he would have noticed the strange speculative look in her eye and wondered about it, wondered what kind of fire was producing it. But she was good at flattering him, so he put it down stupidly to actual interest.

But to be fair, she was persuasive in seeming interested. When he talked about making the mirror. And Maggie, whom he missed. She especially liked hearing about the funny predicament of being in Kansas while wanting to be anywhere else. She appreciated the Story of the Tragedy of the Oat Field; it was the first time he had ever told it from start to finish, and it struck him what a good story it was, how satisfying a tale in some way, now that he had ended up here. All the while her big flashing eyes were on him. "Oh, Kansas," she said, "you must have just about said a *bad word*."

And he answered, "I said *both* of them."

And she laughed, all right. And maybe it was just a talent she had, but he couldn't help it, he felt a little bit admired. Under that sort of spell he told her everything. And when you do that you make attachments, one way or another. You are loyal to the people you tell your secrets to.

So he was along when Alan and Mary signed their marriage papers, on the second floor of the city hall, and he put his name on a blank line as well, indicating that he had served as the witness, with Felix DuPrie as the officiant. Clyde had been to a few weddings in Streator in the bosom of his family, where there were more cousins than he ever could keep track of and every summer it seemed someone had got old enough to do this. He knew it meant you got to see someone with their clothes off and that everyone allowed it, and like so many familiar things it became wildly strange to him after a while and especially once he got interested in this himself. Then he could not help imagining his cousins and their husbands or wives naked and facing each other across a room, patches of hair sprouting and the shades drawn. You got married in order to be able to do this, very obviously, and for a while anyway it seemed like it was a fair swap; then you got old and didn't care any longer, but you needed someone around for other reasons, if his grandparents were any guide. The marriage of his parents he preferred not to think about, though he had recently become the brother to a new baby sister, according to his mother's letters, a strange unfriendly feeling as though his family had gone ahead with this without consulting him.

What happened in March 1929 was not a wedding in any usual sense, though DuPrie brought some champagne and they drank it in the little paneled chamber in the city hall where the marriage was made official. He had never seen a girl as beautiful as Mary Barber, so he counted it just good luck that he would meet one here in Flagstaff and that she would become his friend. Barber swallowed hard with happiness, it appeared, and in the lonely dim room with the American flag fringing its gold tassels to the wooden floor Clyde discovered the other reason people got married; you got married in order to enter society, to be a part of things, to have friends, and to be able to ask people to take account of you in a serious way. And Clyde considered himself asked. And sure, he would do anything for Barber, for Mary. All it required was loyalty. He could be very good at loyalty. It didn't ask anything except that you sacrifice yourself to someone, and it didn't matter if they cared or not, and anyway there was little danger of rejection as you weren't asking for anything in return. He watched Mary toss her head and look around the room with a startled air as though expecting something else, and her eye caught on him gratefully; and he decided he would do anything for her at all.

If he was good at loyalty then something in him also inspired it, his apparent guilelessness possibly. Later (much later, years from now) he would cringe coming across one of Slipher's letters to Roger Putnam:

We think he is going to develop into a useful man. He has several good qualities that are going to make up we think for his meager training. He is

looking forward to the arrival of the new objective and is eager to be work-
ing with it. He has good attitude; careful with apparatus, willing to do
anything to make himself useful and is enthusiastic about learning and
wants to do observing. We believe these qualities will after a time largely
overcome his deficiency of schooling and training.

How close a thing life is, always, at every turn. And it is usually better
not to know what people are saying about you.

When the Metcalf lens at last arrived in its crate and was painstakingly installed in the empty orange-painted barrel that was to house it
there followed a period of testing (Clyde observed the goony figure of
himself upside down in the perfect mirror of the 13-inch, he had never
seen anything like it, not even Carreau's work had produced such a pool
of absolute machined perfection, and he stared rapt until Slipher, kneeling, slid the cell home into the armature). He expected to get going right
away, but for an outfit with such high associations there followed a surprising number of stupid mistakes. First the worm gear was discovered to
introduce a hard jolt to the drive at 85° right ascension, and it was he himself who clambered underneath with a flashlight and after banging his
head on the iron mechanism asked for a plumber's wrench and concluded
that Sykes had set the tension on the gear too high. It required a couple
days of fine-tuning, but then the telescope tracked true. Next they discovered that the focus slot was much too sensitive for comfort, that Brashear
in having designed the thing had placed the slot too high on the barrel,
the upshot being that the objective had a tendency to slide out of focus at
the least touch, so a maddening delicacy was required, and you had to
walk on tenterhooks around it. When this was accommodated as well as
possible, they discovered that because the photographic plates for the 13-
inch astrograph were so large (17 inches by 14), the images at the edge of
the plates tended to blur. So Dr. Slipher built a Petzal holder, a device
which bent the glass plates just slightly so the light would strike them correctly all the way to their edges. The thumbscrews on the corners of the
plateholder had to be turned exactly four times, with the last half turn
requiring a little muscle. The plates themselves were so big they nearly
filled the developing pan, and along with Barber he watched Dr. Slipher
joggle the whole pan as the plate sat on the bottom like a thick pane of
ice. When they developed the first plate with the Petzal curvature set

correctly, a few bright specks began to emerge at once, and then there was a general darkening of the whole plate, and after another ninety seconds it was so completely flecked with star points it appeared diseased. Slipher slipped it into the fixative and after a minute in there he drew it up and set it in the angled drying rack with the red light behind it.

"Holy moses," Barber whistled.

"Well," agreed Slipher, in his rubber apron, leaning in with a loupe, "could be worse."

Barber said, "There must be thirty thousand stars on there."

"What is that, down to 15 or so?"

"I'd say that's about right. Magnitude-15 objects, Tombaugh, how do you like that?"

"I like it fine," he said.

"I'd say that makes this just about the most sensitive planetary-search instrument ever developed."

"Yes, sir."

"Thirty thousand stars at a go, Tombaugh."

"Possibly twenty-nine thousand nine hundred ninety-nine."

"That's the spirit," Slipher said.

They looked at the plate, teeming with possibilities. Any one of those could be a planet, in theory.

"But, brother," Clyde sighed.

It woudn't be bench work, maybe, but it wouldn't be that far off.

So his labors began. The first test plates had all been of Gemini—using Lowell's old coordinates—although in practical terms they were useless, since Gemini had moved well out of opposition by March. Even if a planet were by chance captured, it wouldn't appear to be moving at all against the background stars.

"Don't even try to blink them," Slipher said. "But maybe they'll come in handy one day."

So they filed those plates away and began at opposition, in Scorpio. If something was moving there, they could see it. You look where the lamp-light is best. With Barber he slowly learned how to expose a plate in differ-ent weathers; it was a nerve-racking matter of judgment, and he ruined his share of plates by ending the exposure too soon or by not covering up when a haze came over. And then there was the matter of developing, which was another skill entirely; he couldn't see the Rochinal chemicals at work and so got suspicious of whatever was going on down there invisibly, and he took weeks to get the hang of it. But once he had that figured, the job itself wasn't difficult. He just stood there and followed the stars, exposed the plates, listened to the motors make their little concentrated humming, and considered his life, if he happened to be of a mind. There wasn't much else to do. In the cold he thought about his father and his mother and old Roy, and even Kelly the dog, and Charlie and the grinding post, whose simple routines he began to miss, the small problems of it, and the intimate pounding of the thresher and the feel of the wheat shifting in his arms. As the summer approached he had a funny itch to be back on the farm when all along he'd wanted to be gone from it. You couldn't leave the objective, so you couldn't read a book or write a letter, and the radio was off the air at this hour, and it was considered bad form anyway; it was just you and the sky, the machine, you and the animal textures of the buffalo robe. So he had time to think. A boy alone at the telescope. He constructed a few scenarios involving Lily Gooden, but in fact she paled next to Mary. Sometimes he could use this to advantage, in that he could be above it all and she would find this interesting. But really he had raised his standards. This was one way in which you could not really compare life here to life there. He was the one who took the photograph of the comet Florence when it came over on April 27, although it was just a smudge, nothing more, not all that impressive even at its closest. Alan wouldn't even look at the plate. "Longest hangover in recorded history," he groaned.

And when Mary saw the photograph she scoffed. "What a stunt," she said, laughing. As though you knew people who named comets all the time. But she peered at it, all right, the little hard white knot with the milky trail extending from it like a horn. It was a good photograph; he had gotten proficient at it finally. She ran her fingers along the comet's trail before she handed the plate back to him, saying, mysteriously, "It looks more like *me*, anyway."

As the summer came on, the viewing got hazy some nights, so he was able to make up some ground at the comparator and still spend some time in town horsing around with Mary and Alan. Now that they were married he felt a little more at ease with them; it gave him a sort of kick to be palling around with a couple of married people as though they were just like everybody else. During lunations, when the moon made it impossible to see anything, they went to the movies and sat with their feet up and ate peanuts and hooted at the screen like idiots until they got warned by an usher in a red organ-grinder's cap, and once they climbed Sheep Hill Summit with their canteens banging on their hips, slipping on the dusty trails. He still got antsy when they got higher than about five hundred feet; he could feel a sort of momentum gathering at his back like a stretched rubber band just waiting for him to slip so it could sling him back to earth. But he made it to the top, where the trees gave out and they had a view that went on forever, north toward the Grand Canyon and south toward the plateaus of Sedona. Arizona. Sure as hell you didn't have this in Kansas.

"Brother," he breathed.

A long way below they could see DuPrie's dig, the cluster of white tents on the red soil.

"Doesn't look like much from up here, does it?" Alan said, tying his handkerchief over his head.

Mary was tugging at her shirt. "I ought to take him out there, Jim," she said.

"Show him off, you mean," Alan said.

"Sure, he's a rare specimen," Mary sniffed. "Not every day you find a real-life boy from the year zero."

He went warm all over; he would accept this from both of them forever. "Aw, dry up, you two." He grinned. "I happen to know you can learn a few things on a farm."

If you imagined an advertisement that went BECOME A REAL-LIFE DINOSAUR HUNTER! then DuPrie had really done it. As it turned out to make those dumb pitches come true all you needed was about a million dollars and you could be whatever in hell you wanted. You wouldn't peg him for a DuPrie in that hat and beard, sweating with all the Italians and grunting as he swung the bucket of plaster off the lip of the pit. And just think, back in Streator Dr. King wouldn't even go out in his carriage when it was raining.

"Pleased to meet you, Mr. Tombaugh," DuPrie nodded, when Mary introduced him.

And he thrilled, imagining how he would tell it to Roy. "Likewise, Mr. DuPrie," he returned.

Looking down into the pit Clyde was reminded of his root cellar, naturally, and watching the men go at it for a few minutes he could see that even the excavation was not complicated work, only required you to be methodical, and Clyde decided that if it all came to pieces at the observatory he could come down here, hat in hand, and ask for a job.

It was here, visiting the dig, that Clyde first noticed real strangeness from Mary. He knew her well enough now to know she had peculiarities, that she did not like to be walked up on from behind, that she did not want to be the first person into a room, ever, but he attributed this to being a girl and being beautiful and being able therefore to act generally as she pleased. But on the sloping dig she walked twice around a small square pit, staring in at the scoured-up dirt, then refused to get down into it, although two of the Italians were making room for her.

"That one's not for me," she said.

Clyde was humoring her and said, "You let others do all the tough work, I guess."

She only shook her head gravely. "I can tell when there's a chance it might be a bad one."

He looked and saw nothing unusual. But he followed after her. From behind she had a bright, hurrying walk, bouncing along, the walk of a girl down a dark alley, looking straight ahead toward safety. And he scurried along behind, as always willing to follow her anywhere.

This was the week when otherwise he would have been sharpening the thresher's great blades; and that other self, marooned back there, was vivid to him, as vivid as though he had been split in two. If Carreau had not been so disbelieving, Clyde might have had the courage to change his mind and accept the job after all; or if Clyde had not written to Slipher at all; or if Slipher had not wanted him—well, but surely then he would have found something else; he would have found some other means to escape, if only to vanish, as Mary's brother had—to get up and disappear. Surely.

Anyway he hoped so. He shuddered to think of himself stuck on the farm, not seeing *this*, not doing *exactly these things*. They had assembled a picnic lunch, and Clyde had brought along a pair of sunglasses which met with Mary's laughing approval. "You look like an heiress, Kansas," she pronounced.

They picnicked on the bluff above the dig, chicken and potato salad and coffee. Not his mother's, but it would do. He lay in the sun wadding his jacket as a pillow and peeking glimpses at Mary as she ate table grapes one at a time, with the playful deliberation of a child; he would add this to his long list of things he liked about her. Alan carved their names into the rock: MARE—JIM—KANSAS 1929. Then the sun reddened Clyde's vision, and Clyde tipped his hat over his face and inhaled the stewy stink of his dirty head. It was nice, no, it was heavenly, to be outside in the sun away from everything; you had to have a break once in a while if you were going to take care of yourself the right way. He imagined his father wondering what the hell kind of crowd he'd got himself involved with, lying around in the sun like a barnyard cat. But this was the way people really lived, wasn't it? They worked as hard as hell, and then sometimes they didn't.

He woke to a pecking, scraping sound. Mary was gouging away at the wall of the bluff with a butter knife and talking, thoughtfully, to no one; Alan was asleep, and she was just speaking to the air: "Any time you become part of someone's assignment," she was saying, quite reasonably, "you end up with a responsibility. If they're after you, you end up being part of *their* assignment, you end up in *their* job. And then you never know when it's going to happen. So you don't let that happen, you do it backward, you end up being the one who makes them part of *your* assignment. If you go after them, you're always at the advantage; that way you don't let it come to you but it's the other way." She went on in this nonsensical vein for a minute before she removed with a satisfying entirety the rock she was intent on. "There," she said, demonstratively, and seeing Clyde peering at her from beneath his hat, she said, "This is a creature who used to swim."

He took it. It was a rock.

"It's not the usual kind," she said.

"I guess not."

She took a deep shuddering breath and took it back and tossed it blindly over the side; a little fist of dust rose far below on the sloping terrain.

"*That* one won't be back anytime soon," she concluded.

Well, it was the strangest thing he had seen or heard in a long while. A little bit of sunstroke, maybe. But he had the sense that he had interrupted her in some private reverie, and that anything he saw would be bad manners to comment on. And he just admired her so much, he couldn't imagine anything could possibly be wrong with her; so he kept it to himself.

The final feature of the summer was the periodic arrival of a handful of mysterious telegrams from Cambridge, beginning in July and going through September, each bearing a long list of ecliptical coordinates. Alan came to him with the first one, his face dead white and solemn, and handed it over to him. "It's probably nothing," he said. "But let's take a look at these."

When they had the first plates out Clyde nodded and said, "That was one of my suspects, all right. It looked good for a while, but the third plate—it's just a pair of variables."

"But you thought."

"It looked just right. But there's nothing actually moving, just one of those cases where there's a pair of variables apparently close enough, and you happen to catch one first and then the other the next week so it looks like movement. I did the third plate on that just to be sure."

"You're sure it's nothing."

He was. "So what is this?"

"This is that little number named Florence Morrow," Alan grudgingly began.

"_Her._ Competition?" Clyde whispered.

"I'm afraid so."

"Does Slipher know?"

"Slipher knows all about Florence." He took the telegram back and folded it down the middle and tapped it against the brass lip around the edge of the comparator. "But this could be trouble. That was a real suspect. Who knows what that means exactly except she's on the hunt. Every one of these must be another suspect."

"They're not that uncommon," Clyde answered. "There's one or two of that sort on every plate."

Alan turned this over and pocketed the telegram and said, "Anyway. Full speed ahead, Clyde."

So, put together with the constant inquiries of Roger Putnam and Constance Lowell, it was enough to keep him lashed to the wheel. You looked at the whole of the night sky, like looking into a dark bowl swarming with invisible life, a hundred billion souls on ten thousand worlds; you could picture the sky infested with monsters and princesses and crystal palaces, with ray-gun fighters and million-year wars. For a while, sure. But eventually you couldn't tell yourself it was anything but drudgery, plain and simple. You photographed at opposition; you checked the worm gear; you kept alert to all the things that might go wrong but usually didn't. Then when the sky set, you shut it all down and took your plates downhill to the Main Building and stowed them in the basement and lugged yourself upstairs to get a little sleep. In the morning you developed a plate or two in the basement and then sat down at the comparator for the long day's work. Now and then he would run down one of Florence's images and find it was something he had already arrived at; and every time Alan would have that frozen iceman look on his face. The fear of being scooped on this one was terrible. What would you say afterward? What would you do with yourself? And once in a while he couldn't stand it, and he would go to the movies alone or go spend some time with Venus in the barn or with Sykes in his shed sorting screws or up on a ladder oiling the joints in the goofy old Clark dome. Meanwhile in the library down the hall Alan was at work on the residuals, and except for the occasional visit to the comparator room from Slipher or Lampland, just checking in, Clyde was left with the Planet X search in his hands alone, crawling across the night sky like a spider across a ceiling.

After a while it began to seem familiar, as though it reminded him of something; something from long ago; and it bothered him until at last he figured it out. Once, with the harvest in, he and his father had lured young Roy out snipe hunting. Stay here, they instructed, handing him the empty feed sack, hold still and we'll drive the birds your way. Three hours later Roy walked back into the kitchen with his pants full of burrs, finding his older brother and his father waiting for him.

"Fine," Roy said, and walked through, went upstairs, and locked himself into the bedroom.

It had raised some bad blood—conspiring, brother against brother, for the father's favor. You should have seen Muron Tombaugh grinning meanly at the footsteps on the porch. You didn't witness much emotion from the man, and now here he was delighting in this ugliness. How it shook up so much between Clyde and Roy, really, now that he thought of it. That one scene, the oilcloth on the kitchen table, the dinner things put away, the stove polished, and the firebox full. This was when Roy began to mock him in earnest—began to take him less seriously, anyway, as a big brother worth consulting. Not the best son, Clyde, and not the best brother, either.

Well, Clyde knew, of course, that the whole operation couldn't possibly be a stunt; plainly the telescope was a real object, the plates cost money, he was drawing a real salary, and Alan Barber was from Harvard; but he was unable to shake the idea that something was off about the whole deal. He argued with his father in his head. *Watch out for bench work.*

But it's not bench work, pop.

Well, it just wasn't.

Finally in September he went to Alan with it worrying him like a tooth. "I guess I just don't want to be anybody's patsy is what it comes down to."

Alan didn't even look up, figuring, figuring there in his gray herringbone and soft collar and smooth hair, his cup of coffee. He said, "I don't think you're a patsy, very much."

"But who says there's *anything* out there?"

Alan screwed out his cigarette and heaved back in his chair and said, "What the hell, Clyde."

"It's all just a *guess*, isn't it?"

"I suppose. But an educated one."

"Now you throw that at me, all of a sudden."

"I'm not throwing anything. It's a guess made by people who know what they're talking about. Me included. There are a lot of people who know what they're talking about who set this whole operation up because they were convinced there'd be a payoff."

Clyde said, "I *had* that offer in Wichita. I could have *had* a job, you know. Anyway, if I work a couple more months I'd have almost enough money to go to Lawrence."

Alan sighed. "You're not thinking of quitting."

"I don't know. I see myself stuck here doing whatever this is. Every night. All day at the comparator."

"I know it. But you're here at Lowell Observatory, Clyde. On the Planet X search."

"Sure. If it's even out there." Then Clyde ventured, "And actually you don't even need me, with what you're doing, you're just going to find it anyway sitting in here doing *that*."

But Alan was looking at him with a sudden worry. "Say, pal, you can't seriously run away on me. I need you."

"That's a laugh. You need that twitch back in Boston. Or you need her to lay off, anyway."

Alan looked to the edges of the library and lowered his voice. "It's not just that, Clyde."

"What, then?"

Something was clotted behind Barber's eyes, and then he decided out with it: "It's Mary," he blurted, "she's in a little trouble."

He felt himself going red. "Aw, gee, I didn't mean—"

"Not like *that*. She's got a nervous condition," Alan rushed on, "it comes and goes, and actually, Clyde," he said, as a look of terrible sadness came over him, "you can't tell anybody, but she was in the asylum once, and I'm just trying to keep her out of it; that's all I want right about now is just to keep her on the level. So I've got this and the Atlas and I've got you in there, but if I have to take over for you—"

Another flush, deeper this time. What the hell did he know about real life? "But she's so nice looking," he said, stupidly.

"Sure," Alan said, "glad you noticed."

"I guess I mean"—he deserved to die—"you can't tell anything—there's nothing you can see. You look at her, and she just looks fine."

"She hides it."

Clyde nodded furiously. "Sure," he whispered. And so now it all made sense.

"And," his friend swallowed, "Florrie's out there on our tails, too, just to make things a little more lively. Not to mention the widow Lowell putting her thumb down on everyone."

In the dome-ceilinged library the two clocks ticked, overlapping, intersecting. Not to turn away from *this* brother. And to be summoned, called to sacrifice, lifted a banner in his boyish heart. "I didn't know, Alan," he said.

"I know."

"I'll stay as long as you want."

"Okay," Alan said. Then, muttering into his papers: "Thanks, Clyde."

Shyly, Clyde whispered, "Is she going to be all right?"

And Alan lifted his gaze to him and sent him back only the bleakest, saddest look in the world; then returned to his figuring.

Anyway, the banner was raised. Alan needed him. Mary did too. And all right, he was just a farmer somewhere deep down, what did he really expect from the world but mute unending labor. He redoubled his efforts at the comparator. He went all out. He would find the damned planet, and then he would turn to Alan and his sad beautiful girl and say, *All right, that's done, let's get on the train, what do you say?* at which Alan and Mary would take him each in an arm and say, *You bet, kiddo,* and together they would jump the noon train west and land out in California, lie in the sun all day, and live out at the beach where it's always warm—

He wakes. Staring at a field of black flecks. He has fallen asleep at the comparator again. Straightening, he shouts with his mouth closed, then rubs his eyes and straightens and feels the pinch of his new shoes.

Aw, but try to stop him. You do anything for your pal. Anything for the girl. You're a straight-up fellow, all the way down the line. That's the way you operate, all right. Watch him leap light-footed over the bad guys and come bounding up to the rescue.

Captain Clyde Tombaugh of Burdett, Kansas, miss, at your service. She is the princess of Mars Hill, isn't she, and he'll do anything for her. What simplicity in such devotion. How much it solves for him.

He still has half an hour before he needs to dress for dinner, and he lifts the grease pencil and goes at it again.

25

An hour later Clyde is in a quiet panic trying to make sense of the forks and the glasses (only water is served at dinner, but everyone else looks longingly at the mysterious wineglass which is never filled, but which is nonetheless in front of every setting, like the empty horse at a military funeral), and Mrs. Lowell is presiding in her imaginary blindness at one end of the table, and Felix DuPrie sits upright in his beard beside her, as custom dictates, and his tiny ancient mother is propped beside *him*, the little old woman trying gallantly to keep up with the courses as they come, one after the other: pineapple and orange cocktail; steamed halibut in shrimp sauce with parsley potatoes; roast stuffed turkey with cranberry sauce; pear salad; and Clyde fearing each new dish as it arrives, expecting it to hold some monstrosity, boiled shark or jellied polecat; he is wearing his blue suit and tight shoes and feels fine, despite the peculiarity of all of them seated together at the table, the Sliphers and the Lamplands and Mrs. Fox and even Stanley Sykes in his old-timey mustache, and Mary holding down the far end and casting a secret frightened kidding glance Clyde's way every now and then, *Look at us*, and Alan with his jaw set in permanent distaste.

Look at them all! He can hardly believe it himself. What Lily Gooden would say! What his father would!

"Pay attention, Clyde," Alan breathes into his ear, "you get to see how the world really works."

The way it *really works* is, Mrs. Lowell talks and everyone listens. Actually he is not too surprised at that. After the dinner has been removed and they are awaiting dessert, Mrs. Lowell, at the head of the table, says to the air (the subject of dogs has come up), "Now *I* used to bring my dog Surrey, but he was always eating everyone's food, Mr. Lampland you'll remember this, and rolling around in filth and tracking it around everywhere. I didn't want to keep him on a chain, but he *wasn't* very well behaved."

"We don't miss him," Slipher says.

"He's long gone, Mr. Slipher. As *so* many dear ones are. You know it's funny to encounter you out here, Ann. I suppose you must remember good old Harcourt Amory."

Mrs. DuPrie says, "Yes, a little."

"Well, what a dear. He was very helpful to me when I needed him. You know I've had a terrible, terrible amount of *difficulty* since Percy died. No one really understands the kind of difficulty I've faced. And when I start to go on about it they're very, very dismissive."

"I was so sorry to hear of the trouble with your eyes."

"Well, that's a nuisance, too." Mrs. Lowell smiles. "But I've learned to live with my troubles. Not many people do, Ann. Though you seem to have done all right."

Mrs. DuPrie considers her fork and says, "We've come around, I suppose."

"For me it's really especially difficult when I'm *here*, you know. He always seems so close."

Clyde is not going to say word one at this table, count on it.

"It's awfully hard when they go, isn't it?" Mrs. DuPrie reflects.

"Well, it's *something*, isn't it, Ann? I always personally thought that the air here holds ghosts more easily; they can travel through the air more easily because it's *drier*. Also we *are* so high up here; that's the other thing a ghost will do, it will *rise*, I think, very slowly, they're not attached to the earth any longer so they're very slowly . . ." She does a sort of harem dance, lifting her wiggling fingers into the air. "You know, the earth is where *living* things live. You can't be too careful out here; you'll end up seeing things you don't want to see."

Now Mr. DuPrie says, "I know just what you mean."

"Well, I guess you're the only one. Percy always thought I was at least eighty percent crackers. If only I could see what you look like. Ann, does he look like you?"

"Oh, no, he's very handsome. And now he's got a beard, too."

"Mr. Lowell had a *mustache,*" Mrs. Lowell says wistfully. "Now, of course, we *are* up very *high.* That's why I'm talking about *ghosts* and *spirits.* You know Percy and I used to sit out on that porch, and we used to talk about all sorts of things. We came to know one another rather later in life, so we had a lot to talk about. We had a lot to *tell* one another, you know. When I could get a minute with him, I mean, when he wasn't holed up somewhere working, we used to talk about all the spirits on all the other worlds. I know you can't prove it from here, but I think it's very likely that the other planets are spirit homes for us."

Slipher lets out a long, unconscious sigh, at which Mrs. Slipher kicks him sideways.

"This is only a *way* station for us," Mrs. Lowell goes on, "this planet, and we all begin in the sun, as pure spirit, and we move, you see, from planet to planet; we begin on Mercury and then Venus and then we're born here, and from here we move on to Mars, and so on. And so the last planet, Planet X, is the place where we all go, that's what Percy and I always believed; *he* believed it *secretly,* of course; no one would have taken him seriously if he'd ever said such a thing out loud in public. He had enough trouble with the question of Mars. But I think that once we're done here we rise, you know, we . . . *rise.*"

An appalled silence settles over the table, into which Mary, after a moment, proposes, "I guess that's what happens when you consider *advancement,* isn't it?"

"Just so," Mrs. Lowell answers. "It's *advancement.* Everyone has a plan for advancement, and this is what the universe has for us."

"But some people are stuck here," Mary says.

"Well, I suppose that's possible," Mrs. Lowell responds. "Yes, now that I think of it, you may well be right."

"For example, if you have too many bones," Mary goes on. "You can just become too *heavy.* Or if someone wants to grab onto you and ride you away at the end, you can't rise."

"*Yes,*" Mrs. Lowell says. "That's a *problem.* And then what do you do?"

Mary replies, cannily, "Well, don't ask me. I mean I know it's all imaginary, except that doesn't mean it's not real."

Mrs. Lowell turns to Mary now with a cruel, predatory smile. "Whoever you are, dear girl, you've just put it *exactly* right."

"Mare," Alan says.

"Well, but you must be really looking for *something*," Mary says, turning to Alan now. "That's what Florence *was*, wasn't it? You were trying to put her up there before she wanted to go. That's why she got so mad at you."

"Don't, Mare," Alan whispers.

"But Florence isn't there. She isn't *there* yet."

"Why yes," Mrs. Lowell smiles again, turning all her attention to Mary. "I think you've got it exactly *right*, my dear. She didn't want to be put up there at *all*. She had already been claimed by someone else, hadn't she? Before your husband put her up there against her *will*."

"Ma'am," Alan interrupts, down the length of the table.

"*Yes*, Mr. *Barber*," Mrs. Lowell replies, full of mock solicitousness.

There is a pause, an electric suspension around the table. In the sudden quiet Clyde can hear the kitchen staff clinking dishes behind the polished door. Upright in her chair, Mary is full of desperate comedy, her face alight, her expression alive with mad wonder—and Clyde cannot mistake it, he sees in her staring amazement a cousin of that intent preoccupied look she was wearing that afternoon on the bluff as she dropped the rock over the edge. Across the table from Clyde, Alan rests a calming hand on his wife's arm; he appears to turn over a number of possible lines before he leans forward a final degree and says, simply and softly, "I wonder if we could drop this subject, ma'am."

At this the old woman tips her head in gracious, cruel deference, her veil clinging to her face; and, while Mrs. Lowell grins meanly down the table at them all, the kitchen door swings aside, and Mrs. Wroth enters and turns out the electric light above the table; she is bearing a cake on which a handful of white birthday candles are burning brightly, and the orange light fills the room.

"Well, and I see you brought me a *cake*," Mrs. Lowell states, in her queenly satisfaction.

Then freezes, her mouth dropping open.

But she can't see that, can she?

A momentary current runs around the table, no one sure what to do. Then Slipher gives one hard, incredulous bark of laughter, then heaves himself back in his chair and remarks, "Looks as though we did, Mrs. Lowell." Lampland reaches uneasily for his cigarettes; Mrs. DuPrie offers, her voice elderly and frail, "I had my girl make it for you, Connie, she's sort of a wonder. It's a Lady Baltimore cake."

But Mrs. Lowell is paralyzed.

Slipher says, now all conciliation, "Why don't you put the cake down, Mrs. Wroth, before you catch fire."

"Ye-es," Mrs. Wroth decides.

She sets the cake before them, all its candles still alight. Mrs. Lowell's mouth slowly closes. The candles smoke. An eerie light decorates the ceiling.

"I don't know what you people think you're doing giving me a *cake*," Mrs. Lowell intones finally.

"Oh, for pity's sake," Slipher mutters. "Mrs. Wroth, would you cut it up, please?"

Mrs. Wroth only withdraws to the edge of the room.

Silence.

"*Well*, Connie," begins Mrs. DuPrie, brightly, "we just thought it would be sort of festive. Actually it was Felix's idea, since we were all sort of— fellow travelers, I guess. All of us out here alone, away from home. He came in today with the idea, and I asked my girl to make it for you and then I asked Mrs. Slipher to hide it at her house so it could be a surprise. The candles," she smiles, "were my idea."

No one is looking anywhere in particular, but they are all aware of the old woman at the end of the table. Clyde tries to catch Mary's gaze, but she is visibly elsewhere, peering intently at the shadows dancing on the paneled walls. And Alan beside her, a hand laid on her arm as though to keep her in place. To keep her fastened to the planet.

"Well, if you ask me," the old woman exhales at last, "I think it's a terrible idea. We're not *celebrating* anything. Mr. Lowell's birthday isn't until *March*. And none of these people have *found* anything worth talking about. So what is it we're supposed to be *happy* about."

"*We've* just finished the Stegosaurus," Mr. DuPrie notes, a little stiffly. "Which may be worth a celebration."

"The *what*?" Mrs. Lowell asks, full of acid. "Am I supposed to know what in the world that is?"

The bearded man only blinks mildly. "It's a Jurassic dinosaur, ma'am," he explains.

"Would you care to blow out the candles, please, Mrs. Lowell," suggests Mrs. Wroth.

But Mrs. Lowell does no such thing. "Everyone throws their money around like it's going to last forever, but it's *not. You,* Mr. DuPrie, out there on the desert, and Mr. Slipher's like that too, I happen to know. *All* you people are, in fact."

Clyde grows even more motionless in his chair, continuing to gaze off in a carefully indeterminate direction so as not to attract attention. He notices the pattern of blue ivy around the rim of his plate, seeing, with some surprise, that it is the same pattern as one of his mother's kitchen bowls.

"In fact, do you know what, Mr. Slipher," Mrs. Lowell continues, coolly, "perhaps there are a few things it is about time you *hear.* Since apparently what you people have decided to do is to make me into a laughingstock, why don't we just go ahead and have it out right now. As it seems to me, for the last few years you've conspired against me with Mr. Putnam. You've not only secured funds for the Planet X search without consulting me but you've spent just terrible, terrible amounts of money on other matters without securing *any* kind of approval from me, the only Lowell you ought to be answering to if you had any conscience. I know there's no love lost between the two of us but at least you agree I have the best interests of the observatory always at heart. And of all the bad turns you've delivered to me over the years, Mr. Slipher, hiring these two *boys* is among the worst." She aims an accusatory finger down the table, which Clyde does his best not to notice. "*Boys,* to do the work that Percy spent the balance of his adult life pursuing."

Slipher says, without heat: "As you well know, Mrs. Lowell, both these gentlemen are hard at work."

"But Percy *solved* the residual problem in 1915, Mr. Slipher, that work has already been done. So what this young man thinks he's doing by going over everything again is absolutely beyond me. I suppose you imagine you'll find some mistakes, Mr. Barber."

"Frankly, Mrs. Lowell," Alan says, "what I'm finding is my own goddamned business."

Mrs. Lowell goes abruptly red with indignation. "Well I don't know *what has happened to this operation,*" she spits, through the eddying smoke. "You've hired this terrible *person* to check my Percy's math and you've hired this absolute *child* to run this telescope that you've paid for behind my *back* and put Percy's name on, and you've made a fool of me in the eyes of any number of Percy's dear old friends, those who will still consent to work with you; of course dear old Amory wouldn't stand what you asked him to do and you had to resort to putting your hands all over Guy and now of all people *Roger Putnam*, who I happen to know would sell his own mother for a nickel. Do you know what you are, Mr. Slipher, you're *not loyal*. Percy was your greatest friend in the world but since Percy died you've done nothing but make trouble and *get in the way* of what he wanted to do. It's only *my efforts* that have made any sort of *respectable* work here *possible*."

At this even Lampland has to disguise a guffaw.

"You and Roger have done your best to trick me out of everything that's rightfully mine and I'm only a poor old blind *widow*. If that's your idea of Christian behavior. And *you*, little schoolboy whatever your name is, you must think this is some sort of charity program, when I'm here to tell you it's *not*. You might as well just go back your bags and get ready to take the next train on out of here. Go on back to your farm, wherever it is."

She is staring right at him.

And it is the mention of the farm, possibly, that gets his back up now. What gives her the right. What the hell does *she* know. "Well, ma'am," Clyde says, levelly, "I guess I had that idea already a few times, to be honest."

"*Did* you?"

"Well, I guess once or twice."

"Oh?" she sneers, "do you think what you're doing is just a bunch of malarkey, Mr. Tootoo?"

He doesn't, does he? Only sometimes. The room is staring at him. The candles are burning down to the nub. "I don't know, ma'am," he answers, "just sometimes it occurs to you, maybe there's nothing really there."

She gives him a wicked smile. "Well—do you know what, Mr. Tombaugh? Mr. Slipher, Mr. Lampland, Mr. Putnam, all of them are too cowardly to say such a thing aloud. So I suppose you've got a lot of bravado. But in fact I've got news for you. Something I've never had the heart to tell you before, Mr. Slipher, but I think you ought to know it, since it seems you've guessed it already." She draws back her veil and sets it on her broad ridiculous hat and faces the table with her eyes closed. Seen naked now her face is clear, unbothered, pretty. "Just before he died, Percy made a confession to me. His confession was that he believed there *was* no Planet

X. That he had been *wrong* about everything all along. That it *wasn't there*."

"Oh, Constance," Slipher sighs.

"Well why do you think I've spent all my time trying to keep the *money* from you. Because it's a ridiculous project. And it always was. I mean if we're suddenly being honest here."

"Well," Slipher says.

"You *know* it's true, don't you. And do you know what he was doing, really? Do you know what old Planet X was really all about?"

A silence settles. The candles hiss, still burning.

She says, "Planet X was the excuse Percy had for getting away from *me*."

Slipher says, unsteadily, "I'm sure that's not true, Constance."

And Mrs. DuPrie says, "Oh, Connie."

"You be quiet, Ann, you've got your share of secrets too. At least I'm honest enough to admit it. You're obviously not very well, and I'm sorry about it, but that doesn't give you the right to feel sorry for me. He was *tired* of me, Mr. Slipher," Mrs. Lowell states bravely, her eyes now nearly opening. "So he made up a little project to get him out of the house. That's all it was. You've been going on for years over that man's sad little desperate *invention*."

Mrs. Lowell is moved by this declaration and seems, for the moment anyway, to believe it. And you do not doubt the old woman lightly.

And then Mary tugs her arm out from under Alan's hand and, tossing her head with an air of resolution, stands and walks around the table and kneels at the side of Mrs. Lowell's chair and, grappling, takes the widow's hands in her own. Mrs. Lowell resists, surprised, but then instead of struggling or pushing Mary away she lets her remain. It is a gesture of attempted comfort, it seems to Clyde, as though Mary wants to make the old woman feel better somehow; and then Alan is standing as well, going toward them both; and then he slows, and they are all watching this strange tableau, for it is entirely unaccountable, and no one knows what to say.

Her own brother, Mary must be thinking. How people go away without reason.

Clyde, paralyzed, is suddenly missing Roy with an aching need. His mama. And that porch roof, and that gorgeous Kansas sky.

And all at once—they all sense it together—a palpable uneasiness travels around this beautiful rustic old room. Something in Mary's posture, possibly, or some quality to the silence, or to Mrs. Lowell's pained and suffering expression—but they all feel it at once, a swift sudden fear that maybe the widow is finally telling the truth after all. And that they have all been fools, every last one of them.

And then all the candles go out, and the room falls mercifully dark.

Clyde doesn't want to believe it. Later on that night he stands in front of the comparator with his tight shoes still on, but he can't make himself sit down. Because what the hell does he know? Maybe she's right. He would sure believe her if the evidence is anything to go by.

Upstairs he takes the dirty cards out of their hiding place in his suitcase; this usually will serve him well, but they are getting to be pretty old hat by now. He has begun to notice not only the pebbly nipples and the simple amazing fact of a woman with a man's organ in her mouth (he has tried to imagine this so many times, how it might happen sort of by accident one day) but the details of the background, the carpet-pillow under one girl's rear that must be prickly and the preoccupied *how's-this* expression in another girl's eye as she looks off stage left obviously at someone's instruction. Tonight, his new jacket slung on the end of the bed, he searches without success for something new he hasn't seen before. It is funny how this feels all right suddenly, not the worst thing anyone has ever done. If they have all been duped into hunting for a planet that doesn't exist, well, that would be worse.

He hasn't even the heart for this, it turns out. He tucks the cards away. In the suitcase still are the boxes of Carborundum, of emery and grafting wax. He takes these out instead and sets them in order on his desk, not knowing exactly why. They smell like the barn and the grinding post, and his old smudgy fingerprints are on the paperboard boxes. They are his prints, but they are the sign of a vanished time. There is a nostalgic gust at his back somehow. You are in too deep and you want to go home.

But he can't go back. He can picture his father waiting against that pillar in the station, satisfied that the world answers to his expectations after all. What a lunatic thing it had been to go west to Arizona. So no, he can only go forward, into whatever comes next.

———

The next morning, when Clyde is back at the comparator again, Alan comes hurriedly in, unshaven, his tie askew. "She isn't *here,* by some chance," Alan asks.

"Mrs. Lowell?"

Alan shakes his head, his expression wild. "Mary."

"No."

There is some trouble. You can see it pressing against the inside of Alan's face as he tugs his tie aright. "I think I'm going to need a little help, Clyde," he says.

"What's wrong?"

His friend moves to explain but instead says, "You'd better just come down and see this." So Clyde gets up from the stool. Outside he slings himself on the back of Alan's motorcycle, embracing him from behind as they bump cautiously down the rutted switchback road to town. They pick up speed on the pavement, and in a minute they are at the dig office, where Alan opens the door and passes inside.

The place is not a ruin exactly, but crates are jimmied open everywhere. Straw and broken plaster are scattered on the floor. It takes his eyes a second to adjust to the dark, but then he sees it. Against the back wall someone has constructed a rough, rearing monster. A dinosaur made of a hundred disparate parts: fossil bones, scrap wood and other miscellaneous clutter, a broomstick spine and two hammers for hands, eight feet high at least with the skull of something terrible grinning out at them, a composite skull with parts from three or four different beasts, all of it lashed together with tight loops of baling wire and balanced delicately like a horrible mobile. It is obviously the work of many hours.

"Holy moses," Clyde says.

Alan lets him have a good look at it. Then he hooks Clyde by the elbow and hustles him out onto the motorcycle again. They swing over the brick streets, and in a minute they are at DuPrie's door. The morning wind is stirring up chilly from the desert, and a low cover of clouds is skidding in.

Felix DuPrie himself comes forward to the screen, his beard shining and his red hair marked with the crease of his habitual Stetson. His face is gray and narrowed, and he is none too happy looking himself. The night before did its work on him as well, it would seem, and, going by the man's haunted look, presumably on Mrs. DuPrie too. "Mr. Barber," he mutters. "And Mr. Tombaugh. Good morning."

"Good morning," Alan answers. "I'm sorry to trouble you. I'm hunting Mary, actually. She's not here, I take it."

"No." Mr. DuPrie considers them each in turn. "She's not at the office?"

"Not now she's not. Although she's *been* there. Been and gone. You haven't been over there today, I guess."

"No."

"Well, I'm afraid she's made a pretty good mess of the place," Alan says.

"A mess?"

But suddenly Alan can only nod, helpless, desperate. He claps his hand to his mouth and nods.

Mr. DuPrie says, gently, "It was a mess before she came, anyway."

Clyde doesn't even want to look at him; they are all at a loss together there, at the doorstep.

"You think she might be on the dig," Clyde finally suggests.

"The dig," Alan whispers, his hand still on his mouth, "sure."

"That's where she is." And Clyde knows it in a flash, for a certainty. That rock, that mad conversation on the blufftop. "I bet you anything."

"The dig." He looks at them in despair. "But I've only got the Omega."

Mr. DuPrie reaches into the drawer of a table by the door. "Maybe you'd like to take the Stutz."

"The *Stutz*," Alan breathes.

"Yes, I bought it," Mr. DuPrie admits. "Had it fixed up a while ago." Now he holds out the gold key, a look of solid fellowship in his eye. "I guess you know where it is."

26

The Stutz. It sends a spike into Alan's heart. It's parked in the same old barn where a million years ago he went with Florrie and Dick; he knows just where it is. When he and Clyde whump the canvas back, the same cloud of hay dust comes swirling out and he sees there is a raw repair to the right front fender and axle. Clyde runs his hand over the metal in his assessing way. "Butchery," he says.

"I guess it runs. Come on."

Clyde is a little reluctant, but he snatches off his hat and lowers himself into the car and at once says, "Jiminy, what a ride."

"That's Florrie's seat you're in right *there*," he tells him.

"All right," Clyde says, feeling the seats. "But don't think I'm going to give it up to you."

He smiles despite everything, and they drive out into the light. The Stutz is a jumping, purring machine; it surges forward underfoot. Coned and arrowed by the open windows, a swirl of haydust comes slipping up from the back seat and snakes between them and pebbles itself on their trousers, seeds and flecks. They make the drive with the powerful car horsing itself up and down the ruts. On this Sunday the dig is a scalded empty hillside churned up it seems by a greedy hand. And sure, there she is. A relief to find her here: she hasn't gone far. But Alan sinks, too, to see her alone, helpless against whatever now possesses her. She is wearing only her cardigan over her dress, clutching her elbows and bending over sort of curatorially as she paces the bottom of one of the big holes.

He pushes open the car door and big-legs down the hill and puts himself at the edge of the pit. She doesn't look too bad, considering. Only some shadows under her eyes and in the eyes themselves a look, too intent, wild. But she's still dressed and shod.

"Say, Mare," he says.

"Hi up there, Jimbo."

He scans from horizon to horizon; beyond the tents it is only empty scrubland. "Sort of a long way out, aren't you?"

"I'm just looking for a certain *part*, Jim," she tells him, all sweet reason. "There's going to be another part to him."

"That thing back there," he supplies.

"Oh," she cringes, "well, that's just what he's become in the meantime. I'm sorry about that. He won't be like that forever. He's going to go on and develop."

"But Mare," he begins.

But what is he supposed to do next?

He has no idea; only he figures he should bring her home somehow.

He stands for a while, watching her pace the pit. Even now she does not look stark raving mad, only a little worried, preoccupied.

"Some car you came in," she notes, after a minute. "Who's that in there with you, Florence the Avenger?"

"That? That's just Clyde."

"Not the men in the white coats?"

"No."

Clyde is getting slowly out of the car now, coming down the hillside, his hands stuffed in his pockets.

Mary's sweater flumps in the wind. None of it is entirely strange by itself, but added all together it's very bad. "What are you doing, Mare?"

"Oh"—she shakes her head quickly, that old beautiful motion—"I'd tell you what it was, but then it'd be giving away the whole plan, wouldn't it? And if I told you that, then you'd be about a mile ahead of me. Hello up there, Kansas. I guess you're not really part of this operation. On the other hand, maybe you are. I guess it's too much to ask if it's just a coincidence."

"Hello, Mary. You must be freezing."

She gives him a swift smile from the pit, then does away with it as not the thing. "There's a way about you, Kansas, that people like. You sort of have a straight-ahead way with you. Even if you did sort of replace yourself with my brother somewhere along the way. If I could open you up just a little bit, maybe that's where he'd be. He had enough skin to cover you about twice over."

Clyde says, "I'm just me, actually."

"A farmhand. What a thing. Nothing surprises you, does it?"

"I don't know," Clyde answers. "Lately, most things do."

"I bet you have an idea of where he is, at least. Don't tell me you came all the way from Kansas and you didn't keep notes on everything. I know what a big one you are for notes and so on. I thought for a while he might be out here buried, you know, or that someone'd put him in one of my boxes. But that would just be too mean, wouldn't it? Nobody would really do that, put my brother in a box. I think he's still *out* there somewhere. I get the weekly updates from the local investigators, but they're not having any luck, according to them. But I'm starting to think they really know where he is. So, that's what the *thing* is for."

Clyde says, "I never met your brother."

"So you *say*." She is down on her knees now, scraping at the dirt with what looks like a hooked knife she has drawn out from somewhere. Alan was not expecting this. She works at the dirt for a minute while they watch, making calculations of how easily they might grab it from her, and then she aims the tip in a sort of lecturing fashion at Clyde and says, "That thing back there is a *hunter*, Kansas. In case *you* ever get any ideas about running off."

It's not a knife, it's a claw.

Beside him Clyde parries, trying for sense, "If it makes it any better, I've got a brother I haven't seen in forever myself."

"You only *think* you have one, then, Kansas. If you haven't seen him, you don't know if he's still there. He might have gone right into the ground." She aims the talon down. "Down right there into the darkness, old Kansas. That's where it all ends up, which is not news, I guess." She starts scraping away again at the dirt. Not violently, just curious little scuffs. As though she has all day long.

And how long are they going to stand there watching, anyway?

A wind climbs up the slope.

"Come on up, Mare," Alan says.

She sends him a sheepish glance. "All I need, you know, is just the last *piece.*"

Finally he says, "What should I do, Mare?"

"Well," she answers, "you can come down here and start digging, for one thing, or you can go ahead and just turn me loose, for another; it's no skin off my nose, actually, it's happened before. What I really need is to find old Holly and have him come back because this is the area that's his *specialty,* you know."

"I don't know where he is, Mare."

"He got *tired,* didn't he, Jim?"

"I don't know."

"What I worry about, actually, is that the underground chamber is going to be the place I end up. You know what happens there, you're always in there with everyone, you can probably see out a little but everyone's down there, and I'd end up mashed down in there in all the *darkness.* That's what you've been looking for, isn't it? The dark outer, the dark outer place, the last outermost place?"

"I won't leave you, Mare," he says helplessly.

She gives him a wan smile.

"Why don't you come up here with me," he says.

"I think I'm going to stay right here, Jimmy."

"Maybe, Clyde," he says carefully, "you might go get us the car."

Clyde hears the horse-wrangling tone and smooths off up the hillside. Mary is sensing the trap closing around her, but she is not about to go. From her squatting crouch she gazes up out of the earth from under her eyebrows.

"*You* might be the boneman, Jim," she says now. "I never thought of that before. It might be *you.*"

"I'm just me, Mare."

"But how do I know about *inside*?" she says.

"Just me," he says, "all the way down."

Clyde has almost reached the Stutz.

"Come on, Mare," Alan says, his heart breaking, "it's just us here. Nobody else." Under the desert clouds it seems truer than anything has ever been. "Nobody's here but us."

She stares at him one more long moment. What on earth is she seeing? Something from another dimension.

"No," she corrects herself, now, sternly. "It's *not* you, is it, Jim. It's *him.*"

And at this she springs out of the pit with a leaping grace and goes sprinting past him, up the hillside, between the yawning tents. She dodges the little hollows and heaps of soil and runs uphill toward Clyde. He turns and runs after her as Clyde observes the whole thing from his frozen post at the driver's door, ready to accept her embrace or something.

Then she lifts the talon to strike at the boy's eyes.

Alan reaches her just before she arrives at Clyde, and he wrenches her elbow away so somehow it is he who gets the claw in the side of the face instead. He recoils while like a horseman Clyde instantly has her pinned and the claw pried away with two hands. Alan claps his hand to his cheek and feels the blood sliding down. He can't tell how bad it is but there's something wrong with his face all right. Then Clyde hands her over to him and Clyde is behind the wheel now and has the car started and Alan puts Mary in a one-armed bearhold from behind and wrestles her into the back seat. She screams and writhes until they are both smeared with blood. It is more blood than he has imagined is in a body. It is slicking down his face and into his collar and everywhere on his shirt and all over Mary, but he manages to hold on to her, saying her name over and over again, just her name, interrupting himself only to croak their destination to Clyde. And the car surges forward mightily, and then he is glad for the Stutz.

Mary is unloaded at Bel-Aire—two hefties manage to wrestle her out without much trouble, they are used to this sort of thing; she is not exactly screaming, but she does kick and mutter under her breath as they hoist her up with no regard for the blood and sort of scoot her along across the parking lot. And Alan follows her in, but one of them puts a firm hand on his chest and directs him with Clyde instead into a little white room, and that is the last he sees of Mary for now.

In the waiting room he unpeels his hand from his cheek, and Clyde's eyes widen. "She sure got you," Clyde murmurs.

It is a white examining room of the better sort, with chrome and glass fixtures, very bright and unstained. He stands stunned, not wanting to get anything bloody. He is a mess, for sure. He examines his gory hand. His clothes.

Mary.

That raised talon. He gasps a little with the memory of it.

"There's a mirror," Clyde points, gently.

He leans in. His green eyes are pinned open in shock. Gingerly, he moves the muscles of his cheek. There is a four-inch gash like a second mouth. The wound does not cut all the way through his cheek, but it goes deep. His stomach turns a little.

"Gee," Clyde whispers.

A nurse pushes open the door. "Mr. Barber?"

"Yes," he says dully.

The nurse arrests, not expecting to see so much blood. "Some morning for you, it looks like," she says, recovering.

"Just a little shaving accident," he answers, with a great effort.

The nurse grants him a kindly smile. "She had a knife?"

"A claw, I think." He crooks a finger. "From a dinosaur."

If this surprises her it does not show. Studiously avoiding his gaze now she takes a glass jar of cotton balls and a bottle of ethyl alcohol from a cabinet and directs him to the examining table.

"Are you hurt as well, sir?"

Clyde starts. "Oh, no, ma'am. This is all just secondhand blood."

Away in the upper reaches of the building comes the thud of a body hitting the floor. *Darling.* He makes to get up, but the nurse checks him with a slender hand.

"It's going to be all right," she tells him.

"It can't be much worse," he says.

She gives him a numbing shot in the cheek. Then there is the painful business of cleaning his wound, after which the nurse gathers the gory pile of swabs between her two hands and tosses them into a sort of standing wax-paper basket. Then she goes out in search of Dr. Yost, leaving Alan sitting there with a strange airy feeling to the side of his face.

"Oh, say," Clyde mentions into the quiet, "thanks."

It takes a moment to figure what he means. "Oh," Alan says. "Well, I guess that would have hurt, to get it right in the ocular."

"Maybe just for a second, but then it'd have been all done with," Clyde says. "That was a nice sharp object she had going there."

"I guess it was."

"Actually, come to think of it. Just where I was getting it away from her. I hardly touched it." Clyde unfolds his own hands now. A long ribbon of flesh stands open across both palms. "Gee, look at that," he says.

"What the hell, Clyde."

"I just noticed it, I think," he says, going to the tap. "I was watching that nurse."

Then Yost bustles in. "Mr. Barber," he states, gravely. "Let me see what she's done to you."

"Where is she?"

"She's upstairs," Dr. Yost answers, "where she's in very good hands." Yost fits a needle with a length of smooth black thread and lays his hands on Alan's face. "Do you have any idea what happened exactly? Was it a complete surprise that she should do this?"

He feels a twinge of disloyalty when he says, "She's been in the hospital before."

"*I see.* Hold still now." The needle slides in with a peculiar pressing sensation. Then comes the strange tug of the thread. Yost's eyelashes are blond, nearly white, and seen at such proximity his skin is marred with a million tiny pits and roughened with countless sunstruck discolorations. "I'm assuming you're committing her to psychiatric treatment."

"I think so."

"You ought to know, before you agree to it, that at Bel-Aire her commitment means two weeks of mandatory no visitation, in order to give the patient time to stabilize."

He says, "All right."

"And where was she in before?"

"Belmont. In Boston."

"*Ah.* Really." Yost lays those big hands over his cheek again saying, "Well, that's *very* reassuring. They're quite excellent there." When Yost is done he tugs and ties off the suture and wipes it clean again. "Well, it's not pretty," he says, "but in a few years you won't notice it from down the block." He applies a bandage and tapes it down, then rolls back on his wheeled stool. Then he catches a glimpse of Clyde, who is at the sink, dabbing expertly at his hands with a cotton swab. "And she got you too?"

"It's not much," Clyde shrugs.

Yost takes Clyde's hands in his own, turning up the palms like a fortune teller before returning them. "Not too serious. Why don't you head next door to have Patsy doctor you up while I talk to Mr. Barber here, alone, if you don't mind."

"Suits me," Clyde nods. At the door he turns and says, "I'll just wait for you, Alan."

"All right."

Clyde goes out and closes the door tidily behind him.

The white room, the silence.

"Now, Mr. Barber," Yost says, rolling forward again with softening seriousness, wiping his bloody hands on a cloth, "why don't you tell me what you know."

Later Clyde with his bandaged hands is leaning against the door of the Stutz. "I sort of didn't want to get in there," Clyde says.

You see what he means, all this blood in the car. On the gray ceiling and the smooth gray seats and smeared all over the walnut steering wheel. Like one of Machine Gun McGurn's projects.

He'll have to explain it to DuPrie, he supposes.

On the drive back they come up the long rise toward town, and DuPrie's dig lifts into view. A single tent flap balloons out in the evening breeze. A moment later all the flaps on the hillside whap out with a nautical slap. In the red desert glow he sees them as a fleet of ships caught eternally on the down-falling side of a frozen wave. A lost fleet. At the observatory he noses the Stutz against the Main Building and without looking left or right plunges through the library and into the basement with Clyde beside him. Standing by the giant furnace, he pulls off his shirt and stuffs it into the flames. His pants have to go too, and Clyde says, "Let me get you something of mine to wear."

He stands nearly naked by the furnace grate. Shivering as the truth of it all comes home. He has lost her finally, as he feared he would from the moment he first saw her.

It is too much.

He pulls himself together when he hears Clyde coming back. Clyde hands over pants and a shirt, and Alan buttons himself into the new duds. They fit just fine, smelling of the observatory laundry service.

He and Clyde climb two flights of stairs to the dormitory wing.

Here is Dick Morrow's bed and the window with the view of the mountains. He lowers himself slowly to Dick's old mattress. He still has the feel of Mary in his arms, struggling against him; he is going to just lie here for a little while and feel that. It is all he has left of her now. Clyde hovers there at the door for a minute, then he goes.

Alan doesn't sleep much that week while Clyde retrieves some clothes for him from the house and feeds McGurn and brings up other things from town. Slipher asks no questions, but the word is out; everyone knows everything. His stitches are a hard lacing in his face, and he swabs at them, wincing, with a cotton pad. And he is left mostly alone, except now Mrs. Slipher will deliver him a little basket for lunch, leaving it with Mrs. Fox, who leans an indicating finger at it while pretending to attend to the mail.

There is a letter every day from Bel-Aire assuring him that everything is all right. Signed *Yost*.

So he works. All night, all morning, wandering dozily up to bed. He hardly notices when Constance Lowell and Mrs. Wroth depart, a week later, the station wagon roaring into the parking lot again and ferrying them both downhill to the depot without a word of good-bye to anyone. And the B.M. locked up tight again, the shutters closed.

"Gone," is all Slipher says, at the library door, before vanishing again.

And then, at last, just ten days after he committed Mary, he comes to the end of his massive calculation. It is three o'clock in the afternoon, and the mountain light leans in through the library door. He heaves himself back, surveys the length of the table.

For all the good it does him now, he thinks.

But he reaches into his pocket, tugs out an index card. He writes the solution in pencil and carries it down the hall to the comparator room, where Clyde is blinking, endlessly blinking.

Clyde takes the card. "I'll be damned. Alpha Gemini."

"You've got those plates, Clyde."

Clyde is already at the filing cabinet. "Right over here." And in a moment he has them out. So it is that on a late October morning in 1929 Alan clips the Alpha Gemini plates into the comparator and moves the ocular to the right coordinates. Then he steps forward and puts his eye against the eyepiece and turns the blinking lever once. The opposition is ideal. The differential very good. Clyde has turned into a hell of a photographer. He turns the lever again.

Again.

Again.

"Well," he says.

It is just another field of stars. A single streak races toward the sun, a lonely asteroid. Not even as good as one of Florrie's red herrings. He sighs and rests his forehead against the hard brass ocular.

"Nuts," he says.

He steps back and lets Clyde see.

"Nothing right there," Clyde agrees. "But I'll blink these for you now. It might be nearby."

"No," he says. "I mean, go ahead and do them in order."

"I can skip around a little. I'm almost to Gemini."

"No," he says, "just do it your way."

He slumps to the stool. So he is nearly ready to admit it—that there is nothing there. Percival Lowell madly convinced of his own genius, or running away from Constance, or both. And everyone playing along because he had the money. But in the end, in the objective light of the comparator, there is no such thing as Planet X.

Well, but he will do what he can. Clyde has found hundreds of asteroids. He will calculate their periods, determine the swing of their orbits. And all the bigger ones need a name, don't they? And if you put them all together, they add up to most of a planet.

So ignoring Clyde's looks of sympathy, he slides off the stool and pulls an armful of plates from the cabinet and carries them down the hall to the library. He lugs a lightbox in and sets himself up with a new red ledger. They will be the Marian Objects, that's what they'll be. Nice simple soothing work. Keep you occupied. Until you can go see the real object herself, at least. Because now what the hell else is he supposed to do with himself but this.

He is still at it two days later when Clyde, covered in dust, comes into the library and thumps down a wooden crate marked PLANET X—SUPPLIES.

"Just found this," he says, wiping the grime from his hands, "way the hell in the back, under an upside-down wheelbarrow. Hope you don't mind I borrowed that key."

"How about that," Alan says.

"They even nailed it shut," Clyde indicates. "Those ungenerous bastards."

"Well," Alan says, casting around for a tool.

But Clyde tugs a hammer from his belt and with the claw end goes about the business of opening the box. The nails cry against the wood, and splinters spray over the lightbox. Finally he has it loose, and with one last effort he wrenches off the lid.

They peer in.

Inside, nestled in straw, are two fat green bottles of champagne: 1907 Heidsieck Goût Américain.

"They sure had their hopes," Alan says.

"Soon, pal," Clyde answers, full of fire, "we're going to drink this. You and me. I promise you."

"You don't even drink, Clyde."

"Yeah, well, not usually," Clyde growls, lifting the crate into his arms, "but I'm planning on making an exception."

IV

THE ELEMENTS
OF ORBIT
1930

27

By the time the train is halfway to Arizona, Edward Howe has committed the letter to memory. Black typescript, white onionskin paper, a neat blue envelope postmarked January 1929, almost exactly a year ago, and Mary's tight black unmistakable signature at the bottom, written it seems on the surface of his soft old heart. *Dear Scotty,* it reads,

It's only every so often I can admit reaching an extremity but to all appearances that's what we've got here. As you can see I am now in Flagstaff Ariz. where I have found myself attached to a paleontological expedition under the direction of a genuine DuPrie. Probably one of your old pals and this sounds grand enough but mostly I am a sort of secretary and he is a cowboy with a million bucks behind him. I type and file the junk away while he goes riding off into the sun, rise and set.

But imagine my surprise when Holly jumped ship on me on the way out here. I know the two of you parted not exactly pals but I wonder if for old times' sake you'd help a gal out. In the middle of Kansas Holly disappeared from the train, believe it or not, and nobody has seen hide nor hair of him since. A real Houdini act. It has been a few weeks and we have heard nothing and I am at my wit's end. I'm angry of course but more I am worried about him. You know how he gets when he's down and he was missing you, I think. If you've seen him please let me know as I promise not to pursue him, I just want to see he's all right. And on the other hand if you haven't seen him, please let me know that as well, if you would be so kind old man old horse old sock etc etc.

I'm holding on but it ain't easy. I'm all right for now but you know how it goes.

And the hell of it is he can hear that voice of hers—that lovely instrument. The hope behind it. And the fear. And now without Hollis to lean on.

This DuPrie fellow better not have got any ideas.

He folds the pages again into their envelope. Silently he urges the train forward. What will he find in Arizona, after so long?

He will knock on her door—stand enormous before her—she will fling herself around his neck—they'll go off together in search of Hollis, wherever he is . . .

Kansas rolls past. The series of tiny towns. Sylvia, Stafford, Macksville. They do a little two-step heading out of Hannah so he can notice that this name goes the same either way, and this strikes him as a good omen: what is done might be undone. A gray mountain of clouds fills the western sky. The newspapers carry the latest bad news, more Wall Street boys jumping out the windows and the margin buyers called to account. But you can't tell anything has changed out here. Into Wyoming it is mostly rangeland. Every so often the houses cluster into dusty towns. Brown cattle drift on the scrub. You can stand on the rear platform and see the rail glinting like a filament of silver behind, the frailest thread upon which these forlorn places are strung. But with Mary before him his thinking grows hopeful. What goodness is revealed! What concentrated human effort! How difficult, how honorable, to make a living from the dry and unforgiving soil! Here are people in the abstract, and he feels that old public stirring in him, vigorous, full of dumb optimism. Something he has almost given up, after all this time, and that now comes expectedly upon him again. Mary, again, making the most of him.

Almost exactly eighteen months it's been since he put down the telephone after speaking to the brother. After hearing nothing from Hempstead for the whole of that terrible morning, he called again, and no one answered. You stand there like a chump waiting with that goddamned tube in your ear and all you hear is *no, no, no*. You stand there all helpless. Louise peering around the door. He put the phone down and saw suddenly how little he knew of Mary, really. From Pennsylvania, but where? This card of Hollis's without an address. Helpless, he waited all afternoon and all night for her in that shadow-haunted apartment and went to the flower market the next morning, where he stalked the corrugated sheds with their hanging lights. Nothing. Unshaven, he visited the Hall of Records on the way into the office (the streetcar! the lifeless streetcar, without Mary in the wicker seat!) and discovered that Hollis Hempstead had no official presence on the tax rolls. He did not possess a license to operate a motor vehicle; he had never been arrested, never applied for so much as a fishing tag. His address was unlisted in the reverse telephone directory; you could be unlisted for a dollar if you wished.

Here he had kept a file on all the fighters down to their sisters and none at all on his girl. Of all the goddamned foolish oversights. He had the sense of a superb con game having been executed around him, all unknowing.

But that was crazy. And what the hell was the con anyway?

He wanted to swing at someone, but there was no one to swing at.

He found the artists' supply store where Hempstead had worked, dredging the name up from memory. Weber's. He described himself as a man in need of a portrait. He hasn't been in lately, they said, but they would pass on the message. But *no*, my word, they didn't know where he lived. They were lying faggots every one of them, and he wanted to smash some of their fairy heads, but it would do him no good so he played it straight ahead. He waited outside the store a few mornings, a sandwich wrapped in paper beside him as he hunched down behind the steering wheel of his Buick, but Hempstead never appeared; when he asked the clerks again a week later, they said he hadn't come in, and now they were worried, and he could see this time they were telling the truth.

The homosexual angle was not something he could investigate himself, but he knew whom to send. Frankie was happy to oblige. Looking for a froggy-faced fellow. Silver suits. Red ties.

"Everyone's got a red tie on at these places," said Frankie.

He paid Frankie twenty dollars to ask around and he came back with bags under his eyes but with no news. "No one's seen him," he said.

And naturally he went out to Belmont, following Isabel's lead, but he was always turned away at the desk. For a month, at odd hours when he could afford the time off, he took himself out on the car and passed into the garden-green bughouse lobby and waited to see if Hempstead would appear or Mary, but no dice. Edward despaired. What the hell good was he? First Isabel had thrown him over for a hatmaker, and now a beautiful young girl like Mary had gone nutsy on his watch. The apartment was lonely and full of the missing Mary, and in the press of everything he began to get fat. He sought out Lucian in order to have his suits altered. Something had been stuffed into the wings of his throat, his neck too small for the amount of blood that wanted to course through it. His face grew florid. His shirts creaked against his torso.

Everyone knew what had happened to him, his girl had run off, and there was a funereal silence around, rumors she wasn't right in the head somehow; how people discover these things he didn't have the first idea. People never let on what they really think about you, but they think it anyway. His new secretary was a blonde with an underbite. She opened the mail on the wrong side of the envelope and called him Mr. Howe. You treat him nice, honey. Old man Howe, has-been and former champeen, he's Suffered a Blow.

Well, you give up sometimes. You try to go about your business, but you're less and you'll always be less, but at least you know your outer limits, the sort of happiness you could have had if it had all lined up just right for you. Maybe you reach back for something good that's left. In the Carson Avenue Gymnasium for Boys and Men you inhale the smell of sweat and rubbing alcohol. He felt all right in here, it was the real old stuff, all right, and he was most himself, once, long ago, even before Isabel, in places like this. The sunlight fell at a slant through the high windows, lighting the long room in yellow, and from the corner came a thud as their kid John Coughlin worked the heavy bag. Off in a corner in the elevated ring two boys were circling each other, one slipping out a slender arm as though testing the temperature of the air. At the lockers Edward levered off his street shoes and gonged them on the metal floor of the locker open in front of him. He unthreaded his watch from his wrist and lay it upside down into his right shoe and changed into his sweat-clothes. It was the old familiar, and it came back even in his weariness. He buttoned himself into the high fighting boots he had worn when he was twenty. He slung his sparring gloves over his shoulder. Coughlin was still whomping away at the heavy bag, and beside him Joe Hass teetered on a stool. The old man grabbed Edward's arm and slid himself off to the floor. "Hello, Mr. Howe."

"Well, there he is," Edward said, "Crazy Kid Coughlin."

"I didn't mean anything by that, Mr. Howe," Hass said, quietly.

"Sure. I know it, Joe."

"Now that I think of it, *Mean* Kid Coughlin has a sort of ring to it."

"You're right, Joe."

And Joe reached way up and whomped him on the shoulder with his little hand.

What you put up with. Still, the kid had a good reach and an accelerating power in his stroke, which he delivered unblinking, his eyes fastened in front of him. It was the plain, natural cruelty in his gaze that Edward had first noticed and that he noticed now again, as though Coughlin had an ancestral hatred for the bag, for the stuffing that filled it and for the ropes that held it in place, for the world that had made the bag necessary. He was a good one, all right. His arms were ropes and he was slender through the stomach and legs, but a firm pack of muscle had developed between his shoulders. This was where his power now came from. His red hair rose up from his head in a pluming crest, and his broad eyebrows were furry. Freckled all over his shoulders and up his throat and onto his face like a rash. See him flare. The Red Kid, maybe. He had already had his nose flattened, so that his breathing came with a chuffing sound to it. He plainly did not mind getting hurt. Because of this he gave off a definite air of menace. It was something you either came equipped with or did not. Beat him to hell, he didn't care.

"All right," Edward said, grabbing the heavy bag, "do it again."

"You want me to leave it all down here." Coughlin's voice was thick.

"You've got more."

Coughlin began another angry round of jabs. When this was complete he stepped back, winded, and spat onto the mat. Edward slipped his sparring gloves on and held them out for Joe Hass to tie. With his teeth he adjusted his wrist-laces, then he climbed into the ring and lifted the rope for Coughlin, who climbed in with a look of sullen obligation.

"You look all sad, boy," Edward said.

"I ain't sad about anything but you showing up today."

"You better be sad," Edward said.

Without looking up, Hass rang the bell.

Coughlin said wearily, "I had a night last night."

"Mr. Joe Hass," Edward said, "this boy thinks he had a night last night."

"Ask him does his head hurt."

"Does your head hurt, kid? You got a little headache or something?" Edward was much the bigger man, and as he advanced on Coughlin he sensed the long power in his own arms, the size of himself. But older and cautious, and Coughlin could hurt him, all right. The stringy redhead and his sloppy red lips and the freckles, he was dangerous. Maybe those wary old bare-knuckle fighters Edward had admired as a boy had just been old. Their hesitation had not been strategic, just protective. He closed with Coughlin, who set up a polite series of soft hooks into Edward's torso.

"Come on, you little pissant," Edward said.

"Aw, leave me alone, Mr. Howe."

Edward put a short fist on Coughlin's chin, but Coughlin pushed himself away and fixed him with his heller's eye. Sure, the kid could kill him and knew it, but the kid didn't care to. What's the use? And you did not push John Coughlin into anything he did not want to do himself. They sparred like this in silence for a minute until the bell rang again. The yellow light angled through the windows and caught Coughlin's red hair ablaze. Crazy Kid Coughlin, not too bad really. Well, you could go on like this all afternoon if you wanted; you could spit and spar and take the blows you had coming and make your way down the ladder of another day.

These were Edward's only happy times, when he almost didn't think of her.

He finally asked Louise to box up Mary's things, as he could no longer bear to see them. She hired a man to pack it all away in the cage in the apartment basement. For days afterward Edward felt a desolating sorrow, and in his mind he was always explaining, taking it all out again. Looking for her on the street. On the streetcar. That lively, hurrying step. Those narrow calves. In the mornings he shaved his old discouraging face with extra care, in case Mary should return. She did not, reliably, every day.

And sitting upright in his chair behind his tumbled desk it seemed he could feel the world sliding out away from him, away through the wall and gone. The whole world was vanishing before their eyes. Wall Street crashed and suddenly everyone was a little tight with a buck, and more to the point the Boston Garden was about to open for business and putting on two-dollar fights for a thousand head in a grange hall suddenly seemed like the saddest most old-timey stuff. They would put Coughlin up but how many more boys would they manage? How many more newspaper-men would they be able to cuff around? How *precious* it had all been, he felt suddenly, to have had Mary in the outer office going about her errant, peculiar business! How terrible to sense her ghostly figure stalking in only garters around his office, bending over that desk—walking in to announce that she had written her reply to Jim Gardley without using the letter *s*!

And Hollis—*If you need me, please let me know. I'm happy to drop everything for her sake, no questions asked.*

As though it were that easy.

And then one day he reached into his drawer and took out the man's card. Blue ink, ivory stock.

And he had a thought.

A good one, though. The people in stationers' shops were less suspicious than those at the bughouse. When he asked around he pretended he only admired the man's taste, that he would like to have some made of the same sort, and hadn't this man Hempstead come in here to have them done? His mind was addled, you see—why, he suddenly couldn't remem-ber—it had been *somewhere* around here, surely! And in this way, after a week of searching, he discovered that Ballinger's had done Hempstead's cards, and that Hempstead had not paid for them himself.

Oh? asked Edward.

"No," said the clerk. "A Mr. MacAllister."

Edward fixed the order card beneath his fingertips. Noted the address. Scott MacAllister.

"How many would you like?"

"Just this one," Edward said, pocketing the clerk's slip.

The address was at Seahome, an hour away. He steered the Buick north as the January moon came up. Soon he could smell the ocean. The evening air was heavy and chill, with a dense marine flavor to it, and the light was glossy and serene and fell over the enormous houses and the long lawns with a silvery entirety. The MacAllister house, lit up at a few of its uncountable windows, was a vast cottage on a moonstruck lawn. He parked. Gravel crunched underfoot.

He wasn't hoping any more, he was past hope, but he felt he was on some track. Pushing forward to the next thing. He went up the walk and rang the bell. An ancient man came to the door. Two Airedales swirled around his legs.

"I'm looking for Scott MacAllister," Edward said.

"Are you! Well, how fortunate. There are *three* Scott MacAllisters here for you to choose from. From the looks of you I don't think you have any business with me, at least I hope not."

"I'm looking for a man named Hollis Hempstead."

"*Hollis.*" The old man searched his memory. "I suppose you'd better come in," he decided.

Edward entered. It was a fine old entryway with a candlelit polish to the paneling. Rooms reached into other rooms. He could live in a place like this.

"Will you be staying?"

"What's that?"

"Will you be *staying?*"

"I'm looking for a man named Hollis Hempstead."

"Oh, yes!" the old man cried. "And you're looking for a Mr. MacAllister to talk to. Well, just a minute, let me try to find you one. I think I can guess which one you want."

Within a minute a slick flop-haired fellow appeared in a gray suit. "I'm Scott MacAllister," he said.

"Edward Howe."

They shook hands; MacAllister's grip was faint and flimsy. "You're looking for Hollis?"

"Yes."

"And what do you want with him exactly, may I ask?"

"I was engaged to his sister."

MacAllister halted. "Well, so you were, sir. I remember now. The fighter. Is she supposed to be here, as far as you know?"

"No."

"You don't know where she is?"

He swallowed. "I guess you could say that."

"Well, neither do I," MacAllister confessed. "In fact I haven't seen either of them in a very long time. Would you come in?"

And what was it that allowed him, now, in the lamplit peace of this big house, to tell this floppy fellow MacAllister everything? He was exhausted; he had been holding himself together so fiercely; and now he put himself on the sofa in the octagonal library at the end of the hall, where the old man sat under his own lamp, staring vacantly at his book without turning a page—and with these two men as an audience he described it all, while a fire burned in the fireplace, now and then attended by a manservant in black gloves.

The hairpins, the terrible emptiness, the loss. He swiped his hands repeatedly down his tremendous thighs. He had evidently lost all vestige of shame; and despite the air of effeminate sympathy radiating from MacAllister, he held nothing back. How could a queer hurt him? And besides they had each lost something. "Do you know how I met Hollis?" MacAllister asked at last, throwing an arm over the back of the sofa. "It was a moment of embarrassment. I had been on a car and—oh, I don't know, I was in some sort of mood or something, and my stop came up, and I just swung down as the car was going off, and I was—oh, I was trying to be *graceful*—and I just swung myself right out of my *shoe*. And there was my shoe on the *car*, and there I was in my stocking on the *pavement*, and there . . . goes . . . the . . . car." He drove a flat hand away. "So there I was, one shoe off and one shoe on, dibble dibble dumpling. And I turned, and Hollis just stepped right out of the shoe store. Like an act. And he offered to give me his old shoes. And they fit. And that was how we met."

A log settled in the fireplace. This man missed Hempstead, and dully Edward noted that it turned his stomach a little to imagine what they went off and did together; it pained him to think of what dirty stories Mary had been forced to hear. "Why the hell'd you leave, then?"

"He left me, buster." MacAllister pouted. "I was busy setting up the Napoleon Club. Knee-deep and deeper. You can't leave a growing concern like that and allow someone *else* to grab all the glory." MacAllister adjusted the fall of his cuff. "He loves that sister of his. More than he loved me, I think."

Edward could only look away.

"You're a very big man, aren't you? I remember being terrified of the idea that you might come hunt us down. With those great big mean fists of yours."

"You can keep your eyes elsewhere, maybe."

"Point of fact only," MacAllister answered easily. "You know he did those." He indicated a series of paintings, three gray portraits of the house, lopsided and amateurish—

And another, of the sea and the lawn, this one somewhat better—

And another, of one of the dogs asleep on a chair—

And another, of Mary. He sat up. There she was, her legs tucked beneath. A gray background. Blue light over her shoulders.

"Mary," he breathed.

"They're everywhere," said MacAllister, and Edward saw that they were. Mary. A dozen times. And a long green estate car. And a snail on a rock that had turned out purple. And Mary again. And Hempstead himself, gazing with distaste from the canvas. And Mary, over and over again.

Mary. Mary. His heart on the walls.

"They're not very good, but I miss him very much, you see. It's really all I have left."

"Where is he?"

"Promise me you won't hurt anyone."

"Yes," he whispered.

This flop-haired boy rose now. "Come with me," he said. "I want to show you something."

They returned to the entryway. At the far end of the space—above the stairway where he had entered—hung a portrait of Mary. Different from all the others. A telegraph pole growing from the top of her head, draped with wires. Her expression was pained, burdened, brave. She had been unfairly saddled with this grotesque appendage, she seemed to say, but would wear it nonetheless.

That he should do such a thing to his dear, lost Mary!

And yet—how true the portrait seemed, how strangely right—

"That's his best, I think," MacAllister said. Then: "You're still in love with her."

"Who wouldn't be?"

"As far as I know, she and Hollis are no longer in touch with one another," MacAllister said. He reached into the drawer of a side table and removed an envelope. "But this may help."

He whipped it open and read it, his hands shaking. *Arizona*. What on earth.

"I don't know." MacAllister shrugged. "I wrote back and told her we hadn't seen him, but I never got another letter from her. She may not be there still."

"Sir," he said, and shook the man's slippery hand, and an hour later he was back at the apartment, packing for the morning train, and the next morning when the housekeeper Louise came in she saw the expression on his face and the letter and the suitcase and she cried, "Oh, sweetheart," and fell into his arms.

Before he left he scrubbed his face with salt to toughen the hide and broke two eggs into a glass and covered them with honey and milk and stirred them up together with a fork and drank them down. He filled an envelope with cash and opened the door to the chill morning and with his little suitcase set off down to the streetcar. He walked a minute. Then, ignoring the lead in his knees, he broke into a heavy lope. Two blocks of awkward running. The air scalding his lungs. The suitcase banging his thigh. His toes numb in his boots. Running, Edward filled his lungs and went harder down the sidewalk. The beautiful old neighborhood of his ancient vanished happiness. The naked winter trees in their morning fog. And the empty chamber of his heart, filling again with a fighter's blood.

Now Flagstaff as it unfolds is a shabby, worn-out burg, crusted with January snow. It saddens him to think of Mary here. A hole in the ground. The Monte Vista Hotel is a broad brick dump with a slanting frame porch and in the warm front room two old duffers chewing their cuds in cane chairs. One raises an arm as frail as a chicken wing. The hotel is full of spittoons, and the walls are painted a frontier red, and the whole joint smells of coal gas. The desk clerk is two inches taller than Edward and a hundred pounds lighter with deep creases around his eyes. He sports a white shirt with a blue stripe and a checked jacket that saw better days under President Taft and a string tie fixed with a turquoise clasp. He eyes Edward now, top to bottom. "Well, howdy do," he says.

"I'm looking for DuPrie. The dinosaur people."

"You missed them right out there in the front room, if I'm not mistaken."

"Mary," he inhales, turning.

"Naw," the old man laughs, reaching after him, "just a coupla dinosaurs. That's what passes around these parts for humorous banter, mister. Luther knows who the hell you mean, though. If you can get him to stand up once in a while. You in there?" the old man calls.

"I most certainly is," says a boy's voice from behind a bead curtain. Through it now emerges a dark, scowling figure, swatting the beads away. "You want DuPrie, he's out on the dig."

"You headed that way?"

"I might be," the boy says. "I'm late out there anyway, although I guess it don't matter any more. But you'd have to convince me to leave my card game."

"How about a dollar?"

"A whole dollar," Luther says. "Well, fancy that."

The boy leads him out into the daylight and to a ruined truck. Edward tugs a coin from his pocket, hands it across, and Luther holds it into the light, amused, and in a flash it has disappeared somewhere, a sleight-of-hand trick. He wrenches his truck into motion and starts them climbing across the desert.

"You law?" the kid named Luther asks.

"No," he mutters. "For chrissake, I'm not law. I'm looking for Mary Hempstead."

"Oh," Luther says with a wise nod.

"Where is she?"

Luther considers. "I'll take you to DuPrie," he says. "He'll get you fixed up."

So he is close. His heart is racing. They ride the rest of the way in silence. Finally they arrive at a sad little churned-up hillside. It is nearly empty, only two men visible, each with a defeated aspect in their posture.

"Which one?"

"The beard," Luther says.

"What exactly is he to her?"

"Him? DuPrie? To her? He's nothing. I don't know *which* way he goes. Or if he goes at all."

This is some good news, at least. "You sure?"

"Sure," Luther says.

Edward wrenches open the door and steps out and takes himself down the sandy slope. DuPrie is a manly fellow, bearded. Dirt is ground into the creases of his eyes, and he offers a squint from beneath his broad Stetson. Hard to believe this is a DuPrie of Maryland. He fields Edward straight ahead and accepts his name and offers his own while shaking hands. Hard, callused palms. "What can I do for you, Mr. Howe?"

He says, "I'm looking for a particular girl I think you may know."

He looks Edward over again. "Well, I'll spare you the wisecracks. How can I help you?"

"Her name is Mary Hempstead," he says, and a gulp of sorrow clenches his throat. "Very pretty, dark girl. I got word she was working for you. From her." His heart flipping, he takes the letter from his pocket and hands it shakily across. In the light of day it is an embarrassing article, a piece of worn underclothing.

"But you're not MacAllister," DuPrie confirms.

"I'm a friend of his."

"And what's your interest in the girl, exactly?"

He says, "I only want to know she's all right."

"Well, she's all right."

"I'd like to see her for myself."

"I don't know who you are, mister," DuPrie says. "I guess you understand my position."

"We were engaged, once." Worlds ago, it seems. "We go back a fair ways."

DuPrie says, gently, "She's married now, Mr. Howe."

"Married." He has almost been expecting it, but still it lands solid enough. "Sure," he cries. "All right, okay!" All he can do, he has taken a blow to the gut, he sinks to the earth, crouching. "Married," he says, from the dirt. From some vanished world he hears a count begin. You use it, soak it all up, all the room it gives you to judge the state of things. "To who?" he asks.

"A man named Alan Barber. Works at the observatory. Over the summer they married."

"You sure?"

"I married them to each other," DuPrie says.

Down in the dust he groans. He crouches there like a child. Mary! Out of reach forever! But he has to see her again, he must. He knows his own bulk argues against him, even huddled in the dirt. "How is she really?"

DuPrie hesitates. "She misses her brother, I think."

"I'll find him," Edward says. What else is he going to do? "I'll find him and bring him back. Where is she?"

"Well, sir, she's frankly locked up right now," DuPrie tells him. "In the local asylum."

"Oh, darling," he whispers. And he is lost. From somewhere he hears DuPrie give Luther an order, and then Luther is shepherding Edward back to the truck and they drive away again over the hills. There is a crate in the truckbed now, and it gives the truck a swinging heaviness, like the train, and he feels the train under him again, the pouring glory of the prairie clouds, the silver trace of the railroad across the empty plains— all his foolish imaginings dashed—his heavy softhearted longings shown at last for what they have been all along.

Some chump, he is.

But as the white building comes into view he knows his mission. He'll find the brother and bring him back to Mary and make her better. And then he'll kill himself, that's what he'll do. It is the biggest overswing of his life, but as always it seems fitting at the time.

He has never made it past the front desk of a bughouse before, but this one appears pretty decent. And as it happens he is lucky, he catches her at a good moment: she is downstairs, she is aware, she is not too fraught. And she doesn't look too nutty, only very small and frightened by the windows of the common room, absorbing the January sunlight. Well, so there she is, you correct your vision a little to account for the particulars (she is fairly tanned now, even in winter), but she is still something else. A vision. She stills his heart and gives him peace. Even seeing her here.

"Why, Teddy," she says, quietly.

He gulps, "Hello, Mare."

"This isn't Boston," she remarks after a moment.

"No. It's Arizona."

"Funny," she says.

"Well," he says, "it had to be somewhere, I guess."

"Did he follow you?"

"Who, Mare?"

She shakes her head. Crazy thoughts. He watches as she puts them aside. "I'm sorry I ran out on you, Teddy. They were making plans for me, and I decided it wasn't the best idea when everyone started to get the news."

"You're married."

She stares at him. "Someone's been broadcasting."

"That's all right," he says. The love of his life, anyway, it's nice to have such a thing settled. Never need another one. "I learned about you," he says, "I mean the time before."

"You understand, then," she says. "Why I couldn't."

He doesn't. But it's over and done with now; there is no going back. So he says, "Sure, Mare. I understand."

"Anyone could tell it's already happening," she replies. "If he comes back dead now, that just means he's somewhere else. But if he's *alive* and then comes back, there's a chance he's trapped inside someone else. So you can't be too careful. Even you, maybe." But she considers. "But no, you're too *big* for him to get into like that, I guess."

You put a girl in your heart like this, and you can't stand to have her unhappy. Because she's part of you and you want her to be happy because of it, because there's no difference between her happiness and your own. "I'll find him, Mare."

She is so *still*, that is what strikes him, very still and quiet as though not wanting to disturb something. "He ran away, Teddy."

"I know. I found MacAllister. That's how I found you."

"Scotty," she says. "Well, how's he doing?"

"All right, I guess."

"He hasn't heard anything? Not that he'd care to tell me; I know what sort of doings he gets up to in the meantime when nobody's looking."

"You want me to find your brother? I'll find him for you."

"We decided he got off the train between Hutchinson and Abbyville, Kansas," she tells him, with pacific clarity. "That's where I'd start."

"All right. I'll bring him back, Mare."

"I'd like that," she says, "if you can make sure he's just *himself.*"

He has seen that suffering expression before: the terrible painting in the MacAllisters' hallway. He has only the whole damned country to look through, that's all. "All right," he says.

She says, whispering, "Bring him back up, Teddy."

"I will, Mare." It is his exit line, and he takes it. He grants himself this: he leans forward and kisses her sweet soft cheek. It is a feat of fabulous strength that he now walks out and doesn't look back. It feels awful at first and his eyes fill, and then it feels better than anything. He is still one tough son of a bitch. Look out for Teddy Howe, here he comes. Striding out through the scurrying nutters and out the white corridor and into the January sunshine.

And now he has a reason to see her again, when the time comes.

Well, he will earn his keep, that's all.

28

By now, near the end of January, Alan has grown used to it, almost; but it hasn't come easily. Approaching Bel-Aire in the Stutz, he still feels powerfully that he is nearing a place of terrible danger, that the building is full of monsters and the damned. He has come to know the old worn road: the rough slow climb to the ridgeline, the Stutz creaking like a galleon over the rutted washboard; then the smooth decline, past DuPrie's mostly shuttered dig, to the open territory beyond, and the first view of the place, as white under the winter sun as a palace on the moon. And with everything else to think of, he can almost, but not quite, ignore the news coming out of Wall Street, where all the fancy folks have lost their shirts. DuPrie among them. And not just them, but all the conductors and taxi drivers and bartenders who have taken to buying on margin and who have now been called to account. No one is sure what it means exactly, only that suddenly no one has the sort of money they thought they did.

The Lowells, of course, are immune to all this, as Slipher assures them. But Alan finds himself hoping to hear bad news about the Morrows. Surely they deserve a fall. Something that equates, anyway, to his own. Coming to this place every day for so long, and seeing his wife in such pain.

She has been there for nearly three months. The two weeks of enforced no contact ended, but she hadn't wanted to come downstairs; it had been another two weeks before Yost took pity on him. "Come on up," he said, "you can see her for yourself."

At the top of the stairs, a stark white hall. Bars on the windows. A row of cells. Some doors with a single window—made of reinforced glass—and others simply numbered, with a spyhole. As he followed Yost down the hall he caught momentary glimpses of a few empty white rooms, white bed frames, sheets with a plain blue pinstripe—

And then there she was. A locked door with a window.

"Can I go in?"

"No." Then: "It's not the time yet."

Her room was a small chamber with a gray floor and a barred window that looked out on the lawn and the canyon below. Beside the bed was an upholstered sitting chair. In this chair was Mary, turned three-quarters away. She was rocking back and forth. What he could see of her face was set in stern concentration.

"Terrible thing that brother of hers did, without knowing it. You do think he's dead."

"I hope to hell he is."

"Of course we do see it a lot. That kind of abandonment. It gets to be such a burden." They both gazed at her.

Beautiful. Still.

The ceiling was gouged with horrible scratches.

"She did that with her shoes, we think," Yost said, following his gaze. "The first day we didn't take them from her. Although how the hell."

Alan noted the scratches with a creeping unease. The tusk would have done that, he thought. Madness. "She eats?"

"Oh yes. She eats; she drinks; she's capable of taking care of herself more or less. I mean in many ways she's quite lucid, as far as it goes. We allow her to use the bathroom alone, which is a privilege not many of her fellows share. This is a secured ward, as you can see; she can't get out. But she's not interested in going outside. Or downstairs." Yost turned to him. "You want to know what I think, I guess."

"Yes."

"You won't like it."

"I don't like much of this."

"No. Well, Kleist, it usually runs a certain course. The previous episode lasted about three months. We're at about four weeks now. If the past is any guide, we've got a little while before it begins to abate. She'll still be somewhat delusional, but she'll be moving toward the back end of the labile curve."

He would just stay here at the window, watching her.

"On the other hand, she's lost her brother now," Yost continued. "Which introduces a new element. My hunch, although it's difficult to tell with what she's told us so far, is she's simply become fixated on him, and it's something she uses as a sort of precipitant, a catalyst, without being itself organically related to the cause of the trouble, which is more fundamental. For example, I've never been able to get from her exactly what it is her brother would do for her that, for example, *you* couldn't do."

"He's a link to home," Alan supplied.

"But a link who ran away from her." Yost squinted at him. "And *you* didn't cause any of this, you know."

"Oh, spare me."

"All right. Some people worry. No, the real answer is we'll just have to wait and see. I've been in communication with Bob Miller, whom I happen to know a little bit. He remembers her distinctly, and he has high hopes for her. And so do I. Usually what happens in these cases, especially a second episode, is they resolve on their own after a little while. Usually the second episode runs a little longer than the first episode, I warn you, but they do resolve. Already she's nearly always able to dress herself and get out of bed. If that's any comfort. I hope it is. It's quite a bit more than some of our patients can do for themselves. She still has her delusions, of course, but she's now talking about them a little bit. That's often the first step with Kleist; you get someone talking about the things they know are delusional, and it gives them a certain perspective on it all. It's tedious work for a person, but it does succeed. When you met her she was not long out of Belmont, if I remember rightly."

"That's right."

"And you didn't see any of that then. She had it managed, didn't she?"

"Completely, as far as I could see."

"So, I can only counsel patience. She'll find her way out eventually. She wants to." Dr. Yost touched him companionably on the shoulder. "She wants to find her way back to you, sir."

You did not learn about this in school. No one ever broke the news of madness to you behind the fence the way one learned about sex; this was territory no one ever spoke about. A blank space on the map. That house at the end of the road, the witch inside, the windows pierced with brambles. So, sure, he gave himself credit for performing as well as he could. He was a scientist at heart, and there was some scientific explanation to what had happened to Mary, psychological or physiological he didn't know, but he resolved that it wouldn't scare him too much. There was mystery here but nothing mystical.

Still, of course, it pained him. His girl, locked upstairs in this house of the afflicted. She didn't come down. He came out anyway, just in case. He grew almost used to the groups escorted across the lawn, not just madwomen but recovering bronchial cases, frail asthmatics, dried-out drunks. He no longer cringed at the sudden startled moans from an old woman in a wicker chair, as though just awaking to where she was, dying of senility and sitting at an empty card table. In the afternoons the lawn of Bel-Aire was dotted with white figures walking in twos and threes. Every afternoon the same nurse would greet him with a cautious smile. "Mr. Barber," she said.

"Hello, Patsy. Clyde says hello."

"And how are his hands?"

"Still just fine."

She smiled and gestured around the corner with a long manicured fingertip. "You know where to wait."

As always when Alan appeared at the doorway a dozen heads, all of them patients of one kind or another, swiveled to look at him. He settled himself on his customary ladder-back chair, the nearest thing to the door. He was conscious of the room's examination of him, but he sat without expectation, his feet flat on the floor before him, his hat on his knees.

His good old hat. In trouble again.

He would wait an hour, always in vain, then get up to go. And how it pained him to abandon her again. What Hollis had done once, on an impulse, he now did every day at exactly half past four in the afternoon, when visiting hours ended.

Finally at the beginning of December she came down. She was half better: subdued and clear-eyed. Recognizably herself. But still plainly troubled, tipping her head back and forth strangely. The terrible tusk. He could see it there himself, nearly. She was well-kept, however, her hair in order and her clothes tidy. Her voice was low, modulated. "Hello, Jim," she whispered.

"Mare."

"Ooh." She eyed his scar. "That must have hurt."

He did not know whether to embrace her, but she came forward and buried herself in his arms. Warm, this shape, his Mary. Never leave.

"Oh, Jim," she whispered, "I'm sorry."

He could only shake his head.

"How's Clyde?"

"He's fine. He's all right."

"Is the old lady gone?"

"She's been gone for weeks," he told her. "We chased her out, Mare." She gave him a little laugh at this and sat down beside him and grasped his hands. He did not know what to ask or how to look at her except to pretend that it was all a joke between them, a sort of grand practical joke they were both playing on everyone. You could not just be serious about it because what good would that be? *Show some gas, Barbie.* "That was some cake," he said.

"Some cake," she agreed, with a little laugh. Then, calmly, she began to explain: "What they've done, Jim, is they've taken me out of harm's reach. They can't fix everything at once, so they start with the basics. For example, *you* can't get in here unless you can prove you're *real.* So everybody I see here is actually a real person, like *you.* But oh, your *cheek,* Jim."

He soldiered on: "Something else, isn't it?"

"Oh, Jim." She cringed.

"It doesn't hurt any more."

"It wasn't my fault," she said.

"I know it, Mare."

She stared bewildered at the scar, something churning in her. Then she erupted, "I can't help it, Jim, he's not *in* there, is he? I know it's crazy, but he's not, he's not *inside?*"

At her urging he opened his mouth, stretched out the tender cheek. His dear sweet Mary, eyes wide. He would stay like this as long as it took.

———

At the end of the glassed-in porch was an old saloon piano. So sure, he sat and played, no one prevented it, and the old ladies snoozed and the dryout cases listened with desperate attention and Mary sat very still on a cushion, her hands folded in her lap. He might play for an hour, on a good day, without design or intent. "The Good Son Shuffle." "The Happy Traveler." He joined it together artlessly, the eighty-five songs of his mother's *First Songbook for Home Enjoyment*, and down deep at the bottom of the well the old *sean nós*, the old notes holding some trace of his father in them, for might he not have been in his father's lap when he first heard them? The old progressions and dismantlements still unwound in his fingers with a rolling simplicity; he could do this all day long.

But did she ever get any better? He couldn't swear to it. As far as he could tell she believed herself safe inside, safe from the dried-out old rider; but she asked after Hollis, and still wondered if Hollis might have been taken over by the little man, or that the little man might be able to hide inside other people who came to visit her.

"It will pass," Yost told him, although he sounded less sure of himself.

Christmas came, and New Year's Day 1930, and the snow fell and the winter sun lit the world white and glaring beyond the tall windows. She was as beautiful as ever to his eyes. Then, one day at the end of January, she seems suddenly more upset, more cautious. She stands at the doorway watching him carefully for a long minute before agreeing to sit down across from him. She asks, as she always asks now, "Any word from Holly?"

"No, Mare," he has to say.

"It's not that I expect anything. I just wonder what the likelihood is of *finding* me. If they start coming now, I know that's a sign that things are about to happen again."

"I don't know where your brother is, sweetheart."

"I *know* you don't, Jim. I know what happened to him; he went inside somewhere. Inside and *down*, zoop, right into the dirt. But do you know who *was* here?" She is so still, so motionless. "*Teddy.*"

It takes him a moment. "The boxer?"

"That's right."

"When was he here?"

"A few days ago," she admits. "But he looked *fat*. I guess he missed me."

"He was really *here*, Mare, here in the room, like I am?"

She laughs, a little sadly. "I *know* you think I'm crazy, Jim, but it was really him. A *version* of him, anyway. He'd come all the way on the train."

"How did he *find* you?"

"Isn't it spectacular? He'd got hold of one of Scotty's letters. One of the letters I mailed. The one I mailed to Scotty."

"What did he want?"

"Oh, just to see me. He knew we were married. He said he'd find Hollis for me."

"Well," he offers, "that's awfully nice of him."

"Poor Teddy," she says. "Oh, it was *strange* to see him come in that door. It was like another life coming in, from another world, just walking in that way, that life I used to have before everything happened."

"He said he'd find Hollis?"

"Well, he said he'd try. I believe him."

It is enough to give him a little spur of hope, actually, after he confirms the visit with Patsy. He has known about her letters but gave up expecting anything to come of them after so long. And now this. "Is he still here?" he asks Mary.

"Oh, no, I don't think so. I think he left right away. To Kansas."

"That's a start, anyway."

"I know. I meant to tell him about Clyde, but then I thought that'd just sound crazy to him, my theories about why Clyde came because he had Holly inside him. I mean I know they *are* crazy, Jim. I just thought you should know I was thinking about it and didn't tell him."

"That's good, Mare."

"I know." She sighs. "They go round and round like that, those stupid ideas." She twirls a finger in the air. "Like you, you go round and round."

He wipes his hands down his face. "We're still looking."

"You still think it's there."

"I don't know, Mare. Clyde does. I've named a few asteroids after you, anyway."

She beams at him, plumps herself upright. You can still flatter her; it is interesting to see that. "Well *that'll* throw him off the track, anyway," she grins.

———

You can count on finding Clyde at the comparator just about any hour of the day now. When Alan returns he discovers Clyde peering forward, the room full of the endless *clack-clack*.

"Patsy says hello," he reports.

Clyde blushes and sputters a little, then holds out another telegram. "Your old girl says hello too, I guess," he answers.

From Cambridge. Alan slits the envelope and extracts the blue paper. No, not Florrie this time. Dick, maybe, just having fun. He wouldn't put it past him.

WE HOPE YOUR FINANCIAL POSITION REMAINS STEADY

Funny, how he finds himself disappointed. He was hoping it was another set of coordinates. And the right ones, this time, so they can be done with this. But no, it's Dick rubbing his nose in something else. He's survived the crash, it would appear. No surprise there, of course. He thinks of Edward Howe, a man he's never met, on the train to Kansas. Urges him on as he folds the telegram in half and slips it, for safekeeping, into his breast pocket, and returns to the library. Wishes him well. He can use all the help available, he thinks.

29

Beneath the single white cover with its many sewn eyelets Felix's mother has suddenly shriveled alarmingly, living on tea and an occasional piece of cake. And alarming too, in a different way, are the fond, glad looks his mama gives him, so that without warning he can look up and be confronted with a loving gaze, full of fulfilled gratitude.

"Desist, mama," he finally protests. "You make me feel like a lost puppy."

"But you *were* lost, Felix," she tells him.

There are times when he enters the bedroom after his timid knock to find her flat on her back, her mouth in a lifeless O, the lace nightgown collar unmoving at her throat—times when he is sure his mother is dead. He hesitates. Eventually she stirs, gives Felix a look of embarrassed recognition. Caught. And beneath this: fear.

"You want to go see Yost, mama?" he asks.

"No," she croaks.

"Just a social call."

She accepts this with a faint rustling smile. "He's not as much fun as he thinks he is."

There is also the question, suddenly, of how they might pay for her to go. Their ruin is in the newspapers back home, where dozens, hundreds of others are also ruined—the Dentons, the Victors, the Farquhars of Providence, on and on. He takes some comfort in this company, and in the notion that their calamity is shared. Still, it is terrible, and he feels the stunned blankness of someone who has been in an explosion, who has lost a limb suddenly, the size of the blast and the shock of the wound erasing, for now, anything like pain. But you try to move the missing article and you feel something strange all right. For example you go to wire money from your last active account and you receive a dropsical look from the boy at the Union Bank counter when he slides you the wire back under the grille: SIR NO FURTHER FUNDS AVAILABLE SINCERE REGRETS. And then you get a funny twinge, all right.

"Sorry, Mr. DuPrie," the boy says.

"They're all like that now, aren't they?"

"Yes, sir, I think they are."

"Something going around, I guess."

"Must be catching pretty bad," the boy replies. "You ain't the only one."

So now he is really absolutely broke, every scrap of property in mortgage down to the sofa buttons and no cash but what he has on hand and therefore nothing really but what he's standing up in and can put his hand to locally.

"All right"—he tips his hat—"much obliged."

He turns and goes out again in his good old snakeskin boots, in shame surely and embarrassment but also a sort of puzzlement. How in hell do you operate when you don't have money?

He emerges into the daylight still holding the wire.

He does not often leave his mother's bedside now. Prudencia is there to perform certain offices and to manage her person, but he has to think of what Prudencia costs them. Two dollars a week, which will buy a certain amount of plaster, a certain amount of flour and sugar and coffee, too, come to that. And he will have to give up renting the warehouse.

"You think Dr. Yost would mind a visit, anyway?" he suggests.

"Felix, I'm not going to go up there. I don't want old Mitts looking at me while I lie around like a mummy. She's going to live until she's a thousand years old, and I don't want to give her the pleasure of my company at the moment."

"Mary's there now."

This pains his mother. "Oh, but Felix, all the more reason *not* to go. She wouldn't want me to see her like that. In fact I doubt she'd permit me. I can't imagine what that must be costing."

"It can't be cheap."

His mother hoists herself up from her pillows, staring out from the caverns of her eye sockets. "Felix, you have to promise me, if her husband can't do it, that you'll help him pay for it out there. You have to promise me that."

"We haven't got anything ourselves, mama."

But she will not be deterred. "You have to promise me, Felix, that you'll make sure she can stay there as long as she needs."

"Yes, all right."

"That's what Larry is underneath it all, Felix, he's a psychiatrist. Drying out is only a lucrative sideline, and mummy tending, you know, that's only for the money too. Maybe he'll even take her for free, because she's so interesting. But promise me."

"I promise, mama," he says.

"All right." And she reclines again, satisfied. "If you don't do it, Felix, I'm going to *haunt* you."

"I believe it, mama."

"I'll come at you in chains, and it will be very embarrassing to explain to the neighbors. What you didn't do when you should have done it."

It is torture to watch her decline like this. You cast around for something to provide with: you've got the house and the dig now shut down and the life you've lived behind you. The Hundred Club, the lightning rod, those great illustrated volumes with their color plates, his father's banded hole, the *Tarsal*, that night in the rowboat and his fury, the heaving sea, the sobbing of the universe behind a stone door it seemed. Against his mother's leaving, it is all too puny to believe. Darwin says, *The suffering of the lower animals throughout time is more than I can bear.* Count it all up, the striving and the triumph and the pain, and somehow it all contrives to vanish, unbelievably, all this feeling-matter exiting from the dimensions of known space and entering the eternal zero.

A fine pickle you've gotten yourself into, isn't it!

At dawn he will leave her side and ride Sissie out to the dig. *Suspending* was the word he used, but the crew knew the real story, all right. One after another they shook his hand and went on their dark way.

"I guess they can go ahead on," Willoughby says. He and Felix are on horseback, surveying the tents, the hastily buried pits. "But I must confess I've grown to like it pretty well around here."

"I have too."

"I guess we work together all right," Willoughby proposes.

"Sure. Well, I guess we do."

"That's still all Morrison Formation out there." Willoughby waves. "And right here. Still who knows what to find. And we still got that lease for another year, don't we, all paid up."

"Maybe Isenbright might come through," Felix suggests.

"Stranger things."

"Just so we're clear, Will, I can't pay you anything."

"I understand it. I got a little bit saved. I'll be all right for a little while yet. We can go halves." Willoughby gives him a curious squint. "You really busted?"

"Busted as Ben Doney."

"I mean all the way down, busted busted?"

"All the way down."

Willoughby considers this. "You really going to stick it out?"

"I guess it's as good as anything. We can make a little bit of a living out there."

Willoughby adjusts his hat and scans the horizon. "It is the Morrison Formation."

"It is."

"You know what it's possible to find out in the Morrison Formation, don't you?"

Felix says, "I guess I do."

Willoughby grins now and says, offhandedly, "I mean in the way of certain ores and minerals, Mr. DuPrie. Carnotite. Shistovite. Other matters such as these that we might still turn up, if we explore enough. Thought you might have a ghost of an idea."

"No."

Willoughby shrugs. "Well, maybe it's a long shot this far south. Most of what we've found so far in Utah's been associated with the real main-line of the Morrison. But you never know what we might turn up. Find ourselves a breccia pipe, we might just find ourselves a little bit of uranium ore." And he shoves his hat down on his head. "It can be a pretty rich country, in fact, if you know at all what you're looking for."

"I see," Felix answers.

Willoughby leans over from Picobel to shake Felix's hand. "You want to go partners? You still got the lease in your name."

"Sure, partners," Felix agrees. "However you want to play it, Will."

Willoughby smiles. "You didn't think we were all out here just looking for *dinosaurs*, now?"

It is business, and he knows it is done this way, and so it should satisfy the fading ghost of his father. And this new angle might show certain facts in a new light. Those shouts from the dig face. That odd remark of Bryce's. Maybe even Willoughby's interest in the Sinagua.

But none of it seems that vital any longer. After all, Felix has been down that road. And he knows where it goes. What will it bring him? Cars, houses, boats. And the freedom to act like a perfect idiot.

So maybe he is really set loose, he allows himself to think. From all that back there.

And blasted free like this in the silence that has followed his great ruination, he finds his mind moving in what seems to him a new fashion. What he has been waiting for all along, maybe. In the early morning when he hoists the saddle onto Sissie's back and cinches her belt tight around her belly, waiting for the brown balloon of her abdomen to contract before he pulls it snug, and fills the canteens with water, and packs her single saddlebag with food, he finds he is simply—what is it?—*content* is not the word. Nor is *attentive*, although this is closer. The light, unforced focus that he tried so hard to bring to bear on the deck of cards in the Staunton he now brings to bear without effort on this firm green apple with its black scaly divot where the blight skipped through the orchard. Feel that with the rasp of your thumbprint, that's all. And the oiled pistol, hard as a bone against his side. It's all here to be seen and felt, and you're here too.

You *accept* everything somehow, maybe; you sort of accept the fact of the world.

He is getting a little Hindoo out here possibly; it's been known to happen.

Ten miles from town, from the top of a desolate plateau, Arizona can be seen to continue forever. In the winter wind the snow fringes the scrubby pines and the cactuses. And away to the south the canyonland is a muted pink and orange. A titanic wintry vacancy. The mind travels out into the landscape and, finding nothing, returns with the sense that something really is in residence there: something huge, silent, eternal. It is an absence so complete it becomes a thing in itself.

Sit atop your horse and look out that way.

Whatever it is. The last thing that awaits him in this place. A great emptiness.

30

It is a mild, snowless February in Wichita, as though Nature herself is waiting for what happens next. The whole country has its breath held to see if it's just all going to get worse. Even the gangsters are quiet. And if you have something in hand at the moment, you don't spend it without a good long thought. In something of the same fashion Edward Howe decides to stay in Wichita until he's scoured the town from top to bottom. What is in Boston for him now? He arranges to have Frankie and Fitzsimmons and that whole bunch keep an ear to the ground for Hempstead, and they place advertisements in all the newspapers, and he writes a single letter once a week to Arizona that of course Mary never answers.

He doesn't care, maybe.

And Hempstead *was* here, at least briefly. He is sure of that. The station agent's description of him was exact. Now, if he can only pick up the man's trail again.

It had begun easily enough. The stringy, sun-tanned station agent in Abbyville remembered a man lingering strangely in the midnight station around the correct time, and the man had answered to Hollis's description; and he remembered him asking after a bus to Wichita.

"Kansas?"

"Yes, sir, Wichita, Kansas. Said he wanted a place to settle down a little bit out of the way."

"I'll be damned," Edward said. "You're sure."

"Yes, sir." The station agent lifted an eyebrow: "We don't get that type around here too often."

So he had headed off to Wichita full of hope. No one remembered Hempstead at the bus station; but the city did strike Edward as a quiet, decent place to be—just the sort of place to hide out if you wanted to. So he spent the first few days in Wichita, after he had bought a cheap old wood-sided car, a Ford, driving very slowly up and down the side streets, leaning out to read mailboxes and making inquiries in rooming houses and the YMCA and the post office. At the end of the day he would sit and have the fifty-five-cent dinner at the Wishing Well. It was not too bad and you got enough meat anyway, but the dinners always left him feeling as though he had been kneed in the abdomen. He was not really cut out for a bachelor's life for as much as he had lived it; in the absence of female company he grew lousy with self-pity and a heavy hammy lassitude as though his muscles had turned to sand. But it helped that he was on a mission, and after dinner he would go to the movies and sit still for a while in the dark, eyeing his fellow patrons from behind, or find a club where he could settle his stomach with a beer or two and cast a slow eye over the crowd, mostly little businessmen and their hot nights out.

He was not naive, he knew Hollis might be long gone from here; but it was a place to start, and he had nothing better to command his attention. He sent word to Fitzsimmons that he would be back sometime but that family pressures made it impossible, et cetera. He knew such a letter would mean the end of him in Boston, at least with his own outfit; but their time was up anyhow. And there was nothing he would rather be doing. Mary, sitting very still at her window; he could help her. He could.

But if it was possible to come to a city and leave no mark on it, Hollis Hempstead appeared to have done it. After a month in Wichita Edward had visited rooming houses, hotels, speakeasies, police stations, libraries, cemeteries, hospitals, dance clubs, art supply stores, analysts, tailors, employment agencies, and post offices—and found nothing. A man accustomed to living a secret life, Hollis had managed it expertly here as well. And Kansas was looking less like the place to be; there were dust storms in the news now, you could hardly credit it, nothing in Kansas yet, but in

Oklahoma and Texas you heard of it and saw the photographs, little towns being overwhelmed by great tumbling clouds, like something from another world.

On the other hand, Kansas was not so different from anywhere else, he began to suspect; listening to the news and going to the movies, Edward began to sense that some critical nerve had been cut somewhere, as though the life had gone out of everything American. The speakeasies were still doing business, but there was a new, serious tone to the drinking, and you saw more and more men just skiffing along the sidewalk looking busy but avoiding your glance. A whole class of men gone truant. Going up to doors and knocking, just as he was. But not looking for a man—looking for work. And the rooming houses, carved up into a dozen rooms that opened nonsensically off one another, babies screaming from the top of the stairs and everywhere a smell of boiling laundry, and spiders patrolling the basins, and the side yards were full of snow and glinting shards of busted metal, as though someone had tried to run a car into the house.

And to all these places Edward presented himself as a possible tenant. He tipped his hat and ducked under the lintel into a gray room with a rag rug coming unwound underfoot, and he was invited back into a kitchen for coffee, and there was Mr. Mitchell, who taught at the trade school until he lost his position; or Mr. Jenkins, who lived on a railroad pension and occupied the upper rear room with the view of the water tower, poor sorry suckers who looked at him with all their mustered dignity and cracked wise about the food and the neighborhood and the work they had once done.

And the poor duffers had never had a chance. Hard times had come to Kansas, all right. And still these were gentlemen who looked you in the eye, and this stirred something old in him. And sure they drank too much and told hard-luck stories when he didn't want to listen, and they wiped their drooling lips with the backs of their hands, and they hadn't seen the business edge of a decent razor in a week, and some were simply ornery no-good sonsabitches, but what the hell was he? Just one of these men who'd had good breaks all his life, never mind Isabel and Mary and that he'd never won a belt.

Who the hell was he, in comparison to them?

As winter bore down in February, and as he had looked nearly everywhere he could think to look, he began to slow his operations. Three expeditions a day turned to two, then one. Edward walked by the YMCA one afternoon and found himself drawn, as though hypnotized, through the swinging doors and into the low light of the gymnasium with its familiar smell of sweat and leather and the rhythmic whirring of a man skipping rope in the corner. He began training again, an easy routine meant to keep his body, lazy dog, in reasonable condition, and as he addressed the seamed speedbag he felt something large and final had begun to settle in him, some giant satisfying sadness whose outlines he could not see from where he stood, because it was still too new, too near. And as February cycled through, and as a huge warm windstorm filled the air with a continental roar, and as the windows of the automat grew wet with everyone's breath, he felt he was cultivating this sadness, keeping it warm and quiet, sensing that it was related in some fashion to his notions about the duffers in the rooming houses and to the new mood in the country; he felt suddenly and for the first time entirely in tune with things, with the country itself, where a vast melancholy had settled down on all forty-eight states all at once. Even the wits on the radio were strained and played to an audience whose laughter was quieter, more qualified, so that when he did visit a stinking rooming house or fleabag hotel to ask his rote questions he felt ever more certainly that he was trespassing into some tender, secret part of things, that everyone had dropped their fancy acts and good lines and was looking, at last, to one another for the thing they had always been afraid to ask for before, some sort of hand up. Because now everyone needed a hand somehow.

And it is early March of 1930 when, visiting one of these houses—not too lousy a one—he glances up and sees, in a far corner of the kitchen, a painting of a man behind a desk, glowering. It looks strangely familiar, and he feels a funny instant sympathy for the man in the painting, a big blockheaded fellow staring up at you because you were bugging him, all right, and then he recognizes his own bronze swan lamp and his zinc cigarette lighter, and then himself: his own broad squat aggrieved body and his heavy black head.

He grabs the landlady's arm. "Say, who painted that?"

"A tenant of mine."

"Name of what?"

"MacAllister was the name he gave."

"MacAllister!"

"He left that for me because he knew I liked it." She looks at him levelly, and he releases her. "It does look like you a little, doesn't it?"

"When'd he leave?"

"Oh, months ago."

"You got an address for him?"

"I think so." She gives him a long curious look. "You know what he is, don't you?"

"Yes, ma'am, I do."

"He kept it out of my house, though. And he didn't drink. He liked to paint, but I made him take it in the yard, because of the smell. He wasn't here very long." She eyes him suspiciously. "You want to have your portrait done or something?"

"Something like that," he says.

She sniffs disbelieving, but she gets him the address: 451 Dunbar. He knows Dunbar, all right. He draws his collar up around his throat and turns to take his aching carcass back down the icy porch steps. And despite himself, his soft old heart—oh, he can hardly stand it—is poised for one last hopeful lunge.

31

Clyde finds it is nice to have Alan as company across the hall; it is almost like having Roy there if he doesn't open his eyes and ruin it. Back in October and November Clyde watched Alan pick away at the bandage, then swab it free of crusted stuff. It was gory but seemed to Clyde it was also somehow his *own* wound; it was meant for him, after all. And it allowed him to think of Patsy, who had dressed his wounds so nicely and said, "You've got nice hands, Mr. Tombaugh," and presented them back to him all fixed up.

All this has added up to a hunkering intensity, a continued concentration. The crate of Lowell's champagne sits in the corner of Clyde's bedroom, often draped with his stray undershirts or stacked with his half-read magazines. He has been at it nonstop, on behalf of Alan and Mary, since October; and he has kept it up through November, December, January, now February. Getting through the Taurus plates at the galactic center has taken him forever; they are so dense as to be nearly unblinkable. Great freckled swarms, uncountable tens of thousands on every single plate. It is terribly slow going, and you have to count all the variables and asteroids besides. The Taurus plates have taken him six weeks on their own going twelve hours a day. And still if the planet is there at the moment, he fears he'll miss it, that it's going to stay hidden forever.

He would have jumped ahead to the Alpha Gemini plates had Alan insisted, but he had not. And it is just as well, for when he reaches them, easier going now, there are no suspects anywhere in view. Methodically he goes through Alpha Gemini and Beta Gem and Gamma Gem, nearly all the way around again to where they began photographing so many months ago, when the constellation was out of opposition; it is the afternoon of February 18—a Tuesday—when he finally reaches Delta Gem. He sits on the stool, his eye at the eyepiece, the rhythmic *clack-clack-clack* of the comparator filling the room. Three hours into the day's work, something flickers.

Following procedure he reaches down and turns off the automatic blinker. Then he puts his eye to the objective again and blinks the machine manually. There is a tiny black fleck, no bigger than a grain of salt, much too small to be a planet.

He flicks the plates manually. The speck dances back and forth a few millimeters.

Well—it's small, anyway.

With a dawning excitement he reaches into the desk drawer and pulls out a ruler and swings the viewing mechanism up and out of the way. The two plates stand at their canted angle, side by side, illuminated from the back. He lays the ruler on first one plate, then the other.

"Three point five millimeters," he says aloud.

He checks the dates again. January 23. January 29. He makes sure which is which. This one on the left is the first exposure. This one on the right is the second. So yes, whatever this thing is, it's moving. And not only moving, but retrograding. And nothing retrogrades unless it's also orbiting the sun and you're going past it on an inside track.

And it is in Gemini.

"Also I took that disaster on the twenty-first," he says, to no one. He stands, lays his hand on his forehead. "It would have to be that one."

In the file drawer.

Now don't drop it, you dumb hick.

January 21, a cloudy night, off and on, he had to close the shutter more than once when the clouds came ragging in, keeping a watch all night, and the exposure came out lousy, a little blurred with atmospheric haze and overexposed, lousy enough that he decided to start over and do two more plates of the same location. Lucky now, it turns out, because it means he has a third check-plate already to hand. No good but better than nothing.

He crouches and gets it out and removes the paper wrapping and checks the label and holds it to the light. The same area of sky. He exchanges this plate with the January 23 plate and bends over the machine. Funny how your hands start to shake. Nothing left to drop at this point, but he snugs his hands into his armpits and crosses his arms across his chest as he leans over the ocular.

Well.

So.

Well, so, there it is again, one more millimeter to the east. Moving just the way a trans-Neptunian body would move. But it is just the faintest possible light: a tiny 15th-magnitude flyspeck. A tiny, tiny thing. Nowhere near as big as Neptune. Not even close.

But without a doubt it is out *past* Neptune. And it is bigger than any asteroid could be. Especially way out there. There's nothing out there.

He stands for a long minute, staring at the two plates.

"Well," he says.

He crosses the hall and knocks on Lampland's door. Lampland has his giant square Frankenstein shoes up on the desk and is busily noting something in his ledger, his spectacles on his forehead. "Mr. Tombaugh."

"I think I've found your Planet X," he says.

Lampland's eyebrows go up, fetch his glasses from his forehead, and bring them neatly down onto his nose. "Have you now."

"There's something in Delta Gem."

"Delta Gem." Lampland sets his ledger carefully aside and swings his feet down and follows him across the hall. In the blinking room he leans in and activates the manual trigger once. Again.

"I don't see a thing."

"Just north of the star," he tells Lampland.

Lampland clicks again. Finally he lets out a long descending whistle. "Two days either way, you'd have lost it in the glare."

He stands bent for another long minute, flipping plates back and forth.

"Well, it's awfully small," Lampland notes.

"Yes, sir."

"Amazed you ever saw it. It's not an artifact of the plate."

"No, sir. It checks out on the third plate too."

"And it's retrograding."

"Yes, sir. There's no doubt about that."

"You're sure these dates are right?"

"I'm quite sure."

Lampland straightens. "Well, you'd better go tell Dr. Slipher."

"I'm getting Alan first."

"You get V.M."

"No, sir," he says, "I'm going to get Alan first."

He finds Alan upstairs at the library table, a stack of plates before him and an electric viewing box plugged into a floor outlet and an open ledger at his elbow, at work on his endless asteroid catalog. Alan looks up wearily. But at once he catches something in Clyde's face and says, "Oh, you're shitting me."

"I don't think so."

He jumps up and comes around the table and stalks forward across the room. "Where?"

"Delta Gem."

"God*dammit. Fucking* Gemini."

"It's tiny, though." They are already into the corridor, then at Slipher's door. Slipher is already up, a pink india-rubber eraser in his hand. "We've found something, sir," Clyde says, and Slipher rushes forward and past them both and hurries down the hall ahead of them in his shirtsleeves and braces. You hold on to a thing for thirty seconds, and then it is taken from you. Well, he had it once. Had it first. Lampland steps aside. The director's expression is fierce as he bends over the eyepiece, still holding the eraser. "This is Delta Gemini?"

"Yes, sir. Just north of the star."

Slipher is frozen for a long moment. He clacks the comparator once, twice.

"Oh, Percy." Slipher sighs.

"That's eight days, sir."

"Well, it's moving the right way, all right," Slipher notes. "But it's *small.*"

As a body they all check the window. A thick blanket of gray clouds covers the sky. Then all eyes return to Slipher. He has straightened away from the comparator and now is facing Clyde. The director sags with what appears to be despair. Clyde takes a step back into the corner. Fifteen years, and the kid from Kansas finds it. Of course the man would be upset.

But then a moment later the expression is gone. In its place, a look of resolve. Of something having been decided.

"Sir?" Clyde asks.

"That's our boy, all right," says Slipher now. "No doubt about it. But we can't tell a soul until we're sure. No one knows. No one. No telegrams, no cables, no telephone calls, no letters. I'll bring Shapley in once we get another look at it. Maybe if we're lucky, the deck'll clear tonight before the moon's up. Tombaugh, you're not to say a word."

"No, sir."

"Not mom, not dad, not nobody."

"No, sir."

"If we get lucky tonight, Mr. Lampland and I'll go after him with the 42, see what we can see. Barber, how soon can you have an orbit?"

"Couple hours."

"No need to rush it. Work it up with what you've got. Tombaugh, you'll go hunting for it on other plates."

"Yes, sir."

Slipher, calculating, says to Lampland, "Be nice if we can get our ducks in a row by March 13. Three weeks. The hundred forty-ninth anniversary of Neptune's discovery. Percy's birthday, too, only fitting. That'll give us time to get some more pictures and to work up a reasonably good orbital path. I think that's within your capabilities, Mr. Barber?"

"Yes, sir." Alan is looking at it now. "Sheesh, Clyde, how'd you ever in the world see that?"

"I've spent half my life poking around in Gemini," Slipher sighs, "I must have seen the thing a dozen times." Then the director turns and extends his hand. "Congratulations, Mr. Tombaugh."

He shakes. "Thank you," he says.

"I suppose you'll want to name it Clyde."

It is a joke, of course—Clyde knows it at once—but he can't speak. If it is what they think it is—well, and it just has to be, there's nothing else out there—then he's found a new planet. It's beyond Neptune, it's retrograding; it is the missing planet. He's found it. And as he stands there he feels—he could never have guessed it—the giant weight of the rest of his life descending on his shoulders.

And he feels that it's *wrong.*

Wrong. It's simply too large a thing to ask him to accept. Now and forever, the kid who found Planet X. He puts his hand to his mouth. He was well-suited to search for it forever. But it strikes him that he is very ill-suited to be the one to have actually *found* something.

"That's a joke, son," Lampland puts in.

"Yes, sir." His voice weak in his own ears. "I know it's a joke, sir."

Slipher regards him curiously.

"A joke, sir," he repeats.

"Mr. Barber," says Slipher, taking his arm, "why don't you find this fellow a nice place to lie down."

Clyde can barely walk, suddenly. Alan says, "Come on, Kansas," But he hardly hears it; because all at once he is full of dread for the future and he's thinking, *Oh, no, what have I done?*

32

Halfway down the corridor to the library Clyde turns to him and says, his face a mask of horror, "Look, Alan, I'm sorry."

He says, "Forget it. Go grab the first Gemini plates we did together, all right, and start blinking them. And don't *drop* anything."

Clyde stands at the head of the basement stairs.

"The first Gemini plates," Alan urges.

Clyde only stares at him. "This wasn't what I was supposed to do," he says. "I wasn't even supposed to be here."

"Go on," Alan says, gently now; at this, Clyde turns like a mummy and goes back to the comparator room. Alan watches him go. And sure, there's something wrong, he knows it. Something wrong at the root.

Because that image is too damned small to be anything like a planet. No matter how the hell far out it is.

For simplicity's sake Alan begins by considering it a two-body problem— a distant body orbiting the sun alone, without interference from any other bodies. As later data become available—as Clyde digs up older images, over the next few days—he will refine his numbers. But for now, simplicity.

To determine the size and shape of the orbit of this object, he will as usual need to determine:

e, eccentricity

a, the semimajor axis

T, the orbital period

t_0, the time at perihelion transit

ω, the angle between the perihelion and the ascending node

Ω, the longitude of the ascending node, and

i, the angle between the ecliptic and the orbital plane,

the last three elements being precursors to the transformation from the orbital plane system to the heliocentric system. Once these values are determined, he will insert them into the further equation

$$\frac{a^3}{T^2} = \frac{(M_\odot + m)}{G\,4^{\,2}}$$

with $M_\odot$ representing the mass of the sun and G representing the gravitational constant $2.95912283 \times 10^{-4}$ AU^3 $M_\odot^{-1}$ d^{-2}, to determine a preliminary planetary mass, *m*.

He can do it in his sleep. He dreams it, sometimes, in fact.

So, feeling a fateful tremor under the amber light of the Saturn lamp, he launches himself from the top of a page, beginning the long work of translating three images into an orbit. The evening passes in this way, with Clyde down the corridor at the comparator, searching for earlier images on old plates, while Alan patiently stalks his game. At eleven o'clock Slipher ducks his head in.

"Anything yet?"

"Getting closer. It'll be rough."

"That's fine. We just want a little bit of an idea tonight. Tombaugh's still working over the old plates," Slipher tells him. "No luck yet."

"Hard to believe he saw it in the first place."

"Small, isn't it?" Slipher winces.

"Small," Alan says, addressing his papers, "and *faint*."

"You noticed," Slipher says. "So my first thought was, well, all right, maybe it's just got a very low albedo."

"Sure," he answers. "But what sort of gas doesn't reflect light?"

"And then I thought, Well, maybe it's all frozen out. At that distance."

"Maybe."

Slipher says, "But that's not likely, is it?"

Alan lays his pencil down. He knows what Slipher wants. What the best thing is, for all of them. He fingers his scar, slick across his cheek. Still, he musters some vestige of resistance. He says, "It doesn't look right to me. No disk at all. Magnitude 15."

Slipher nods at his shoes, acknowledging it. "You can get us a mass."

"Not too long."

"At least no *canals*, please," Slipher warns, and ducks back into the corridor.

Ten minutes after midnight, soon after a light snow begins falling—the clouds will not break tonight—he has it figured. By his numbers, this object has barely a tenth of the mass of Earth—just .106 of Earth, give or take. Which means it is smaller even than Mars. Smaller than any of the other planets by a long measure. And nothing like Neptune, whose mass is equal to about seventeen Earths.

Too small, all right.

He takes his papers to Slipher's office. "I don't know, sir," he begins. "It doesn't make a lot of sense."

"Well, that would be about par for the course." Slipher is bright-eyed and chewing his pipe. "I'm sure Constance and her people will be delighted to hear that."

"It looks like it's got a period of about 241 years. About 38 astronomical units out. A rough eccentricity of 0.23. Tipped way off the ecliptic, although fortunately not for us at the moment, out to maybe about 14 degrees off."

"Boy-o."

"It's an oddball, sir. Now, this is all just sketching."

"Right."

"But with that eccentricity, at that distance, it actually goes *inside* Neptune's orbit. It goes in and out. It'll cross over to be inside Neptune's orbit in fifty-two years or so. Then it passes back out again a few years later."

Slipher grunts. "He'd perturb like hell."

"If he's big enough, he would." Alan swallows. "But I get a mass of .106."

"You do, do you?"

"From what I have so far, anyway."

Slipher says, "Well, that would be one reason he's so faint, wouldn't it?"

"Unless I'm wrong, this is something like a cometary core. Or an errant moon or something captured somewhere along the way and slung into this oddball orbit. My best guess is, it's a very large captured comet, sir," he finishes, "and not a planet at all."

"*Not* a planet."

"At least not as we think of planets, sir."

Slipher turns his pipe. "No, but that's very odd, isn't it? Because you both put it right about there. In fact Percy was closer, wasn't he?"

"A little."

"But you both had him right there, didn't you? With a Neptunian mass."

"Yes." He sighs. "And that's the part that doesn't make sense."

Slipher's Jesuitical gaze goes deep as he stares at the wall. Snow taps softly at the window.

"Well." Slipher sets his pipe aside. "Our friend Shapley sent us a wire." He hands it across. It reads only: CONFIRM.

Shapley. It would be nice to show him, anyway. And Florrie, too, for what that's worth. Constance, certainly. "He won't say anything to anyone yet?"

"Oh, no, that would be in violation of every known code. I've wired Shapley and Putnam, but that's the end of it."

"Still," he says.

Slipher smiles. "Worried about your Florence getting wind of this."

"With reason."

Slipher shakes his head, eyes closed. "No. Absolutely out of the question. Put it out of your mind. There is *some* honor left in the world, Barber." Slipher steeples his fingers and aims them prayer-style at him. "But we've got a little situation, don't we?"

"It looks that way."

"Because what you're telling me, Barber, doesn't really make any sense *whatsoever.*"

"No, sir."

"Because we now have not one but two residual reductions putting the object just about exactly where Clyde just found it. But at the same time you've brought me a mass that's nowhere near where it has to be to account for that possibility. Correct me if I'm wrong, I'm no expert in such matters as you know, but surely a body that small would never perturb the way you and Percy both say it has."

"That's right, sir."

"No. Now, I understand you have a fair bit on your plate these days. But I need you to get this right. Otherwise, Barber, I'll probably just have you killed. And to be fair about it, I'll probably have to kill you myself."

Despite himself he smiles. "Yes, sir."

"Like I used to kill chickens. With my own bare hands."

"Yes, sir."

"Ccchht!"

"I have no doubt, sir."

"There's some explanation we're not thinking of," Slipher suggests. "Maybe it's a dwarf star."

"Not with that orbit. You'd knock every planet out of the sky."

"Then you need to fix this, Barber," he says, mildly. "Either you've got the orbit wrong or you've got the mass wrong, and I can't help you with that. *You* need to make this make sense for us, all right? That's what we hired you for, after all."

"Yes, sir."

Slipher goes about the business of lighting his pipe again, his narrow head bent to the work. "What do *you* think we should call it? Not that I should ask you anything about naming things."

Mariana. "Tantalus," he says, off the top of his head. "Helena."

"The inspiration of a thousand desperate voyages. That's us, all right. I happen to like Persephone, but it's taken. So's Minerva. I like Pluto, also. God of the Underworld. That dark bourne from which no traveler, et cetera. Actually I wish we *could* name it after poor old Percy somehow. He'd like that."

"Well, Percival Lowell," he says. "Actually. That goes with Pluto. You know: P - L."

"Well, yes," Slipher acknowledges, "that's right, come to think of it. Constance would like that."

Alan plucks his pencil from his pocket and leans and sketches a symbol in the margin of Shapley's telegram. "Notate it like this," he offers:

P

"That's not bad," Slipher says. "A little hidden message, sort of. That way we could honor him properly. Secretly name it after the old gasbag, after all."

"If it is a gasbag," Alan says.

There is a complicit flicker in Slipher's expression. "But you and Percy both put it about right there, didn't you?"

He nods. There is no denying it.

"So it's got to have some kind of near-Neptunian mass to it, no matter what it looks like at first. If it's going to perturb as it seems it did."

"You'd think so."

"Maybe, Barber, it's some sort of superdense material we haven't yet discovered. Or a ball of pure iron. All the more interesting, is it not, to have discovered not only a new planet but one with such a curious set of characteristics, wandering alone out there among the giants!" Slipher sniffs. "There must be any number of reasonable explanations, it seems to me."

They eyeball each other for a second, each figuring the other. Alan gets it, all right. It's a planet, period, that's the story they're going with. That's the story they need. They all need, for different reasons. And it's up to Alan to figure out how to make the case. And sure, it is a puzzle—both he and Lowell putting a planet right where they found this, more or less, and with a Neptunian mass. Maybe he's got something wrong. Or the image is deceptively faint for one reason or another. Something.

He turns and heads back down the hall, carrying his papers. He has a flash of Mary here, strutting down the hall ahead of him, crowing at the beauty of it all. She'd get a kick out of him, anyway, stuck like this, serious and burdened. Up against it, to be sure. *Poor old Jim!*

He flips back through his papers steadily. Nothing obviously amiss.

He will walk through it again, just to be sure.

That's my Jim.

An hour later, Clyde shouts from down the hall. A clatter of footsteps. "Found another image," Clyde says, swinging breathlessly around the doorway. "You won't believe where."

"Oh, don't tell me."

He swallows, nods. "On those first goddamn plates, the ones we couldn't blink." Clyde's expression is wild. "The first goddamn plates of Gemini. We had him, Alan. We got him the very first time we opened the camera."

He takes the position from Clyde, a good one—from almost a year ago, after all—and plugs it into his calculations, which he does with extreme care, checking and rechecking his work as he goes. He is at it all night, slurping coffee that Slipher brings him, hoping to come up with some sort of answer to the strange paradox he is confronted with. If there is anyone in the country best suited to do this work now, it is him. But there is no accounting for it. He takes down Poincaré and Leister and fingers his way through their multiple-body shortcuts but sees no advantage in their methods, so he shoves them aside. By the time morning is breaking through the windows, he is just where he was at midnight.

He stands and finds Slipher has gone to bed. Clyde is asleep at the comparator, and the room is filled with the rhythmic clacking. He turns the machine off but leaves Clyde asleep on the stool with his face planted against the brass ocular. A farmboy, he sleeps anywhere you put him. Alan tugs on his gloves and wraps his coat around him and the scarf Mary knitted him (it is the only thing she ever finished) and emerges into the chilly dawn. Nine planets, where yesterday there were only eight. He tries that on for size, whether the sky feels any different.

Nine is a more interesting number, really, he decides.

And Clyde sure deserves credit for something. They both do.

He slings himself down into the Stutz. The dials are fuzzed with dust, and the smell of cigarettes and old shoes is in here, and he rests his head against the walnut wheel. If they call this Planet X, they will make a name for themselves, all right. But somehow they will have to account for the missing mass, and he knows already it will be impossible. There will be no way around it except to keep mum and hope no one notices anything funny.

And at the moment, his forehead on the steering wheel, he doesn't much care. It will be close enough. It will be the most Planet X–like object ever discovered, anyway. No: really, he just wants to be done. He misses Mary, he misses home, he misses the trolley car to the river with his mother swaying beside him, a picnic lunch on the floor beneath her shoes. Summer in Ohio. Sleeping until the sun strikes you and turning over in a warm bed. Sun, and the day.

Just a blameless good life—he sighs—that's all he wants.

He wakes when Jennings grinds the truck out of the shed and into the lot, snow clotted in its tires. The windows of the Stutz are frosted with ice. He turns the key and cranks over the heater. In the mirror he is a fearsome creature, gray all over, so he stops at home to wash and bolt some breakfast before he follows the familiar road out to Bel-Aire. Mary is a long time coming down to see him, but she comes. "Hello, Mare," he says.

He is there earlier than usual, and she is groggy. Her breath burns with some acidic metabolic process, as they still dose her up with paraldehyde pretty well. "Hello, Jim," she says.

"Listen," he says, "you'll never guess."

She inspects him.

"Top secret," he says.

"All right." Her eyes flare.

"Well, we found something."

"Who?"

"Clyde did, actually."

"Clyde found who?"

"Not *who*, Mare," he says, "*what*."

"What?"

"It's *X*," he whispers. It is the moment he has been imagining all along, and here it is, and of course it is nothing like he hoped. "We think."

"*X*," she repeats; then, catching at some skein of sense, or memory: "Oh!" She pinches her lips together, shakes her head. "I'm sorry, I was thinking about something else, you know."

"I know. But we've found it."

"I haven't heard anything."

"Just yesterday afternoon. Clyde found something. We've been up all night trying to get an orbit. And find some old images."

"I was wondering why you looked so worn out, Jimmy. I can practically see all the way inside you."

"I'm fine, Mare. You're looking fine, too."

"They're trying to get the questions out of me, but it's not the best way they're going about it." She sighs. "Once in a while they get a standard answer, but most of the time they're broadcasting too frequently. I guess that's the problem with hiding like that; you have to broadcast to everyone so you make sure people hear the question."

"Anyway, Mare," he manages, this is still very much par for the course, "I wanted to let you know. We're keeping it secret until we get a good orbit and maybe another couple images, but I thought it would be all right to tell you."

"Who'd believe me, is the persuasion you're asking about."

"Exactly," he says.

"Not exactly," she answers. "That was just something I thought about." And with the impression that she has delivered a closing line, she rises and goes out again and disappears into the patient area where he cannot go. If the past is any indication, she will not be returning. But he is so tired; he waits a little while. It is comfortable here, he's so accustomed to this chair, the little burble of broken women conversing. The clatter from the kitchen, hidden behind a wall somewhere.

The big open view, over the canyons.

Maybe Dr. Yost would let him stay here too, just for a little while.

Anyway, he gets up. Collects his hat and scarf and gloves. And out in the parking lot he discovers he feels pretty lousy, after all. Because Clyde found the thing, whatever it is. And he guesses he won't get any credit for that, no sir. And here he is, under this winter sky, alone. Eight or nine, it makes no difference down here.

For the next three weeks, they make no progress. Alan takes his place beside Clyde at the comparator, but together they find nothing further on the old plates. The new images from the 42-inch reflector show a yellow planet without a visible disk—useful, as it seems to confirm the object's small size. But what could be as massive as Neptune and as small as this object appears to be? None of the exotic objects that fit this description—a very small dwarf star, for example—look the way Planet X does on Lampland's spectrometer, where it produces the signature of an icy rock, without atmosphere.

So he is stymied. He has an orbit in hand, nearly the same one he came up with the first night, with minute adjustments given the images from Lampland's new plates. The new positions are of only marginal help in refining the orbit; much more valuable would be an old image from the days of Ross and Greene. But these are not to be found; their tiny 5-inch plates never had a chance to detect a magnitude-15 object. He just wants one more: one old image, maybe from the trusty old Clark, and then he can admit that the object's position is nothing more than outrageous chance; that, as unlikely as it is, Clyde happened to find something where both he and Lowell thought there would be something to find.

It would be such an outlandish coincidence he can hardly credit its possibility. Of course it would mean that he and Lowell have been chasing ghosts all these years, and that the residuals are nothing more than artifacts—insignificant. Or not even there to begin with; just irreducible noise in the data. He resists these disloyal thoughts. You don't want to admit that Constance was right, that Planet X was a project Lowell invented to get out of the way of her madness, that the man was in fact miserable for all those years.

Because these days that kind of idea just hits too close to home.

But it is unavoidable, this line of thinking. Even Clyde seems to get wind of it; he comes to Alan's bedroom one morning, seating himself on the end of the mattress and huffing a few times in preparation, hands squeezing his knees, before asking, "It's not what it's *supposed* to be, is it?"

"I don't know, Clyde," he admits. "I don't think we know what the hell it is."

"What if it's not a planet at all?" he says, quietly.

"Someone's missing moon, you mean."

"No," Clyde says, "I mean what if it's something else entirely?"

"Like a comet? It might be. Although it's awfully big."

"No," he insists. "Like something *else*."

"Like what, Clyde?"

"Like a *ship*." Clyde's eyes expand behind his tortoiseshell spectacles. "Did you ever think, maybe that's what Lowell was after all this time? He was after the Martians. And that's their escape ship. And that's where they went; they abandoned their planet after the atmosphere disappeared, and now they're coming back to Earth to take us over. That's why we've found them now. Because they're getting closer."

He groans and lies back. "Clyde," he says, "don't be a ninny."

"What if they know we've been looking?"

"How would they *know*, Clyde?"

"Maybe rays," he whispers. "Secret rays somehow."

Clyde sounds so much like Mary suddenly that he has to laugh. "Oh," he cries, stuffing his pillow over his face. "Secret rays, Clyde!"

Clyde takes this; you can't get to Clyde so easily as that. "So what are we going to call it?" he asks.

"I don't know. Slipher wants to call it Pluto, which suits me fine."

"Not *name* it," Clyde says. "I mean what are we going to say it *is*?"

"Oh, it's Planet X, pal," he answers. "Get that through your head."

"But it's not, is it?" Clyde asks, his voice wavering. "It's not really."

"It will be," he answers. "And you'll be happy about it. Get that champagne on ice, anyway."

"The hell," Clyde says.

"And you'd better hide those dirty cards, too. Because there's going to be people all over this place."

At which Clyde gets up swiftly and disappears across the hall.

Finally Roger Putnam sends a telegram: MOST EXCITED ABOUT YOUR NEWS DONT BE TOO CAUTIOUS ABOUT PUBLICATION.

"Easy for him to say," Slipher remarks. "It's not his pecker on the block."

But then it is the night of March 12, and no sensible orbit has been computed, and the paradox has not been resolved. And they are going to go ahead and announce it anyway, because there seems no point in waiting further, and because tomorrow is Lowell's birthday.

"Gentlemen." Slipher grins in his office, looking up from his typewriter.

"Sir," they answer.

The director types for another minute, pipe in his teeth. Finishing, he rests his hands on his thighs and leans forward to examine what he's written. Then he unrolls the paper from the platen and hands it across to Alan.

"What think you of this?"

Alan reads it.

THE DISCOVERY OF A SOLAR SYSTEM BODY
APPARENTLY TRANS-NEPTUNIAN

Systematic search begun years ago supplementing Lowell's investigations for Trans-Neptunian planet has revealed object which since seven weeks has in rate of motion and path consistently conformed to Trans-Neptunian body at approximate distance he assigned. Fifteenth magnitude. Position March twelve days three hours GMT was seven seconds of time West from Delta Geminorum, agreeing with Lowell's predicted longitude. Position March 12.14 G.M.T. R.A. 7h 15m 50s Dec 22° 6' 49".

"All but saying it."

"We won't have to," Slipher says. "They'll be calling it Planet X by tomorrow morning."

And sure, Alan has done everything he could. And still:

Some weeks ago, on plates he made with the very efficient new Lawrence Lowell telescope specially designed for this particular problem, Mr. C. W. Tombaugh, assistant on the staff, using the Blink Comparator, found a very exceptional object, which since has been studied carefully. In its apparent path and in its rate of motion it conforms closely to the expected behavior of a Trans-Neptunian body, at about Lowell's predicted distance. There has not been opportunity yet to complete measurements and accurate reductions of positions of the object requisite for use in the computation of the orbit, but it is realized that the orbital elements are much to be desired and this important work is in hand.

"Good?" Slipher asks.

"Your prose style stinks, if you ask me. This whole business stinks, a little. You know why there's no accurate reductions, because the whole thing doesn't make a lick of sense."

"That's about it," Slipher agrees. "You want me to put that in, too?"

"No thank you, sir."

Slipher flushes and yanks the paper back. "Well, what the hell else do you *want* me to say, that you couldn't account for what we *saw*? You'd like my prose style a hell of a lot worse then, Barber." He goes past them down the corridor to Mrs. Fox's desk, and they all follow. Mrs. Fox is waiting for him, threading on her eyeglasses.

She turns on the telegraph machine.

"Ready, Dr. Slipher," she says.

"We'll want to call Putnam," Slipher tells her. "And make sure he tells Constance in person."

She nods. "I've already done it."

"Good girl. Then put us on the map, Mrs. Fox," Slipher orders, handing over the sheet. "For better and for worse. And now, where's that champagne?"

Mrs. Fox has it ready. Slipher pops the cork and tips a little measure into some old glasses. An experimental taste. But it is Lowell, all right: smooth as silk and full of bubble, and they all exchange a look as Clyde bolts his without a word. They stand around watching Mrs. Fox work the telegraph. Alan knows he is supposed to be celebrating; but it is a sickening feeling in fact. Beside him, Clyde is breathing hard. Alan turns and observes the look of wild alarm on the boy's face, and says, through a rising clot in his own throat, "Congratulations, Mr. Tombaugh." At which Clyde, making a noise of incredulity, leans forward and embraces him with a desperate strength. "I'm so sorry," Clyde whispers. And there they stand, embracing, the two of them, Alan suddenly laughing despite himself as Mrs. Fox keys his friend into history. That it should happen like this, after all. Some show.

Some show it is. The reporters get into everything. By noon the next day the parking lot is jammed with cars. You can't go ten feet without finding a stranger with a notebook out trying to make sense of a telescope or of Alan's own picturesque scroll of paper left artfully displayed on the library table or of the discovery plates which Clyde has obligingly returned to the comparator. In his bedroom Alan finds a man wearing a green checkered jacket and running his finger along the closet shelf like a ward nurse. There is an old flask up there from the reign of Dick, and the reporter shakes it and finds it empty and hands it over.

"Long nights?" the reporter asks.

"You're in my bedroom, pal," he answers.

The reporter smirks. "Not much action up here, I'm guessing."

"Oh, no sir," he says, "we're all just a bunch of innocent astronomers."

"Hell of a scar you've got. You get that from a little green girl somewhere?"

Alan blushes but holds his ground. He is strangely tempted to spill his guts, but of course you want to present a certain front and the reporters want to build the story up too, so you just give them enough to go on. Anyway, it's a hell of a story. They knew it would be big, but the interest surprises everyone. Look at Slipher slicking back his hair with the heel of his hand wishing he'd got himself a more recent trim. You pose for the photographers with their flashbulbs that smell of scalded tin, and you pick your way around the movie men with their spidery tripods whose nickel feet gouge the floors. Pass Slipher's office and see a dozen men leaning across his desk, each with a pencil in one hand and a notebook in the other. They photograph Lowell's tomb and the telescopes in daytime, and they arrange Clyde at the stone wall of the 13-inch, where he poses in all seriousness, his tie tucked into his shirt buttons. Telegrams of congratulation arrive from every observatory in the world, from Yerkes and Palomar and Athens; and there is the sense of having done something that no one has done for 149 years.

Never mind the notion that maybe they haven't done it either. Not exactly. They won't mention that. Not even among themselves, not any longer. It is not a con exactly, but what it is Alan isn't sure. And he doesn't mind too much. Anyway, what the hell use are his doubts now? Don't take it so seriously, that's all. He hears Florence in his ear: just pretend it's sort of a gas, you can get to enjoy it even if it's phony, you grin at the camera as the lights come on and you give a good quote and get off a good line, and suddenly all that time among the rich at Harvard comes in handy, doesn't it? All that time spent pretending to be someone he wasn't. Never mind that it feels awful.

He's showed Florence, anyway, sort of. Because there is no word from her; only a great freighted silence.

This important work is in hand. Observatories everywhere are now frantically about the business of hunting for old images of Planet X, and when they turn up, as they inevitably will, orbits will be forthcoming from all quarters. And this is a little bit of a nasty feeling, another sort of trespassing, as though someone is digging around in his sock drawer. And no one else will have to contend with the paradox he does, that the orbit he has calculated makes no sense given the residual reductions he's arrived at.

He knows too much, in a sense, to be of much use here.

But at least Clyde has been given his credit, and Alan is happy for this. And everyone who matters knows that Alan was involved all along. Shapley sends a telegram to him personally—NEVER MIND WHAT I SAID STOP—which Alan folds once the long way and inserts in his breast pocket.

"Contrite, is he?" Slipher asks, opening the other mail.

"Not exactly."

"Well, we convinced him so far—enough to pass, anyway. I imagine he'll continue to agree to toe the line. Ah, and here's one from Constance, too, for your pleasure."

He reads:

Roger Putnam has written me about the intensely interesting observation that you are experiencing—that it may be Planet X I pray. Mr. Putnam asked me if I had any thoughts about the name. He said he had thought of "Diana." If it is not to be Lowell or Percival, my choice is Zeus. Being the father of Aries—Aries being identified with Mars—it seemed appropriate—and Dr. Lowell was born in the sign of Aries.

Sin yrs

Const Lowell

He shakes the letter. This woman. Why the hell does *she* have all the money in the universe? "Write her back for me, will you? Tell her we named it Pickering."

"We are going to have to name it *something*." Slipher peels a letter from the stack on the desktop. "'Dear Sir,'" he reads aloud, "'I respectfully nominate the name Proton for the new planet lately discovered. It is probably the firstborn of the family of the solar planets. It is a name of dignified character. Easy to remember, and of magnificent terminology. George W. Squires, M.D.' What do you think of *Proton*, Barber?"

"Terrible."

"Terrible," Slipher agrees. They have not asked for suggestions, but the letters and telegrams come flooding in. The list of names is now crawling onto a second sheet.

Splendor	Amphitrite
Pax	Salacia
Ariel	Athenia

Maria	Pluto
Eva	Cronus
Nuevo	Idana
Utopia	Tantalus
Amor	Perseus
Electra	Zymal
Peace	Atlas
Victory	Nemo
Maximum	Osiris
Vulcan	Vulcran
Minerva	Virgo

And the letters offer more suggestions:

It seams to me the name of a deity of the underworld would be most suitable, because of the remoteness of the planet from the source of light. Then, too, it is beyond Neptune, and we generally think of the kingdom of the underworld being more remote and below that of Neptune. For these reasons I would suggest "Erebus," which means "Darkness." He was the son of Chaos and Nyx, who ruled before the world had shape or light.

Our class has been thinging about this and we suggest that the planet be called Xenia which means the gift of friendship which we think is a very rightfull name, it is the Greek name and be in line with the names of the other planet's. Also it sort of connects up with the observatory itself; because if I am not mistaken a great friendship prevails as Mr Tombaugh say's between the Junior and sinior members of the observatory and we seriously ask you to please try and give the new planet the name of Xenia.

In view of the fact that this planet was discovered by United States observers in the United States of America, why not combine the first letters of these words and call the planet "Usofa." The pronunciation could be broken after the "U" and after the "f" and that would carry out, to a certain degree euphoniously, the pronunciations of the names of many of the other planets.

Gentlemen: —I have the name "Arthemis," particularly in mind for the new planet. If I win a prize please with your courtesy send it to Mr. Howard Hulla. The name I give to you, bears the special features of "Lady, and Goddess of Hunters". Yours very truly, Howard Hulla.

"Here." Slipher hands half the stack across. "Make yourself useful."

"Thank you, sir."

"So far, votes in favor of Minerva are out front. But we can't use that."

"Asteroid."

"Asteroid. Number two people like is Pluto."

"I think that's the one," he says, "if I'm allowed a voice in this."

Slipher says, "Given your history, you shouldn't be. But that's my pick too. Shall we call it that?"

He says, "We'll want to ask Clyde."

"No." Slipher shakes his head. "Not on this one."

"You're really asking?"

"Yes," Slipher says, "I'm really asking."

"A little consolation gift for me?" he asks.

"Well," Slipher says, "it seems to me I already gave you a comet, didn't I?"

He is struck. Did he? But he remembers, now, in a rush, Slipher guiding him right toward it that long ago summer night. It had never occurred to him before. The softhearted director, offering the gift of a comet to a kid who'd just had to bear Florence going off with Dick Morrow into town. "I'll be damned," he laughs. "So you did. I never thought of it. Hell, sir, you play the long game, don't you? Thank you. I think. Or, damn you to hell, sir, look what you made me do."

"You're welcome." Slipher grins. "And second time's the charm, sonny. Try to get this one right."

"Okay," he says. "Pluto."

Slipher nods. "Pluto it is. Pluto the planet."

"If you say so."

"Oh, it'll probably pass," Slipher guesses. "Actually there's a funny letter here somewhere from Clyde's old pastor. You'll never guess what *he* wants to name it—Burdett!" Slipher gapes, showing his dark back teeth, and does what Alan has never seen him do: he laughs aloud.

"Poor Clyde."

"Poor Clyde is right. What do you think we ought to do with him?"

"Send him to college," Alan says. "That's where he wanted to go in the first place."

"That's my idea too. He's superb with the equipment, but that'll only take him so far. I don't want to mention it *now*," Slipher whispers. "I don't want him to think we're giving him the boot. He's having such a good time."

But that isn't quite right, Alan thinks. In interviews Clyde obliges the newspapermen with his pleased recitations: Kansas, the telescope, the long cold nights, why they managed to catch it this time when no one had ever managed before. But now in the corridor outside the comparator room he takes the letters from Alan's hand with a distracted stare. "Just a line or two," Alan indicates. And Clyde turns, puzzled, without objection. Not exactly happy; more like he's been hit on the head with a frying pan.

What they've done to him—you could almost start to feel a little uneasy about it. As though it would actually be a mercy to get him out of here.

Well, it is all too swift. In a month, the moment of glory, when the whole world is watching Flagstaff, passes. There is other news. A man named Gandhi marches to the sea. Three hundred twenty prisoners burn to death at the Ohio State Penitentiary in Columbus. The first night baseball game is played in Independence, Kansas.

But for Lowell Observatory, everything has changed. No longer is it known for its fifteen-year quest for imaginary Martian canals. Tourists come in gigantic numbers, causing nearly as much havoc and asking as many dumb questions as the reporters did. *How long would it take to get there on the* Spirit of St. Louis? *Why did God make it so far away?*

There is new equipment now, too. A new drive-clock for the 13-inch reflector. A Velox enlargement processor. An electrically humming ivory-keyed teletype. And with all this a new quality to everyone's step, an unmistakable air of triumphant self-rescue, a pervasive, delicious sense of having proven oneself out. Of having gotten away with something. And for Slipher and Lampland, a welcome relief, their dignity restored. And Clyde is not only scouring the ancient plates but also doggedly continuing his photographic search of the ecliptic, despite the lousy late-spring viewing, broadening the scope of the 13-inch search; for if the orbit of Pluto, as it is now called, carries it out to 17° beyond the ecliptic, what other objects might still be out there, waiting to be discovered?

Alan, alone among the staff of Lowell, feels a little at a loss. Nothing much has changed for him. So when June comes and nighttime seeing is unreliable, and feeling he has stared at enough ancient photographic plates in hopes of catching another old image, he asks Slipher for a week's vacation. Slipher sits back at his desk and says, "Why not take a month?"

"I don't need a month."

"Look, Clyde's going to head off to Kansas for a few weeks himself. Go ahead. It's summer. The seeing's horrible. Take a month. Take two. I can bring somebody in for the summer to pick up the blinking work. Take a vacation, Barber. Now that we're famous, people actually *want* to come work here."

"I always did."

"No one will ever forget that," Slipher assures him. Sure, and hear that valedictory note.

He takes the Stutz to the Grand Canyon for a day and enjoys the stares he receives as he steps out. A Lowell himself for all anyone knows. He hikes down into the canyon vastness. And every morning he goes to Bel-Aire and sits in the common room or plays piano, and afterward most days he just drives out into the wildnerness with a knapsack of food and water and hikes the hills. He throws a bedroll into the back of the Stutz and a kettle and a skillet and sleeps out under the stars. He lets his beard grow out to cover his scar and gets dark as a coolie and sweats his guts out on the hillsides, the loose red scree clattering under his boots. It is a hell of a big place. Fall off a cliff or break your leg in a hole, and that'd be the end of you. He comes to see this as an option, in a funny way. But he's careful and he's always within an hour or two of Bel-Aire, and he'll roll up stinking of camp smoke and a night on the desert, but he's there, all right, every day. And once a week or so he'll stop by the observatory and see what's cooking.

It is on one of these days that Jennings catches him and says, "Someone to see you."

"Who?"

The big man shrugs.

He figures it is a tourist, and he heads into the library to the big front doors. But even silhouetted against the sun there is no mistaking her. Up close she is thinner, her cheeks more drawn, a hard dried-out tiredness around the eyes. But still just fine.

He stops.

"Florence," he says, finally.

"Hello, Alan."

"Slipher," he spits.

A look of shy triumph, there is no disguising it, though she has the grace to try. "I found some new images," she says.

"When?"

"Just recently. And then they asked me to come out for the summer. I wouldn't have come, but they said you weren't working here right now, I mean you were on vacation. That's the only reason I said yes. It really is. I hope you don't mind."

"Where's Dick?"

"Getting us settled down at the hotel. He's a little uneasy about showing himself, in fact. And you look like you've gone sort of native, I guess. That's some faceful of whiskers."

"The hell'd you send those telegrams for."

She is delighted. "You *got* them. Well, I kept solving it approximately, and then I'd match my solutions with the Variable Atlas, but I didn't have any way of checking whether something was really a false variable or not. So I guess that was the idea; you'd look and see if it was any good."

So he was right about that, anyway. "You kept solving the whole thing."

"Well, with different parameters, you know. *Roughly.* It seemed really like a ridiculous exercise but then I thought, well, *Barbie's* doing it, maybe there really is something to it. I didn't know I *could* do it, actually, until I started trying following you." She has done something new to her hair, he sees: shorter, more pressed into place. The new style. Like the terminator line, it has arrived in Boston but will take some time to make its way west. "But you can't detect anything at .106, it's impossible."

"That's right."

"So we were all off on a wild goose chase, I guess," she says.

"Lowell too," he says. "All of them, actually."

"You know what *I* think," she says, her voice quieting, "I think it's possible there aren't any residuals at all. I think they all just add up to"—she lifts one hand softly, airily—"a sort of ghost in the numbers. A certain set of errors that you can't effectively reduce."

"I think you're probably right."

"Spooky, though," she admits. "That it was actually right there all along, right where he said it would be. It makes you wonder."

He nods at his shoes now. As if by wanting something badly enough, believing in it hard enough, you can make it come to pass. Create it out of nothing. The universe answering your devotion.

Well—maybe if you're a Lowell.

"But what is it really, Barbie?" she asks cannily. "If it's not Planet X?"

"Damned if I know. Just a big wandering ball of ice and rock."

She takes this in. It's a victory, of sorts, if he hasn't found a planet, after all. Sure, she'll use it somehow, at some point. Or maybe she won't; maybe there's still something like feeling between them. He finds he doesn't much care. "Alan," she says now, gently, "they told me about your wife."

"Well, then, I guess you know everything."

"I'm sorry. I mean everyone's heard back there, too, that's all I mean. Everyone sends their best wishes." She faces him timidly. "Everyone says what a good thing it is you're doing," she offers.

"Well," he drawls, "that's fine, isn't it. Coming from them."

"Do you get to see her?"

"Listen, Florrie," he says, "I'm not your friend. I'm not here to give you a bunch of gossip to go spreading around. You got your problems, too, I bet."

"Not really," she says.

"Well, then, I guess you chose the right horse, didn't you?"

She demurs. There is nothing left to say. Then: "Will you introduce me? I half think they asked me out here so they could shout at me about Dick."

"Maybe they're trying to see if they can get Clyde to run off with you."

"That's nice, Barbie. They're expecting me now. I'll go in on my own if I have to, but I don't want to."

"Wait right here," he says.

He goes down the corridor to Slipher's office. The director is there, making notes into his new Dictaphone.

"Her."

Slipher blinks. Placidly he flicks the black toggle and lets his glasses drop on their ribbon. "Actually she'd been at it for months, according to Shapley. It made sense to me, anyway. It's only temporary."

"Says you."

"Says *you*, in fact. You wanted a vacation. You keep showing up here, on the other hand, so maybe you don't want one. Anyway, the viewing's shot. Clyde'll put her on the comparator to get her training wheels off. It's just labor, Barber, that's all it is. Also, she found an early image."

"So I heard. Which must mean she's got the orbit all figured."

"Yes." Slipher sniffs. "It's what you had the first night."

So it's true. Only an impossible coincidence. His work, and Lowell's, pure fantasy. "Well, that's sort of a capper."

Slipher says, "You're one of us now, all right. Like it or not."

"She's here, anyway. She says she's scared of you."

"Boo," says Slipher.

Alan beckons her into the office. Slipher stands. "Mrs. Morrow. A pleasure to see you again."

"Thank you, sir."

"How is Mr. Morrow?"

"Just fine, sir."

"Still sleeping it off, I imagine." The old farmer doesn't glance his way, but this is for Alan, all right. "We sure did wonder what had happened to him. We thought maybe he fell down a mineshaft or something. You hear about that sometimes around these parts."

"Yes, sir."

"All right, Barber," Slipher sighs, "show her around." So they go down the hall to the blinking room, where Clyde is standing with his eye to the eyepiece.

"Say," Alan calls, "I've got something for you."

Clyde straightens his glasses and shakes her hand. Look at the firmness in the kid. He's taken it all pretty well, it appears. "Heard you were on your way."

"Hello, Mr. Tombaugh. Congratulations."

"You ever worked one of these?"

"They don't let me near it at—no, actually." She is stepping forward, her attraction to good machinery defeating any pretense of shyness. "We've still just got the old Hedder. This is"—she leans into the eyepiece—"oh, I see you've got an asteroid."

"Two," Tombaugh corrects.

She stands motionless, the vulnerable nape of her neck exposed. "Oh!" she cries. "*Two.*" And her look of plain happiness produces in Alan such a complicated mix of affection and jealousy that when he says, "I'll see you later, I guess," there is such a peculiar trembling to his voice that he has to turn and go at once. He will bet anything both asteroids were visible, that she only pretended not to see the second one. And he can't bear it. He takes himself into the hall. He will go see Mary. That's where he belongs, where he always will: with her. And with this understanding a settled rightness comes into him. Where he belongs. He can be good with Mary, good without effort, good because he wants to be, because he cannot help it. So it is what he has to take away: a life with Mary. Lashed to her. For better and for worse, and forever. His life.

He steps outside into the sunny lot. And there is Dick, hoofing into view. The same old grasshopper head, the lean loping frame. But he's trimmer, upright, full of horrible Yankee vigor. "Say, Barbie," he calls. "Some whiskers! I see you've got my car out for me."

But the DuPries have vanished, so it is with a certain satisfaction that he says, simply, "It's my fucking car, Dick," and gets in it and drives out of the lot and down the hill to be with his good, his brave, his lost and beautiful girl.

33

The news of the new planet penetrates most places; it is in all the papers and the newsreels, on all the radio shows for a while. It is one of those good stories that you turn your attention to so as not to think about what ails you and your country and what worse might be in store, which means there are sure as hell no naysayers doubting that good old American astronomers have discovered a new world! No sir. The discovery of Pluto by a genuine farmboy from Kansas is only the first example of what we might be capable of, no matter what else comes along, no matter what catastrophes might be waiting down the line . . .

But as it happens Edward Howe is too wrapped up in his mission to do much but get from one place to another, and he does not have much of a scientific bent anyway; so it all escapes his notice, for the time being. At any rate he is still innocent of the information when he arrives at 451 Dunbar, a tall blue Victorian with a slate roof and an iron fence full of spears. A sign in the window reads ROOMS. The proprietor looks Edward over at the doorstep.

"Well," she says, "I've got to say you don't look like one."

He leans to peer around her into the depths of the house. "I'm the strong silent type," he says.

"I guess you must miss him real bad."

Edward reaches into his jacket for his billfold and extracts five dollars. She looks at it like a ruffled owl, then plucks it cleanly from his fingertips.

"Wait right here," she says. When she returns a moment later she is wearing half-moon spectacles on a chain around her neck, reading a slip of paper. "Well, this says McPherson. A little town north of here about forty miles. You got a fancy friend in Mr. MacAllister," she tells him.

"He's not my friend," says Edward.

"Takes all kinds," she answers, and shuts the door.

The road to McPherson is a two-lane farm highway. In the March sunshine he overtakes a pair of nightmarish threshing machines drawn along the road by teams of twelve horses—giant, dangerously rocking contraptions full of wooden platforms and reinforced canvas belts and shining blades, each of these machines occupied by a man seated high up in its complicated rising, like a man in a choir loft. At McPherson he inquires at 22 South Forest and finds a green weed of a man in a pink silk vest. "Oh, the painter!" the landlord recalls immediately. "Well, easy come, easy go. Said he wanted to find a good house to paint. Thought he had one picked out. Then a week later he changed his mind. I said I thought there might be one like the one he wanted down past Hutchinson to Reno County." The landlord extends a card. "I sent him to my sister's place, a ways north of there. Place called Langdon, past Partridge and Arlington."

The highway passes through Suston and Panuth and Darling, winter-gray crossroads towns, each with a grain elevator by the railroad, a water tower, a sleepy downtown. And then the next town is Langdon, and that nervous flutter rises up behind his sternum.

Langdon is just another modest encampment on the prairie. The main street runs two blocks; the Orpheum theater bulks like a toad beside three churches and a park surrounded by an iron fence where a bare willow tree shades a frozen pond. At the filling station Edward leans out the window and asks to be pointed toward Easton Street, and the boy regards him with pity and says, "You're on it, fella."

"Where's"—he still has to check, though he knows it by heart now—"number 92?"

"Way out down the end there." The boy turns and directs him forward.

"Last house on the right. Mrs. Bale takes people in. Maybe you're looking to stay a while."

"Not if I can help it."

The boy spits. "You and me both, brother."

But as it turns out he could have found it without asking anyone. Number 92 is a rambling old white shingled affair, like a great seaside cottage that has been added onto again and again. The yard is fenced with white pickets, and a brick walk leads to the front steps. The porch is broad and trellised, with six wicker chairs along its length. There is an air of permanence and of never lacking for anything and of time suspended forever and ever. And as he sees at once, 92 Easton Street is a close replica of the MacAllisters' house, a dreamlike echo here in the silent middle of the prairie.

Edward swings down from the car and pushes open the gate. He knocks.

After a minute a woman, about sixty, comes to the door. Mrs. Bale. She is about five feet tall. She wears a dark blue cotton dress with a white lace collar. Her hair is firmly set in a series of crisp waves. "What can I do for you?" she asks.

He tells her.

"What do you want with him?" She shifts at the doorsill. "He's paid for a month."

"Is he inside?"

"He's not here," she says.

Edward's heart drops. "Did he say where he was going?"

She looks him over again. Anyone might be a suspicious number, all right, in this day and age, and his bulk argues against him. But he knows he can put on a decent hangdog air. "Does he owe you money?" she asks.

"No. It's more of a personal matter, ma'am."

"I see."

"It's his sister," he adds hurriedly. "She's in a bad way. We want to bring him back to her."

She weighs the truth of this and finally relents: "Come in."

It is a silent cool house. Orientals cover the floor, and a green tiled fireplace takes up half a wall. The light is distant and gray. A mantel clock ticks. On the hall table sits a single brass bowl, in which lie two keys marked #1 and #2.

"He's out back," she says.

He follows her down a corridor and into the kitchen, then through the kitchen and the pantry and into the yard. There is a dormant kitchen garden, and at the edge of the yard stands a wire fence, and, beyond this, stubble.

Away in the center of the brown March field, at a distance of about a quarter mile, sits a tiny spot of green.

"That's him out there. You can lift up that gate. Make sure you close it. And watch out for the bull. They let him out there sometimes without advance warning. And he isn't too particular, if you know what I mean."

"Yes, ma'am."

"Is she badly off?" Mrs. Bale inquires, at a whisper. "The sister."

He turns to her. "Yes, ma'am, she is."

She crosses her arms against the cool wind. "Tell him, if he wants, he can have his money back."

Edward lifts the wire loop and pushes the fence open. The figure in green seems to stop what it is doing, then goes on doing it. When he gets closer Edward can see that the figure is sitting on a stool before an easel. The goddamned fool is painting. Of all the goddamned fool things to do while his sister suffers. The brother has on a broad straw gardening hat, which must be Mrs. Bale's, and is sitting in a green barn jacket and heavy twill trousers. When they are close enough to shout he calls the man's name, and Hollis looks up. He is gaunt and wasted now, but more than this, it becomes obvious, he has endured something hard, his face is taut and the eyes press up from the bottoms of two pits, and only the strange wet out-turned lips are as Edward remembers them.

"You goddamned fool," says Edward.

Hollis, silent, does not dispute this. Above them stands a vast empty sky.

"I've been afraid of this for so long," the man croaks, finally, his voice full of gravel. "Is she dead?"

"No," answers Edward, "you dumb son of a bitch, she needs you."

A great final sigh from Hollis. A sagging collapse of his upper body until he is swaying forward, staring at the paint-spattered stool he sits on. "I didn't mean to stay away this long," he murmurs.

———

It is true; he didn't. He didn't mean to stay away at all. Only, he was so weary of it all, poor Mary's neediness, and yes, he put her away and got her out again, and had botched it with Edward Howe, and then he helped her along until he found Alan for her, and then that California light had beckoned and while Scotty had been too involved in the Napoleon Club to uproot himself ("And everyone in the world is *here*," he said, simply) Hollis had felt something drawing him west with her, some instinct—but on the train—well, such a lot of effort it had all been, and there at the dining car table she seemed truly happy for the first time since their parents had died, truly content, and he only stepped off—without even his overcoat, just his cigarettes and his matches—and the freezing midnight stillness hung there above the platform, the silver train standing idle, producing the strange silence that a train can, the sounds of coughing and papers shifting, the hot oiled smell of its undercarriage penetrating the chill, and he only dared himself: what if he didn't get back on? Only that. But in that instant the notion seemed to blossom, becoming irresistible, as though it had been there all along waiting for him to let his guard down—and of course he was only playing a game, because he had his duties, after all, and he could not leave her alone like that.

The train jerked. He watched it creep forward. He could just take five steps now and swing up. It began to move faster and he could still catch it, only he would have to quickstep it a little, and in a moment it would be his last chance, and then he would sprint and catch the final car as it pulled away and he would look back at the station where he had stood as the train took him away into the darkness—

But instead he watched the train go and finished his cigarette and watched the red light of the last car diminishing, and the rumbling died away, and he was standing in silence and the frozen stillness and he felt—oh, just wonderful, such a bewildering lightness, as though he had just cut himself loose from the bottom of the sea and was rising now, *plunging* toward the faraway light—!

He waited for remorse to strike, and it did not.

No, at first he was filled with such buoyancy he could hardly stand it. He warmed himself in the empty station hall—four benches arranged in two facing rows, in echo of the vanished train compartments—and regarded himself in the darkened window glass. He had no notion of where he was: western Iowa somewhere.

A glowing clock above the doorway read 11:45. Abbyville, Kansas.

He had never done anything like this before. After all *he* had gone back to take up Mary when their parents had died. *He* had tended her for all those months. And now he had abandoned her.

He did not know what to make of himself, exactly. Only—what *freedom*!

"Is there a bus somewhere?" he asked the station agent.

"Next bus to Wichita is seven a.m., sir," the agent offered, eyeing him dubiously. "If you like a *quiet* sort of place for the likes of you."

He spent the first night of his removal on a narrow hotel bed with a freezing draft knifing under the window. But it didn't matter, he couldn't sleep anyhow—he was too elated, too mystified, by the thing he had done. Finally he rose before dawn and made his way down to the bus station and boarded in the morning chill, more than a year ago now, and tipped his hat back and watched the snowy prairie towns sweep past, and he was free, he was gone, he was *happy*.

In Wichita he found a cheap room and resolved to stay just a week. It was only a vacation, he told himself. And every morning he woke with a guilty start and resolved to send a letter. But every day he didn't do it. And with every day that passed, it became more impossible to do. The hotel was a brick tower above a downtown corner, and the room was spare and good, with a bed and a bureau and a bath down the hall and a window that looked down on the streetcar line, so he could see it coming from two blocks up the avenue. He had one hundred five dollars left to his name.

After the first week he found work in the Hammond-Willer vacuum cleaner factory, where he sat at a bench for ten hours a day using a hydraulic stamper to punch holes in a suction disk. He made two dollars a day, and this was enough to keep him fed and mostly away from his capital. After two weeks at the Marlborough Arms he took a room in a house at the edge of town and once he had settled there began to buy paints. He missed his paintbox, but he relished too the starting over. Tincture White #22, Yellow #9, Palmer's Perfect Black #1, Light Blue #8, Real Turpentine. From the factory he took sheets of cardboard and with two hinges and three wooden posts he made an easel. Then he spent fifteen dollars and bought five good brushes of different gauges, #10 for washing and #6 for broad strokes down to the #½. Then he needed a strap for the easel and a sack for the paints and brushes, and he was set.

On Sundays, then, he woke at six to catch the first outbound street-car at twenty past the hour. Ten minutes later he got down at the edge of town—in the opposite direction of the vacuum cleaner factory, near the stockyards—and walked an hour or more into the countryside until he found a good house to paint. He had never really got it right at the MacAllisters' or afterward, but now on the old cardboard with the printing still evident on it he began to get better. He was only an amateur, he reminded himself, but he wasn't bad, and he wasn't a show-off; he told no one at the factory what he did on the weekend, and he did not consider himself an artist, and he was not secretly hoping to be discovered after his death, and yet—well, he liked the figure he cut there, he supposed, the solitary figure he presented only to himself; he liked to think that if you looked close enough you could see the penitence in his posture, his expression. But no one ever came to see him; only now and then a farmer's car would pull up, and a group of faces would peer out over the sills and offer comments.

"You forgot the pig," they might say.

He was lonely, of course. For Mary, and Scotty, and everyone.

This idyll, or whatever it was, lasted almost a year. Then when Wall Street crashed, the factory closed—with strange suddenness, as though everyone had been waiting to be told bad news all along—and he looked for work for a while, until the winter came on, but no luck, and then he packed his few clothes and new paints in a box and left the paintings behind with Mrs. Stephenson, because who would ever want to look at them? And went off to Hutchinson with his easel and paints on the advice of a man he met named Harry Pearl, who had family there and who said there might be work, but there was none; then, once the disappointment of this passed, he was able to appreciate that possibly the house he wanted to paint was even farther out there somewhere, under an even larger sky, and then he had gone through Hapsburg and finally come to Langdon and Mrs. Bale's perfect house, and now he had painted it thirty or forty times. He was using house paint now because it was all he could get.

And all the while—all the while—he had thought of Mary and won-dered how she was and loathed himself and wondered what had possessed him. How he had stood there and smoked. And watched the train pull away. And not then, not immediately, made it right. Had waited, instead, for punishment to seek him out, to decide that he was worthy of it. What a selfish bastard he was. All those forwarding addresses. Leaving a trail, if someone ever cared to follow it.

He has waited, waited for his punishment. And now it has come.

Edward manages to get him up from the stool and back to the house. The brother is so much thinner than he was that Edward twice has to stop and hold the man out at arm's length and convince himself. The hard-luck winter tan and the sunken eyes—but no, it is his man. Once they are inside Hollis shakes him off rudely and announces he is going to wash before dinner. "I'm very sorry about your sister," Mrs. Bale says, and Hollis shoots Edward a murderous look before vanishing upstairs.

"Are you staying?" Mrs. Bale asks him.

"Yes, ma'am," says Edward, "if you'll have me."

"Supper is at six o'clock."

"Does he have a car, ma'am?"

"No," she answers. "He hitched a ride here." She knows it is not proper to have an interest, but she is losing the fight. "You said his sister was sick. Is that true, or was that just a story?"

"It's true, ma'am."

"Where are you from?"

"Everywhere," he sighs, "lately."

"I've been feeding him and feeding him, and he just doesn't fill out." Then, catching herself, she says, "The sitting room is yours from four o'clock until dinner."

He figures the odds of going to town to send a wire. He cannot see Hollis staying put now, and he does not like the idea of dragging the man along. So he will wait until the morning.

When Hollis comes down for dinner he looks stronger. He has washed and shaved and put on a new shirt. The furrows of the comb's teeth shine in his hair. Dinner is quiet, served by a girl from town. Hollis eats steadily, a cornered fugitive, not looking up.

"You're a cowardly son of a bitch," Edward says once. "Pardon me, ma'am."

"You go to hell," the brother answers, without heat.

After dinner Hollis excuses himself and bids goodnight to all three of them. Edward stands at once himself and follows him upstairs and confirms his door shut with the man behind it. The second-story windows are too high to afford escape and sealed behind storm windows besides, and this is the only door to the man's room. Edward sits there outside the door.

Mrs. Bale says, "That staircase creaks like you wouldn't believe," but he resolves not to sleep that night, and when the house is dark he sneaks down the staircase and with his heavy tread passes the jingling china cabinet and lowers himself onto the sofa, where he can observe the stairs from this strategic angle.

In the darkness the mantel clock whirs and chimes on the quarter hour as he reclines on the sofa with his boots off. The wind blows up a gust beyond the window. It is a long room, in shape very like his own living room at home, and after a while he has a strange sensation of having Mary near him, taut with unseen suffering but present, alive in the air. Then this vision is confused with a vision of that golden octagonal room— the white dogs—that old man beneath the lamp turning pages, the room's hidden heart—and then he is asleep.

When he wakes it is full morning and light is streaming through the lace curtains and across the red carpets and tasseled lamps. He curses and bolts up from the sofa and races upstairs. Hollis's door hangs open, and the drawers have been emptied.

"No," he moans, and bangs down the stairs, a frustrated poison in his gut. In the dining room he comes upon a surprised Mrs. Bale. "Why, he's out in the field," she tells him. And nods at the distant figure.

Edward squints and watches long enough to decide that it is Hollis, all right.

"He wanted to paint one last picture before you took him home. And I said that was fine. He's not going to run off, Mr. Howe," Mrs. Bale assures him, setting a place. "He knows he's done his sister poorly."

He recovers himself. "About time."

"Time enough," she says. "You go ahead and wash up and help yourself to some breakfast before you two get on your way."

He eats while through the dining room window he observes Hollis without pause. It is Hollis, all right, even at this distance there is no mistaking his gaunt haunted frame. Edward pegs him at about 125 pounds, an easy featherweight. Hollis stands now and then to stretch his legs, walking back and forth for a minute or two with his hands in his pockets. Then he sits down again.

The morning passes.

"Did you see?" Mrs. Bale queries, tipping the paper toward him. "They've found another *planet.*"

But he has no interest in anything but the figure in the field.

How long does it take to make a painting? Edward doesn't know. Fifteen minutes, an hour, six hours? But by lunchtime Edward has decided it is time enough. He has kept an eagle eye on Hollis the whole morning; he has been sitting steadily at his stool for a good half hour now, so his work must nearly be done. He jams his hat on. He crosses the grass and lifts the wire loop and opens the gate and sets off in his boots across the stubble.

The easel, and the figure under the gray Kansas sky.

Oh, but something's wrong, isn't it?

He suspects long before he arrives there what he will find, but still he makes himself walk on, arguing, cajoling, telling himself it cannot possibly be true, there is no possible way, his boots laboring in the clotted soil and his ankles turning in the ruts. The stubble pokes at his shins and calves, and the smell is one of perfect mineral emptiness, water and soil and nothing living in it.

When he gets to the easel he sees the stool placed there in the dirt, and the square metal box of paints, neatly shut.

And an empty figure on the stool. Its green jacket and twill pants are stuffed with muddy stubble, and it is wearing, like a scarecrow, Mrs. Bale's ridiculous hat.

He looks around at the surrounding field. No footprints.

"The hell," he says.

On the easel is a painting of the great house that stands, much diminished now, at the edge of the field. It is a good painting, Edward notes, wearily. And there is a car: his Model A, with paneled sides. And within, etched in miniature but with fierce, fond precision, beside Edward's face, is Mary's—lit bright, full of wit and promise. And at the sight of it Edward feels something set itself suddenly to rest in him. That's her, all right. She looked just like that.

Well, the bastard finally got her right, anyway.

He turns in all directions to make sure Hollis is nowhere to be found. But there is no one racing away naked across the field. Only a total, patient emptiness. And up through the soles of his boots Edward, in his vast sorrow, feels a new flush of power come into him. Goddamn the man then.

Let him stay lost.

Mary is better off, it is suddenly plain, without him. And Edward—*he* is of no use to her either.

But *she*—*she* is of use to *him*, still. Forever. To mark that outermost place, the highest and most generous measure of himself.

He pulls the painting off the easel and slings it over his arm. He'll take this one, for sentimental safekeeping. And over his other shoulder he slings the empty doll of Hollis, the rustling scarecrow full of straw. He puts Mrs. Bale's hat on his own head. "All right," he declares, to the empty Kansas fields, "we'll just see about that." Because he suddenly has a vision—faint at first, but coming swiftly into focus—of standing on a platform. Giving a speech. He could be an alderman. Hell, he could run for Congress. That old Rooseveltian heartiness is still there, all right. He only needed a chance to find it again. All those poor lost duffers in the rooming houses. All of them. Everyone, so lost. But it didn't have to stay that way. The field swells beneath his feet, an uprising sea. The sorrow is in it, but something else, too. What *love* he has, suddenly, for Hollis, for himself, for all of them! What stupid, powerful affection! What an overswinging *chump* he is! What an absolute *palooka*!

He labors alone across the field in his hat, smiling, carrying his several burdens.

34

Through a crack in her bedroom door, left ajar as though to invite visitors, Felix catches a glimpse of his mother in the lamplight. Limping from bureau to vanity, she wears a gray slip, an inch of ivory lace tracing the hem, and around her neck hangs the necklace of segmented Languedoc silver. Her old calves have been reduced almost to nothing. A great purple stain wraps what remains of the muscle of the left one, a mark so livid and intricate he thinks for a moment it has to be a tattoo, the mark of some secret membership. But of course not. Only purple capillaries burst beneath her skin.

He knocks, averting his eyes. "Mama?"

"Just a minute." Then, presently: "All right."

He enters. She has put on the black kimono. Her tiny wrists jut like a doll's. She continues her puttering, breathing hard. She has gathered a small heap of jewelry on the marble vanity-top; now, standing before the top drawer of her bureau, she plucks fitfully at its contents. She puddles a necklace of ivory beads in one palm and, tottering over to the vanity, adds it to the pile.

"I want her to have these things, Felix," she breathes, placing a hand on the heap. "I won't be needing them."

"All right."

"What time is it?" she asks.

"Four o'clock."

She considers this. "We can't ask Prudy for breakfast now."

"No." He pokes through the pile of jewelry, some of it paste but not all. "I'll put a basket together."

She nods into the closet, flipping through her dresses. "I'll be down shortly," she rasps.

He creeps down to the kitchen. By the light of a single bulb he uncovers a heel of bread and a pan of apples and pours them all into a canvas sack. Then, taking things as he sees them, he adds two bottles of Coca-Cola, a fist-sized hunk of ham, a jackknife, a metal tin of Ho-Horum Dinner Crackers, and a block of cheese. He snaps this bulging load shut. Then he fills two canteens at the sink.

Outside the sky is lightening, the air crisp. The chickens are asleep in the henhouse. Gently he calls to Sissie, who he has tied up here overnight. She swings her powerful head around to examine him. A joking, disbelieving expression plays around her eyes.

She *knew* he was up to something, all right.

A formal impulse has won out and Felix is wearing a summer-weight morning jacket for this occasion, and when his mother appears at the porch rail he sees she has put on the dress she made such a fuss over and then never wore, the pinkish-orange organdy tea-dress with matching orange shoes and a small diamond clasp in her hair, as though she is on her way to a party. Around her throat is the necklace of Languedoc silver. He goes to her, his heart sorrowing.

"Well." She holds out her hands. They are hard, ferociously insistent as they grapple at his. "We'll show *them*."

In front of him on the saddle his mother makes a comfortable, gently rustling package. Her crispy hairdo, coming just to his chin, gives off the odor of lavender.

"I haven't been on a horse in an *age*," she sighs.

They pass the empty Black Cat, the brick front of the Orpheum. No birds sing. The dark courthouse lawn is empty of everything but the shapes of the two shifting cottonwood trees and the ancient unringable bell in its white display housing. They ride east out of town along Santa Fe Avenue and toward the road to the dig. At the sight of the open country Sissie prances a jaunty two-step to let him know she approves. "I'm sorry to put you to the trouble," his mother whispers. "I would have done it earlier, but I just ended up without the strength."

"We'll just see," he tells her softly, "what we see."

They climb the rise and after a time they come in view of the dig. Dormant now and half dismantled, it gives the impression of an ancient encampment. "That was a *good* idea you had, Felix," she says.

The land begins to slope into the Sinagua canyon and she notes it with interest; but it is too near town for their purposes, and after a while they are out of it again onto the open plain. Before long the sanitarium comes into view, high above them on its great single bluff. "The poor girl," his mother says. But even this seems held at arm's length in order to give her room to do this thing she has vowed to do.

"She's safe now."

"You won't forget. Make sure you pay that one when it comes. I used to know Larry's father, you know."

"I know, mama. But I think they'll be all right now. He won't ever lack for work, at any rate."

"I suppose not. But poor little Mary." And then they are riding on the broad floor of the desert with the building out of sight above them.

As they ride the daylight comes up around them. It is a perfectly cloud-less April morning. They are bearing south, toward the real canyonlands. He keeps Sissie traveling as quickly as is comfortable. The idea is to get far from town before their absence is judged important enough to act upon. And by then it will be too late; they will be lost.

At first there are no opportunities to lose themselves. But then the lit-tle ridge they are following begins to rise, and then it becomes a wall, and then there is the first side-canyon, such as it is, only a foot wide where it cracks the bluff and choked with scrub. But then comes another, wider.

He stops Sissie, and they peer in. He has the sense of a corridor stretch-ing away. He thinks abruptly of the little Mexican church where they washed up—its gray interior extent, surprising him, and the voice sob-bing in the night. His own voice, of course. Though in memory it remains a thing from without.

He looks back the way they have come. Their tracks are indistinct.

"Well, mama, this looks interesting," he says.

"I couldn't agree more, dear," she answers.

Now he sees that the high canyon walls are exactly the color of his mother's dress—a perfect match.

And then he sees—of course—that this is no accident. No. The dress is meant—was always intended—as camouflage.

Not this—then what?

So now he knows.

His heart aching, he urges Sissie forward into the divide.

Late in the afternoon—they have been gone from Flagstaff for twelve hours—they come to a likely spot. A ledge, ten feet up, flat, clean of any debris, as tidy as a porch stoop, accessible by an easy series of boulders. Within five minutes he has placed his dozy mother there and tied Sissie to the wizened branch of an ancient juniper. He takes the Indian blanket and spreads it over the floor of the ledge. For a pillow he puts an empty waterskin to his mouth and inflates it.

"What I like about this neighborhood," she croaks genially, "is the lack of busybodies."

Without making a show of doing so, he sets the food and the water between them. She has refused it all day, but possibly she will change her mind. Then he sits and removes his jacket and slings his holster off and folds the holster, with its pistol, into the pale green lining of the jacket and sets the package on his other side, away from her.

"Comfortable, mama?"

"Oh, yes," she says.

He knocks a single pebble over the edge with his heel.

He is tired, all right. The job of keeping his mother upright and comfortable on a horse all day kept his body at pointed attention and now, in the cool still air of the canyon, he feels a shivery weariness.

He is not as young as he once was.

He lies down too on the smooth stony ledge.

A clean ribbon of evening sky runs cool overhead.

His mother sighs.

They watch a single black bird sail diagonally overhead.

"What will you do, Felix?" she asks, after a spell.

"Why, I'll stay here, mama."

"What will you do with the house?"

Some searching tone tells him she means the house in Indian Head. "What would you like me to do?"

A hand rises feebly. "I'm sure I don't care. We had our times there. But it was just something we were expected to have."

"I don't know if we really have it any longer, exactly," he says. He thinks of its gray withdrawing bulk, the silent oily cavern of the garage. In those rooms he counted pegs with her while she mourned his father. And so his mind is drawn back, as it is so infrequently now, to the moment when she plunged into the sea after him, to the desperate love that overtook her, her head bobbing amid the waves.

Who will help him remember these things, when she is dead?

Her mind has been moving parallel to his. She says, "I still see that church sometimes. I have dreams about it."

"I do too."

"I'm always waiting for something to happen." Her mouth, dry, forms the words with difficulty. "But we *survived*." They are not only Maryland DuPries, she means; they are made of tough stuff, through and through.

In the dim cool hour after sunset the canyon comes alive. Lizards scoot after the insects that rise from their nests within the stunted junipers. A platoon of bats storms up the canyon in a darting mass. Sissie stirs at her post. And just as night falls, Felix sees—thinks he sees—the low liquid shape of a mountain lion lurking past. Sissie makes no move, and the shape only pours forth up the canyon, deeper into the labyrinth.

His mind perfectly empty, the creature known as Felix DuPrie sleeps.

In the first gray light of morning his mother's face, darkened already by the previous day's travel, seems a brown mask of death. But then her eyes open and, as if surprised, alight on him.

A look of confusion subsides as she remembers where she is, and what she is there to do.

He is painfully thirsty, and hunger sits at the top of his stomach like an ache. But he will not drink while she watches. He clears his throat—dry as dust.

"Would you like anything, mother?"

A blink, no.

A distant bright smell of water moves down the canyon. He sniffs it greedily.

Overhead the first raptors go gliding down the morning updrafts.

He sits beside his mother as the light increases. His thirst burns his throat. The bones of his pelvis ache from the night on the rock. He stands and stretches and as he does Sissie steps back and observes him. She tosses her head inquiringly but he ignores the horse. The soil in the bottom of the canyon shows no tracks. Whatever beast passed last night, if it was not an illusion, walked only on the stone.

He sits again. His mother is peaceful, breathing evenly, her mouth open. Now and then she opens her eyes and seems to see him, but her expression does not change.

The morning passes in this fashion until finally he can stand it no longer, and, turning away, he unscrews the stopper of the canteen and drinks. When he sets the canteen down she has opened her eyes.

"Water?" he asks.

She seems not quite to see him. "I would like to be alone," she whispers.

A chill lances through him. "Mama."

"Baby," she answers.

He waits for more—a last pronouncement—but nothing comes. He leans over and kisses her dusty forehead.

"Good-bye, dear," he says.

He clambers down to the canyon floor. Then he charges away, walking hard and fast. He rounds a corner and then another, he is breathing quickly, something rising in him, the understanding that this is real, it is the dreaded moment arriving now, and with this a burst of sobs erupts from him, his body so dry his eyes burn from undiluted salt. He does this for some minutes before the thought comes that in the last throes she has changed her mind, and while he argues against himself his love wins out and he hurries back to the ledge.

She is already dead. She is clutching to her face the material of his discarded jacket, as though to inhale him one last time. The pistol—in his haste to leave her he forgot it—lies untouched on the stone. His heart breaks, his heart, he falls to his knees beside her.

He stays with her body in the canyon. He lies beside her and stares. He stares at her curly gray hair and the slack surfaces of her ancient face. What he wants he doesn't know. He watches her motionless until at last the light begins to fade. After two or three false starts he manages to make himself rise. His mother no longer looks like herself exactly, her mouth open and her few remaining teeth visible down to the roots. She would want to keep the jewelry, so he leaves it in place. Also she would want him to take the blanket from beneath her, so he slides it gently out and leaves her there, perfectly orange against the orange stone, just as she planned. His mama, to the last.

Back down on the canyon floor he loads Sissie with his remaining supplies. When he is on her she canters sideways and awaits his direction.

What he is leaving back there. He has a terrible image of her awaking— sitting up horribly alone and lost.

After half an hour he reaches a turning. He marked each of them— there were four—with a cairn of pink stones and an arrow, scratched into the wall of the canyon, pointing him back toward home.

The arrow directs him left. But he has another day's worth of water, at least. And Sissie is game.

He turns into the labyrinth.

That night he sleeps in a shallow cave five feet up the canyon wall, and when he wakes the next morning he finds a tarantula pacing its way along the edge of the cave as though deciding what to do about him. He knows they are good jumpers, so he sits up slowly. At this the spider turns and crouches on its hind legs and seems about to spring.

He hurls himself out. He lands on his feet on the canyon floor. Sissie stands off a few yards, enjoying it.

"Nuts to you," he says.

He is thirsty, but he divides half the remaining water with his horse and feeds her his remaining apple. She takes it noisily into her brown teeth. It is a cool morning, the sun just up. He slept hard, and now after two nights in the desert he is coated in red dirt. His hair is jackstrawed, and he runs a finger into his ear and works the grit around. His trousers are torn at the right knee, and he wears his shirt unbuttoned at the top, and he folded his jacket and the shoulder holster into his saddlebag long ago.

The Mexican snakeskin boots, however, are holding up well.

Quality will out.

He mounts his horse and turns her deeper into the canyons. A quick calculation shows he has enough water left to last until three that afternoon. If he does not find water by then, he will turn back. He does not intend to die here, only he does not want to return, not just now.

He thinks of his mother, the spiders investigating her sleeping form, and a slow dreadful sadness moves through him, like a single piston stroke. It doubles him over for about a minute, this sadness, and then it lets him go again.

By midmorning he is smelling water. Sissie picks it up as well. As they go on the canyon floor changes texture. Where before it has been rough dirt, it grows smooth. Water has been here. Sissie's hooves make soft, perfect impressions in the earth. A breeze buffets down the crevasse. The blue sky is only a narrow strip. They are easily fifty feet down, the rock striated in orange and red bands to the sandy lip.

He is hot under his silk shirt. His tongue is thick. A faint sulfurous smell comes to him. Smoke, possibly.

He drinks most of his remaining water, leaving about a cup's worth. He presses his heels into Sissie's flanks, and she trots forward.

His thoughts arrive all unconsidered now. His mother and the fact of her lying dead in the canyon. If he could rise like a bird she would be only minutes away. Lift above the wrinkled channeled canyonland. What the buzzards would do to her. Rancid creatures, their feathers groomed with rotting fat. He has seen them hopping around the corpse of a steer. The steer missing its eyes and its tongue eaten out through its cheeks. Small cuts in the steer's black hide as in a mishandled suitcase. The buzzards' talons yellow and cruel. An impulse to wind his way back to his mother's body and to bury her decently. But her wish was to have been left out in the air. He is embarrassed by his weakness. His mother was stronger than he all along and is still stronger in death. He is soft and has always been soft. Possibly now at last he is just getting harder.

He presses on.

The canyon floor is still smooth and sculpted. A few stones in the soft soil. The smell of water more distinct and with it the smell again of smoke.

He rides through noon. Sissie slows to a protesting stroll. But the water is nearby surely. The scent of it has grown only stronger and the canyon floor grown thicker with what now seems a kind of silt and the stones embedded in it grow larger as the silt grows deeper. Then the stones begin to become very large and are of a different character. They are sharp and conical and ridged yellow and brown like great shattered teeth. He dismounts and kneels in the dirt. They are heavy and made of accretionary limestone, and it takes him a minute but then he recognizes what they are.

He stands and, taking Sissie's reins, leads her forward through the white and massy jumble. It has the appearance of a marble city, a city of the moon, ancient and in ruins, shattered pillars in smashed repose. Now he begins to hear a burbling. The canyon turns and there is the head of it, and standing beneath the high cliff is a round blue pond, not large, about the size of the Dartmouth pool. Around its edge animals stand and drink. A dozen antelope and four haggard coyotes and the lion stand lapping at the water. A stork is standing a few feet in, its eye canted into the depths. Eight or nine buzzards hop shifting at the edge.

Sissie jerks the reins from his hand and canters forward to drink.

Underfoot now he sees the remains of fish, some torn and eaten and others rotting into the sand. Among them are the white segmented remains of a crustacean no bigger than his thumb. Once he cottons to these, he suddenly sees hundreds of them everywhere.

He seats himself on one of the larger white conical stones and unlaces his shoes. He strips naked and approaches the water.

The crustaceans are too many to avoid and crunch delicately underfoot. But he steps between the fish. Whistling peaceably through his teeth, he comes up from Sissie's right flank. He wishes to avoid the coyotes, and everyone is content to leave the lion alone on the far side of the water. The stork eyes him as he steps into the pool.

The water is icy cold around his ankles. He gasps with the slipping chill, then moves deeper in. The bottom is smooth and silky, and as he walks he stirs up clouds of mud beneath the surface. Around his calves now he spies the little flashing forms of fish. He wades until the water covers half his thighs, and then he sits down in the water.

He takes a deep breath and slides beneath the surface. He is encased in a frigid film. He opens his eyes underwater. He has kicked up mud, but elsewhere the water is brilliantly clear and he can see the slender rootlike leg of the stork ending in its talon and the spinning, glancing schools of fish. The fish are eyeless. The little crustaceans are cave creatures, white and blind. The water is from underground, of course, and now and then it wells up and the canyon floods. The white conical stones in the canyon are broken stalactites, washed down the canyon in some long-ago cataclysm.

He puts his feet down. Stands, surfacing. Wipes the water from his eyes. Sissie is still drinking.

No one pays him any mind. He has vanished, and yet here he stands, naked in the watery desert.

Pushing off, he ventures farther into the pool. The water grows deeper. His feet find freezing depths, an absolute iciness that begins to numb his legs. At the center of the pond the sandy bottom vanishes entirely, and he is looking down into a black well, about five feet across, the source of the water from the cavern below.

He aligns himself and takes a series of swift breaths, then lets himself drop. He sinks, sinks, and the bottom of the pond rises up around him like a collar and he catches a last glimpse of the stork's beak piercing the surface and the cliffs refracted upside down. Then he is slipping into the darkness.

He lets himself drop ten feet into the cave.

Above him the circular opening glows. A cone of light falls from it as around him the eyeless fish dart into and out of the light, unknowing. He cannot see the edge of the cavern or the bottom, but he has the sense of being suspended high up near the ceiling of an enormous dome. Looking down between his feet, he sees nothing but blackness. But then at the very edges of the cavern—just hinted at—very far away . . .

Shapes of some sort, hard to see . . .

He sinks farther to get out of the light.

The pressure grows crackling around his eardrums. His lungs throb with the effort not to breathe.

He drops until the sunny opening floats far above him in the darkness like a great glinting open eye. The Eye of All-seeing.

He hangs there, kicking, while his vision adjusts.

The great immensity of the cavern takes shape around him—dark, gigantic—he strains through the darkness to see . . . tiny shards of glinting light, thrown back to him at a variety of shifting angles as he hangs floating in the flooded cavern. He has seen this sort of thing somewhere before. And then he remembers: that tiny quartz-lined chamber from the flood catch. Gaetano's tiny skull.

He is inside a giant geode.

A giant skull.

And then, as though his understanding has disturbed it, he catches the sense, at the edge of his flickering vision, of a great dark benign presence fluttering away, vanishing in the way a dream would, before being entirely seen. As he turns to face it, the presence moves farther into the shadows—a shy, withdrawing thing; immense, retiring—ghosting off like a thought . . .

He will never know, of course, whether it is really true. Or whether he is only imagining it because he so badly wants it to be true. He hangs there another moment, in the darkness of the great cavern.

Waiting, staring into the dark.

But then, enough. He needs air. He will never know; it is not a thing subject to knowingness. This is what he has come to, and it will have to be sufficient. Have to last him, from now until the end.

With a fierce lunging, his lungs bucking, he kicks up toward the light, toward the world.

35

Clyde buys a second-class passage for Dodge City, and for most of the trip he has the compartment to himself. When he grows hungry he opens the basket Mrs. Fox prepared for him and pulls out biscuits or an apple he sections with his penknife. For dinner he goes sideways down the aisle through the third-class cars, where the rows of staring eyes and the sea of hats make him wince. It is possible they know him from the newsreels. But no one calls out and he makes it to the club car, where he buys a ham sandwich with potato salad which he carries back with him on a paper plate, and once he has negotiated the sliding compartment door he sits and arranges the food on the little chrome-rimmed tabletop and alone with himself Clyde Tombaugh, discoverer of Pluto, watches the emptiness roll by.

Hot-diggety-dog, he done found himself a planet.

He smiles to himself at the wonder of it, and the dirty sense that they have gotten away with something after all.

The trip over the mountains from Flagstaff takes thirty-six hours. He arrives at the long dusty brick Dodge City station at noon and steps down. After a moment's searching he spots the face of his father.

"Pop," he says.

"Clyde," his father replies.

"Well." He shrugs.

His father says, "You look fine."

"So do you, pop."

"I've been worse," his father says.

Seeing his father now after so long, Clyde can measure him for what he is, a short slight man with a farmer's canny sinew. Just a farmer from Kansas who's survived this long and will manage to survive a little longer. Never mind the dust storms in Oklahoma and Texas, he will make it somehow. Clyde is unexpectedly pleased to be near his father, who has made it this far, and also pleased to have something to hold over him. Over everyone.

You can't tell Clyde a damn thing at the moment.

The car is comfortable and runs like a dream, and the drive to Burdett takes an hour, Kansas unrolling past the windshield in high dry summer. The ditches are whirring with insects. White farmhouses and galvanized barns and their accompanying silos stand at the ends of long dirt drives. If hard times have come here, you can't much tell the difference. Times have always been half-hard. Only it is dustier and less finished than he remembers. Dried-out cottonwoods clump along the streambanks and far away to the west a set of summer clouds is thumbing its way over the horizon. The fields are wanting rain badly, but there is nothing to be done about it. The Tombaughs are now lucky not to own in a sense as they can pick up and go if necessary. In the face of this, his father's old defeated indifference appears useful, just damn-it-all no matter what, and now you don't look a fool because you've always known. As they drive, his father keeps up a steady chatter. "I guess you know the movie people were here."

"Yes, sir. Out there too."

"Well, boy! They got into everything. When we saw it at the Bijou, you could hardly hear it, people made such a clamor. And I guess you know they dug up those pictures of you in your track suit."

"Kind of them, wasn't it?"

"Mother couldn't believe it. She said, Well, I've got a whole album of decent posed photographs that don't show anybody's spindly legs and why do they need those."

"I saw you looking through the 9-inch."

His father nods, sheepish. "Sure enough. In the middle of the day. Like a fool. Well, it was exciting around here for a little while, wasn't it?"

"Some show out there too."

"I guess it must've been," his father acknowledges.

They are close to town when Clyde manages to say, "Well, they're going to go ahead and pay my way to college, anyhow."

His father nods. "Clyde, I think that's fine."

"I'm going to study astronomy."

"Well, that's fine."

A while later when they are nearly home they pass the Goodens' house, and his attention just snags on it.

"Gone," his father says.

"No."

"Well, he just gave it up. He didn't have it in him. Now *she's* still here over to the Usterhalls. But," he finishes.

Not Clyde's fate, he means. Clyde was always cut out for bigger things.

He just wants to say, into the air of the car, *I discovered a planet, pop.* But this is not the sort of thing you say without asking to get a cuff in the head. So he doesn't. And furthermore he is still not sure if it is exactly true.

So there is the house, looking just the same. Roy has arranged to be working on the front porch shingles so he can hook the hammer in his belt and pluck the nails from his lips and come on sauntering forward. "Say, big brother," he drawls.

"Hello, Rooster."

"Guess you had enough of all that business."

"Surprised you're still here, anyway."

Roy blushes a little. "I guess it's not as bad as it could be."

"Anyway, it's good to see you," Clyde says.

"All right!" Roy protests. "That's plenty."

There is his mother and Charlie, and here is his new unseen little sister Paula, already upright with a head of blond curls and fat feet like clenched fists, and best of all here's Maggie behind the wire going about her old business. He gives her a whistle, and she comes up sideways, looking at him askance. "Hello, old girl," he says.

Well what have we here she asks him.

"Sure," he says, "it's me again." And hearing his voice a second time, she ducks forward to accept the hand on the muzzle and the slap on the neck, and then she's off cantering on her toes, a little trick she learned from somewhere to let you know everything's all right again.

———

He means to stay only a few days before returning to Flagstaff. But by the end of the second day—the sky so vast, the clouds hanging forever at the edge of the horizon, like the landscape of a dream—he drives into town and cables Slipher and lets him know he will be away another week or two.

It is all right to be there with his brothers while his mother fusses and flutters around. Because you've proven yourself, and all at once the things of your life take on a glowy simplicity. There is some solitude also of his last youth that remains here, some essential Clydeness that he wants right now to remember, who he was before he was anyone. He has the sense that it is leaving him, and he regrets its going. So one afternoon he takes a leftover glass blank to the grinding post, and after donning the apron and rubber gauntlets he prepares a paste of Grade 40 Carborundum and distilled water and applies it with a tongue depressor to the grinding disk. Then he starts to grind. Push, push, push, turn. He can still do it in his sleep. After thirty minutes of this he sponges away the 40 and goes to a 60. By dinnertime he has finished the 120, and the disk has acquired a definite concavity and the glass taken on a scrubbed clouded appearance, and it feels alive and giving under his fingertips. And then his mother is calling from the back porch, and there in the yard he feels a kind of beautiful satiety; he is cared for, and the barn just ten yards away is a creaking old rustic cathedral of hay and machinery, and now that he doesn't have to run wheat into the feeder or worry about his oats or whether he's going up to Lawrence or not, he wants to stay forever, suddenly. In a few hours he will write a letter to the pretty nurse who fixed his hands, Patsy, telling her about all this, one of those good old romantic letters you can hardly stand to look at later for all the passion contained in it, but that does the work it needs to, you know, it really seals the deal. His granddaughter will get it out of him, though, you can count on it.

But the letter isn't written yet. Because what has to happen first is this: after dinner his father takes himself to the barn and busies himself with the usual small repairs, and Clyde is still ripe with that excellent fullness, and feeling the old pull he follows his father to do his own ancient chores. He sweeps Maggie's stalls and tosses the soiled hay on the manure pile behind the barn, the pitchfork balanced loosely in his hands, and the smell of the summer earth surrounds him, a smell like good green bread baking, and on the breeze the smell of Kansas rain, a promise. It has been awful dry, his father tells him again, as they swing shut the stable doors.

"We'll last it out, though," his father guesses.

"Sure, pop," he answers.

"I was wondering," his father mentions, latching the door, "maybe you might want to look into mechanical engineering up at Lawrence. Seems they get a lot of work."

"Yes, sir."

"Well, that's all I want to say about it. Well, and also, Clyde," his father says, and then his father can't help it, there is suddenly a huge smile on his father's face, an undisguisable joy, "gee, but I'm awfully happy for you, son."

Clyde turns from this.

"I'm just awfully proud of you," his father says, and offers his hand.

And all at once, spoiling everything, up boils this terrible anger—hot, spitting fury. It's a whole part of him, in a great horrible chunk it comes vomiting up, all of it at once, no way to swallow it down. "What the *hell* do you think you *know about it*," Clyde hisses.

His father does not act as if he has heard but turns away at once into the shadowed depths of the barn. You leave the kid alone with himself for a while. Let him come to his senses. Meanwhile the impossible weight of what Clyde has done—what he has discovered, and what he knows about it all—comes newly alive to him beneath the old timbered roof, shivering in the little breeze. "What am I supposed to *do*," he whispers. No one else in the world alive has done what he has done. No one in the whole world can he ask for advice. The wicked shapes of the old dismantled Dodge and of the ancient cream separator throw themselves in shadow on the walls. The smell of the iron sesquioxide comes gusting to him from the windy farmyard. It ain't fair; not fair that it was he who found it. He didn't ask for it. Not any of it. He's only Clyde.

I'm only Clyde. He begins to say this, first softly, a sort of offering, an explanation, then with increasing volume, until he's shouting, louder and louder—and he goes on calling, long after his father has gone up into the house and made his shrugging excuses and told everyone to leave him be. He's only Clyde. What the hell's he supposed to do with the rest of his life? What can possibly come up to this measure? What? He's only Clyde. And it's all this—anyway the beginning of all this—that Clyde will sit down and in his perfect blue handwriting describe, later tonight, to the woman who will soon become his wife. There's always solace somewhere, if you know where to look for it. Even now, outside, where he cannot see them, the stars are out in their countless thousands, out sailing above the earth; they're tipping up from the east and making their patient eternal ways across the Kansas sky. They've been there forever, they'll be there forever afterward, and they, at any rate, will never expect anything of him. They never expected anything to begin with. Sailing on unperturbed in their permanent orbits, you can be sure they're just not at all in that line of things.

V

THE PRINCESS OF PLUTO
1990 (and after)

After he has read his pages out the astronomer steps down off the stage, one step at a time. He goes to Sarah and she takes his arm again and brings him up through the parting crowd and escorts him back into the pink house. There is an old man in the mirror, all right. Him. He splashes water on his face and returns to face his granddaughter.

"You all right?" she asks.

"Tired out," is all he says.

The sun appears, and he has a turkey sandwich on a paper plate, and he shakes everyone's hand again and drinks a Diet Coke and conducts the business of being Clyde Tombaugh while Sarah stands by. It is the usual hubbub, but he is newly struck by how much everyone seems to love him, his story, what he did. And he is in turn struck, for the first time in many years, by how questionable the whole matter really was. And is.

But he won't breathe a word of it to them. Why would he? It would only disappoint.

Still, when he's finally done and Sarah takes him back to the A-frame, he finds it impossible to keep quiet. He lowers himself with a groan to the creaking bed and starts to talk. He talks as she packs their things and calls through the doorway as she cleans the little bathroom with a dry washcloth (she is like her grandfather in this way; she does like to leave things neat); he talks all the way down the funneling, hurrying freeways into Boston, in the rental car shuttle van with its muddy rubber floor, in the line for the x-ray machines, at the gate, the whole featureless flight back—he talks.

For the first time, he tells someone everything.

He went up to Lawrence to college, finally; he took the Union Pacific, resting his feet on his suitcase, watching the miles roll past. You can appreciate the beauty of a thing when you don't have to have too much to do with it, possibly; anyway Kansas felt like home to him now; leaving it and coming back had done that to him. And there would be time, he figured, to patch things up with his father, in whatever way he could. And then he was at the steepled station and swinging down and setting off on foot for the campus, for the room Lowell Observatory had helped him foot the bill for, for his new life.

It is a strange thing to get what you had once wanted so badly, to occupy the dream life when it becomes real; there is a permanently installed distance between you and it, so you are never quite enjoying yourself without also noticing that you're here, now, *actually*. But he walked the pretty campus and eyed the brick Agriculture Building where the cornfed giants stomped in and out with the horticulture textbooks under their arms, the Dust Bowl only beginning truly to take hold, so that it was still almost possible to believe you could grow something at a profit in Kansas. He sat in the back in the astronomy lectures in Dyche Hall with his new Masterpiece All-Leather boots in the aisle, taking notes while he fingered the soft collars of his new shirts; and, when it came, he accepted the small fame that his fellow students allowed him. The depression had come by then, but he was comfortable, would remain comfortable as long as he stayed in school, thanks to Lowell's sponsorship; so he was suddenly, and unexpectedly, effectively a rich man. And the discovery *was* too large an accomplishment to really account for, and people were shy around him; what few friends he had were fellow astronomy students, and with them he labored through the math he would need, and had never got.

He was lonely. He wrote to Alan and especially to Patsy. He took his courses, proceeding through them with his typical methodic absorption. And around this time he started to think maybe he ought to take some notes down about what happened to him. It was a project that kept him busy, anyhow. He started with himself, but then he branched out to every-

one else, too, what he'd heard from Alan about Dick Morrow and Florence Chambers and life in Belleville, Ohio, and what Alan had told him
about Mary, and what Mary had heard from Mrs. DuPrie about their
adventures; about Edward Howe, and all the rest. You end up somewhere
so unlikely you want to know what happened to get you there. And he was
such a thorough man; you start a project like that, you keep going until
you get it all down.

As for Alan, he took a job teaching mathematics back at his alma mater,
Indiana University. Cogshall was still there, but a new generation had
begun to appear, and Alan was part of it. Alan was alone for almost a year,
waiting until Mary was well enough to come with him, but she was, eventually, and they found a little house in Bloomington and settled down.

So Alan came to think, sort of, that he had prevailed. He had the life
that Shapley had predicted for him, yes; but he and Mary were together
again, and what else could he want? She wasn't well, and in the years to
come she would be hospitalized again several times; they never found
Hollis and never heard from him again. But they managed. She would not
consent to having children, and he didn't press; but he discovered, to his
surprise, that he liked teaching—the linoleum-floored classrooms, the rising tiers of students creaking in their one-armed desks, the plain recitation of things he knew by heart. And from time to time Alan would catch
the eye of some kid who resembled Clyde and be reminded of the boy
laughing aloud at the idea of Planet X, and be overtaken by a gust of sudden
nostalgia. The ancient elms stirred the air, and great continental clouds,
full of their freight of rain, sailed in fat-bellied from the west, and when it
rained the earth gave up its good dark smell of rank fertility, carried to
him from the surrounding prairielands. Late summer thunderstorms of
incredible violence threw broken branches to the sidewalks and plastered
the bricks with green leaves ripped from their stems. And one afternoon,
taking shelter from one of these storms beneath a stone bridge, Alan felt,
suddenly—with the thunder echoing off the granite blocks of the bridge
stanchions—the truly planetary reach of the weather: that each individ-
ual storm was a result of a greatly complex weather system that never
ceased, a system that expressed its solutions in storms and winds that
came to be because of a near infinity of variables. In his mind's eye he saw

a mathematical problem forming, one of such titanic complexity and difficulty that it could never be solved. His sort of work, in other words.

And his other project, the tracking of the Marian Objects, took his time as well; all the new theories suggested they had been, once, a planet, a missing planet between Mars and Jupiter. That it had come apart, or never assembled itself properly to begin with; and that all the asteroids that now orbited the sun had once been something more whole; of course this appealed to his idea of things, and he was the first to publish a convincing account of this theory, using the data he had assembled, first at Lowell and later at Indiana.

And he continued to play the piano and even to sing. At a lunch meeting with the chancellor's wife, a dreaded event, he was dragooned into attending an afternoon choir concert in the university's little stone chapel. He resisted, wanting to be back at his desk—new readings had just come in from the wind stations he had set up on the roof of the Agriculture Building, and he wanted to be at them. But in the interests of good citizenship he went along with her, her many rings pressing into the flesh of his fingers. He should not have been surprised, really, to be so terribly moved by "O Sanctissima," but he was—the plain pure unaccompanied voices, eight of them, proposing to the universe this linear language of knots and spaces, like a pioneer's string calendar. It had been Cecilia Payne's song—now Cecilia Payne-Gaposchkin—and it struck some tender old chord in his heart. So he came back singing into the house, and from then on he was to be found in that little chapel every Sunday, a thorough disbeliever, throwing his voice to the universe.

So when Alan and Mary came to visit Clyde and Patsy in Lawrence every few years, he would be a singing figure, bearing his strange and beautiful wife and steering the creaking Stutz under the elms. And later, in Albuquerque, when Clyde and Patsy had their first child, Alan would sing to her under the big New Mexico sky, full of a kind of precarious happiness, up on his tiptoes, clutching his heart and crooning his father's old *sean nós* over the picnic blanket and looking for all the world as if he was trying to sing her into the air while Mary stood by, rolling her eyes and clutching comically at her heart. He was a ham, was old Jim. There are photographs of this tableau to be pored over, and although if you ask her about it today Sarah's mother will admit she has no memories of Alan doing such a thing, who's to say his singing did not in fact have some influence? Our lives intersect, and interfere, and there is no telling where certain beauties might come from. Some song in her heart, where otherwise there wouldn't have been one. And in Sarah's too, passed on down.

So the last thing there is to tell is about Alan and Mary.

In 1937, in Indiana, Alan made one thousand two hundred dollars a year and paid thirty-two dollars a month for a mortgage on a house at the edge of the campus. One early morning—he and Mary were in the back yard very early, before dawn—a bright river of flaming green light came streaking overhead, bright enough to illuminate the yard. Mary grabbed his arm, and together they watched the trail—it was greenish white, with interesting momentary eddies and swirls, glowing and fading—pass silently overhead. Mary stood still and watched it diminish into the distance.

"How about that, Jim?" she said.

"That was a big one."

They had the same idea at once. A crazy idea, of course, but Alan had long since grown accustomed to this kind of accommodation; he had become, you might say, voluntarily crazy himself, when he needed to be. So they drove west and south, west and south, following the path that he could still see in his mind's eye, etched on the sky. Calculating that trajectory, all right. All morning they drove the farm roads, joggling down the state, Alan craning his neck and peering into every field they passed. And then, at noon, he stomped suddenly on the brake and flung the door open and whispered, "There it is, Mare."

She was still nervous about open fields, about things that were buried in the ground. "I don't know, Jim," she said.

"It's all right," he assured her.

They were in the middle of nowhere—far on the horizon a silo showed—and the earth was furrowed and barren underfoot.

"Look over there."

In the middle of the field a dark streak of dirt had been torn up.

"That came from above," he told her. "Not from below."

Alan took her hand.

The field seemed to go on forever, furrow after furrow, and when they finally came to the gouge in the earth there seemed to be nothing there.

But Alan went to the far end of the gouge and began pawing away at the earth. After a moment he uncovered a black stone as big as a head.

"Gee," she said, and backed away.

"No," he insisted. "It's all right."

The soil was hot under his fingers, and when he touched the stone itself his fingers came away scalded. When the meteorite was finally sufficiently cool to carry, it was very heavy—it was nickel and iron, quite dense—and even after having been buried in the earth it gave off the sweet, metallic smell of deep space. He gestured to her, and she agreed to help him. Together they struggled with it back across the lumpy ground. They passed it through the barbed-wire strands, then wrestled it over the lip of the trunk as the Packard dipped on its suspension.

"That one's yours, Mare," he said. "Little planet all for you."

They stood at the back of the car together, silent, alone, in the middle of nowhere, the open country spread out around them in all directions, as alone in the world as though they had just been born there in the weeds at the shoulder of the road. Alan's hands were still clotted with soil and the feel of the wire was still alive in his hands, and Mary stood, hands in the pockets of her long purple coat, flapping her wings, watching as he whumped the lid of the trunk closed. The stone that had sailed for eons in the outer dark had now come to be lifted into their own possession, secure in its bulk beside the road flares and the spare tire and tire jack. A planet all for her. Wish for it hard enough, and it will come to pass. It is a foolish proposition, and untrue, but now and then it does seem the universe works this way; once in a while it answers you. And when it does, you feel a rightness, you sense that you have a place in things; and you feel the scale of the universe as well, the interlocking workings of its great dark machinery, and you know your place in its vast mechanism is a very small one. This is a good feeling, usually, and often a feeling of peace; it is peaceful to feel oneself a part of something so large so completely; and right there, just for a minute, Alan and Mary felt that peace as it entered them without effort and without price. Certainly they did not have much of it otherwise, from day to day; but here was a measure of it, all unexpected.

And then they understood—both of them at once—that they had no idea where they were. Mary, realizing it, smiled broadly—a real smile, something that was becoming rarer and rarer—and faced Alan with a fond, familiar amazement. "Jim!" she cried, laughing, "we're lost!"

But it was all right (there were maps in the car, after all); and, together, they would carry a portion of that peace back with them in the car; and in the years to come he would remind her of this feeling by patting the meteorite on its hard nickel head as he passed through the living room, grinning unkillably at her as she lay in her robe on the sofa, smoking, suffering the things she would suffer. It was a tiny gesture, and it would have meant nothing to anyone else, but they both knew just what he meant by it. He meant everything, and especially everything unsayable.

And a lot happened after, and there is naturally more to tell about everyone. But by the time Sarah and Clyde's flight lands at the Albuquerque airport, Clyde is exhausted. He has at long last run out of words. He dozes in the wheelchair all the way back through the concourse to the car, and he sleeps against the passenger door all the way home while Sarah keeps watch on him from the corner of her eye. (Oh, and what does she think of him now? Is he still of any use to her at all, now that she knows the whole story? But of *course* he is—of course, and much more so. Gripping the wheel, she decides she will tell Dave everything. Or . . . no, she will not. Or maybe one day. Or, no, she will have to think about it for a while, among the grasses in Indiana, tending to her own tender crops; possibly she will want to write it all down for herself eventually . . .)

Well, no wonder Clyde is so tired; he has not spoken that way to anyone, ever, not even to Roy in the glory days when the two of them craned to hear the music of Chicago bubbling over the horizon. It is late afternoon as Sarah pulls the car crunching into the driveway. The astronomer's wife emerges into the late light, wiping her hands, relieved to have her husband back, smiling—how she has missed him! Then she sees Clyde's sleeping form, sees his face dead slack, and her expression grows worried. But Sarah leans over and whispers, "He's only worn out. He talked the whole way home."

And more came after this, too, of course—even as Clyde goes on sleeping in the car, his innocent mouth agape and his windbreaker turtled up around his shoulders as the women go inside, deciding to leave him be for a little while, there is more to tell. The story goes on into the future, as everyone knows; but it is a fair bet that the man who discovered Pluto would prefer that the story end here, this way, at this juncture, with the planet he found still up in the sky where he put it, circling round the sun, tugging imperceptibly at its neighbors and being tugged at in turn, turning its freezing surfaces alternately to the faraway sun and to the imponderable depths of space—the least of the planets, and the outermost, and maybe the hardest-won; and so end here it does.

AUTHOR'S NOTE

This is a work of fiction. While the general outline and a good number of the particulars of Clyde Tombaugh's life in Kansas and in Arizona are carefully adapted from historical accounts, I have, throughout, shaped and altered the historical materials as has seemed useful for my purposes. The same is true of the matters touching on Lowell Observatory, Constance and Percival Lowell, Vesto Slipher, Roger Putnam, and other real-life figures and places.

I am deeply indebted to the staff at Lowell Observatory for their generous hospitality and especially to Antoinette Beiser for her excellent and enthusiastic guidance through the superb observatory archives and through the observatory's many glorious spaces. Needless to say, all errors and omissions, conscious or otherwise, are my own damn fault.

ACKNOWLEDGMENTS

This book would not exist without Janet Silver's indefatigable patience and incredible faith over the many years of its assembly in her several roles as editor, shepherd, agent, and all-time best reader. So her name is first here.

I also owe deep thanks to the University of Pittsburgh and the University of Michigan for providing regular employment and friendly places to be, and I owe particular thanks to Dave Bartholomae, Chuck Kinder, Lewis Nordan, Cathy Day, and Phil and Susan Smith at Pitt, and of course to my buddies Eileen Pollack, Peter Ho Davies, Linda Gregerson, and Nick Delbanco at Michigan; to the many friends, students, and fellow writers who offered company and encouragement along the way; to Tim Seldes; to Helen Zell; to Sid Smith; to Joanna Campbell; to the excellent folks at Holt, especially the remarkable Webster Younce and the outstanding Marjorie Braman; and to Charles Baxter, nuff said.

And unlimited love to my wife, Susan Hutton, as well as to the unsurpassable Hazel and John, hello guys, and endless thanks for making everything, you know, just so *lovely* all the time.

ABOUT THE AUTHOR

MICHAEL BYERS is the author of *The Coast of Good Intentions,*
a book of stories, and *Long for This World,* a novel. Both were
New York Times Notable Books. He has been a finalist for the
PEN/Hemingway Award, won the Sue Kaufman Prize from
the American Academy of Arts and Letters, and received a
Whiting Writer's Award. A Seattle native, he now teaches creative writing at the University of Michigan.